this exquisite topology

a collection of happy abstractions

naomi simone borwein

chun hyon lee

angry gable press

angry gable books

Angry Gable Press
www.angrygablepress.com

contents

introduction

Naomi Simone Borwein and Chun Hyon Lee

If you are reading this, you are 'holding' a copy of *This Exquisite Topology: a collection of happy abstracts*. It's a volume of weird, fantastic, absurd, humorous, amorous, and horrific stories and poems. When we made the call for this book, we defined topology loosely. Topology can be understood as "the study of geometric properties and spatial relations unaffected by the continuous change of shape or size of figures" (Oxford Dictionary).

Within narrative spaces, somewhat like mathematical ones, "[o]bjects can be stretched and contracted" (University of Waterloo, "What is Topology?"). But in these stories and poems, we see textual environments that create "material spaces of hope" and reveal the multiple "topological inflections of things" (Barba Lata and Duineveld 2019, 1769).

The call required that writers include happy abstracts or moments of joy. What we received were pieces that slipped from reveling in delight to powerful depictions of serenity, romantic or familial bliss, intoxication, tranquility, ecstasy, obsession, and pleasure. If you came here for traditional happy endings, I am afraid you are holding the wrong book. However, if you continue reading, you will find pieces that engage in the pleasure of strange love, oceanic calmness, artificial joy, sex and mathematics, and even magical woodworking! With our definition of speculative topology comes connectivity, mutability, intermediality, and happiness found in the oddest of locations.

Featured in this anthology are winners and nominees of prestigious international awards like the Hugo, Nebula, Rhysling, Ignyte, Stoker, Elgin, Aurora, and many others. It was a delight to bring this unique collection to life, and we hope it will take you to places you never considered going before.

Naomi Simone Borwein
Chun Hyon Lee
July 2025

fresh

. . .

Saundra Mitchell

There's an orange on my bed.

This wouldn't be remarkable, except I've been alone in this field station for three months, and all the fresh fruit is gone. I'd tried to savor the last orange in the last case; I'd held onto it far longer than I should have. Its flesh had desiccated at the edges. Age diluted the meager juice; the only thing that orange had going for it was its perfume, because its fruit disappointed the tongue.

I dried the peels on the same radiator I use to dry my clothes. They're browned, curled strips of leather now; they only give up their sweetness if I rub them and hold them to my nose. Some nights, I huff them, like a fruit junkie desperate for a fix. I convince myself of the perfume, even though rationally, I know it's sense memory at this point.

My contract has three more months on it, and I have all the supplies I'm going to have. I have more than enough freeze-dried, flash-frozen and canned meals to last me. This lush fruit is simply impossible. It cannot be here. It isn't real.

There had been training videos about the effects a winterover could have on a person when I first got the job. Long term solitude during the Antarctic night had been known to cause anxiety, depression, insomnia, mania and hallucinations. I guess I'd never expected hallucinations to come in the shape of a fat, no—*abundant*—orange, one so bright and fresh, I see the dimples from here, with a bit of stem and a single, celadon leaf still attached.

Because my hands are half-frozen, I fight my way out of my coat and gloves like a frantic toddler. When my left sleeve refuses to cooperate, I yank at it until I twist myself into a full circle. When I flap, I grunt, and I kick the solid steel door frame, because mild violence is sometimes the solution. When I finally free myself, I force myself to hang my coat and gloves, but I keep my boots on. There's no one around to judge me and I'm the only one who will be annoyed by the snow I track into the station.

I kneel on the edge of my bed. The orange rolls toward me, its leaf a helpless flag of surrender. I never thought I would need to describe the sensation of a citrus kissing my knees, but now that I do, it's fucking *magical*. My nostrils flutter, anticipating the fresh, bright bite and my mouth doesn't just water. I drool; deeply embarrassing even without witnesses.

This is what it must be like to stagger through the desert, burned by sun and wind, sand smoothing every exposed surface, and then suddenly, in the distance, an oasis appears. I swipe the spit off my face, then reach out. *Oh, please orange, please hallucination, please don't dissipate. Please be improbable but real, please, please* and then my palms cup around it, capturing it like a butterfly.

I raise it to my face, and god, it smells of summer and windows open and fans clicking in their fixed orbits. It smells like sno-cones and creamsicles; it smells like a push-up pop shared with a lover, now that the sheets are on the floor and the sweat has evaporated. Experimentally, I touch my tongue to the flesh, and I feel its irregular surface; I order myself not to bite. *Not the peel, do not, absolutely do not bite that peel.* It would be bitter, but my teeth want to rub and nip and nibble so I decide it's time.

My thumbnails are short, but they find a crevice by the stem and break the flesh. The rind exhales a tiny hiss, the sound of cellular walls breaking, breathing volatile oils into the air. Creamy white pith clings to the fruit underneath. I peel off a stripe of it and pop it into my mouth. It tastes of nothing, but the bouncy, foamy freshness of it wakens my pulse. If this is all in my mind, my mind is incredible, and I love it.

New, gingery, spicy bright—it's so bright, I laugh. As recently as yesterday, I'd been huffing the sad, mummified remains of the last orange. I hadn't remembered rightly at all. It was a ghost of a moment, now resurrected, truly alive. Light gleams through the vesicles, translucent stained glass ordered in the same honey-glow shade. This is summer in the Mediterranean with my wife; this is standing in wonder at a glory so great, our ancestors called it god.

So I eat it.

I gobble up every single piece of it, in juicy, open-mouthed carnage. Sticky face, sticky hands, sticky fingers, spots of juice on the blankets, where no ants will ever find it. Sprawling back in my bed, I trace my booted toes against the floor and throw my arms over my head. Sucking the taste from my lips, I probe my teeth with my tongue in search of any leftover bits. Saving it for later had only led to disappointment, last time. I learn from my mistakes, even if I'm not the smartest woman on the Poles.

That's not modesty. I'm not a scientist; it's my job to maintain the station until the scientists come back. They're looking at the radio waves in the universe, trying to capture a billion years of history in a graph, in an equation, in runes I couldn't hope to read. But today I ate an impossible orange and fell in love with my wife and felt the firmament move with the first taste of worship. If I'm losing my mind in Marie Byrd Land, Antarctica, then it's lost.

The summer in my belly will see me through 'til I find it again.

an intergalactic kraken's greatest woe

. . .

Devan Barlow

Why, oh why?!
My dear, distressing sourdough
do you defy me?

I've gathered yeasts from the furthest fastnesses
shrouded by shadows of fulgent nebulae
Collected warmth from last
gasps of stars who perished of fright
at beholding my tentacles
Accumulated the last breaths of tyrants
and keepers of obscure solar secrets
Harvested wheats whose grains feast upon the frozen
corpses rife within blasted forgotten plains
Amassed water dripped from icicles older
than the dead gods of the last
exoplanet I terrorized

I've stirred and mixed with force
sufficient to churn the deepest oceans
Forged you a container from
plundered planetary rings and

molten exoplanet cores

Yet! Oh!
You thwart me so!

As often as not you give me
useless muck worse than
inchoate, inclement sands
along the shores
of unrelenting estuaries

Thus I toil on
pilfering more texts and chefs to gain
the wisdom I require

Alas!
You have me in your grasp
For I crave
the oh-so-soothing comfort
of returning to my trans-dimensional
vortex-lair at the end of
a long celestial rampage
shaking off the day's ichor

and preparing
a loaf of homemade sourdough
in my oven
powered by the triple quasar
I've slaughtered to protect

For all you thwart me
I know one day your love will
prove

as true as my own

complex alice in the riding hood

. . .

Geoffrey A. Landis

What Red Riding Hood hadn't noticed, hadn't known, was that
the big bad wolf wasn't really a wolf at all, it was a wormhole in
wolf's clothing.
When the wolf swallowed her, Red Riding Hood (whose real
name was Alice) was not eaten up at all, but followed her grandmother through the mouth of the wormhole, which is to say the
rabbit hole, into another world.
Later, when the woodsman cut open the wolf, which is to say,
performed a branch cut on the embedding function in the
complex plane, who is to say that it was Red Riding Hood (that
is, Alice) who popped out,
and not one of innumerable other Alices
from innumerable other woods
on other sheets
deep in the complex plane?
Most certainly, Red Riding Hood returned changed.
But then, being swallowed by a wolf will do that, with or
without wormholes.

stone lions

. . .

Cliff McNish

Davina props a hand under her chin, gazes adventurously into my eyes.

"I'll start this time," she whispers.

"Go on, then."

"I love you."

"I love you, too," I respond.

"I love you more."

"No way."

"Yes, way. Definitely."

"How can you know that?"

"Because I'm deeper than you."

"Oh really? You feel things more deeply than I do?"

"Yes."

"Prove it," I say.

"There's no way I can prove it to you in a way you'll understand because you're shallower than me."

"You could prove it to me *physically*."

"What, you mean a kiss?"

"Well, I think you can go one better than that."

"To show how much I love you, yes?"

"Exactly."

"I think you're mistaking gestures of affection for real love again, John."

"Am I?"

"Yes."

"I'm a shallow bastard, then?"

"You are a bit."

"But you still love me?"

"Yes."

"Doesn't that make you a little bit shallow yourself?"

And at least she laughs. Davina's full-on laugh is always an event: like a horse snorting the wrong kind of grass. Couples on nearby tables straighten, but not that much. They're too wrapped up in the same kinds of conversation. The pair to our right are playfully exchanging love similes. While I kiss Davina I listen in:

"How much do you love me?"

"Um. More than chips."

"That's quite a lot for you. You can never get enough chips."

"How much do you love *me*, then?"

"I love you... more than a cat loves its tongue. I love you more than a werewolf loves its... um... hair."

Her partner plucks at his lip. "I love you more than a toad loves its stool."

She giggles. "I can't believe you just said that."

"I did, I just said it!"

Davina and I exchange a look. You're not supposed to steal love-conversation ideas from other couples, but everyone does. New material = more points.

"I love you more than a birthday cake loves its candles," Davina says to me, and the couple to our left nod approvingly.

While I'm thinking of possible similes to respond with to that a waitress arrives. It's the fruit juices we ordered to keep our throats lubricated. They're free, thank god, and, taking a sip, Davina makes a melodramatic lunge for my knee under the table. Good move. Spontaneous physical tenderness = multiple points as long as your partner looks genuinely surprised. I make sure I do.

I kiss the tip of her nose. There are eighteen tables in this café. Every café in the city, in fact the world, is now occupied twenty-four hours a day. Gender is optional, but everyone has a partner. Only the dying are exempt, and moves are afoot to limit even that to final days.

"I loved you the first moment I set eyes on you," a woman at a table behind me whispers desperately. Her partner, a woman, nods, raking fingers through her greasy blonde hair. She looks exhausted. The two of them are clutching onto each other's arms to avoid sliding off their chairs. They'd better get their act together. They've been faltering all evening. So have we, though. Davina's fighting a chest infection that just won't leave her alone.

She coughs, and we get a warning twang. We've delayed too long exchanging loving thoughts and emotions. The app-generated itch that follows is mild initially. A sensation like your arteries filling up with thistles. Left any longer and your skull starts screaming.

It's unusual for Davina to be struggling like this. Normally it's me she's rescuing. She seizes on the lifeline the female couple threw out.

"I loved you the second we met," she whispers, and the sound of her voice linked to the word *love* dampens the itch. "You walked into the living room at Geoff's place, remember? You were lugging two full carrier bags of beer."

I bring the party back to mind. "I remember you," I say. "Legs crossed like his." I show her. "You were wearing a scarlet dress. Short. A bit tarty."

"But you liked it."

"Oh yeah."

We've done this first-time-we-met routine a hundred times before, so it earns limited points, but it's a start. I link hands with her across the wooden grain of the table. "And from that first moment you fell madly in love, huh?"

"Not quite," she says. "But I felt something." She smirks. "Lust. And you made me laugh."

I doff an imaginary cap. "And how much do you love the jester now, my queen?"

"Oh, *more*," she says with a flash of her teeth. "Much more."

I admire her performance under duress. Even feeling crap, Davina plays the love game with practiced facility. Despite which, she can't quite make herself sound as effervescent as some of the younger couples around us. Which is ironic, given that many of them are entirely inventing their affections. A lot of the youngest have been hooked into the love game since their teens, when it first became compulsory. They're far better at *fake-real* than oldies like me and Davina. All around us is love: love old, love new, love brash, grave, false-innocent and, occasionally, true.

But next year there must be more. It's built into the app. More love is required. We must move forward. How will we achieve it?

We do achieve it. People are ingenious. Next year we manage more fondness and tumultuous affection than ever. The app assists us. Version 6.3 arrives with extras that tether directly to our limbic and endocrine systems. Eye-dilation and voice timbre pick-ups have been significantly upgraded. *"We can now measure the quality of love in your breath,"* says the app manual cheerfully.

Which is not great for me and Davina. Until now we've been able to rely largely on our wits, cheating almost all the time. The new incarnation of the app permits everyone to do that occasionally, but its allowances are stingier. Points are deducted for clear inauthenticity. What inauthenticity means is never conclusively defined.

The app improves the following year. Orifice implants. Aside from work, love becomes all we do. Love jumps off the walls. Love slides off the backs of dogs. The cafés burst at the seams. Homes ring with passionate declarations. People who have never loved a thing, not even themselves, learn to do so.

Being *liked* is officially ditched as inadequate, even on the junior app platform. Scientists figure out ways for teenagers to get their jiggly pre-pubescent hormones jacked up and sizzling sooner.

Throughout August, Davina and I make love until we're sore and talk about love until we're hoarse.

"Have we done enough?" I ask wearily, watching tonight's clock.

We're due our first break shortly. We've been playing without an interval for an hour already, and this is our seventeenth straight evening hooked into the app.

"Whatever souls are made of, yours and mine are the same," I say, adapting Emily Bronte, just to keep us talking.

"Ah, sentiment," Davina mutters, stroking my hand. "But I suspect we can love beyond the reach of souls. We'll simply upgrade human beings. We already are. Incremental but constant improvements. And we'll make up for any emotional shortfall between people by bringing in more love of'–she waves a hand, plucks something out of the air–'*inanimate* things."

"Inanimate?"

"Like the weather. Whatever the weather's like next year, we'll decide it's lovelier. We'll imagine the whole world is literally glowing with loving light, everyone back-lit by olive, mellow, evenly distributed warmth "

"You can't love an inanimate object," I object. "You can fetishize it, but you can't be deeply concerned for its welfare."

"Why not?" Davina says. "Toys are lovable, aren't they? Kids love them. Adults love their cars, their patios, their phones.

People often love their possessions more than they love their own families."

I smile. Davina is a pro at the love game. Her excursions are publicly available, as is all love-game discourse. She's down-loaded by other anxious gamers regularly. She's taught me a lot, but what I'm mainly good at is riffing off the cooky love ideas she lobs me. Her last remarks utilized the word love six times across five sentences. That gets us a payoff. For a few moments we're both entirely free from pain.

Then a new love category flashes up on the app board:

Humor: Next Year.

Every couple in the café stops whatever conversation they were on, and begins again.

"Next year," I begin at once, grateful that we've already edged into this jokier tone, "not everything will be about love, but lovely things will happen. Knees will be less knobbly, for instance. And middle-aged spread will even out."

Davina nods. "And nobody deserving love who rides a bike will suffer a puncture."

"And dictators will still dictate," I add, "but only love poems to their political opponents, whom they have freed and compensated big-time."

Davina coughs into her sleeve. "Yeah, it'll be awesome. Even animals will quit killing each other."

"You reckon?"

"Yeah. Cats will stop maiming mice. All the love they're now brimming with will make the very idea of tearing the entrails out of rodents completely out of the question. Panthers will befriend guinea pigs. It will actually get pretty confusing for a while in the animal kingdom because all the species will want to be together in a big love cave. Physical love itself will become more awkward for us humans too," she continues smoothly. "We'll be falling head over heels in love with hamsters and camels and salmon, and those creatures will be trying to make out with us, too. It will be tricky when a loving priapic walrus meets an ambitious banker. But everything will be handled in a spirit of such tenderness that no permanent harm will be done," she adds. "Or, if it occasionally is, all will be forgiven by the crippled animals and people concerned."

Davina stops. You get a lot of added points for such left-field quixotic references, and the app signifies its appreciation by giving us both a dopamine hit and a silence interval. Two minutes without penalty.

Even before the itch begins again, however—a reminder to re-start–I see that Davina's struggling. Her face has gone slack. It happens to us all. *Love stuckness*. Nothing left in the jar. Everyone has their own personal coping strategy when this happens. The truly desperate just say the word 'love' over and over until their session is over.

Mine and Davina's love interactions this evening have been petering out faster than normal. Nineteen days every month on the app is now compulsory, and this is our last stint. All couples teeter on the brink of collapse during their final few days. Especially people who really love each other, as we do. Davina and I were married before the love app became legally obligatory. Most of the younger couples around us in the café had never set eyes on each other before the app brought them together.

"Next year…" Davina starts, then falters again.

She's weeping. That's not unusual during the love game. In fact, it's almost a disregarded reaction, being so frequent. In former versions of the game, smart couples were permitted to link tearful outbursts artfully into their love routines to continue scoring points. Psychologists had argued that all acts of weeping are categorizable as *expressions of love* on the basis that, even at its most mundane level, weeping represents love of self, of one's own welfare.

But the app's latest algorithms ignore tears entirely. Weeping is now classified as a *multi-sourced emotion*, with no dependable link to love. A bout of weeping is technically designated as a *pause*. Pauses are spaces without love. Pauses represent at best hesitancy. The truly in love have no truck with hesitancy.

Davina grits her teeth, drags her lips open. Fifteen minutes left to go on the creative humor category.

"Next year numbers will become sentient, just as mathematicians and accountants always dreamed they would," she says. "And the numbers themselves, not to be left out, will fall in love. With us, yes, the numbers will definitely get crushes on us, when our fingers write them out, when our fingertips turn them and move them and transmute them thus and thus. But mainly numbers will fall in love with each other. Sensuous zeroes will fall in love with binary 1's, but 5's will also bump slyly against stocky 4's. Huggy catchments and agglomerations of 9's and 6's will abound in oceans. Number 2s will become great dancers, toodling end over end on their angular bases, a rocking motion, solo dancing in front of large audiences, gyrating so ardently they'll not care or notice we're watching at all."

Even for Davina, this is an unusually surreal passage. She looks gaunt. Looks ill. What's the matter with her tonight?

We could just start kissing. It's everyone's standard stop-gap when the going gets too tough to talk. Body love, if engaged in with sufficient intimacy = top marks. But our lips are already red-raw from kissing today and yesterday and the day before. I raise a finger, our sign to fall back on even closer contact. Davina picks up the message, shakes her head. Too sore. We rarely have sex outside the game any longer. Few couples do. The erogenous zones only have so much to give. They're never fully recovered before the month's new schedule begins.

Placing a hand on Davina's cheek, I take up the slack.

"Next year the moon will be extra silvery and ghostly. Full moons illuminating lovers will last longer. And squirrels will be beset by their own serious love issues. Being already nuts about nuts, they'll come to love nuts so much that they can't abide to eat them any longer."

Davina appreciates the break.

"Next year... next year... every word in the dictionary will head like a headless chicken towards the page containing the word love," she mutters, an acerbic tinge to her voice the app will definitely pick up on and deduct points for. "And the word death will come to mean love. And the word love itself will have equal weight with all other words, as everything tumbles towards love. Sometime around October, all canned vegetables will free themselves of their tins, and join up to become part of a great love-in soup. And bizarrely, we'll begin to love insects, simply because, well, we never have. Bug-love and caterpillar love will thrive. Arachnid adoration will blossom. Aphid love will become a craze, replacing that enduring craze of all previous years–that of creating endless webs of human lies and deceit."

I swallow, watching Davina closely. She's losing it.

"Next year or maybe the year after that," she continues with defiant relish, "we'll all start tracking toward patches of dingy water, because why not, we love everything else, why the hell not dingy water? But no matter how early we set off, we'll hardly ever make it to those dingy patches, because there'll be too many distractions along the way. We'll be running towards everything, in love with everything, hugging everything or trying to. Cuddling the air, old bits of chewing gum, homeless peoples' shoes—"

"Davina? Honey?" I raise an eyebrow, give her a sharp glance.

Luckily we still have one 10-minute emergency time-out left. It's a massive points loss to claim it this late in the game, and will necessitate another full additional day next time we resume, but it is available to us.

Davina shakes her head vehemently: *no*.

"It won't be perfect next year, of course," I say, to fill the silence. "Next year everyone will try out mime. Next year everything—for a time—will lovingly rhyme."

I dry Davina's eyes with the edge of my shirt-sleeve, and we clutch each other. Passive holding of this kind = low points, but they trickle through.

"Next year trumpets will blow," Davina splutters. "And bugles will blow! Basically you can rely on the fact that everything will fucking blow. We'll all stand side by aide and blow anything we have to hand because we're all so fucking happy."

I put a hand across her lips. Somehow I've got to switch her back to playfulness.

"Next year serial killers will take up knitting," I say, "and, when they realize they're just knitting things to strangle people with, they'll come over all bashful and stop. And next year bashful people will be even more bashful because they're lovely, why should they change? Likewise stutterers. And all the ditherers and procrastinators, in fact the hesitant generally, will be celebrated like the emperors and empresses they always were. And next year every sentence will be left unfinished, because when you are full of love and try to talk about it, you just—"

I get an originality points boost for this dubious outburst. It chimes in both our ears. Feeds us five full minutes of dopamine peace. It's within the rules of the game to offer the full drug-share entirely to your partner, so I do.

I'm getting seriously scared now, though. Davina's long doubted we'd make it to the end of this year, but I've remained hopeful. Naively believed that, despite the odds, the true love between us would get us through to December. But while some people can pour out endless marathons of fake emotion, Davina is not one of those. And without her I'd be hopeless.

We have three more hours to endure in this session. I stare at Davina and say, "Forget the rest of the world. Just concentrate on our love." Our code for, *I'll keep talking, you rest.*

Davina nods gratefully. Every couple still surviving on the new version of the app sacrifices this way at times for their partner. Davina won't be able to just sleep while I prattle on, however. Between micro-naps she'll need to say *something*. Individual silence is permitted for no more than 90 seconds while the app is actively running.

"Picture us as an elderly couple in a living room," I tell her. "Wouldn't that be wonderful?"

She nods, scrunching inside the duvet. We've left the café now and are at home in bed, which is permitted so long as we continue talking during the journey back. It's dangerous lying down, but I can see Davina needs to.

The new category the game's thrown at everyone currently playing is: *The future loving couple.*

"We're in our loving dotage," I continue, "and we're sitting a little apart on the couch. Our old legs tend to get tangled up if we get too close."

"Do we still sleep together?" Davina nestles into my shoulder.

"Of course."

"Nude?"

"Always. Well, *you're* starkas anyway. I insist. I still can't get enough of that body of yours."

"To my dying minute you'll be begging me for sex, yeah?"

And we both laugh. Honest laughter this time. Should be extra points for it. There won't be.

'So we're propped up in our chairs,' she says. 'We're watching TV, I suppose. Too enfeebled to do anything else.'

'You're right about that.'

'What program?'

'Lurve island.'

'Of course.'

'It's a special episode,' I tell her. 'We were two notable contestants in a series four decades earlier. The show is a special *Fifty years of Lurve Island* retrospective, where couples like us come on to talk about how the rest of our lives have worked out.'

'I suppose we're vain as hell.'

'Not at all. Even though we met in the media circus of the show's hot studios, we're still madly in love.'

'I like the sound of that,' Davina murmurs, laying her temple against the brushed cotton of her pillow. 'What are we like in our old age, John? Are we deeply inspiring to less experienced couples?'

'You bet we are! They're all insanely jealous of us. Even in a future bursting with love, no-one can believe how ridiculously in love we still are. Nothing—not nuclear fallout, not a resurrected Jesus–would strip us from each other's side. I'm one hundred and eighteen years old. Science has no idea how I can still be alive, but of course love is keeping me alive, only love.'

Davina's eyes flutter half open. She leans against my shoulder. 'Where do we live in this far future, John? I suppose we just have a brittle celebrity existence, dashing between international studios desperate to film us?'

'Far from it,' I say. 'We live modest lives in the countryside. Some unpretentious rural spot where we can just be in one another's gaze without interference. But that's not quite enough for us.'

'It's not?'

'Not for me, anyway. I remain a burning cauldron of devotion to you, and have no choice–I have to broadcast it.'

'How do you do that, John?'

'I take snapshots of you on my phone and send them to the passengers of passing trains via wireless 9G. They take the images of you into greyed-out and mysterious regions we don't even have yet in the world–cities and towns called Knolfski, Ariest-tremaine, Snordakai, and other such places, because fifty years from now everywhere will have been renamed along principles of whim decided entirely by people in love. The passengers themselves take the snapshots of you onward. They take them into their own homes, heartlands which are a million miles away because future trains are interplanetary and go all the way to Neptune.

'Yet,' I say–Davina is basically asleep now, but needs to make an interrogative, so I nudge her–'yet even that's not enough for me.'

'No?'

'No. Sometimes, defying science, I bound after the trains. I sprint. God knows how, but I leap right onto the speeding carriages. Tear off their doors with my bare hands.'

'Sounds dangerous,' Davina drawls. 'What if a kid's behind that door, and falls out? Don't you check who might be there first?'

'Never,' I say. 'I clamber aboard the train, not even noticing the tiny children tumbling behind me on the rails. They know it is all done out of love, which always takes precedence, and give me a thumb's up. I sit down–a little out of breath–next to the first passenger I see, man, woman, child, it doesn't matter, and I tell them how amazing you are. And they carry my words with them. They ferry them to Mars, to Jupiter and its moons, and Saturn, whose craggy inhabitants, geno-adapted to live in the planet's dusty, light-drenched rings, are now crazy for your welfare.'

Davina wriggles her toes under the blanket. 'I guess the cult you initiated for me on Pluto is still going strong?'

'It's led to savage wars, unfortunately. I tried to hide your Athenian loveliness. Failed. They each want you for themselves.'

'And you look equally glorious, I suppose, my love?' she murmurs. 'More youthful prince than mature king?'

'Of course,' I say. 'In your eyes I do, anyway. In actuality, I'm a flatulent, corpulent thing, but to you my liver patches are beauty spots, which anyway you claim are basically hidden inside my still-childish dimples. To you, I'm beautiful. To you, my lopsided, stroke-affected grin still has the dazzle of a serial killer whose victim is all trussed up and ready to dispatch. We're fundamentally content, Davina, that's what I'm trying to say.'

'Do we still like our tea?' she slurs.

'Oh, we love our tea. We love drinking it and we love looking at each other. That's about all we need now. Tea and looks.'

I gaze down at Davina and she blinks sleepily back up at my unshaven chin. Her sleepiness is contagious, and I nod off too. Big mistake. We both wake at the same time, being viciously brain-spiked by the app. I check my watch. Still nearly two hours left.

'Go on, John.' Davina bends across. Gives me a tender kiss on the one part of my forehead than hasn't been kissed already into permanent soreness.

I rub my eyes. My energy levels are fading. I need to continue, but I'm suddenly love-stuck. Shit. *Come on, come on.*

'Imagine a gate through which only starlight can be seen,' I say, pinching my cheek. 'Imagine your tongue curled around that gate, holding it open. Imagine my tongue on the opposite side of that gate, doing likewise. Active tongues. Both of us are stone lions. We're the guardians of the gate to Heaven. We stand miles high, only the good and the just may pass beyond, and we alone decide. A solemn, awesome responsibility. And yet we keep forgetting about all of that. Our feline mouths hang open. We're panting and laughing. We can't stop giggling. We can't stop looking at each other, either. You keep glancing away from the gate to make me laugh, and each time you do that terrible sinners pass through into Heaven in droves, but I don't care because I'm watching the wind traverse your flung mane.'

Davina nods, but sadly. It's an old story, old imagery. I've used it before. Not many points for repetitions. I tried to amend it half-way through, but couldn't come up with anything fresh.

Out of ideas, I stare at the mattress. And remember how, decades ago, long before all of this, straight out of my teens, I came to live in Norway where Davina was working. I'd met her at *Infernos* night club in London, and contrived a totally unbelievable excuse to see her again. Told her I just happened to be on a Scandinavian holiday the very next week, taking in the fjords. That I was staying on my own in her hometown of Oslo for two nights.

I had no money for that holiday. I had to take a circuitous

Ferry route via Denmark's Hundested-Rørvigvia port and a sleeper train across southern Sweden before I finally got to Norway's capital. Armed only with an address, I travelled for eighteen hours straight, and when I finally turned up at Davina's door she met me in a little black cocktail dress because, she said afterwards, to wear anything more after such a journey simply wouldn't have been trying hard enough.

Private reminiscences, unfortunately, don't count on the app. Real = Public. I'm being bayonet-spiked again, and so is Davina. She valiantly pretends she's feeling no pain as she gazes at me from those widely green and provocative eyes of hers, and I recall when everything between us was not about love. When there was room for other things.

'Do you remember where we keep the feather dusters?' she asks, and I'm shocked, but not entirely. It's code again. Our death code this time. Agreed in the dark hours, as everyone's is, when the app is turned off. And when Davina gives me a confirming look—*yes, I mean it,* I'm surprised to find the weight not adding to but lifting from my shoulders.

I nod. Get the guns out of the side table. Davina switches the app off. The penalty for premature ending of the session is an extra week on it, but that doesn't matter now. We take the head-links and aural bobs out.

Davina cuddles me, then reaches slowly for her gun. Cameras in service of the game are placed in every house, and such a move is always a prompt for live audiences to dive in from love conversations elsewhere—even those actively playing.

Will love go off with a bang?

'Wait,' I say to Davina. 'I want to say something.'

She smiles. Curls her toes around mine. 'Only if it's about us,' she says. 'Truly about us.'

'It is,' I tell her, and suddenly she's wide awake as we cheat the home-installed cameras and audio devices. I whisper in her ear under the sheets, and she whispers back. Words they'll never know.

We've not forgotten the guns, however. They're on the mattress, close to our hips. The guns are, in fact, part of the game. Intrinsic, indeed, to its essence. Killing yourself for your partner gives them a year off the app. The ultimate love sacrifice. The real question is... who will pull the trigger first? We've both insisted we will. We both mean it.

We raise the muzzle of the guns to our foreheads, and a silence falls between us, It is one that stretches and stretches. Davina strokes my face with her free hand, and stares at me. And I stare at her. I stare at her the way a child does an ice-cream in the hand of another child. I stare at her hands especially. She's always had lovely hands. When we were young they were strong as badger claws, and all over me.

'It's OK,' I reassure her. 'It's fine. You'll be fine, Davina.'

I place my gun deep inside my mouth.

And she places hers inside hers.

bewitched border

. . .

Lisa M. Bradley

Las Bruja-jas—troublemakers all—
met at Maribel's botánica
determined to deflect
the newest hordes
of National Guard ordered
to the border to force
back asylum seekers.

Each witch came armed
with their family tree
and a potluck dish.
After pozole, enchiladas,
rice, salad, and beans,
before mesquite shortbread
café con miel y
Abuelita hot chocolate,

the members—women, men,
and neither or both—
formed a circle in the back room

Lisa M. Bradley

amid yerba buena in bulk,
incense, and saint candles.
Holding hands, they called
upon the ancestors, invoking
loved ones from ten to fifteen
generations ago—

before the wall
before the state
before the border

—and added their own outrage,
copious,
to the true brew
of "don't tread on me."
Weaving together memories,
family legends, and newspaper articles,
they built an invisible bulwark
against the northern invaders.

A mountain of dissent
erupted just beyond
the Falfurrias checkpoint
and those following
arrogant edicts
crashed their caravans
against boulders they could not see
or stalled out each time
they tried to push through.
Even on foot, the Guard
found themselves repelled,
boots striking the rampart
and sliding down, as if
against glass.

Journalists
tipped off to the plan
snapped some fuzzy footage
of the stymied soldiers
and compared it to their own
easy passage through
the new border.
The witches cackled
when they tuned in.

Well nourished, the Bruja-jas'
ancestral barrier lasted
long into the night, long after
the witches commenced
their tradition of trying to foist
leftovers on one another.

The next morning, the Guard
reported a breakthrough
to their higher-ups, now
able to breach the no-go zone
(though their trucks still suffered
invisibly rocky terrain),
they were on their way to bar "illegals"
from the American dream.

Las Bruja-jas,
up with the roosters,
gathered at a cafe to watch
the news and click their tongues.
Even miracles have expiration dates.
Maybe, they speculated
over cafecitos,

next time they could hold the line
a little longer, torment the soldiers
a little more. After all,
Las Bruja-jas had the power and
"The ancestors aren't going anywhere."

the joy factory

. . .

Liam Hogan

They check on me every five minutes. "Everything okay, love?"

"Everything's okay," I happily agree, beaming back. But it's not. If it was, I wouldn't be here. I'm serenaded by the soft babble of electronica, the chatter of circulating nurses. I gaze out at the other half-dozen patients, each donation station taking a bite out of the room as a whole. Some watch videos. You might assume from their hoarse laughter they're watching a comedy. Others listen through headphones to music or audiobooks, or thumb their phones one-handed. They laugh just as often, and just as loudly. Or smile contentedly at the choreographed movements of the staff as they dance in and out of the bays, delivering paper cups of water and squash. One elderly lady attempts a novel, though turning the pages is comically awkward. She ought to try a Kindle.

Our movement is restricted, but not as much as it *feels* like it is. A line comes out of the crook of one arm, and a line goes into the crook of the other. In between, a machine hums and purrs. Takes my blood and does something clever with it. Filters out the stuff that shouldn't be there. The stuff that would kill me if not removed, though what a way to go. The *happy* stuff.

It's manufactured, so the doctors told me as I sat, grinning at the news barely a month ago, by a growth in my hypothalamus. A brain tumour. *Cancer.* Buried deep, it's a particularly difficult area to operate on. The blood filtering is a stop-gap measure while they deliberate over the course of action, debate the cocktail of chemo, map out the precise target for proton beam therapy.

I might suspect other reasons for the delay, were I cynical. If my blood wasn't so full of oxytocin and other valuable hormones. If I wasn't so blissfully happy.

It's not all it's cracked up to be. The genie does not play fair. If you wished to always be happy, the genie would make you the village idiot. Because who else is full of joy *all* the time?

It isn't just because this world is full of things that bring you down—brain tumours being but one of many. It's human nature to balance things out, to find ways to fit the square peg into the round hole. The multi-millionaire who has everything he could possibly want is no happier than the minimum wage drudge— less, if that drudge has a little unexpected fortune, a work bonus, say, or an heroic win by their football team. It seems ridiculous that this is true. We normalise good and bad fortune; each of us has a base level. When we're at it, it doesn't take very much to change our mood. A random act of kindness, or a thoughtless slight, from someone we regard. What makes us happy or unhappy are events above or below our individual status quo.

Unless your body is cheating on you. And then... *well.* There are side-effects to being too happy, for too long. As I glance around the room, I see them reflected in my fellow sufferers, just as I would see them in me, were a mirror placed at the foot of the reclined and padded chair. We are dangerously thin, because happy trumps hungry, every time. Sallow eyed, because happy trumps tired. Some of us sport bandaged limbs or other dressings, because all those nerve endings whose job it is to warn us when we are accidentally hurting ourselves, can't be heard over the incessant clamour of *Joy! Joy! Joy!*

As for our careers, our relationships, our families... best not to talk about *those*. It can be quite the ordeal, being with someone who is deliriously happy, 24-7. In small doses, it's lovely. Like being surrounded by a litter of puppies. But just as time consuming, and just as messy, and always as utterly exhausting, once the novelty wears off.

It's not unusual for the partners of joy sufferers (there probably ought to be a better term for us!) to try to sabotage our mood. They know how brittle happiness is, how easily it is burst. Except ours *isn't*, driving them to more and more extreme acts. And still brain chemistry triumphs, as the relationship plunges over a cliff and into the abyss beyond.

If only I could share a little of my excess joy with those around me!

And that's the really remarkable thing: I *can*. My blood is being purified, yes. But the stuff being taken out is also, effectively, purified. And that stuff, for want of a better handle, is pure joy. Undiluted happiness, in a bottle. Or glass ampoule, anyway.

Despite the best attempts of a number of pharma companies, the extracted blend of our out of control hormones is more potent, and more effective, than anything lab-grown. Our joy gets given—in small doses—to terminal patients. It is used to reset the emotional compass of those with severe depression. And yes, it creeps out onto the black market. While being happy all the time is debilitating, being happy on demand... Who wouldn't want that? Those multimillionaires who ask *is this all there is?* now have an answer, as well as the money to pay for it.

I can hardly complain. Because while I'm not financially benefiting from spreading my joy, I am, *medically*. I'm about half way through today's collection, based on previous sessions, which occur three times a week. After forty-eight hours, the amount of happy hormones in my blood makes my mood undentable, makes me feel like a hero, even as I car-crash my life and everything around it, all with a cheery smile and a floating-on-clouds air.

There'll be a comedown at the end of the treatment. The harvest stops when my response to the nurses' "Everything okay?" isn't quite so chipper. When my infectious smile collapses. I'll leave here grimly sober, squinting into the sunshine, wondering at the blackness that lurks behind everything, wondering why I no longer fit as well as I did before, the angles all jagged and sharp. But I'm not there yet, as the machine continues to whirr. I lie back on my pillow, watch the world go by, and muse on my peculiar situation.

The honest truth?

I couldn't be happier.

adventures

. . .

Devan Barlow

As the eldest, I was always so busy
cooking, cleaning, chopping firewood,
trying to convince my younger siblings
there was more to life
than dreamed-of adventures
Perhaps this is why
when birds who insisted they were kings
came to the house seeking brides
they never chose me
Instead they flew off with all three
of my sisters
It seemed there was to be
no fourth bird-king for me
Once the girls were gone
my brother left too
convinced he had a fortune to seek
sure I would manage
as I always had

Something cracked apart in me at that
like a paltry twig atop a fire

I left the cottage,
then the village,
stepping beyond the extent
of the world I knew
Good fortune crossed my path
with that of traveling players, who needed someone
to stitch, sell tickets, soothe the stars,
shift scenery on occasion
At least now I was paid for working hard
and would see some of the world
Such was the troupe's fame that soon
we set off on a ship
Yet one night when the waves and winds churned
with the tantrums of underwater monarchs
we wrecked upon an island

If anyone else survived
they were on a different bit of beach
For I woke alone
Nearby, upon the churned-up sands
a strange box, once buried, could now be glimpsed
as though left for me, from the storm,
by way of apology
I unearthed the box
Inside, bizarrely, were
animals upon animals,
once inside another
somehow still alive
Each scampered away as I uncovered them
until at last there was only a duck
Was this, at last, my feathered groom?
Yet this bird did not propose
or promise me palaces
Instead the duck vomited up an egg
before waddling away

The egg's shell possessed a dozen textures
a hundred colors
a scent like nothing I could name
This all seemed a very long process
for a very small meal
but I wasn't in a position to be picky
Expecting albumen and yolk
I cracked the egg open
Instead —
Death spilled into my hands
feared and treasured, hidden here
abandoned for so long
Stewing in the type of power
that comes from old, intricate enchantments
and the breaking thereof

A power that now
was entirely mine
Turns out
I adore adventures

a flat white ribbon

. . .

Elana Gomel

I was invited by my friend Drago Drago to discuss my new theory in the company of the most discerning physicists of our time. The North Hemisphere Society for Spreading Light and Knowledge met regularly after dinner at one of its members' country houses to consider new hypotheses, exchange ideas, and engage in some harmless but delicious gossip, lubricated by their excellent beetle wines. I had never been invited to these gatherings until now. Being an immigrant nobody, I did not expect to. So, I was overjoyed and a little apprehensive when Drago casually dropped in a conversation that I would be welcomed to join him and a select group of friends for an evening meal on his estate but of course, if I had prior engagements… I assured him that I happened to be perfectly free. It was true as it was true every other evening.

Drago's estate was some way outside the Capital, and I had to take a train to get there. I disliked trains for reasons I did not feel compelled to share with anybody. But there was no choice. Despite my university position, I was too poor to afford a car. Not having any family estate to fall back upon would deplete even a generous salary, and mine was far from it.

To distract myself from the gentle rocking of the train, I

busied myself with going over my notes. It helped to calm me down. So, I finally dropped the scribbled pages onto the wobbly table tray and allowed myself to stare out the window.

The day was almost done, and the sky was of a beautiful purplish rose color. Today was a Butterfly-day, and the forecast for tomorrow was the same. Clouds of multicolored insects were settling down in the squat hive trees that lined the tracks. I still remembered the embarrassment of my arrival in the Capital when I naively asked somebody on campus why all the trees were shaped in the same cuboid fashion. I thought they were topiaries and admired their precise cutting. The man's eyes grew wide. Fortunately, he was just a lowly janitor and probably attributed my question to a scientist's eccentricity.

I could see the bright orange dot of the rising Sunmoon through a swarm of butterflies. Their colors were hard to distinguish in the twilight glow, but I knew that they obeyed no discernible rule. Different species mixed together, brown swallowtails with black and red monarchs. They had no concept of uniformity here.

Butterflies and moths would rule the air for another cycle or so, and then the forecast spoke of a Mosquito day. There was enough time to buy a new net for my window as the old one was torn when a portly rhino beetle tried to push through a couple of cycles ago.

I lowered the rattling window to let the outside air in. It was as warm as boiled milk at bedtime; the blazing heat of the Sun settling into the caressing comfort of the Sunmoon. A swirl of butterflies drifted in, and I shivered as they brought back the memory of dancing white flakes nobody but me had a word for.

Drago met me at the station, and we embraced, to my surprise and delight. I never thought we were close, though I would call him as a friend. To a lonely man, even an acquaintance becomes family by default. I always told people I had left my childhood friends behind when I came to the Capital. It was true, in a way.

He had a car, a rattling turquoise contraption with a foldable roof. Now the roof was down to let us enjoy the rush of warm cinnamon-scented evening air. A large stray moth that lodged itself in my hair was a small price to pay for the pleasure of feeling the gentleness of twilight. I carefully disentangled it and let it fly out. Drago chuckled.

"You are a kind man, Santo," he said. "I never saw you kill an insect."

"I use baits and sprays like everybody else," I said quickly, trying to sound casual. "It's just not efficient, killing one creature out of millions if you want to exterminate all."

"The dream of total extermination is just that, a dream," Drago sighed. "I wish it were not, especially on a Mosquito or a Tick-Day. But I will let our friends from the Biological Society ponder these issues. You and I are here to solve a much greater mystery, right?"

"Yes," I said. "The overall structure of the Universe."

***

The men that gathered around Drago's dinner table were some of the most illustrious minds in the North Hemisphere. I knew most of them by name and reputation; with some, I had had brief professional exchanges. My relatively low rung on the academic ladder meant I was protected from the worst viciousness of scientific squabbles. I noticed that Hildur Hildur, a visiting scholar from the Physics Enquiry Institute of the South, was absent from this gathering. I was not surprised: the political tensions between North and South were rising, and milky-skinned Southerners were occasionally harassed in the streets.

I should have been petrified. The circle of glittering eyes and pursed mouths surrounding me had the power to make or break my career. Though I had tenure, and the Society was but an informal gathering, these people had the clout of words and reputation. The thick aura of respect hung around them, as palpable as an insect cloud. I was a nobody, a stranger, even if they did not know how much of a stranger I was. And yet, I was perfectly calm. Being intimately acquainted with your own death makes you immune to petty anxieties.

I took a sip of Drago's excellent beetle wine, unfolded my papers, and started talking. At some points, I made use of the slate board that he thoughtfully provided to scribble down my equations.

I was so engrossed in the truth of what I was saying that I barely felt the pulse of my audience. When I taught, I was as attuned to my students as an actor on stage is attuned to his spectators, adapting my pitch and delivery to their shifting mood. But here, the equations themselves were all I needed. That–and memories.

I do not know how long I went on, except that my throat got sore, and I had to wash it with another sip of wine. And then the final formula was on the board, and I surfaced out of my trance. I looked up at the faces around the table.

I saw what I had envisioned as their reaction before: surprise and rejection, mixed with thoughtfulness. In truth, there was more of the latter than I had expected and less of the former. But one man seemed to be puffed up with indignation. It was Onto Onto, head of the Astronomy Department. He and I had met a couple of times at various university functions, and I had a vague liking for the man because his complexion was mahogany like mine. Skin tones grew deeper the further North you went on a smooth gradient, so people often assumed we were born at the same latitude, which of course was not the case. But now his face was even darker because it was swollen with blood.

"It's preposterous!" he thundered. "Nestled universes! Macrocosms contained within each other like roasted birds served at fancy banquets! Are we talking physics or culinary arts?"

Drago cleared his throat, embarrassed at this outburst, and now as I regained my ability to tune in to the mood of the audience, I saw, with surprise and apprehensive delight, that most of them were on my side. Even if they did not accept my theory in full, they were impressed by the flawlessness of my math. And even more so, I realized, they had come here to enjoy the fragrant countryside after the butterflies had settled and flowers opened up in the gentle radiance of the Sunmoon. The intellectual discussion was but an addendum to the rich food and rare wines. They regarded science as they did their cigars. They had no idea how deadly science could be. Or maybe they did not care.

I responded to Onto with more math and though I did not convince him, the polite impatience of the rest of them, eager to end the lecture and take a stroll in the garden, wore him down. With a scatter of compliments to my "originality", our meeting dispersed.

A servant showed me to my sleeping quarters, but I wanted to enjoy the gardens before sleep, hoping that a walk would tire me enough to grant dreamless sleep. I went down the side staircase and exited into the orange and pink twilight as the Sunmoon climbed higher into the luminescent sky, glittering with the infinitude of closely set stars. Branches rustled as the butterflies settled deeper in and moths started to emerge. The trees looked like cubes cut out of jet, glimmering with an occasional wave of motion as a synchronized twitch went through the ropes and clusters of insects.

A figure stepped out of the arbor. It was Drago.

"Can't sleep, old chap?" He addressed me jovially. "Well, your presentation was amazing, just what I expected. Not that I buy it, mind you. Our models are just beautiful stories written in math. The real world has no need of them."

"Stories have power," I said.

"Words are words, not reality."

"Words can kill."

Drago snorted. He was slightly drunk, I noticed, and apparently wanted to eliminate "slightly" in this description. He invited me in for a nightcap, and I accepted.

He poured me another goblet of his famed beetle wine, the golden bullets of beetle bodies diving and surfacing out of the dark purple of the foamy liquid. I took an appreciative sip.

"You know," I said, "there was a time in my life when I would find drinking wine with insects in it totally disgusting. But this is wonderful!"

"Seriously? How come? Even the albinos like their liquor, though they put caterpillars into it, which is a profanation."

I noted that he used the pejorative term for the people of the South. It was becoming more and more acceptable. I could not understand the growing hostility as the South was a separate continent, and the people of the two landmasses seldom mixed. Politicians on both sides could not claim the impurity of blood.

"Where I grew up," I said, "wine was made of plants."

Drago sputtered.

"What? Where? I never heard of such a thing!"

I had a strange feeling then, as if stepping off the precipice, feeling the exhilarating rush of surrender as gravity takes hold.

"I was not born in this world, Drago," I said. And then I told him.

I cannot stand white. The reason is that it was snowing when they took us to the ravine.

Nobody here knows what snow is. The Sun and Sunmoon, the axial tilt, the flat plains and shallow landlocked seas, make for a warm and humid climate. There are no polar caps, no glaciers or snowstorms. But my first memory is of making a wet snowball and laughing uncontrollably as I tossed it at my older brother Tonnie. My brother who was one of the first to be killed.

In our world, which we, of course, called Earth just like this one, lava flows and earthquakes were common, and so were sharp differences in temperature. There was no Sunmoon, and in Northern countries, the Sun would disappear for months at an end. It was cold where we lived, and I did not like it. But I liked everything else: my family's big house full of servants and tutors for my brother and me, and our mother's art studio where she would occasionally let us sit and watch while she painted. She was a famous painter, and Tonnie wanted to follow in her footsteps. But I studied physics, to my father's delight. My father was an accountant, not a scholar, but he had a deep reverence for science.

That was why he was so deeply upset when Blood Science became popular. He could not quarrel with thick tomes filled with tables, and data, and calculations. If it did not affect us personally, I am sure he would have accepted all of its conclusions and would have become one of its most fervent acolytes. He would have carried out the practical applications of the theory with no hesitation, just like the people who later on showed up in our house. Unfortunately, it did affect us, and my father was a lost soul, torn between his respect for words and figures and his horror of what these words and figures meant for our family.

"You see, Drago," I told him, "in my world as in yours, people have different physiognomies. But here skin tones get redder as we are going North and milkier as we are going South. In our world, there was no geographical rhyme or reason, and complexions were all mixed together."

"So, you lived side by side with albinos?" he asked. I could see that he did not believe a word of what I was saying, treating my story as a sort of fable. But he found it entertaining, and that was all that counted.

"Yes, only there were more different physiognomies and body types. Skin colors were as varied as those of insects, and there were people with all kinds of body shapes. Some people were pink like newborn piglets and small and rotund. Others were indeed thin and white, paler even than the Southerners.

There were some with emerald-toned complexions, and those were rare, and considered beautiful by some cultures."

"Like June-bugs," Drago snorted and poured me some more wine. A beetle climbed onto the rim of my goblet, and I crunched it with my teeth. It tasted like licorice or what I remembered licorice tasted like.

"Imagine humanity like moths and butterflies, with different colors and even different growths on their bodies. For a long time, it did not matter. In the Dark Ages, nobody paid much attention to physiognomy. There were wars, of course, and the occasional massacre, but it was all for land, or resources, or religion."

"Religion is a bane of humanity," Drago opined. Like all members of the Society for Spreading Light and Knowledge, he was an atheist.

I shrugged. I wished I had retained my faith in the solar gods of my childhood, but they seemed rather irrelevant in the multi-colored twilight of the Sunmoon.

"Science can be just as bad," I said. I realized I was getting seriously inebriated, but I just did not care anymore.

Drago lifted an eyebrow.

"You, a scientist?"

"We believe in science because it makes the world compre-hensible. But what if it's not? And when our explanations fail, we get enraged and try to force reality into making sense. We tame chaos and purify the disorder. By violence."

"Tell me more about this world of yours," Drago said. He did not want to get bogged down in a philosophical discussion, and truth be told, neither did I. Once breached, the dam of memories could not hold.

"Anyway, there was a man, a biologist. He came up with what he called Blood Science. He believed that all those different skin colors and body growths, like additional limbs or double noses–these were quite common where I grew up–were a sign of an underlying disease that was eating away at humanity. The blood that flowed through our collective veins was impure, contaminated. He had a plan to purify it."

I swallowed. I did not want to go on because suddenly it was not about words anymore but about the whiteness that hurt my eyes, and the implacable cold that stole through my bones, and the acrid smell of blood in the snow.

"Sounds like a good idea," Drago said.

"It did sound like a good idea to many, my father included. Until they started arresting people who did not fit the biometrical profile drawn for each specific community. Deviations were allowed but only within statistically established parameters. So, our family, being too red for our province, were singled out."

"How can you be too red?" Drago was indignant, his complexion, enhanced by the wine, almost glowing like a ruby. Here the more your skin approached pure vermillion, the more attractive you were. I had received many offers from marriage brokers, all of which I rejected.

"You can be if you stand out too much, breaking the smooth graph of variation. It was not a specific color or shape they came after. It was exceptionality. Difference.

The arrested people never came back. And then soldiers came home from deployment and told stories of ravines in the snow forests filled with corpses. We did not want to believe it, of course. By this time, though, Blood Science was taught in every school and university. There was an election, and the party that promised to make it the cornerstone of domestic and foreign policy got an overwhelming majority."

"Democracy in action," Drago said approvingly. The North just recently moved away from an autocratic Council of Seven to a parliamentary system. The South was still stuck with a hereditary ruler.

"Our neighbors started avoiding us. And then my brother Tonnie went missing."

I took a deep breath and glanced outside. The Sunmoon was glowing with rosy radiance through the lattice of branches, and I thought I saw movement in the gloaming. Would it be a rare Luna Moth Night when night insects swarmed under the light of the Sunmoon?

"The thing was, we did not know what was actually involved in purifying the blood. Words can be slippery, you know. This is why I love math. It is not as ambiguous as language. Words, though… they can mean so many things and you can be hypnotized by their beauty without trying to delve into their correspondence to the world. Purification sounds good. Who can be opposed to purity, after all? But when Tonnie did not come home from school, I slipped out and stole to the outskirts of our town where the train depot was. By this time, it was common knowledge that arrestees were taken there, loaded onto trains, and taken into the deep forest. You see, Drago, our plants were different from yours. They grew by themselves, without symbiosis with insects, creating gigantic plantations of wild trees where one could easily lose oneself.

I saw the people standing in two lines, shambling toward the open doors of the train cars. They were herded by uniformed soldiers. At first, I thought they were shackled together but then I realized that the flexible ropes that connected their wrists were not restraints. They were tubes. And they were filled with blood."

"Transfusion?" Drago asked. His joviality was gone. My story was impacting him as the picture, so clear in my mind, was being built up in his brain, word by word. I did not want the power of storytelling but somehow, I possessed it–or maybe it possessed me.

"Yes, transfusion. This was how they were trying to purify the blood, to normalize the wild variance of traits. Two random people would be shackled together, their blood mixed, circulating through their conjoined bodies. The belief was that the variance would be diluted, the differences smoothed over. Only it did not work. The people would either go into shock and die or just remain as they were, their blood mixing but their physiognomies still the same. So, they were taken into the forest and shot. Blood Science was infallible. If people did not respond as they should, the problem was with them. Their intransigence, their inner corruption, their evil. It had been proven by that time that the power of pure blood could be countermanded by impure thoughts.

I saw my brother Tonnie. He was shackled to an older man with a strange, pale yellow, jaundiced complexion and a small third eye in his forehead. I did not know who he was. He was drooping, and Tonnie was trying to support him. The tube linking them was swollen with blood like a leech.

Tonnie saw me and waved frantically at me to run away. I did. I came back home and told my parents what I had seen. My mother tried to kill herself in the evening, but my father stopped her. They came for us the next day.

The soldiers were polite and professional. They separated me from my parents, and I never saw my mother and father again. I knew they died exchanging blood with strangers.

They took me to the train station. It was unbelievably cold. I cannot describe to you, Drago, what it feels like. You have never experienced a cold like this. It leaches life out of you and leaves you a poor shivering thing, unable to think, feel, or move. They had taken away my coat, and snow was settling on my naked arms. Fortunately, after a while your body becomes as insensate as your mind."

"What's snow?" Drago asked.

"Imagine a swarm of tiny white butterflies or bees, the biggest swarm you can visualize, and it never settles, never goes away, just swirls and roils around you, and drinks your warmth until you are as hollow as a rotten stump. It's just a metaphor, of course. Snow is simply frozen water. But it feels alive.

Anyway, I was not suffering from cold for long because they herded me, along with a whole lot of other people, men and women alike, toward a makeshift station that was set in the depot. It was marginally warmer inside, and I was glad. The station was manned by several harried people wearing white scrubs. In our world, Drago, medical personnel wore white instead of black.

Soldiers lined us up in two rows. These soldiers were not as professional and dispassionate as the ones who had arrested me. They seemed nervous and jittery, and they yelled at us and pushed us roughly. One woman fell and they kicked her. A man tried to interfere and was kicked too. I noticed some familiar faces among the soldiers. They had been in school with me. I could not see much difference between them and myself. I think they realized it too, and it made them angry.

When my turn came, a doctor at the station smiled at me. He was about the age of my father, with a round avuncular face. He beckoned a man from the second row—an old man who I had never seen before. He was one of those whose complexions were unusually pale—much like the South people who you call albinos.

"You two will do," the doctor said with satisfaction.

The needle in my vein hurt so much that I yelped. The doctor padded my hand.

"It'll be ok, son," he said kindly.

When the blood started circulating through the tube, I felt it heavy in my veins like molasses. It seemed to be reluctant to flow in. You don't think about it, but your blood is viscous, and it takes the constant uphill battle of your heart to keep it moving. The blood did not want to mingle in our bodies, and the doctor squeezed my wrist painfully to force it out. And then he put a flat white ribbon around my wrist, a pressure bandage, winding it and pressing it close to keep the needle and the tubing in place. Soldiers pushed us out, back into the cold.

The train was waiting; the car doors yawning wide, black against the white of the snowdrifts that started accumulating on the platform. I thought that I could run away, roll into the drifts, perhaps escape the rain of bullets that would follow. But I could not. The tube that linked me to the stranger pulsated with my own and his blood, and it was as tender and swollen as if it were an actual part of my body, an artery suddenly released from the confines of the flesh. The thought of yanking it out, of seeing my blood spurt out, red on white, made me faint.

We shambled toward the cars, the old man who was now as close to me as I had been to my mother when in her womb, shambling by my side and cradling his pierced arm. I appreciated it; any sharp movement would cause a dull wave of pain through my body. I realized I did not know his name and asked it.

"Lonnie," he said, "I'm a mechanic."

He also told me his patronymic, but I have forgotten it. You see, Drago, in our world people took their father's name instead of doubling their own.

The train ride passed me by in a blur of nausea and thirst. Every jolt of the car sent a wave of ache through my body. The windows of the car had been covered by cardboard, so it was very dark. We all huddled on the floor as seats had been taken out. At least, it was not cold anymore, as the exhalation of too many bodies pressed together created a miasma of warm stench. People could not use the privy because there was none, and in any case, when shackled by a transfusion tube to another person, you could not move freely. Every movement had to be negotiated with a maddened stranger. I had read about conjoined twins and how such babies were invariably killed by their parents. At the time I had thought it was a barbarity; now I realized they were doing their children a favor.

Finally, the train stopped, and we were ushered out, with curses and blows. Funny how the soldiers' behavior changed the further away we were from the city.

There was nothing there. I thought there would be a medical center of some kind where our cure by Blood Science could be monitored, but there was not a building in sight. Just an icy platform and a track leading away from it into the depth of the black forest. It had stopped snowing, but the drifts were tall around the track. Some soldiers with machine guns milled around, and there was a group of doctors at one side of the platform, stomping their feet to keep warm. They all wore heavy coats and hats over their scrubs.

Lonnie tripped, pulling on the tube and making me cry out in pain. He apologized, but I saw his face had acquired a kind of greenish tint, and his lips were pale. There had been rumors that transfusions killed some people even before they were shot. We stumbled together toward the end of the platform. I squeezed the flat white ribbon that the doctor had wound around my wrist with a kind of reverence. It kept the needle in place, and blood flowing. I felt no ill effects unlike Lonnie; just the opposite, I was beginning to feel warmth radiating from the insertion in my vein, keeping the cold away.

One of the doctors was examining every pair that the soldiers herded toward him, and another one was standing by his side with a clipboard, making notations. Once examined, each pair was pushed onto the track that disappeared into the forest. I heard a dry cracking from the moment we disembarked. I thought at first that it was tree branches giving way under the burden of snow. But it was machine gun fire.

The doctor briefly glanced at Lonnie and me, his eyes sliding off our faces. I remember him well: a young man, his complexion an approved median brown.

"No improvement," he said, and the nurse standing by him made a notation on his clipboard.

I realized, then, that the entire thing was a charade. Of course, there would be no improvement because nobody, including the doctor, knew what an improvement would look like. And yet he was pretending that there was an actual inspection here, that there was a chance for some of us to survive, while knowing perfectly well where that track led. Or did he know it? I am still of two minds about it.

We were pushed onto the track by a bored soldier. Lonnie was drooping, his knees giving way. At some point, he stumbled, turned away and vomited into the snow. He still turned to me and mouthed an apology. Another soldier kicked him down, almost yanking the tube from my arm. Only the flat white ribbon held it in place.

I was focusing on this white ribbon so intensely that it became the most important, nay, the only thing in my world. You know, Drago, the theory I presented today about universes nestling within other universes, macrocosm and microcosm meeting like the ends of a circle, I had been thinking about it my entire life. I have now the math to substantiate it but before I knew enough to speak the language of equations, it was a story, so deeply embedded in my dreams that I did not even know where it originated. And at this moment when I knew I was about to die, I also knew that this story was my only chance of survival.

I kept staring at that white ribbon. It was made of some dense rubberized fabric, slightly ribbed, and it fit snugly around my wrist, cradling and squeezing it with the strength that somehow gave me a reassurance of continuing to exist. It was real. And the more I tried to connect to its reality, the more did everything else–the cold sting of snowflakes, the tug of Lonnie as he crawled on the icy ground, the shuffling of many feet, the rattle of shots–was receding, fading away.

A shot so close that it seemed to reverberate in my ears yanked me back, just as the tubing was yanked out of my arm. Lonnie was lying on the edge of the ravine, his head blooming into a bloody halo, exploded by the bullet fired by a bored soldier. The ravine was full of bodies, so there was no room for another corpse. But people kept coming, so bodies were beginning to pile up.

Blood was pumping out of my wrist and mixing with the bloody slush of melting snow. It did not look different from any other blood.

I squeezed the white ribbon around my wrist, trying to stop the bleeding, just as the soldier lifted his gun aiming at me.

And at that moment, the ribbon expanded, wrapping itself

around me like a maelstrom of white, drawing me deeper and deeper into a funnel of stars. I cannot describe it, Drago. I saw worlds within worlds within worlds, swarming like moths, circling around me. I saw reality as I fell through universes nested within each other.

And I instantly forgot what I saw. Only a pale shadow of that revelation remained, like the melting remains of a dream.

When I came to, I was lying on the warm moss surrounded by butterflies, and a bright pink-orange disk was shining through the lattice of branches, bigger than a star but smaller than the moon. I stared at it in childlike wonder. For you see, Drago, in my world there is no Sunmoon but there is a dead satellite we call the Moon, which gives off no warmth but only silver light."

I ended my tale by discovering that my goblet was empty and the last beetle that had crawled out of it lay on its back the table, legs twitching. I swept it off.

Drago shook his head.

"What an imagination you have, Santo Santo," he said with an expression that I could interpret as either admiration or disapproval. "I see how you crafted this fable to give a poetic form to your dry math. And I believe I see a note of warning in it. But honestly, my friend, if I were you, I would forebear to try to publish it or to tell it to too many people. People are likely to misunderstand it as a political statement, though I am sure it was not your intent."

I had nothing to say but to thank him for listening to me and for his hospitality. It was very late, and the Sunmoon was setting. I went to my quarters.

Standing at the open window, I looked into the sky that was as different from the sky of my Earth as the swarming insects everywhere were different from the stark barrenness of its snowy planes. And I imagined the flat white ribbon encircling the galaxies of this universe, holding it all together, and preventing realities from bleeding into each other–the bandage of creation.

But what if this bandage was unraveling, weakening, giving way?

A swarm of moths rose up from the cuboid bushes under my window. All the moths were white, sparkling in the last rays of the Sunmoon like a flurry of snow.

end of watch

. . .

Charles Chin

Oh, you're awake.

Well, as awake as you can be while still asleep. Yea, look, I know that really doesn't make any sense, but I'm just your Sleep Paralysis Daemon, I'm not used to explaining these things to humans. You're usually asleep until I'm gone. Nevertheless, you won't have to worry about little ol' me much longer. I only have ten minutes left until the end of my watch, and then it's back to the aether for me, and to the waking world for you. Until then, I'll be here, protecting you.

Relax, no need to panic. I can see you trying to move, but I have things locked down from up here on your chest. Can't have you thrashing about when the darkness lifts. This is the most dangerous time, you know. Right here at the edge of the veil. Those beasts inside you have had all night to feed, and without me here, who knows what they would do to you. Or what you'd do to yourself. Your human psyches are such fragile things. It's a wonder you make it through the nights at all.

Actually, this is a pretty serendipitous happening. We really need to talk. It's been a decade or so since I was reassigned. I won't get into it, but let's just say that the last daemon knew someone who—no, I said I wouldn't go into it, so I won't. You don't want to hear about office politics. But now that I'm back, I've seen you've rearranged the place, that space inside your head, and not for the better. You've made it a home for some pretty nasty creatures.

I see one now, one of those pulsing beasts, skulking in the shadows there behind your Ambitions. You've stacked those boxes so far back there in your mind, I'm surprised they haven't topped over from the weight. Don't tell me you've given up on them? No wonder they called me back: the last guy was sleeping on the job, and those little nagging thoughts have turned into full-fledged terrors.

Ah, got it. Here, you see? Wiggly bastard, isn't it? Even with me sitting here, us having a full on conversation, these things still try to sneak out. Well, maybe less a conversation and more of a lecture, but I digress. The trick with these, the ones with the tails and the curved teeth, is to pinch them right behind the eyes. It cuts off the circulation, and they just melt to smoke. There, see?

I can see you're still scared, what with those wide eyes and all, but I took care of him. And hey, look: no one's a lost cause. Take it from me. I've been doing this for longer than-well, come to think of it, I've just always been doing this. So when I say you're going to be alright, you know I mean it. All different kinds of humans from all different walks of life can end up with shadowed minds and lost hearts. I've seen beasts driven from hollower souls than yours.

First things first, we're going to need to rearrange some things. With your Ambitions in that corner and your Joys shoved into the drawers of that cabinet, you've just got this clutter of boxes in the middle ripe for terrors. Look, it doesn't have to be a whole deal, we can start small. Clean out one little box. Like that one there, filled with recent conversations with your sister. The Anxieties crawling out of it are impressive, seeing as it seems to only be holding a month's worth of phone calls. Definitely want to take care of that one sooner rather than later. Those spindly legs of Anxieties leave little holes in the floors of your mind, and before you know it, you'll be leaking essence all over your subconscious. And trust me, getting red essence out of subconscious takes more than just baking soda.

So let's empty that box. Just concentrate and give it a nice push. Good! Yes, just tip it over and let that gray sludge spill out. I've got the bugs, don't worry. My trusty pike here makes short work of them. A little air and look! It's evaporating already. You'll need to do something about the filmy residue, of course, but that's tomorrow's problem. The first step is the hardest, and you're already past that. Oops, almost let one of those Anxieties escape into another box. I got it, though.

Now, just breathe. Let's make it an exercise, yes? See how high you can lift me with your chest, then slowly let me down. That's it. How's that feel? Just one little box and I can see it in your eyes: you feel better.

Well, the veil is starting to lift, and I can see the waking world coming into view. Time for me to clock out. But hey, even a little bit of progress is progress. I'll be back, don't worry. I'm here to build you back up, and once you have the strength, we can tackle some of those deeper terrors. Like the ones hiding in the mirror. That's where the real change happens.

Take care of yourself out there. And when you talk to your sister again, just remember you don't have to hold onto every little thing.

Wakey wakey, eggs and bakey.

experiments in probability theory

. . .

Veda Villiers

We begin with the dice,
six faces, each a trace
of possibility—
one roll,
a universe unfurls.

Chance, the queen of uncertainty,
shakes her quantum cup
and spills
a constellation of numbers—
random as rain,
yet some say the rain knows
where it will fall,
just as my heart knows
its heartbeat– a calculated risk
in this vast equation of existence.

Probability is the ghost
of a thousand futures,
each one unfolding
from a moment of choice,

splitting like light
through thousand prisms—
each hue a path we might walk,
each fog a road we might never see,
where quarks gamble
with dice that rewrite
a crystalline multiverse.
I trace the threads, a pilgrim
through time's mirrored traverse.

In my lab, we measure it:
the bell curve bends
like a black hole
sucking in every outcome
not yet imagined,
flattening the peaks
of our certainties
into probabilities
that hover,
tentative,
above the threshold of knowing.
much like my hope for you—
delicate yet unwavering.

$p = 1$:
Perfect certainty.
$p = 0$:
An empty hand.

But here—
in this sliver of time,
where we spin poised
and the equation wavers,
we live between the edges—
neither certain nor absent—

in the gentle tremor
of chances.

If I flip the coin,
does the outcome already exist
in the ether,
waiting to fall,
or do I create it
with every bated breath,
each choice cascading
like a rolling stone,
down a mountain
that may or may not exist?

And what of you, my love—
your soul, a fragile horizon
in this chaotic universe.
I calculate your chances,
in tender fractions
upon equations of survival.
In this dance of fate,
I hold your hand,
defying the odds,
believing love bends all
rigid laws of chance,
that in the realm of possibilities,
our future is an astral configuration
and your survival
the sweetest outcome
I dare dream.

dark (matter) angels

. . .

Geoffrey A. Landis

Angels are immaterial:
    Crystalline ether
        Substantiation of essence
            Luminous air
                Immanent spirit

Solid matter is nothing to them.
They slip through the world's substance
—through steel through concrete through rock through
    flesh—
more easily than we pass through air

The surface of the earth
circumscribes
    defines
        delimits
            embodies our world
but to angels, it is insubstantial,
like passing through a dream.
To an angel, there's nothing particular about the surface of
    the Earth

than any other location
above or below
interior, exterior is all the same
to angels

Angels fall, and keep falling
Angels fall through the center of the Earth
Circle the center of the Earth like moths around the
    lamplight
oscillating

Astronomers tell us:
        dark matter holds the galaxies together
Invisible, yet ponderable
Falling angels.
    Falling
    angels
            falling
            falling
            falling

the moon smiles at its creatures

. . .

Akis Linardos

the Child was born at night
on a dark and endless canvas
where there existed no land
not even stars

the Child suckled on the breast
of the primordial void,
its belly turning nothingness
to light

the Child blew bubbles
suffused with Its bellylight
but without laws to burst them
they expanded infinitely

the Child's smiled,
face captured in Its creations
reflected on newborn starlight
split within the bubbles' cores

the Child's bubbles sprouted creatures
feasting on the fragmented bellylights
and they know It's watching over,
if they squint up at their moon

when droids dream

. . .

Joe Wood

Is this what humans look like when they sleep?

AN-D wondered about this, as they watched the crew of *The Vera* sleep. The little droid hovered over them in silence. They peered into each pod, making sure that each human slept peacefully. Sure, they could just read their vitals on each corresponding panel—which all looked normal, of course. But AN-D knew better than that. Even with the best maintenance, enough time in space and any machine will eventually break down, fall apart, glitch, corrode, corrupt, destabilize, decay, or make a potentially fatal error. Eventually.

How peaceful, AN-D thought, while the droid watched them sleep.

AN-D worried about thinking too loud in the stasis room. They tried to mind-whisper as much as they could. With so much silence, it was not hard to imagine even a quiet thought echoing off the steel walls.

And we can't have that, AN-D mused to themself, keeping its thoughts at a purely conversational tone. *Can't wake them up yet. We're almost there!*

AN-D pretended that there was a reason to not wake them early, one that had nothing to do with death. Surely, it would be seen as rude by human customs. *Don't wake a deep dreamer,* AN-D mused. It sounded like a type of nursery rhyme–the ones human children got from caring old people in every holotape. Those holotapes would play when the crew first entered their pods, relaxing them until their vital signs began to dip into a lull. While their minds wandered, their bodies went into a cozy hibernation. To wake them, AN-D would have to follow a very specific thawing process or risk sending them into shock.

The droid looked at all four pods quickly, making sure that everyone was safely tucked away, as they were thirty-four seconds ago. Ice crystals clung to the lining of each window. So, AN-D had the faint sensation that looking into each pod felt like peering into their neighbor's window in winter. On their last pit stop 10 ESY (Earth Solar Years) ago, AN-D had gotten a chance to see an Earth winter. The crew had some time to themselves before they needed to use the Warp Door for their mission. So, Captain Fidele, closest to the door on the right, had taken them on a trip to his uncle's farm outside of Buffalo. They had thrown snowballs at each other and his young cousins. Even AN-D got to land a few, since the snow was flaky enough that no real harm would come to the humans (even if they shouted a little when one covered their faces). Captain Fidele kept a brave face, not flinching or tearing up when his cousins had to be pulled off him on his way out. *Just for a little while,* he told them in the same unreadable expression he wore in his pod.

AN-D wondered if Captain Fidele learned to lie from their company *Synchro.* It promised the crew a chance to be among the first humans in a resource-rich world at the edge of known space. The only catch: it was 10 Earth years away from the nearest Warp Door. Not that it would feel like that to the humans of *The Vera.* But AN-D did notice that Captain Fidele's usual smile faded once *The Vera* exited hyperspace.

Across from him, Alis silently called out for help. AN-D knew that was not the case, but even they could have been fooled every time they checked on her. Unlike the others, the resident agricultural specialist went to stasis with her eyes open. Though her EEG readings indicated that she was in the same deep sleep as the rest of the crew, her face had an animated quality that none of the others shared. The grayish-blue lenses were nearly swallowed by red veins that formed most of her bloodshot eyes. While AN-D ensured that all the crew completed the stasis process normally, Alis must have had a sudden, distressing thought emerge as the freezing began.

Poor Alis. What could have scared her like that? AN-D thought as they hovered around her pod. *She was already going to wake up with a searing headache. Now her eyes and throat will need careful monitoring when we reach our destination. I should make her an herbal tea. Yes! A good, strong, gently warm tea with leaves from the garden.*

With that soothing picture in mind, AN-D drifted through the room. Shadows draped over the last pod, obscuring Gemma's face. Shining their headlight onto the glass, AN-D found that the communications expert had laid on her side as she slept. They had cautioned her against this multiple times, rattling off findings from *The Interstellar Traveller* and *Cryogenics* that strongly frowned upon that practice due to its correlation with cardiovascular problems. The response was short and persuasive: *that's why you're here, AN-D. To take care of us.*

Those words echoed in the droid's mind throughout this expedition. They were loudest in the quietest moments: looking at the stars through the observation deck, crossing the engine room when the beating heart of the ship needed to rest, and traveling from the stasis chamber to the garden across the hall. AN-D welcomed them. Sometimes, they replied out loud, eager to answer the call.

AN-D could neither taste the air nor feel the heat from the garden on their metal shell. But they still knew it was a sanctuary. Nowhere else on *The Vera* teemed with that much life— nowhere on this still, silent mausoleum of a ship. Instead of tapestries, the walls in this room were decorated with flowering hydroponics stations. The minimal amount of water that it took to feed these vines was recycled back into their individual devices through a slow dripping process. Likewise, the fresh air from the garden funneled through circular vents in the ceiling, cycling air throughout the entire ship.

"Good morning," AN-D said. Other than the slight breeze pushing past the curtains of vines, there was no movement in the garden. The droid looked around the room, keeping their head swirling around 360 degrees. Gliding through the spacious room, they stopped only once they reached the center. Light poured down from a circular fixture, illuminating the heart of the garden.

The floating tree responded with its usual silence. Instead of towering over its neighbors in the garden, it was content to turn inwards. It resembled a vast bush the size of a cloud. Cotton candy branches bundled together to form a fluffy pillow in the low-gravity chamber. *It looks so soft*, AN-D thought. *As soft as...* the droid did not know. Though the tree did not need any pruning, AN-D still brushed its branches softly with their hands. Leaves pooled in their palms, so fragile and bright. The answer was somewhere in the tangled vines, something the droid could not see or feel. *Like a dream.*

AN-D loved hearing about dreams. They preferred hearing about those strange stories to watching any holotapes. More than a few times, the droid had wished that there were projectors built into stasis pods, so that they could see the dreams of the crew play out in real time. Often, AN-D would ask them about what dreams they had right after they grabbed breakfast from the mess hall. They assumed that it was part of some psychological reports the droid needed to fill out regularly. There was no harm in not correcting them.

Even though AN-D had their own room (double the area of most standard utility closets), they always felt most at home here. Sometimes, they thought about laying down on top of the tree, closing their optic sensors, and waiting for sleep. Surely, if they followed the mechanics and motions of sleeping, they would be able to have wondrous dreams. Eventually.

"Happy Birthday," AN-D beamed. Then, they pressed the button on a panel adjacent to the tree. Mist rained from spouts in the floor and ceiling. The tree seemed to welcome this gift, glistening like a bundle of stars. Clumsily, the droid wiped the lingering droplets off their visor. As AN-D's vision cleared, they saw a shadow in the corner of their eye. Someone spied on them from the doorway. "Hello?" AN-D asked. As they turned to look, they heard the shadow start laughing.

The ship's Virtual Intelligence Vera slipped through the doorway. A VI was an older model of synthetic life. When Artificial Intelligence gained critical thinking, the advanced synthetic lifeforms were given the necessary bodies to function as droids; all the while, VIs lingered in lifeless places. They shambled through their shackled existences as personal assistants, targeting software, and navigation programs on old ships that were waiting to be decommissioned. This one called herself Vera, after their ship. It was her home, and she was its beating heart.

Every few seconds, a pulse of energy coursed through her flickering, blue silhouette. Her form was an approximation of a human without its detailed facial features, except for two eyes that burned like twin stars.

"Query: AN-D, what are you doing?" Vera asked. Pointing back to the med bay behind the droid, she said, "When was the last time you charged yourself?"

"Oh... within the necessary parameters," AN-D said.

"Which was?"

"A year ago."

Vera leaned into the little droid. "No. Tell me it was not a year ago."

"Well, in that case, good news!" AN-D said. Bobbing up and down nonchalantly, they continued, "I miscounted. It was 13 months and twenty days since my last—"

With one look from their widening, blue optic lenses, Vera cut off the nurse droid's excuses. "I am not sure what reasons you have, or what gives you the strength to keep moving. But you need to start charging as soon as possible. You could just fall over at any moment." The VI motioned for AN-D to follow her.

AN-D protested, saying, "I have been functioning perfectly fine without that. We should be landing on Panthea soon anyway. Until then, I can make decisions with optimal processing speed and working memory. I am fine."

"You need to rest."

"I can't," AN-D said. They looked down into the charging pad, seeing a fragment of themself reflected in the dark pool. "Even when I did start to charge, I never felt any different. When I shut down, I lost track of the ship. Without it, I just float in darkness."

Vera relaxed their grip before they left indents in the other droid. "You're worrying far too much. The humans are safe in their pods."

"Have we ever been in space this long?" AN-D asked. Neither of the droids needed to answer. Both knew. "How many ships have made it to this planet before? Why are we the only ones that are charting a course in this place where no shipping lanes come close?"

"We're the best on a bargain," the VI said.

"But that doesn't mean these humans are expendable."

For a moment, it seemed like the VI was buffering. Eventually, Vera phased through the wall behind her. Even after they set off down the hall, the VI looked at their companion every now and then. On one of those moments, they said, "Alright, AN-D. Do what you need to for these priceless humans. Just remember —you're not exactly replaceable."

AN-D thought about this on their walk. *It would be impossible to purchase another nurse droid on the frontier. Even the black market has not made it out to this section of Andromeda yet. So, I agree. It is currently impossible to find my replacement.*

It was a cold thought, but one that echoed around AN-D's

central processing unit on the short flight down to the charging pad. They swerved to avoid running into Vera, who had taken a post outside of the maintenance closet that held the charging station. With a courtesy nod to the translucent VI, AN-D hovered towards their charging pad. When they lowered themself onto the pad, three blue lights flickered on.

As the charging pad hummed to life AN-D found themself drifting off into their stasis mode. Noticing how the little droid tensed at first, Vera added from the hallway, "Relax. Total recharge should take thirty minutes and 45 seconds. Until then, enjoy your rest."

AN-D fought it at first but soon surrendered to the combined powers of gravity and mental exhaustion. Any resistance they still held dissipated with the influx of energy, which surged from their thruster before rising through their lower torso, central processor, neck, and into their head. All along the wave, their worn-out servos and joints received a welcome dose of soothing power. As they did, each part of AN-D let go.

The last to stop twitching were their fingers and optic sensors, which turned themselves off after one last check on the room. AN-D turned their focus inwards—to a space where they rarely returned. In their mind, unchained by a flood of sensory input and unshackled by their metallic shell, AN-D imagined themself to be far different. With their sense of self broken down to its most raw, fundamental form, AN-D was a being of pure light. They lacked any definite shape. Instead, their psyche condensed into a mass of memories, where recognizable words, places, and faces all meshed into a finite point of experience. In essence, they were a star.

A black void spread unfolded around them. It lacked any dimensions and went on forever in all directions. As AN-D floated in it, imagining that they were the center of this space, they heard whispers call to them nearby. These voices came all at once, making it hard to decipher any one message at first.

Slowly, as AN-D drifted in one direction, some voices became more pronounced. The loudest called out, *Taking a break?*

AN-D moved closer to the sound of SAE-D's voice. As they did, another light emerged from the dark. Inside this star, which resembled a candle's flame, a miniature picture of SAE-D flickered. When AN-D came up next to it, the star grew threefold, so that SAE-D looked down on them with that warm smile they always had.

I'll be right back.

When AN-D chased down this memory, it gave way to another. And another. Soon, there was a whole constellation of memories of SAE-D, connected with vague lines of stardust. Each memory glowed brightly and passed on this light to the next ones. Each jolt of energy that AN-D received from their charging pad sent a wave of light through this map of stars like a thought through a chain of neurons, activating different sections of their memory. By traveling through this web, AN-D saw pieces of SAE-D within the fragments of their memory that they were not aware of during their conscious processing: how SAE-D broke holes in four walls the first week they were on the ship, how they pretended to fire their laser cannons at incoming asteroids before they broke harmlessly against the ship's shields, how they looked so empty when they were told that they would be replaced by a newer model Security and Enforcement Droid...

AN-D dwelt there for longer than the other memories. None of the others around it seemed to be as vivid. Then, another spark ignited from the void. The contrast between its brilliant luminescence and the darkness nearby caught AN-D's attention. They began drifting towards it before they were even fully aware of its pull. This time, the memory was a video. As it played out on a loop, the picture became clearer and more vibrant.

It was the last day before the crew needed to depart Earth. Back on Captain Fidele's farm, AN-D had been tasked with taking a picture of all of them: SAE-D, Fidele, Gemma, and Alis. While the others lined up, waiting for their picture, AN-D had been fidgeting with the archaic camera given to them by Fidele's uncle. In the meantime, the captain had persuaded SAE-D to lift him up, so that he could rest on their outstretched left arm ("so we can all fit in the picture"). From where AN-D hovered, it looked as if he was dangling his legs like he was on a swing set. A moment later, Gemma appeared on SAE-D's other arm. SAE-D said something to Alis, who shook her head. But even she leaned back against the droid's leg, so that her head rested against their knee. AN-D had the camera trained on them, but the focus was blurry. Then, the lighting was off. Then, the camera turned off by accident.

Then, SAE-D called out to AN-D. *You record anything you see, right?*

Right! AN-D said after fumbling with the camera, and gently setting it on a nearby stump. *Do you want me to?*

I want you to get over here!

So, AN-D flew over to them. It had just started snowing, as they had worried that morning. On each of the planets AN-D had visited during their pick-ups, drop-offs, and shore leaves, none of them saw any snow. Though AN-D knew on a scientific level that snow was condensed water and therefore harmless, they still found it disconcerting that on their last day before such a dangerous trip humans expected the sky to start falling. Looking up at the swirling clouds, AN-D was pleasantly shocked. If the sky was falling, at least it did so softly. By the time AN-D flew up to face SAE-D, the snow had started falling so hard that the flakes obscured parts of the recording. Between bits of laughter and cheers, AN-D was able to piece the rest of it together in their mind.

Infinite and irrational.

Facing away from this memory, AN-D followed Gemma's voice. Her words were a whisper in the far-flung corner of AN-D's mind. Getting closer to them meant passing by dozens of other memories of the crew—some of them together, others separate. All of them had something about each that AN-D could love.

Infinite and irrational.

Counting each of them was impossible, as the memories spread out at an exponential rate. They seemed to swirl around AN-D, each reflecting a different part of themself. Experiencing this was both chaotic and rejuvenating. No matter how far AN-D went, or how many memories they perused in the celestial gallery of their mind, they found themself returning to the same one: where they embraced their crew on that snowy day.

Before, taking time to charge meant agreeing to an eternity of darkness as they waited to be functional again. Even if their routine on the ship was mundane, it at least gave the droid a chance to escape the emptiness. Ten years of waiting was torture for a droid that could process the world around them at the speed of light. They had never had a reason—or a desire—to look inside themself like this. In their own little solar system, there was no need to hold onto worries. Vera seemed to have kept her word. There was no trace of her to be found. AN-D was safe, and so were their memories–their artifacts from a better time. Maybe they only noticed those memories now because of the darkness surrounding them. One thought emerged in their peaceful trace: Even if these stars came out of darkness, they're still more beautiful because of it.

Even that happy thought drifted away, let go like a satellite leaving orbit. AN-D just needed to hold onto this memory, which played in a perfect loop. AN-D could watch it revolve around them forever. In this space, AN-D could slow down their processing and savor every millisecond. Time could come to a blissful crawl. They had an eternity to enjoy.

golden

. . .

Colleen Anderson

nectarine, honeydew, nectar in my eyes
I stare into the sun's bright face

its long tongue laps me, tasting
the tears that strayed upon my cheeks

growing thick and tacky, tenacious
grief swelled each one, lemon drops

solar sympathy melts this grief
turns it to iced tea and honey

sweet moments as you alight
upon my mind the warm buzz

your memory fills and sates me
your gift a languid summer song

deus in/ex machina

. . .

Rodrigo Culagovski

The centerpiece of Jake's latest animation project played on his workstation's screens—a story about a young woman named Lilac sitting on a balcony looking out over a glowing green ocean.

She spoke into her terminal as winds spiraled behind her in a storm large enough to swallow the floating city whole, kept at bay by an array of flying weather spheres that created an adaptive-static field around it.

"Such bullshit," she said, "an arranged marriage!" She cut off the call with an angry gesture, ignored the view, and looked instead at a small screen on her lap. A science fiction short video played on it, set a hundred years in the future on the fictional space station *Stella Maris*.

The station orbited the stable L4 point of the Mars-Sun system, growing prosperous from the trade between Jupiter, the Belt, and Earth's former orbit. Prosperity had not brought freedom or joy to the entire station. A handful of people enjoyed the rewards of success—everybody else suffered lives of boredom, subservience, and quiet desperation. The station's authoritarian government recorded, watched, and analyzed everything, and punished people as they saw fit.

"Oh crap," said Yndree, the protagonist of the story, as she saw a pair of cop-bots heading her way. She stood perfectly still, pretending to look out the tiny porthole the station had installed in the proletarian lounge to keep worker discontent down to a manageable level.

The cops walked up to her. "Nice weather we're having, no?" said Yndree. One of the cops swiveled its main camera at her and flashed the color for *watch it, prole*, but didn't slow down. Once they disappeared, Yndree slipped into the off-grid crawl space she'd discovered. She spent her scant free time there reading forbidden full-sensorium comics and playing the proscribed VR games it was her day job to censure as a minor acolyte in the doctrinal purity department. She wished she could live in their worlds instead of hers.

Yndree was playing her favorite game, *TimeFall*, starring a time traveler called MxMx who came from a distant future in which humans had spread out over fifty solar systems yet spent their lives strapped into prosthetic rigs that kept their bodies alive.

MxMx shouted out "One, two three, go!", but there was no one to hear xem—everybody was in one of the VR worlds xyr civilization ran on the computronium they'd broken down their planets and moons into, spending their time in non-sensical virtual sports and bad poetry competitions.

Glad to leave this tedious life, xe flipped the switch on xyr time/space machine, traveling to twentieth-century Old Earth. Xe ended up in a movie theater in Los Angeles watching a movie called *Silver Lights, Silver Life* about cinema's beginning a few decades before.

It starred a young actress, Claudette, who would become famous before falling from grace in a few decades in a drug scandal fabricated to cover up a more complicated and far-reaching sex scandal.

The camera zoomed in on the young actress.

And then things get weird.

In the exaggerated acting style of the period, still closer to theater than film performance, she twists her head around with wide eyes, gasping and bringing her hand to her forehead. She stops, adopts a more natural expression and turns to look at the camera.

She says, "I can feel you, you know. I can see you now as well."

In the movie theater, MxMx says, "Do you mean me?"

Claudette, the actress not the character she's playing, answers, "Yes, you. Why are you watching me?"

MxMx fumbles for a second before saying, "Your story has always fascinated me. It is so different from my own." Xyr phrasing sounds stilted and artificial.

"What about my life fascinates you?" asks the young starlet.

"How brightly it started and how grimly it ended," xe says.

"*Grimly*," she repeats. "Are you referring to the affair my studio head is trying to pressure me into?"

"And how they will accuse you of smoking hemp to discredit you and keep his name unsullied. And your death in the mental institution they force you into."

"Are you from the future?"

"Yes."

"What stops me from changing my future and refusing the studio head's advances before he feels the need to ruin my life?"

"This is the past. It has already happened."

She stops and looks at xem for a moment. "Has this moment happened too? My talking to a time traveler through a movie screen?"

MxMx hesitates. "I do not know. This is new. I have seen this movie many times in the data archives. I have never seen this before. "

"I see."

Claudette stands up and walks off-screen. The film continues to run, showing the empty room and the empty screen, waiting for its protagonist to return.

MxMx is confused. Xyr face shifts between emotions, fear, doubt, and excitement, before cycling back again.

Xe realizes that the past is as unknowable as the future, for the same reason: entropy.

Elated by xyr discovery, xe triggers the jump-back sequence on xyr space/time travel rig, to find xyr society in tatters, the Dyson sphere's virtual reality invaded by a memetic virus suspected to be of non-human origin. All xyr fellow citizens forced into their physical bodies for the first time.

Xyr people don't know how to quell their sense of panic. Unused to managing their limbic systems unaided by technology, they collapse into dysfunctional heaps of flesh and emotions.

MxMx turns xyr head through a fractional dimension and says, "Yndree, I need your help."

Yndree, hiding in the unused maintenance storage space on the Stella Maris station, is surprised. Pseudo-customized games that pretend you're a participant went out of fashion five seasons ago, and she didn't think *TimeFall* would resort to such an unsophisticated trope.

She's about to shut down the game in disappointment when MxMx speaks up from the VR display.

"Wait, this is real. My society is collapsing around me, and I need you to do something."

"Prove it."

"Prove what?"

"That you're real and not a simple chatbot."

MxMx stops and thinks. Or the game's AI simulates xem as thinking. Yndree has no way of knowing.

Xe stares out at her and says, "I have always felt your presence. When I went about my life. When I traveled into the past. I always had a sense of your watchful eye over me, over my friends and family. We need your help, now."

The oddity and awkwardness of MxMx's emotional confession convince Yndree it's not scripted. She reaches into the game's configuration interface and finds a series of sliders she has never seen before. She tweaks the settings and watches as MxMx and xyr compatriots gain control over their emotions, free their bodies from their life support systems, and relearn how to interact in the flesh.

She shuts down the game, knowing MxMx existed as more than mere code on her console.

The walls around her sanctuary collapse. The Faraday field she used to hide from the space station's vigilance breaks up in a loud static hiss. Security bots pour in and rip the VR rig off her head with more force than necessary.

The largest bot hangs back. Its faceplate resolves into an image of the station's head invigilator, Chief Defender of the Faith Irrurizaga, Yndree's boss.

"I long suspected you of harboring heretical impulses, Yndree. I am saddened to see my misgivings were true. There is no place for this . . . *filth*,"—he points at the gaming console and comics strewn about the closet—"in the holy order of Stella Maris Corporation."

Yndree knows her time has run out. So have any fucks she had left to give. "You're a sniveling idiot," she says, "the only reason you have this job is because of who your mommy is."

This is cruel but true. Coco—as he hates to be called—failed his civil service test before his mother, the Chief Executive Pontificate of the station, intervened annulling the test, assigning him the top score, and appointing him to his present unearned C-suite position.

She continues. "Nothing in these games is as disgusting as the way you and your inbred clique exploit the people of the station."

She spits at the faceplate, wishing it were his actual face instead.

Coco subvocalizes a command to the security bots. They rear back, taking some distance from Yndree so they're not affected by the backsplash of whatever they're preparing to unleash on her.

Yndree says, "Lilac."

It's a single, quiet word. It rips the surrounding air apart.

The bots fall to the ground. She feels—the same way she feels Lilac's presence—all the automated surveillance and punishment measures in the station crash.

They won't be down for long, a few hours at most. Enough for the hundreds of thousands of exploited workers to start working on a solution to the problem that is Stella Maris Corporation and its masters.

She grins in a direction at right angles to her reality and mouths, "Thank you."

Lilac grins too, happy for the first time in the past year. She realizes that if Claudette could step away from her future, MxMx could lead xyr people to corporeal life, and Yndree could start a bloody revolution in the middle of interplanetary space, she can godsdamn refuse to spend her life with the entitled son of a family of jellyfish breeders. Especially one whose greatest claim to fame is a series of cruel pranks at the bottom-rung academy he attended after being expelled from every other school of note in the floating city he and Lilac call home.

She doesn't need any outside influence—she is more than capable of standing up to her mother on her own.

She still appreciates an audience.

Jake has watched the series of collapsing realities, so he isn't surprised when she says, "Jake, make sure you record this for posterity," as she walks along the umbilical to her mother's apartments.

He brings the shot in close to show Lilac's look of determination. He's happy that things will work out for her, but it doesn't get him any closer to his own goal—breaking down the doors closed to those of his class and his skin so he can make a living in his chosen profession.

Jake scrubs through the rendered animation. Lilac to Yndree to MxMx to Claudette and back again.

Jake smiles for a minute, then turns and says my name.

whale song

. . .

Colleen Anderson

great blue beyond, diving into the deep
       sounding, where is my song that propels

       my inclination drops, depth charges
beneath the surface pallid jellyfish bloom

lion's mane, sea nettle, marine stinger, more
       toxic thoughts numb momentum

       as I drift, carried formless on chill currents
oceanic lanes vibrate with primitive hungers

alluring tendrils entangle the careless swimmer
       I camouflage, distinguish shadows from caves

       cradling memories, regrets pull me under
the immense pelagic mystery births aquatic gods

where swims the baleen behemoth, majestic
       master of my thoughts, I choose plunging into

life's constant ebb and flow, ideas spraying
soak me as whales breach and lead me home

the soulmate

. . .

A. M. Sahu

Greetings Human reading this missive,

You don't know who I am, and I have absolutely no idea about your existence, but you are reading this because you are my Soulmate.

Yes, you read that correctly. YOU ARE MY SOULMATE.

I understand you are probably thinking my words are senseless and I am a raving lunatic. But fear not, I am ready to prove my existence to you. If you have doubts in you, present this missive to another one of your species. They cannot read it. This is only a mass of unintelligible scribbles to them.

If you are continuing reading at this point, first, accept my heartfelt gratitude. Second, the translation mechanics do not always get it right. Disclaimer.

I am called Xharnolsto (nomenclature translation not working). But do continue reading please. As said already, I am your Soulmate. It is somewhat unwieldy to explain the purpose of soulmates, since each soul is prepared separately and will perish separately.

I have been continuing my search of you for an extraordinary amount of time, in which I assume you would have likely changed bodies many times. I cannot say how many. But one thing I can say for certain is in any of those previous bodies, you did not perceive your soulmate. How could you? I exist in a separate universe to yours. Unlike your universe, in mine, everyone needs to find their soulmate to return to the one energy place and, while everyone I knew had been assimilated into the one energy place, I remain in search of you. It has been a solitary existence to put it truthfully.

In my search, I have learned a great deal about your universe and your planet. It's rather remarkable, how your species has developed values based on lies and deception. Your decision-making system lacks due to the impact of environment and factors unimportant. But I will accept, there is a certain charm how your species goes about their nothing lives and fill up the void with all useless things with no meaning whatsoever. I do have this theory that your species' obsession with futility has you stuck in an eternal loop of birth-death. But sadly, no proof yet.

I understand this must be incredibly shocking for your organs and if you believe you are nearing your reincarnation phase, then I will leave this missive to your better judgement to find it a safe spot, where you can find it again.

If you are still standing well at this point, I applaud your strength.

The day I achieved the soulmate status, it was the happiest day of my existence. I was ready to find and share my life with my soulmate, absorb the knowledge and entertain each other, and one day attain the next level— the one energy place. All my same-agers attached themselves to their soulmates. But my soulmate signal was too weak. It blinked so I knew you existed, but had no idea where.

Much time passed as I continued my expedition to find you. I hopped from planet to planet and scanned my soulmate signal. But in vain. All was lost. My same-agers were now moving to the one energy place, while I was held back. I hadn't even attached myself yet. It was the blackest time of my existence. I was lower than the last realm of time. But I couldn't let it succumb me, even when the solitude wanted to eat me up, all teeth and claw.

I seeked help, guidance, solace to ease my solitude. After much trial and setback, I found a worthy mentor—Brahma.

Brahma is the all-knowing, sage of the sages, giver of life. They hold all the knowledge of attaining the one energy place. They explained to me that I was special, that my soulmate was in a different universe, a tortured place that needs saving. I was to be the frontrunner to help humans escape the reincarnation cycle. That gave me new purpose.

Under the mentorship of Brahma, I learnt many things, which you cannot know just yet. I cannot tell you. You are too fragile, my dear Soulmate. Your organs will cease to exist when the ocean of knowledge crashes on you. You need not worry though. I will wait until such time when your being achieves the soulmate status and you are ready for me to attach with you. As I understand, when the time comes you will know.

With the new knowledge, I devised technology to reach you. Still under progress for verse hopping, so I cannot be with you yet. But this translation missive was one of my brilliant inventions so we know of each other. So, we know we are not alone in the multiversal cosmos. Without a soulmate, it can be a relentless life, short as it may be for you. Nevertheless, it will be relentless.

But knowing you are here, there is hope. A hope for the truth of existence. A hope at the end of the lingering black winding path we all have to lead. A hope that in the end we will be together. Forever.

I send you this missive so you can have that hope too. Hope that will hold your hand through all the solitude. It will not be easy but it is as is.

Until such time, you must not waver from the goal. Learn to enjoy the solitude you have and use it wisely. Don't wander yourselves in futile pursuits like your same-agers on your planet in your universe. You have a much higher purpose, my dear

Soulmate. I have learned that only a handful of humans have ever dared to achieve the one energy place. Most do not even understand what I tell. But you will. You are not the lowly creature as you once were. You have withered many a round of birth-death and now you are assigned as my soulmate. So, there may only be a few more reincarnations remaining for you.

I cannot wait for that day to reach.

Until then,
    I remain,
    Yours only,
    Soulmate

the soulmate experience

. . .

Anne Wilkins

"**H**arry, we *must* do this."

He leans over to take a look at my phone. "Soul-mate Experience?"

"Haven't you heard about it? It's *everywhere*. Everyone is doing it."

I show him the pictures on my Facegram of loved-up couples bonded together.

"Looks dumb."

"No. It's the new thing, look–" I click into their website full of smiling, happy couples.

"Experience love in a new way. Be joined in heart and soul," says the voiceover.

"Ugh! They look like freaks."

"No, honey. The website says it's the greatest experience of love, creating an incredible bond between lovers."

"Is it safe?"

"Of course. It lasts an hour, and you get these epic photos afterwards, see?"

He did see, but it took some time for him to warm to the idea.

We turn up at Soulmate Inc. for our scheduled appointment. Our phones are fully charged, ready to take photos. A machine scans our retinas allowing us entry.

"Welcome," says a humanoid. "I am your assistant today. You must be Angela and Harry. Please follow."

It floats down a long hallway towards a white room while calming music follows us.

"Please undress in here. Clothing, devices, watches, jewellery, and moveable tattoos are to be placed in the storage chute."

"What, we'll be naked?" asks Harry.

"Clothing interferes with the process."

"But we need our phones with us – to take photos," I add.

The humanoid smiles. "We understand your concern. To assist customers in obtaining the ultimate experience, we take all photos on-site. There is a small additional charge to purchase our photos. Would you like to upgrade?"

"Of course," I answer, without hesitation.

"Processing..." The humanoid's eyes flick back into its head. "Done. Thank you for your cooperation. I'll return when you are undressed."

The humanoid leaves.

"Harry, I'm worried."

"I thought you said it was safe."

"Not about that. I'm worried about the photos."

"We just paid for an upgrade."

"I know, but what if the photos are no good? What if the humanoid doesn't put a filter on? My friends and followers haven't seen the real me in years. I always take out the grey hairs, wrinkles, erase my double chin. What if the humanoid won't do that?"

"Look, how about we just sneak a phone in with us? I'll put it under my armpit. It'll never find it."

It's at moments like these that I really love Harry.

• • •

We're led naked into the Soulmate chamber. It's a huge white sphere coated in magnetic particles. Inside it looks like a soft, fluffy cloud with two pods side by side, just for Harry and I. In the centre of the sphere is a small device that is the heart of the machine. It contains a microscopic wormhole that powers the reaction.

The humanoid's talking, but I'm not really listening.

"... and you will experience some disorientation which is completely normal. Any questions?" finishes the humanoid.

Harry and I shake our heads.

"Then take your positions. And enjoy."

The door to the sphere closes and Harry whips out his phone for a quick snap.

"Smile," he says. He gets a couple of shots out the way before we start to feel the machine warm up.

There's a soft humming and then I feel a pulling at the edges of my body. I hear Harry breathing beside me, but then I feel him breathing *inside* me. There's no Harry anymore. No Angela. Our parts intermix, intertwine.

"Woah," I say, but it's not my voice. It's both of ours, a mix of octaves.

This is crazy, I think, but it's not my thought, it belongs to *us*. My atoms fly with Harry's around the sphere in a complex, crazy dance, a sharing of souls.

And then it's over. The machine powers down, and our atoms return to their pods.

But we are not the same as before.

The door opens and the humanoid enters.

"Do you feel enlightened?" it asks.

And Harry and I speak together from our moulded mouths, "Yes."

"Come, see yourself." We stumble after it, still learning to walk.

It leads us to a mirror.

We are perfect. For Facegram.

Our bodies and faces combined. An obscenity perhaps. But only for an hour.

We're directed to try on clothes, silly hats, and costumes, specially built for combined bodies. We clumsily navigate our new body together. Laughing at how difficult it is to step into clothes, to speak, to walk. The humanoid is busy taking photos. Its eyes busy being shutters. We ask for time alone, so we can explore our new body in private and the humanoid leads us to a bedroom. We reach for the phone to take our own photos, but it's gone. The thought is troubling.

At the end of the hour, our time is up, and we return to the machine. Eager to return to our bodies and post photos.

The humanoid's face looks grim.

"The machine is no longer operable. Did you take anything into the chamber with you?"

"No," we both lie. "When do we go back... to ourselves?" our voices echo.

"When the machine is repaired, we'll be in contact. Please note wormholes can take a long time to fix. In the meantime, please continue to enjoy the Soulmate Experience in your own home. A free set of clothes is provided for you. Have a nice day, and be sure to place a five-star review."

We waddle outside the building to our vehicle that we can no longer fit in. The humanoid's photos are already uploaded to Angela's phone. There was an option to add filters after all.

We laugh so hard we start crying.

Intermingled tears run down our conjoined face as we get busy posting to Facegram.

somnambulance

. . .

Kurt Newton

the creak & shuffle of project binders
the buzz & hum of overhead fluorescents
the drone of presentation voices
becomes an incorporeal shadowbox

the connective tissue between worlds ablates
thinner than receding hairlines as sheer as secretarial
    blouses
a hole opens in the office floor
and a ladder takes you down

into a mirror-image boardroom
except with autopsy table lighting
the ghostly specters of co-workers arranged
like a 19th century séance

a cast of runes decides your fate
the buzz & hum becomes a mantra
spirits rise and exit your body
past lives of what could have been

you try to escape but there are no doors no windows
only the ladder ascending heavenward
you wake with a nudge and drool on your chin
it's time for your presentation

just past the petting sharks

. . .

Kurt Newton

how many times will you enter the chasm
where the whispers circle like graveyard echoes
how many times before you find the child
that wandered there far away from home

you descend once again using familiar footholds
and retrace your steps to the edge of uncertainty
each time the landscape appears slightly altered
as if growing new features or slowly dissolving

each time there comes the sloshing of saltwater
the gong of the containment pool where the sharks
    are held
each time you're aware of the inherent danger
as each step closer increases their thrashing

this time however you hear a distant whimpering
and there on a ledge you see the child
dirt-stained and shivering timid and frail
whose face bears an uncanny resemblance

but the void between is too great a leap
and besides the sharks just won't allow it
so you pet their heads and avoid their mouths
as they whisper secrets through their pointed teeth

the awakening

. . .

Kurt Newton

once again you fall into a lucid dream
one so vivid it's like a digital screensaver
the one where you can slip through walls like a magician
the one where you can fly

once again you're down in the depths of the chasm
only this time the petting sharks are sleeping
their eyes turned downward their fins barely moving
as if they don't know you are there

once again you can see the child on the ledge
only this time you're determined to reach him
you lift your arms and give them a flutter
and float up over the void

the boy hasn't aged for all the years you've dreamed him
forever stuck on this ledge in a dark
he clings to you like a son to a father
and you can't help but believe this is real

together you navigate the way out of the chasm
climbing ever-higher toward illumination
when you reach the light the weight disappears
the boy is gone but you're no longer alone
94

love, an act of
terraforming

. . .

Lynne Sargent

Building a house is always an act of terraforming. So what if love is one of the forces I am shaping with? Who is to tell me that the mortar between the bricks of the walls I make is not made of passion; that the excavator with which I dredge the oceans is not powered by the eternity of my ardor. Why should I not begin this worldbuilding with the perfect carbon of your bones?

One wonders if there are, or ever have been, or ever will be, a civilization not so founded—on love, I mean. So, I begin.

I peel your skin free and stretch it into soil, drawing out the terroir of your armpits, the musk of your genitals. I begin the composting process with the drippy inside of your nose and ears, sucking out those tubes of moisture to dampen the dirt. The expanse of your tummy alongside the flayed flesh of your arms and legs become the fields and vineyards, plains interrupted by tufts of hair that will someday transmute into the proper crops with enough time and belief.

(Will the bread that is eventually made here still need salting, or will that already be part of your yeast that floats on the air? How will different grape varieties and the resulting wine express the sweet tang that once was your blood? What new recipes will the people create? What new crops will they breed?)

Once dry and peeled, your bones pop free. I use this cracked frame that once was your scaffold and re-invent it into something new. I take your bones and sculpt mountains, shore up the coastlines with cliffs, mirrors to all the ones we walked together, but strange too— drawn out and spiky. Under my feet they are familiar though, drawn out over miles, a pale echo of the inches of you I traced into muscle memory with my fingers. Each step is delicious to my hungry feet, though you tire me out more in this form. You have always been worth every ache, though.

(How long will it take the people to map you out? Will there always be holes no matter how many workers they dedicate to this task, how many satellites are launched, how many submarines sent into the depths?)

With the cage of bones now gone, only the organs remain: stomach, liver, bladder, intestines, lungs. I take your stomach and make the bogs and swamps, marshy wetlands that are primed to become prized and unique ecosystems. The lungs make the atmosphere, the breeze contains the ghost of your wheeze, but no longer sickly in connotation. Instead, it's a reminder that life exists, that it struggles on, that because of my handiwork I am no longer alone in the silence you left. The heart I shove down deep below the ground, and it becomes the molten core of this place. Your brain, this expanse's call to spiritualism, the drive for the things that live here to remember. It is a subtle partner to my own creator, deist to my witchy, theistic meddling.

(What creation stories will they tell, millennia from now? What teleologies will be invented? How might they re-invent the sciences and re-imagine the arts both in the light of your cosmology?)

Next come the oceans, the lakes—puncturing the remaining organs for their fluids, putting back in what I took out when working the skin. I make it so that acid and salt may support life here. It is not a difficult magic, backed as it is in memory and preservation. After all, you thrived around these things, and so did all the bacteria, viruses, fungi, and other denizens of your body that will now evolve into new creatures, while remembering the hardy single cells they used to be.

I keep your eyes with me, that I may continue showing you the wonder that you are through my own experiences. I walk this land that I created, travel as we travelled in the before place. I find new nooks and crannies and things to love. I am reminded that the capacity for new love, new discovery, this is a constancy in every universe, made or born or otherwise. There is adventure in the strange and familiar both, like a retold fairytale, a song of knees and elbows in Franglais, a fusion of cuisines.

It is a new frontier; it is home, as travelling always was with you by my side. You are the world all around me now, but this is not a new truth. It is still the most sublime one though, even with all my powers and learnings. I will spend another spade of lifetimes mapping your curves, documenting your whorls, recording your strengths and storms. Still, I will not do you justice.

Do not praise me for making you a whole, wide world. The magic only works because you already were.

auragami

. . .

Marisca Pichette

paper forms are magical.

take a piece of air
fold it under your tongue
press it through your
twisted teeth
and send it through the ether

make the leaves dance
under, over, paper forms
flying, folding, bending
tearing.

make a picture
out of algae bones
the hearts of trees
rolled in one—
graphite, phloem,
sapwood, xylem.

wrinkled forms—

stiff, soft, crumpled
in shaking fingers,
covered in microscopic
paper cuts.

galaxies began
with paper sketches

skyscrapers
with paper models

commerce
on paper bills—

Tell me again
the magic
of paper forms.

meeting

. . .

LindaAnn LoSchiavo

i. tonight's the night

There it was: the sky pink as a wolf's tongue, flirting through the windshield, triumphant in its gold fist of early September, beckoning the howl of harvest. How easily nature's devastation and decay coexisted with joy. Never deficient in doubt, his mind today was in overdrive. Perched between the bucket seats, two take-out coffees stood inside the oblong well of the console, bookending a sandwich, tidy in waxed paper. Distracted, he'd walked out with the wrong order, haunted by his unquiet mind and what might happen later. Several hairpin bends—he'd been warned about these—snapped him back to attention, car keys clicking like impatient ghosts. At last, the straightaway, where the black top was sheltered by majestic trees—oaks and conifers—a reminder that he'd neglected his parents' once manicured garden. Like him, it had gone wild. "Tonight's the night," he thought, nodding at the well-tended green giants, which kept the sun out of a motorist's eyes, kept the sky out, kept everyone's secrets in.

There it was: the decision to slam the door. "Tonight," she realized, "is the night." Hastily packed, a suitcase leaned against her bare legs like a bewildered puppy. Noticing a late-model sedan, carefully emerging from a blind curve, she pinked her pout, jutted her thumb.

Usually, he ignored vagrants and hitchhikers. But he noticed a black eye, a fresh bruise like a misshapen heart on her raised arm. The wolf inside him opened a slumbering eye and braked. Pleasant words were exchanged. But as soon as she stowed her luggage in the back and sat down, the back of her neck prickled, suspicion settling over her like a shroud. Wordlessly, like a discreet butler, he handed her the sandwich, as neatly wrapped as a gift, and a steamy offering of dark coffee. Her eyes, still as stone, crinkled her thanks as her cold palms cradled the tall white cup, a bit of warmth she accepted as a good omen.

ii. uncanny

There it was: the purple pledge of sunset, peppered by birds rising in groups, leaning into dusk's deepening colors as if they wished to leave their bodies behind. On a sleek birch branch, a black-billed magpie perched hungrily, biding its time. His car windows took in the panorama of older trees, thwarted by persistent winds and stooped as though in pain, framed in the ambiguous amber glows of early evening.

As his slim passenger crossed and uncrossed her legs, she revealed bruises staking their claim, rotten fruit of the flesh, blunt as a fist. A quarrel that lived its own life of transit and fire and left its "trophy." He recognized her type. Another woman mortgaged to obedience and unable to pay down the devastating debt. A born victim. Every visible scar rendered him empty-handed against cascading remembrances that clawed and clamored, rocked inside him like a Trojan horse, a catalyst for his disease, cursed. Violence: a flexible outlet for throat-dark rage. Many entry-level opportunities led into this infamous brotherhood with its exultation at the loss of boundaries, misogynistic behavior, willingness to brave risks. For decades, serial killers and abusers stood on the shoulders of the werebeast community where strength and stealth were king. How uncanny—night's uneasy depths.

There it was: the day folding in on itself like dirty laundry. At dusk, she would have been at the stove, tending to him, his ogling mouth insatiable as a storm drain. Or walking the dog, pretending to be okay, while caught in a work-sleep-fight Bermuda Triangle. Home. Except this cursed home meant giving her body over to him, always aching with the insistent weight of his presence, her clothing and bed saturated with the scent of him, all smirk and sex. He tapped her like a sugar-maple, eager to drain her goodness, carved his initials in deep. Dug in. Gouged.

There it was: the car commandeering an exit lane, their silence stretching like a road between them. "Gas station," he gestured. "Ten-minute pit stop. Need the restroom?" Friendly voices were always the lamp that lit her dark corner. Uncanny though how his eyes glowed. Surreal. Must have been a trick of the light, she decided. Hurrying towards a worn sign labeled "Toilets," she found herself thinking that he had a strange smell. Distinctive yet unrecognizable.

iii. the meeting

There it was: shadows lengthening, night creeping up the two-lane parkway, swallowing it with its black lips, clotted clouds glaring their disapproval. Her body felt empty not unlike a vase with nothing but desires swishing around. Anxiety made her heart thrum, as though restless insects, caught inside, were hurling themselves against her ribs.

Another exit, then a pause at a traffic light. "Bus depot—up the block." His voice sounded deeper, conspiratorial. "Happy trails!" A thick wad of cash was thrust at her. His stare had an acuity of focus that was unfathomable, almost panther-like. "Thank you…." She paused. "Sorry. Didn't catch your name."

His beard seemed much bushier—or was it? It came instantly: a sinking sensation of shame for paying so little attention to others. "Hey! Running late. Gotta split. Take care, eh?" As she tried to close the passenger door, the vehicle was already moving.

There it was: a waxing gibbous moon peeking through trees like a caring mother. Minutes later, he approached a low structure like a barracks on a dead-end lane. A robust man was waiting, a hoodie shielding his bearded face. "Meeting's just starting." A thick key ring negotiated numerous locks. Inside an easel supported a handmade sign: "*Welcome to Werewolves Anon.*"

other windows, other lives

. . .

Pixie Bruner

We're driving at night down Briarcliff,
Those beautiful modern and vintage homes,
Arts and crafts, transoms, touched by gingerbread,
    postage stamp yards
An ever-evolving city's white elephant architecture
    jumble sale.
The mid-century-modern atomic sunbursts of the
    Space Age,
the many-paned gridded wall of windows that curve
    around the
corner apartments. You've nicely framed art. Sleek mini-
    malist decor.
A cat seated, as if cut out in black construction paper,
a perfect silhouette on someone's backlit windowsill. I
    approve.
I imagine I am someone else, some*thing* else, maybe even
    some*time* else,
a me, whom I don't know looks out from those perfect
    windows at the me passing by,
a link in the chain of headlights flashing past on the
    street

The mirror-ghost I see behind you, waves over your
    shoulder at me
through the fishbowl windows I glance in, as I pass.

(There is no celebration of the senses,
there is no melting, dissolving,
the swordplay of tongues.
There is not molten cores in us.
There is no Rohrshach wet spots to celebrate.
To interpret like the denouement tea leaves or coffee
    grounds of passion.
There is no fusion in the limbs and pulses of lovers.
A head tenderly cupped on the pillow.
But I know there is,<__your name here__>, as surely as
    you do.
Even with enthusiastic consent the level of Molly Bloom's.
"Yes" is such a magical word, even when we say it to
    ourselves.
I love you, <___your name here___>, I miss you,
your delicate loudly-speaking sparrow-like hands
Upon men rougher hairier, coarse, and bigger,
upon women soft silken fragile like spun sugar.
There is still magic in selectively banishing all barriers
    and simply being human and loved.
The greatest of *all* sins is not loving enough!)

I love the cosmos between us.
I love the new rug.
I love the stars behind your eyes, a binary system.
Let me *in*. Then let me **inside**.
I love what you've done with the space!
No sin is *ever* possible in this timeline.
All my heart and passion,
Me
(In/Inside/Outside/A Meteorite/A Comet Passing By)

a craving for incalcula

. . .

M. Lopes da Silva

Finally: the classroom was melting. After so many long hours spent confined learning lock-step behaviors that felt unnatural. After all the failures and one hundred percents. After the instructor smiled and locked our dead masses to one solar system, squarely, and my rage melted horizons infinities *yes I will be gone flying into the dark*. Of course that kettled anger kicking chair backs in front of us had to go somewhere; a kind of chalk dust summoning circle tamped damply into cracked linoleum sigils. Ink-tattooed and compass-carved graffiti epithets on our desks. Yearning for incalcula to disrupt the calculable. For anything to end the confinement.

Is it ego or was it my rage, that unanswered howl, that summoned her? *Yes I will be gone flying into the dark.* Was it my desire for disruption? For the ticking crawling fractal thing to start building trees out of the root systems of my arteries? For the insect hum to buzz my vocal cords low into choir? Didn't everyone want this? To unpeel like fruit or unpeal like a bell?

I am a math problem. I am happily divided. Reduced to my lowest common denominators. Each sin of mine fragments into components I can perceive even though I don't have eyes anymore. Incalcula strings through the abacus beads of us. I hope my classmates wanted this to happen. I am eager to catch a look of happy recognition, a moment of camaraderie, but no one has eyes so this is difficult. Everyone is on holy fire so this is difficult.

I'm melting and gutted but I have acquired buds on the tips of my twigs. I have graduated and acquired tenure. I didn't want any of this. I protest. I pluck myself clean and don't cash the checks. Nonetheless I die.

My death is horribly painful, but pain can be reduced to its lowest common denominators. Numbers run like water and puddle below. Into each digit I multiply myself. I soon am us. My classmates. We are me. We're all laughing. We're all screaming.

Then we coagulate. The process is slow, a primordial pottage of our past states. When we are dry the scabbing wound of us receives a gentle kiss. I am a beautiful sleeping frog prince. I am in her arms, stuck in her spawn jelly. Everything is possible. Anything is possible.

Inside me, tenderly, incalcula reassures me of my rebirth yet to come. Of my fate to be spewed across the stars like so much foam. To survive the journey my form must become a shape so holy-monstrous no one can help but love it. A young goat is brought to me as offering; I slit her throat and devour every piece of her, offal and bone. I feel so loved. I am held close in some place underneath my skin, but above my heart. I suspect she is withholding some vital piece of information but can't seem to make myself care. Yes, I will be gone flying into the dark. Soon. Before I go I hear a laugh that could have been screaming.

the fin stitch

. . .

Marisca Pichette

Atmosphere loved koi ponds.
She sought them out in cirrus clouds
and on the banks of the Seine. She found them
in cathedral windows and
on the underside of classroom desks, when sunlight
and faded pencil sketches aligned.

Atmosphere found ponds at the bottom of vodka bottles
and in snowdrifts flecked with salt. She knew that koi
preferred chocolate to caramel, so while they thrived
in expensive truffles, they shunned Snickers and Twix.

With each pond she visited, Atmosphere counted the koi,
darting between horsetail in a garden in Vacaville,
clustered at the seams of a shot silk jacket
in the back of a mothball-scented closet
—and she embroidered them.

Orange, on her eyelashes. Gold stitched across her scalp.
Red she used to detail her breasts, and black her toes.
She adorned her spine with subtle tones of grey and pink,

while the rarer colors flowed over the inside of her elbow,
and the back of her right knee.

Atmosphere sewed herself sitting on the bank
of a koi pond—in a wine cellar, on a cliffside,
at the base of an empty tin of anchovies.
Her stitches mimicked the turns of the koi,
flashing in the light of her eyes.

Over the years she covered her pores with twisted silk,
replacing her hair with whip stitches, her fingernails
undone by thimbles.
She raveled herself with koi, copying their motion
in needlework.

Beside a wharf where koi circled in the chewed pattern
of a battered buoy, Atmosphere tied a knot
in red embroidery silk, hiding the last of her skin.
She stood, resplendent like the bodies
who paused in their swimming to watch her,
mouths opening, closing, opening
as if to form her name.

She laid her needle down on a faded board
and faced the sea.
All the ponds she'd visited circled and circled
before her, searching for the leak
that would lead them away.

From chocolatiers to traffic stops,
Atmosphere had followed these patterns, etching them
into herself, preparing for the moment
she would break them.

Rippling with stitches, Atmosphere breathed through the

knots she'd tied across her lips.
The koi watched her, their gentle swaying seeming to whisper
of a pond, a pond without a border.
A pond of colors unimagined.
In the gazes of the koi, Atmosphere stepped
into the sea.

Silk threads embraced brine, turning to seaweed as
Atmosphere sank, eyes wide, ready to capture
the koi that swim in the black depths
without restraint.

time is not klein

. . .

Adele Gardner

"So, Noel. You finally killed her," Leon rasped. His ragged trousers were singed, the billowing sleeves of his outlandish shirt charred as if he'd spent too long in-between. The burns stood out against the white he always wore. Leon had the theory that slipping through time and space was easier if you looked like a ghost. It put both you and any inadvertent bystanders in the proper mindset.

I gripped his arms. "What are you talking about?"

"Celine. She's dead. Don't tell me you didn't know." He twisted his arms free. I noticed it then, poking from one ruined sleeve.

"Where did you get that?"

"This?" He pulled it out with a flourish. Rust marred the shining length of the sword-shaped letter opener Celine had given me when I'd arrived. She'd placed it across my palm with a twinkle in her violet eyes—curiosity, a challenge to set her free. The problem with rescuing Celine was, once I set foot in the tower, I couldn't get out myself. I battered myself silly against the stone, trying to slip through. From time to time, Leon soothed me, saying my talent would return—but I wondered. Only he could come and go.

I reached for the miniature sword. Leon jerked it back. "Don't tamper with the evidence!" He coughed. He stank up that little room like a choked-up chimney. Black smoke coiled lazily off his shoulders.

"How did you get that?"

"You tell me!" Leon's eyes blazed.

I braced myself on the round table, so sturdy two people couldn't lift it. Celine and I had tried, wanting to bash out the window lattice. "Even if Celine is dead. Even if I believed you. Even if it's actually true now, and your endless walking hasn't addled your sense of timing. I didn't do it, Leon."

"Your ghost did, then," he insisted.

"I'm not dead yet," I said. "My ghost doesn't exist." Celine and I had discussed that, of course. It was one way to escape this time-trap. The problem was, one of us would have to commit suicide or murder. And we loved each other too much to let that happen.

But flesh was more amenable to egress than iron bars. Late one night while Celine slept, I'd eased the tip of the letter opener under the cuff of my skin, my eyes following the spotted trail it left in the moonlight. My line of breadcrumbs. Only a time machine would turn it into a way home. As I mused, a calloused hand sheathed my wrist. My blood dripped out between his fingers as his palm seared the soft side of my arm with the heat of rapid transit.

"Never take the easy road, boy," he grunted. "It's not elegant enough for the likes of us."

I gasped in consternation. Tears squeezed out, as reluctant as my slowing blood. Celine slept, waxy-white in the moon-light; she had, for the moment, escaped. I wondered if she and I would ever again sit together under trees and blue sky, me with my lute and she with her student equations. I wondered how much longer it would be before I grew so sick of the unending company of my one true love that I slit her throat.

"How long?" I begged the old man. "How long is our sentence?"

"Haven't you been listening, boy? Heaven is as long as eternity—as long as you want it to be."

But this wasn't heaven—my love for Celine chipped away day by endless day, while she slept, her body present, but her spirit as distant as the day she disappeared—imprisoned here. The only thing that had saved us this long was the need to sleep in shifts. Reality slipped away faster when we both slept, unmoored, wandering in dreams.

Whoever snatched her had provided all the civilized amenities: parchment, pens and inks, sealing wax, the letter opener. We had candles, should we wish to set ourselves on fire—and one time we did scorch the bedsheet, laughing madly in the smoke till Leon slid through the walls to put it out.

Our savior. Our jailor. Our postman, whom I'd glimpsed one night bending over the desk. He'd vanished with Celine's mysterious letters. She'd been so coy about them. I'd never received a line, but then, who knew when Leon had delivered them?

And now, he'd come to accuse me of her death. My hunched old mentor leaned forward, peering up at me. "There's another way to create a ghost," he wheezed. "I warned you . . . "

Celine had disappeared from the tower room a year ago. I woke smiling with the sun on my face, not yet realizing our prison was mine alone. I punched the wall, but my arm sank through solid brick. I grew frightened: I glimpsed Celine outside, as clear as day—a bright world full of sun and trees that eclipsed the walls. Our living past loomed around me. "By walking backward," I whispered. "Into myself . . . '

He nodded. Time after time, when I was a child upon his knee, and he the white-robed stranger visiting in the night, he'd told me, "Remember, Noel—you can't go altering things. The loop will catch up with you. You'll trap yourself."

"But what if something bad happens?"

"You bear it and move on."

I'd never been afraid of him, though I'd seen him first as a shadow in my room the night my parents died. There was something so familiar about the way he tilted his head, about that faint smell lurking beneath the aftershave. I'd called him "uncle," though he'd never asked me to.

Now Leon gripped my face painfully between two palsied hands. "Noel, you have to tell me what you've seen! Who's been here?"

"Nothing! No one—"

"Don't lie to me!"

I couldn't stop shivering. Ghosts lined the room, everywhere I turned—slivers of my life. Where was Celine? Childhood playmate, college lover? I knew that Leon must have taught her our secret, while I slept in our tower prison. She'd always been a quick study.

From the shadows behind the tapestry, a bear of a man stepped down into the room, his feet sure. With that shaggy beard and those weathered eyes, he looked about twenty hard years older than I. There was something familiar about the flip of his wild gray hair. He glared through bloodshot eyes at Leon.

"Bring her back to me!"

It might have been my howl. But he was the one who cradled Celine in his arms.

Her white robes spilled onto the floor, along with her blood. I turned to Leon for help—the man who had all the answers. His thick white brows beetled. Then he shook his head. "I'm sorry, Noel," he said. "It's time. You know."

Then the old man did what he does best, and slipped out through the wall. He didn't even pause to look at me, muttering to himself as his torn ghost-shirt floated him to somewhere else, leaving a silver trail, and me caught in the mirror-maze.

I turned on the one who'd brought her. "Who are you?" I demanded.

"Elon," he growled. His red eyes burned.

"You have blood on your shirt!" He also reeked of Celine's perfume, as though she'd hurled the bottle.

He laughed, an ugly sound. "It's yours."

I felt reality breaking up around me. Someone was shaking up the puzzle box. But I didn't care anymore. I locked my fingers around his throat. They fitted nicely, as if they'd been custom-made.

On the wide table, Celine drocped like a dying swan. Her violet eyes fell open and a last note burbled from her throat. Two syllables: my name . . .

We winked, again. I saw her. Green skies—blue fields . . . black specks like crows . . . the bars of a window, the cage of a child's crib . . .

Leon told me once that sanity was the tether of fools, the inhibiting fear of timid men. I called him mad at the time, and he laughed as he walked off, straight through the wall . . .

It's been seventy years since I locked myself in this tower for her good. Time was, and forever. It is time I was on my way.

The table's bare of all but that sharpened glitter. When I found that you had left me . . .

My ghost has done many things. Celine dies, and lives, and dies, but Leon does not come back. The window stands in an unbroken sheet, the iron bars as straight as math can make them.

If not now, then how? That is the question.

If time is not Klein but Möbius, will I get back to you? Even eternity tastes sweet when faced with the alternative.

Each decade in the mirror gives me Noel, Elon, Leon, and loops again.

Lone, I write you this upon my soul with the stylus you handed me, hoping, for your sake, that you won't see this face again.

elegy to a meadow

. . .

Marisca Pichette

your skin grows asters
and burrs that hold and hold—
goldenrod, wildflowers dimpled
with promiseful seeds.

even in winter you're beautiful:
white wasteland adorned in sticks,
haphazard skin holding breaths
awaiting spring's exhale.

walking through you, watching
sunrise, sunset, lying back
counting shadows tumbling from the sky
you know my touch

like the bees, jays, blackbirds
proudly preening red-orange wings.

you know me like the trees that hold you,
guard your edges in their roots,
bless you each fall with a blanket

of spent leaves.

you know I'm shrinking—
my fingers turned to claws,
skin rubbed pink questing
for fur.

you offered me a burrow
and I braided a nest from grass,
touched one end to my back
to place a tail.

I used to hum but now I whisper,
my teeth adept at chewing.

in summertime I sit motionless
counting fireflies in your dark.

I always knew—
from the moment I stopped my car,
left the door swinging wide as I hopped the fence
and knelt in your vastness—

your beauty has the power to change us,
unwind time, bend back the horizon
swirl the stars into new patterns
only mice remember.

curled in my new home
in the heart of you
I miss nothing that ever lived
beyond.

her unerring taste

. . .

Robert E. Stahl

CW: graphic depictions

Sydney jerked awake in the darkness of her bedroom, her tongue darting about in her mouth like a thing possessed. Alarmed, she jerked on the lamp and sat upright. Yes, now that her eyes were open, there was no denying it. There was a tense feeling in her tongue, a *strangeness* that had not been there before. She gritted her teeth, trying to ignore the tongue's desire to move, but the urges only got stronger. Her tongue continued its dance, circling, curling, crawling around as if poking for a way out.

Nerves, she thought. The pressure of being one of the world's most-celebrated chefs. In less than twelve hours, a writer with *Michelin Guide* would visit her restaurant to interview her for a feature. The good press would be a financial boon for La Table Moderne, earning her bistro a place as one of the hottest eateries in town. Yet here she was at three o'clock in the morning unable to think of a proper dish to prepare to knock the writer's socks off, and with her tongue suddenly acting up, to boot.

Hell, it was a wonder she'd fallen asleep at all. Her entire body felt stiff with anxiety. But her tongue! It was alive with restless energy. It wiggled and waggled and writhed like a wonder-filled worm. Eagerly, intensely, thoughtfully, her tongue probed the latticework of bone on the ridge of her mouth before moving on to the walls of her cheeks. There, it stroked the velvety skin like a dedicated lover. Peculiar. She'd crafted award-winning dishes ad nauseam for celebrities, presidents, and kings; had cooked with every meat, vegetable and spice known to mankind; had infused thousands of meals with dizzying flavors such as to bring her guests to ecstasy—yet she'd never tasted *herself* before.

Oh! The piquant brine of her own saliva. The delicate nuttiness of digestive chemicals at work. The mottled tang of potassium molecules mingling amid phosphates. She took a nibble of the buttery skin and crushed it between her jaws. Her tastebuds roared! The morsel was an amuse-bouche of delight. Who would ever have known? Residing there all along in the privacy of her own mouth. How would she ever cook with regular food again?

Her concerns about the Michelin writer gave way to the curiosity of her new discovery. She took a bite of her lip, wincing slightly as incisors crunched through layers of skin, muscle and fat. Her mouth flooded with a surge of warm blood. Intoxicating! The flavors were a roux of enjoyment. The sweetness of protein cells. The metallic twang of copper. The umami of proteins dissolving to their essences, toothsome and savory. Thrashing against the bed in orgasm-like bliss, she could only think of more.

On, the feeding continued, to her fingers, her wrists, her arms. She was chewing on her right toe when her heart finally stopped. Collapsing onto the blood-soaked bed, she succumbed, her eyes rolling back in their sockets, her body shaking spastically before growing forever still.

The world's finest chef, sated at last.

discontinuities

. . .

Madeline Barnicle

Naively, if our pencil never breaks
Contact with paper, then a graph behaves.
But intuition brings about mistakes;
Zeroes will not lie constant in their graves.
So we endeavor, at the least, to label,
To apprehend and classify and sort:
Triage illumines whether we'll be able
To rectify the ways a plot falls short.

A hole draws our attention, and eyes linger;
But singularities can be removed.
The doubting hand, the awed, uneven finger
Refill the void: the bold conjecture, proved.
A jump: the left and right limits don't equal.
Something has ruptured into time and space.
A broken line continues in the sequel
But on a higher plane, an angled grace.

A low-dimension space embeds within
Our solid world. It shouldn't make us feel:
But paper cuts, though infinitely thin.

Depthless projections of my grief are real.
Metrics are inequivalent: my local
Neighborhood is unaltered under most
Deformations that trigger outcries vocal.
Why am I haunted by the flatlands' ghost?

Asymptotes can't be grasped. A boundless slope
Surpasses any limits we would draw.
Beside the infinite, the dimmest hope
Burns bright as bombs, exposes us, rubs raw
Our mispriorities, hacks through the bramble
Of finite goods, now trivially small.
Stacked up against so infinite a gamble
We find they're not a sacrifice at all.

You have no brighter mind or purer soul,
No empathy, no altruistic dreams.
It's only that you're quick to see a hole
In systems, since you're used to axiom schemes.
Math's never driven anyone insane:
You've got causality the wrong way round.
Hypocrisies, injustices, cause pain:
Retreat to the embrace of logic's bound.

Once all the deltas have values assigned
The theorems often seem tautologies.
The trick was never in the proofs, you'll find,
But definitions that preceded these.
The work is in the words, in making formal
The pattern that's apparent to the eyes:
The places where curves bend beyond the normal,
Unfold between the axes and the wise.

the distinction

. . .

Madeline Barnicle

How do you tell your witches from your wizards?
If they're ascetics, sitting atop poles
Heedless of hunger, firestorms or blizzards,
Transcending bodies to perfect their souls—

Well, those are wizards. By contrast, the mages
Who not only bake cakes, but eat each slice,
Who curl their hairs or trim beards in their ages,
Deeming their flesh-dwellings no sacrifice—

Those are the witches, and they both wield power.
Neither is stronger: what requires force
Is parting ways with fashions of the hour
If magic draws you on another course.

Stylites are stylized, skin pulled over skull—
But so too is the full-filled convex hull.

planes of illusory

. . .

Robert Bagnall

Now we request your full attention as the flight attendants demonstrate the safety features of this aircraft.

When the seat belt sign illuminates, you must fasten your seat belt, tightening by pulling on the loose end of the strap. To release your seat belt, lift the upper portion of the buckle. We suggest you keep your seat belt fastened throughout the flight, as we may experience turbulence.

There are several emergency exits on this aircraft: two forward, two aft, and two over each wing. Please take a few moments now to locate your nearest exit. In some cases, your nearest exit may be behind you. Those ignoring this safety announcement may wish to glance around at others assessing the weight and latent aggression of those they'll have to climb over. Forewarned is forearmed, and a hard-spined Tom Clancy can come in damn useful.

In the event of a decompression, an oxygen mask will appear in front of you. Yes, we've all seen *Fight Club*, and their summation is spot-on. To start the flow of oxygen, pull the mask towards you. Place it firmly over your nose and mouth, secure the elastic band behind your head and breathe normally. If you are travelling with a child or someone who requires assistance, secure your mask first and then assist the other person.

In the event of the plane needing to land on water, a life vest is located under your seat. Which, if you think about it, is merely a token gesture. When instructed to do so, open the plastic pouch, and remove the vest. Slip it over your head. Pass the straps around your waist and adjust at the front. To inflate the vest, pull firmly on the red cord, only when leaving the aircraft. If you need to refill the vest, blow into the mouthpieces. Use the whistle and light to attract attention.

But let's be realistic. If the aircraft were to drop from the sky, there's no way on earth we'll be forming an orderly queue and remembering not to pull the toggle until we're safely bobbing in the drink. Or remembering the damn toggle at all. Yeah, yeah, there was that guy they made the movie about, but that was just a freakish one-off. We drop, maybe the family of nine in row twelve all going at once, three generations, will lead the headlines. But not you: you're little people. What have you ever done? Makes you think, doesn't it?

And, whilst we're at it, let's consider the physics of flight. Remember what you were taught at school about the air over the upper surface travelling further therefore being more spread out, hence at a lower pressure, thus sucking a hundred tons of metal, av-gas and self-loading cargo—by which I mean you, bozo— skywards? Hands up who thought, but surely you're just bunching up the air above which must then push back down? For every action, blah, blah, blah. Newton trumps Bernoulli.

And you know what? You're right. The physics of flight doesn't work. It's impossible. It's just superstition that's only hanging together through sheer dumb luck, luck that'll run out when you least expect. But the lizard people don't want you to know that.

The lizard people?

Yes, the lizard people. The ones who control everything. The power behind the thrones.

No, I have no idea whether they're really lizards, or have corporeal form at all for that matter. It's more of a shorthand. Something I thought you may be able to relate to.

I know what you're wondering: what made the lizard people fail to factcheck the physics of flight? How should I know? You think I'm a stewardess. Actually, I'm just a mannequin, hollow plastic with drawn-on eyes, brought to life, animated in the diabolic rather than Disney-sense, by—yes, you've guessed it!—the lizard people.

You've done your seatbelts up, haven't you? I hope not too tight. You'll find you're unable to loosen them. Or release them, for that matter.

Don't you find there's a moment—for some of us it's as the doors are pulled shut, for others as the nose-wheel lifts from the runway—that you know your immediate future is in other people's hands, that there is nothing you can do about how things pan out from here. This is just one such moment. Embrace it.

Where was I? Yes… the lizard people. The best guess I've come up with is they've given you a false trail to follow to hide the real reason birds fly. Which probably means the birds are in on it too. Maybe the birds are the lizard people. I mean, where do they all go to die? If the answer is another plane of reality, that would explain a lot, don't you think?

The chief steward and his team are here for your safety and comfort but, to be honest, their impact is minimal as this is less a jumbo, more a plane of illusory. Your chances of making it out alive in the event of an emergency are, frankly, minimal.

We hope you'll chose to fly with us again.

languid time

. . .

Laura Theis

these days it's all postal weather
an occasional prune maybe

a wednesday too
time's shape vacillates between

a zero a crown and a tiny ball
yesterday a sleepy hare

its brother today a devil's egg
for some reason

oh for a sluice a sword a storm but no
just an identical ballet of round red fur

and a salt swan embraced
by circling shores once more

from coal to coal I notice
blue blank time

pass without plans
sweet and lazy as a river that curves

to meet its own ourborous tail
over and over again

shift

. . .

Laura Theis

I am as wide as the night at four am
running a finger over the cold wet velvet
of the roof's moss-covered tiles

the moon is a neon orange
puffer fish swimming so low on the horizon
it all but disappears behind the neighbouring houses

but maybe the moon is not a fish
not a remote drifting mirror or piece of cheese
not the thumb print of some radiant hand

maybe the moon is the night's ever-expanding and
     contracting ear
listening out for the thoughts and despairs
of the most lost

maybe that is why she has dedicated
her eternity to turning them all
into this one inaudible song of delight

other

. . .

Emmie Christie

Four-year-old Selka tipped her chair back and fell for a half-second. Half of her soul poured out before she caught herself.

She peered around for a bit Outside. Her body shuddered, then a few seconds later, returned to coloring the mermaid in her coloring book. The other half of her soul gestured for her to cram back in.

But she didn't. That part of her hadn't fit, anyway, inside her body; it had tipped out so easy. She followed Selka for years, reminding her once in a while that she didn't possess all of herself, that part of her now lived somewhere else. At those times, Selka saw through "Other's" eyes, leaving her body and all its sensations behind for a moment. At the playground she watched her empty body swing. At the dance she watched Billy Harvey stick his tongue down her throat. He didn't seem to like that she didn't smile, or even frown afterwards—but Other didn't have a body, and couldn't feel his lips, so it wasn't her fault. It wasn't like Other was jealous of Selka, of how she could fit in a body.

Selka herself, didn't mind that part of her lived somewhere else. She had a kind of sister. A silent protector. Her two older brothers had multiplied with wives and children and couldn't understand that she had, instead, divided herself. They didn't understand the drifting, the distant twin-eyes that Other let her peer through. They told her she'd do well to settle down and raise a family. But Selka had no desire for children, or a husband. How could she satisfy another person when she wasn't whole herself?

At 32, Selka lost her job at a promising tech firm. She peered up at the building. It loomed above her, just as her supervisor had. He'd said, "You just don't have what it takes in this fast-paced market. You're always daydreaming."

Other showed her an image of the city from above, from the body of a pigeon. They shared a container again for the first time since they'd been four years old. The tech firm building seemed so small, compared to the sky, that she laughed. *Stay,* Other seemed to say. *It's better here.*

I can't.

One foot in the sky, one foot on the street. She didn't belong in either place. She still craved hotdogs, and the smell of fresh cut grass, and the touch of silk she couldn't buy. Divided. So divided.

Other retreated in her mind, stepping into the headache that began to pound in Selka's head, and then Selka touched back down, in front of the tech firm building once more.

After that, Other drifted farther and farther away. She didn't show Selka visions for several years. Selka trained for a marathon just to feel the wind whip through her hair and sweat to bead her face each day. She craved sensation and the sharp hunger after a run. And yet, the void that Other had left seemed like it consumed her sweat, the wind, the potent perfumes she wore everywhere, the spiciest Indian food on the menu. She tasted the pork vindaloo for a few seconds, then it disappeared into that abyss, the gaping hole where half of herself used to be.

Then, one day at 53, while driving with the windows up, the

wind whispered on Selka's neck, and Other's view filtered over hers.

She had settled next to an eagle in a huge nest. The bird flapped its wings, unsettled, as if it could sense her. Other hopped onto its back, settled into its body a little, and soared through the air. Selka whooped as the air rushed past, sharing in the moment.

Then Other jolted, and screamed, and the bird squawked and flapped away.

Selka didn't understand. What had happened? She tried to call out, and something pulled her back down, but her body wouldn't allow her back in. She felt like toothpaste squeezed out of a tube.

She'd been driving. She'd hit something. A car? Blurry images flashed, and far off pain pulsed. Other hadn't understood that Selka needed her eyes to drive. How could she have known? She didn't live in the substantial.

Her body slumped over the steering wheel. She sidled next to it. She couldn't breathe. And a sense of guilt descended, as Other hovered nearby.

Other *had* known. She'd done it on purpose. She'd wanted Selka with her. She'd missed her. But she couldn't fit in a body, so she'd gotten rid of it, the barrier between them. But now Selka might not want to be with her. Other had been selfish, and jealous, and now she'd ruined Selka's home, and she wished she had tried to slip back in when she was four, but it just hadn't felt right—

Selka joined Other in the sky. She settled into the eagle, merging the parts of her that had lived apart.

"I've missed being with you, too. I'm ready. Will you show me what it's like to be Outside?"

cake

. . .

R.A. Daunton

I t had been a hard-fought battle to get to the house that dwelled above the field.

She had told him that it would be impossible, a suicide mission. That they were better off taking their chances back on the roads. She had pleaded, begged—but he had not listened. The house was too large, too impressive. It had loomed down upon the land with too much authority to be ignored. The pull of that place could not be denied. They needed it. It had to be theirs.

In those times, desperation would eventually make fools of them all.

"Find something to help brace it!" she yelled, pushing her back against the door. Cracked fingernails and rotten flesh sped past her face, clawing at her from outside.

He didn't need to be told twice. Too many years had passed since the Post-Death world had begun. Too many houses just like that one, scoped and scavenged. They had been travelling together for what felt like a lifetime, and it had all become second nature.

Though the room was dark, he knew where to look. After a while, everywhere they went had melded into one. No more surprises, no more exploration. No more wonder, and no more joy. Every house began to fit a pattern: entrance, living room, kitchen, bedrooms, stairs, basement. They were all the same. Same furniture, same foods, same utensils, same tools. Survival became monotonous after everything was looked at objectively. A bed was a bed, it mattered not how comfortable. Food was food, no matter the taste, the brand, or the sell-by date. Everything had become nothing more than fuel for their engine of self-preservation. And it had begun to run low on gas.

***

"Here!" he shouted as he pushed a couch against the door. It was large, luxurious-looking. Unsurprising, he thought, considering the regal appearance of the abode.

There was no time for thank yous or pleasantries during times such as that. There was a long-unspoken rule between the woman and the man that things should be brief, curt, and matter-of-fact during Live-or-Dies. There would be time for sentiment later. If they were still among the living.

A face came through the crack in the door. It was half flesh-half skull. They had slowly been getting worse, she noted. Rotting more every day. She could tell how long they had been dead depending on their state of decay; for how long they had been up and about since Day 1. She could tell that this one was old, maybe one of the first. It had been around too long. It needed to end. It needed to die its second death.

***

"I hate the ripe ones the most," he said. He looked tired and old beyond his years, not uncommon for the living during the Post-

Death age. "Especially when they are surrounded by the freshers."

"At least you can smell those before you see them," she replied. 'The freshers, sometimes I still have trouble telling them apart from the living. What if it isn't one of them? What if I shoot one of… us." The woman wore a scowl, permanently welded to her once-pretty face. "Every little thing helps. The smell, I'll take it if it means not adding another one to their numbers."

The man sighed and nodded his head.

The smell was truly the worst thing about the Post-Death age. Surrounded by the undead, no soap, toothpaste, running water. No showers, baths, nor hot or running water; unless you were one of the lucky ones, and god knows *they* were never willing to share. Lakes, rivers, and streams were one thing, but it was rarely worth the risk of infection. Too much death, all around, rotting, decaying, corrupting everything that it touched.

They loved one another, and that was enough. It helped them to ignore the worst of their stench, their unwashed faces and hair, her lack of makeup, and his ungroomed beard. Their rotting, aching teeth.

Sleep never came easy, even when they knew that they were safe. Even with the windows and doors locked, boarded up, and secured–they could still hear them outside. Banging, scratching, moaning to be let in. They could still smell them.

They held each other and closed their eyes, listening to the hordes and the rumbling of their stomachs.

"Well, at least we found something in the kitchen," he said through a mouthful of Spam. "Now that the sun's up, I'll feel better about checking the basement."

She nodded. Not searching dark, abandoned houses was another one of those unspoken rules. Time and energy had to be expended on securing the dwelling and taking out any immediate threats. There would be time to search if they made it to morning, and they would never make it to morning unless the place was secure.

If they ever got too hungry, if that ever became another Life-or-Death, then they always had The Cake. After all these years, it had still never come to that.

Contrary to popular Post-Death belief, basements weren't the things of nightmares that they were often made out to be. They had heard it all, huddled around campsites with temporary friends and allies. "Don't go down there!", "Opened that door and thirty of them spat out, took out half my group", "A death sentence!"

No, like most things, if handled with proper care, preparation, and respect; their danger could be mitigated. To start with, many states didn't even have them. Second of all, they were almost always locked. Third, if there was one of *them* down there, then it was almost always just a single loved one or family member. Locked away after turning by the occupants of the dwelling, too scared to do away with them in the proper manner. People like that didn't last long, so there was rarely more than one down there. They almost always died upstairs.

The thing about basements is that they almost always housed something good. So, to ignore them, now that was the death sentence. Food, tools, and entertainment. Everything that was needed to keep going. The upstairs of a house, now that was where the danger lay. Attics. People are scared of basements, there's nowhere to run. They don't go down there to hide. They search for the higher ground.

He used his crowbar to pop the lock, and she stood back,

flashlight and handgun drawn. He opened the door and jumped to her side, aiming his rifle into the darkness.

"Check?"

"Hold it…"

The air that billowed out was earthy and sweet. Damp like moss.

"…Check."

The lack of rot upon their nostrils gave them respite, if not ease. He stepped forward through the beam of light. She held it steady, her hands un-shaking. Life for them would have been boring if the promise of death had not lurked around every corner.

"I'm going in," he said. His words were quiet so that only she could hear. Just in case.

"I've got you. Easy does it now," she replied.

He grunted and peered past the open door, the barrel of his rifle pointing inside the entrance. The earthly scent continued to waft upwards at them as if rushing to escape from its subterranean prison. It invited him forward, and he was eager to oblige.

"I don't hear anything," he whispered.

"What do you see?"

The man walked through the doorframe and furrowed his brow. His shadow was projected upon a muddy wall, two or three brief steps from the entrance. To his right were a set of decrepit wooden stairs, leading down as far as he could see, deep into an inky abyss.

"Stairs. They look old. What do you think?"

She stepped forward and looked over his shoulder, holding the torch above her head.

"I don't like it. Do you think this is the only way down?"

He let her pass, and she shone the torch onto the steps. They went down further than the beam could reach, with no end in sight.

"There might be another entrance to it outside, at the bottom of the hill, maybe. But we aren't getting out to check with *them* still out there," he said.

"This is verging on a Serves-you-Right. How many basements have you seen with an exit down below? Not many. We shouldn't even be considering this. We are better than this."

"Exactly," he said with a smile. "We are too good to get caught dead by something like this, that's why it's going to be fine."

"It's the smell, isn't it?"

"It's the smell."

"Fresh. Un-fetid."

"Alive," he replied. "Full of promise. Dare I say it…"

"Don't," she cut him off.

"…Hope."

"Damn, you. Now why did you have to go and say a thing like that?"

"What can I say?"

"Nothing. Just be careful. There's no point trying to talk you out of it, not when you get like this. The first sign that those stairs are going to give, you get right back up here, you hear. If you fall while you're down there, you're dead. I won't be able to get down to get you, and I sure as cats won't be able to carry you back myself."

He put a foot forward, onto the first step. It felt solid, despite its old age. He rolled his shoulders, took in a deep, earthly-smelling breath of air, and began to descend.

***

"See! That wasn't so bad!" he yelled from the bottom of the stairs.

She sighed and shook her head.

"You're an idiot, you know that?" she shouted back. "Can you see anything?"

"Not with my Mag, no. It's dark here, real dark!"

The woman put her foot on the step and looked down. There was no hint of movement below. His voice was echoing up to her, and it had a tone as if the basement was large and cavernous, made of solid stone.

"Stay there, I'm coming down!"

It could feel them inside itself, uninvited and unwelcome. It had not always been so aware of these things; it had not always been so in-tuned with its surroundings. It had lived there once, long ago. Before those days, before that day. The first day. The day that they came and took it all away from it and its kind. Their glory. It had them forgotten. They were once the ones feared. Nobody spoke about them anymore. It never had visitors before then. Now, they were everywhere. Shuffling, moaning. Scavenging and seeking refuge. It was not them, and it was not them. They were not the same. They were not friends. It had no friends. They were not allies. It had only enemies. It wanted to be left alone. It wanted them all to go away. It wanted, it wanted. It wanted, but it could never get. Its eyes were forever open. It had watched for too long. It felt, but it did not feel. It could not understand why it had awoken. But it had always been awake. It was born at the same time, it knew this. But it did not know. It was always alive. It had been there for centuries. It wanted this to end. It wanted it to stop. They were the same, once. It knew that it could never go back. It had never lived. It was not born. It was built. It could never be torn down. It was eternal.

They must be punished.

They must be saved.

They must stay.

They must begone.

They must live.

They must die.

Die.

Like it had died. Like it had never had a life to extinguish.

It knew everything. It knew nothing.

It was the authority, it loomed down, down upon that field, that land.

It had no choice, it was nothing.

———

They heard a rumble from upstairs, somewhere above them. From where, exactly, they could not tell. The house had shaken too, but that had gone unnoticed. They were too deep underground, then. They did not feel the eyes upon them, seeing them even within the darkness. They were too smitten by what they had found.

———

"So, what do you think?" she asked him.

He wiped a film of grease from his chin, looked down at the half-empty can of beef hash in his hand, and grinned back. "Wedding."

"Yeah, that's what I was reckoning. The place must have been used for fancy events of something, way back."

"Catered too."

"Uh-huh."

They smiled at one another as they looked around the discarded mass of empty cans that had begun to pile up around them.

"I wish we could have got married in a place like this," he said. He ran his tongue across the top of the open can, picking up remnants of long-since expired potato.

"We made do."

"Oh, I know. And there wasn't anything wrong with Rev's shack, but you know? The hills of Appalachia aren't exactly the Taj Mahal. Hell, they aren't even Vegas. This place is something else though, huh? At least, must have been back in the day, anyway."

"I've been thinking."

"Uh-oh."

"No, stop it. Nothing like that."

"Oh?"

"Don't be silly. I'm being serious here."

"Silly, me?"

She punched him, playfully, on the arm. "I think we should stay."

"Here?" he asked.

"Where else?"

"But what about all of *them* outside?" he said, his gaze following the silhouette of a shuffling body sauntering past the tightly secured window.

"They won't bother us none. Besides, we can take them out, one by one, you know? From the windows upstairs, probably. How many times have we done this?"

He shrugged his shoulders. "All this food got you thinking, huh?"

"Place is locked up tight, there's more food than we can carry —at least for now—and who knows what else is upstairs? Could be worth a stay for a while. A week or two, maybe. Give us a chance to catch our breath. I'm getting tired, aren't you?"

"I don't remember how it feels to be anything else anymore."

"Well?"

"You don't need to convince me, I'm the one who wanted to come here in the first place."

"Right."

"It's just…"

"What?"

He turned his head and looked towards the stairs. "Nothing."

"Should we take a look around, then?"

"No time like the present, I suppose."

"That's the spirit," she said with a smile.

The scratching, the clawing, the moaning. From outside, from all around. It was ceaseless. There would be no end, but the fear was no longer there. Their feet upon the old, creaking stairs masked the sounds, but they were still there. They sang to them, begged them, called to them. They tried to warn them and remind them of the reality they still inhabited. There are few things more detrimental to the common sense of the survivor, to human beings' survival than a full stomach and a sense of calm. Once the sounds, the sights, and the smells become part of your normal. Once death no longer shocks or holds meaning. Once comfort begins to set in and the struggle begins to dissipate; once one's guard lowers and hope begins to creep, that is when it is all over. Happiness had started to knock, threatening to rear its head. Once invited inside, there was no turning back. There was no room at this table for three.

Fear begets survival. Happiness, in that world, bred nothing but death.

I don't like them, I don't like them, I don't want them. They should not be here. Why why why why why? I we us I us we I us. For so long, had it good. Until *them*. Those *things*. Leave me us alone. I don't like. I don't want. I want. I want. I want.

No.

I feel them crawling over me. They claw at my skin. They run their dirty hands, their filthy feet, their their their their words pepper, their wetness, it slithers across my bones. Too warm. Too wet. Why so wet? I am strong and I am tall and I am dry and I am strong. Stronger than *those*, those who refuse to die. Know your place, your role.

Was I them once? Yes. No. Yes. No. Once but not now. Not for so long.

I am this land. Invaders. Colonists. I am not that. I am us. I am I. I am not I for there is no I, there is no we. There is only is.

How long?

Forever.

Days.

Years.

Centuries.

Hours?

No.

Was I always present? Was I not them once, as well? Why will these memories not answer? My fingers. My toes. My eyes. My ears. Solid now. One with it. It is.

This is only is.

I am strong.

They crawl, they crawl, they crawl. Cockroaches. Filthy vermin. Uninvited. Uninvited. That is what they are. The uninvited. They cannot stay. No guest. No visitors. Alone. I want. Alone.

Thump. Thump. Thump. Stop. Stop. Stop.

Stop treading on me!

We.

Us.

Is.

He held her ankles as she dangled, head-first from the window. This was not a Life-or-Death, not in their usual sense of the term, but there was still no time for words. He didn't like doing this, but it had to be done. She, on the other hand, was having the time of her life.

They marched towards her gently swaying body, intrigued by the display. He often wondered what must have been going through their heads seeing something like this - if anything went through their heads at all. Did they still understand the concept of absurdity, of strangeness? Did the sight of a woman hanging upside-down from a second-story window still register as being out of the ordinary to them?

The Post-Death world was full of strange sights. There was something about the end of the world that led to human beings losing their sense of sense. Desperation, he assumed. He used to write these things down, in a notebook long since lost. He had seen it all; men dressed as clowns, pirates, ninjas, fighting the undead with their bare hands, tuna fish, plastic children's weapons, sex toys—all whilst laughirg maniacally. Humans being torn skin from bone whilst wearing tuxedoes and evening gowns, years after the world had ended. He had seen chariots driven through the streets of Anaheim, pulled by white horses, driven by naked women wearing diamond-bedecked crowns. He had fought off the living gangs of New York, side-by-side with other betrodden survivors, pondering why the locals still insisted on wearing the colours of groups that had long since ceased to hold meaning. He had once lost a friend, a close friend, who had sacrificed his life to save a blow-up doll. In Knoxville, he had almost been killed by a man dressed head-to-toe as Dolly Parton, her dress, her wigs, her shoes; giant, rotting flanks of beef stuffed beneath his dress. The smell of the meat had attracted the creepers, and they had gotten to him before he could finish the job. The man died, singing his lungs out, before they took his throat. He had been stuck with the corrupted, blood-curdling sounds of Jolene running through his head ever since.

She stabbed them through the tops of their skulls as they came close, their rotting fingers reaching up towards her drooping, wispy hair. She would be lying if she said she didn't take pleasure in this. She was a homeowner now, after all. And this was as close to a spring clean as she could hope to get.

One by one, they insisted on coming. Dozens of the things, lurching and moaning towards their doom. They never learnt, never adapted. They just marched, ever onwards, the promise of satisfaction forever just out of reach.

They fell, bleeding into the grass below their feet. Pools of dark, glistening blood shone back up at the man and the woman in the mid-morning sun. It painted a sinister portrait in the grass, mixing with the soil and the dirt. It lashed against the side of the house, licking at it, turning its white-painted wood a muggy shade of brown-red.

Back inside, they smiled at each other over more cans of Spam. A just reward for a job well done. They washed their hands in the sink below fountains of bottled water. They had everything that would ever need, there between those four walls. Food, water, warmth shelter. Each other.

When they made love that evening, for the first time in what felt like months, they never heard the sounds above their heads. The creaking of the stairs, the thumping of the pipes. The strange, ever-growing sound of bubbling, rising from the hill below the house; up from the soil, through the fragrant basement that held their bounty, behind the walls of the dwelling, lashing across the attic beams as if waves dashing against storm-beaten harbour walls.

***

She awoke, cold and alone. There was a dampness in the air, and she could taste copper on her tongue.

"Jacob?" she mumbled, rubbing her eyes. Her wristwatch read 9 o'clock, though the darkness outside the bedroom window hinted that might have meant night, not morning. "Where are you?"

The woman pulled herself out of bed and wrapped her body in the thick, cotton sheets. Luxury that she had not felt against her skin for years. Luxury that she could feel herself getting used to.

"You pissing?" she asked the door frame. The door had been left open, and it was gently swinging on the breeze. There was no reply, but she paid it no heed.

She climbed back in bed, closed her eyes, and went back to sleep.

1 o'clock was when she awoke next, pulled out of slumber by the feeling of wetness on her cheek. "Stop it!" she giggled, playfully waving her hands in front of her face. "No kisses until I've washed, I'm gross!"

Again, she received no reply other than the wetness. The smell of copper continued to dance through the room, and it made her cringe. "Christ, man! At least brush your teeth first!"

Her eyes opened. There was nobody else in the room.

The woman darted off the bed, her eyes scanning the room. There was light, now, outside the window. She touched her cheek with her hand, feeling the wetness. "Jacob! Jacob!" she yelled. She ran to the closed door and pulled at the handle. There was no give, it moved not an inch. Harder and harder she pulled, but it would not yield. When she removed her hand from the handle, her print remained—bloody and bubbling like boiling oil.

She fell backwards, gasping. From the ceiling dripped globules of inky-red viscera down upon her head, spattering against her face and her neck. A pool of red was slowly appearing above her, growing as the rainfall of blood heightened in its intensity. Moaning and thumping sounded from outside, banging and scratching against the windows and the doors. As she stared in disbelief at the pool of blood above her head, she thought that she could hear a voice speaking to her, somewhere deep inside her mind.

"Is," it said to her. "Is. Is. Is."

The blood continued to dribble down as she pulled on her clothes, her pack, and her boots. As she holstered her pistol, she heard a window break from below.

The bedroom door burst open, as the ceiling above her side of the bed caved in. A tsunami of blood cascaded down onto her mattress dent, alongside carpentry and plaster, stone, and rock. There was nothing above her, other than that one place they had yet to check. The one place they never checked. The place within a house that was never worth the risk: the attic.

She could hear them walking through the house. The sound of their shuffling, the smell of their fetid bodies stumbling through her home. The din of windows breaking, doors caving in, tin cans being kicked over, and the moaning of the eternally dammed echoing through the halls.

The cord dangled above, dancing in the rotting air. The house, once such a warming and inspirational place, now felt stuffy and claustrophobic. There was a miasma that brushed the hairs on her face, sticking to the blood.

"Why would you do this?" she asked aloud. "We never do this. Never the attic."

One of the lurchers arrived at the top of the stairs and looked ponderously at the woman. Her back was turned, but she could sense that it was there. She could feel it, she could hear it. She could smell it through the vomitus death breath that engulfed the abode.

It stumbled as it rose its arms and stepped forward, catching its foot on the top step, stubbing its toe. As it fell toward her, she had already dealt with the danger before it hit the ground. A swift insertion of her knife into the soft spot on the back of its head, the end of a life prolonged too long. The well-honed actions of a woman corrupted by a life not worth living. A monotonous existence, with never a dull moment allowed.

The thud of its lifeless shell hitting the floor gave her a brief moment of satisfaction, before passing. This life had left her hollow and cold. Without him, would she even bother to carry on?

Close. Bring her to me, tunnel them forward. Invaders, one and all.

I do not need. I am whole, complete, one with one. I am I and we are forever, alone, as one, complete.

Uninvited, unwanted.

Leave.

Leave.

Leave.

We are not one and the same. We were built, born, not as the same, but become. One. Eternal. Conjoined. Safe.

Uncorrupted.

Unsullied by blood, by filth, by smell and by dirt. Clean, I, we. Ordered.

We were the ones feared. The Before Days. Take us, I, we back.

Strong. Looming. Controlled.

She put her hand on the string. She felt a wetness as it gripped the small, bronze sphere on the end of the string. Sweat, blood. It shook and vibrated in her grasp. It felt as if it was burning her skin, yet it chilled her from palm to sole.

She pulled down, hard. The hatch above her head fell open, followed by the blood.

She climbed the steps, hands before her face, hopelessly trying to shield her eyes from the geyser. It soaked her, and she could taste it on her tongue. Coppery, sweet, vile. It stank of age, of rot. Of aeons past, despair, and pain. Words and images filled her mind as the blood merged with her saliva: END, US, IS, DEATH, BECOMING, ONE, NIL. She battled forward, trying to fight through the despair and disarray. She heard them climbing the stairs below her, reaching the top floor from below. She could feel their fingers, their bone, grasping for her ankles as he ascended the attic steps.

The blood flowed as an endless stream from the mouth of the attic. It bore no relation to any earthly reasoning. There was no body from which it to flow; it merely was. It IS.

She reached the pinnacle of her climb; she pulled the steps up behind her. Her hands were slippery, wet from the blood and the sweat, but they came up easily. The moaning of the *things* began to subside behind her, deafened by the voices in her head.

WE.

US.

IS.

WE.

US.

IS.

She shook her head from side to side, trying to oust the incessant chattering, but it would not relent. The attic was sparse, barren, cobwebbed and dusty. It reeked the stench of dampness and rot. In the far end of the room lay a large, spherical window, crossed with thin iron beams. The moon shone in, dimly, through the window, illuminating nought but a spot within the middle of the room.

Before her, his back turned and crouched in a prayer position, was the unmistakable shape of her husband.

"Jacob?" she stammered. There was no response.

US.

I.

I.

US.

She stepped forward, the floorboards creaking beneath her feet. The entrance hatch thumped and scraped with the sound of bloodied and broken fingernails, but it did not register. She just kept walking, across the room. Onwards, towards Jacob.

"What are you doing up here?" she asked, her hand edging closer to his shoulder. "You know we never do these things on our own. It's suicide."

US.

US.

US.

WE.

I.

Her hand clasped his shoulder and sunk into his flesh. She jumped back, shocked, as his body slumped to the ground like a deflating balloon. As he hit the floorboards, a puddle of pink, gelatinous liquid began to piddle out from below him, seeping down into the house, his shell melting away as if a candle to a furnace.

"Jacob?"

WE.

WE.

WE.

TOGETHER.

She ran to the hatch and pulled it open as the room began to shake. Below her, where stairs had once belonged, now lay nothing but black, abyssal night; stars glistening in the nothing.

She threw her pack to the floor and gazed into the darkness.

A voice rang out, one that she recognised.

"It's not so bad once you let yourself go, Fran. This place is strong and unconquerable. Alive."

WE.

US.

I.

"Nothing can hurt us here. There is no more suffering. No more pain. There is only US."

The moon began to slumber as she closed her eyes. She felt herself melt, and then she felt nothing at all.

The pack lay by the weeping puddle, empty now save for the napkin-wrapped slice of fruitcake inside. Pressed inside the frosting, lay two plastic figures; a man and a woman, hands clasped, together for eternity.

US.

delighted, i'm sure

. . .

Mark Fiddes

Have you grasped how Delight is more slippery
than love or even a fish?
How the afterglow of chocolate or whisky
gets lost past the epiglottis?
How a lover can vanish forever in an Uber.
How the beat does not go on?
If you were a flower, you would use pheromones
or claws to trap Delight's carapace,
to slowly suck it dry.
A camel might store Delight up in its hump
for some quality mammal time at the next oasis.
There is no user's manual on how to bottle it,
then microwave it when you are ready.
You cannot slip it
between DeLillo and Defoe on a bookshelf
for a quick hit when you're low.
Nothing despises Delight more than Time
which stuffs our days into meeting rooms,
rams years into slow trains and rattles our bones,
putting us on hold with robots
for half a lifetime when we should be rhapsodic

and dimly lit beyond past and present,
maybe smoking again.
Yet watch how Delight is ever ready
day and night, spring loaded in the curl of a lip,
on the lip of a glass, or inclined in a semibreve
to serenade us all breathlessly.

zygote city

. . .

D. Matthew Urban

The black-tinted doors reveal nothing of the hotel's interior. When they slide apart at our approach, a blazing hole opens in the night. Everything in the lobby is bright—the chandeliers, the faux-marble floor, the garish smears of abstract art on the walls—but the brightest thing of all is the night clerk's smile. It draws the two of us toward the front desk like moths to a flame.

Moths don't think they're flying toward a flame. The light dazzles them, and they blunder into the flame by mistake.

Off to a bad start. I shoo away the pointless thoughts. This trip is too serious to let nonsense distract me. If things work out, if the treatment does what it's supposed to, it'll be a fresh beginning. A chance to start over. If not…

I'm only halfway across the lobby, and my husband is at the front desk already. I've been dawdling, thinking about moths and flames. Putting on speed, I arrive at the desk just as the clerk takes John's credit card. "One moment, Mr. Brower," the clerk says, his eyes sliding down to his card-reading contraption.

While the clerk's eyes are averted, I snake an arm around John's waist, rest my fingertips on his hip. He doesn't respond at all. No gratified murmur, no groan of distate. Sheer neutrality.

The clerk looks up from his contraption, smiling so brightly the bottom half of his face seems obliterated. "All right, Mr. and Mrs. Brower, you're all set!" He slides a pair of black keycards across the white laminate. "Welcome to Zygote City."

"Is that the name of the city or the name of the hotel?" John asks. "The pamphlet wasn't clear about that." The question would never have occurred to me. I tell myself I'm lucky to have such a practical-minded husband.

"Hmm." The clerk's eyes roll upward. It seems the question has never occurred to him, either. A kindred soul, flighty and distractible. I imagine his thoughts buzzing away like mine do, crazed honeybees eternally circling behind his teeth's white petals.

His eyes roll back down. His shining smile becomes apologetic. "I'm afraid I'm not the person to ask about things like that. Our concierge will be happy to answer any questions you have. She's off for the night, but she'll be here bright and early in the morning."

"Thank you very much," I say. I raise a hand to take my keycard, but John has already snatched up both cards and started for the elevator. I scurry across the faux-marble to reach him before the doors close.

Our room is white-carpeted and terribly cold, the air conditioner howling full blast beneath the window. A framed print hangs over the bed, another on the opposite wall, two indistinguishable swirls of wild and chaotic brushstrokes. I switch off the air conditioner, but its racket seems to linger, a faint after-howl trapped in the room like the sea roaring in a shell.

It's not the sea roaring. It's your own blood murmuring in your ear.

John draws the curtain back from the window, revealing a golf course. Swaths of moonlight gleam on the fairways. In the woods beyond the course, lamps on poles illuminate a clearing where squat buildings cluster.

I point toward the clearing. "That's where the magic happens."

"The famous institute," my husband says in a tone I can't interpret. It could be skeptical, or sarcastic, or just stating the facts—it *is* famous, it *is* an institute. Why can't I understand his tone, after all these years? Why is everything always so full of secrets? Secrets stinging my eyes, tightening my throat. I bury my face in my hands and sob.

"Come on," he says. "It's okay." Is it really okay, or does he just want me to stop crying? I cry harder. He puts an arm around me. I roll my face on his shoulder, leave a snail's track of tears on his shirt.

"It's okay," he says.

"I just want this to work," I say.

He sighs, strokes my hair. "Sure, of course. I do, too."

I don't know if he's saying what he means or what he thinks I want to hear. A picture forms in my imagination: a grass-covered mound, a hole in the mound, a spider lurking in the hole. John's head is the mound, his mind is the hole, the truth is the spider. I wish I could reach into the hole, tear the mound apart, look into the spider's eyes.

I take a deep breath, let it out slowly. I still hear the air conditioner's after-howl. Maybe it's a different air conditioner howling in a different room. I lift my face from John's shirt, look over his shoulder to the window.

The golf course gleams. The institute huddles in its clearing. Among the squat buildings, in the glare of the lamps, something moves. Gnat-like in the distance, a figure—no, two figures—dart across the lit space. One disappears into the trees, but the other stops short, walks slowly along the edge of the clearing.

"Look down there," I say.

"Where?" John turns to the window. I point out the moving figure. "Huh," he says. "Late night at the institute, I guess."

Late night doing what? My thoughts want to buzz in a hundred directions, sip the nectar of a hundred speculations, but I force them quiet. I sag against John's side. "Just another night in Zygote City," I say.

My husband's body shudders against mine. A shudder of tenderness, or amusement, or exhaustion, or revulsion— anything at all. The vermin stirring in its hole.

As promised, the concierge is happy to answer our questions. "Zygote City is the name of the city *and* the hotel," she says. "Some people find that a little confusing"—she shoots a pointed glance at the front desk, where the night clerk is finishing his shift—"but almost everyone figures it out. In practice, there's no problem at all. Just say 'Zygote City,' and all of us will know exactly what you mean." She smiles broadly, as if to show how pleasant it is to know exactly what someone means. Her teeth are stained and crooked, but her smile is beautiful. It warms my heart.

"One more question," John says. "How do we get over to the institute for the treatment?"

"There's a shuttle bus every morning and every evening." The concierge looks at her watch. "The morning bus will be here in one hour. In the meantime, if you'd like to learn more, there's plenty of information in this brochure." She hands me a glossy booklet, its cover as black and blank as the hotel's doors.

We sit in the lobby and wait for the shuttle bus. I leaf through the brochure, pausing every so often to relay some tidbit.

"Why do you think it's called Zygote City?" I say.

John taps his thumb against his knee, pondering the question or annoyed by it. He sighs. "A zygote's like an embryo, right? Maybe the people who founded it were thinking, right now it's just a little embryo, but someday it'll turn into a big, grown-up city, or hotel, or whatever. A hopeful name."

"Good guess, but wrong!" I read aloud. *"The word 'zygote' in the sense of a fertilized egg was coined around 1890, but Zygote City was founded decades earlier, one of many utopian communities established in the early 19th century. Derived from the Greek* zygotos, *meaning 'yoked together,' the name conveys the founders' philosophy of mutual dependence. As one early civic leader, the Rev. Ezekiel Blankart, put it, 'all things of this world are yoked in a common bondage, the chains of each entwined with the chains of all.'"*

"Huh," John says. "What does it say about the hotel? Why does it have the same name?"

"Haven't made it that far yet." I keep reading, but my thoughts are skipping over the words like stones over water, buzzing like insects around a dripping hive. *Yoked together. Chains entwined in a common umbilical bondage.* An infant city is growing in my mind.

I shake my head to still the thoughts. I try to be practical, find the answer to my husband's question. A word in the brochure catches my eye—"hotel." I backtrack, focus, hunt down the meaning.

"Here we go," I say. *"After the founders' utopia fell into disarray, Zygote City seemed destined to become a ghost town, until a lucky business venture gave the community a second life. Charles Sumner Blankart, son of the Rev. Ezekiel, converted the city's meetinghouse into a hotel, which quickly became a popular destination for well-off travelers. Before long, the Zygote City hotel was such a success that the city's residents voted unanimously to merge the city into the hotel. One of the aged Rev. Ezekiel's last acts was to lead his congregation in a ceremony whereby, as he put it, 'the zygotic spirit shall pass from city to hotel, hotel shall open its doors unto city, the two fusing as bonded twins of one womb, tangled chains of each umbilically rooted in the other's most secret penetralia.'"*

John snorts. "Are you sure you read that right?"

"See for yourself."

I hand him the brochure. He stares at the glossy page. "Huh."

Most secret penetralia. The city spreads, houses rising in the valleys of my brain. My thoughts flit and swoop, insects around a carcass. I'm chained to what's hidden in my husband's head, the two of us twinned, everlastingly tangled. *Come out, vermin. Come out, my little darling.*

John flips through the brochure, scanning the columns of type. "Wonder what it says about the institute. There's a city, there's a hotel, there's an institute..."

"And a golf course, too," I murmur. A moonlit gleam, and a squat cluster, and gnat-like figures scurrying.

John stabs the brochure with a finger. "Bingo. *On the eve of the Second World War, Dr. McKinley Blankart established...*"

"Excuse me," a voice calls. Startled, I turn to see the concierge standing in the entryway, the black doors open behind her. Sunlight glistens on the faux-marble. She smiles her crooked, beautiful smile. "The shuttle bus is here early."

The driver plies his trade in absolute silence, his eyes hidden behind sunglasses. Through the trees that line our path, I glimpse the golf course's green blaze.

The woods close in around us, curtains of dark leaves and tangled branches so thick it seems the world ends a few feet beyond the road. I can't imagine a single human being living out here. I say to the driver, "Pardon me, but is the city nearby?"

His black lenses don't waver from the route. "Nope. Other side of the hotel. Some people get confused about it. Institute on one side, city on the other, hotel in the middle. That's what you've got to keep straight." His voice is flat, professional.

"Okay, thank you." I sink back into my seat. I wish I'd brought the brochure along.

The woods' curtains fly apart as we enter a clearing. Close-cropped and freshly watered, the grass sparkles like a carpet of pearls. The road ends in front of a squat building, an off-white cube with a green door and no windows. "Institute," the driver says.

As we exit the shuttle bus, John holds out a ragged twenty. The driver accepts the tip without comment, the bill wrinkled and grayish between his fingers. I tell myself I'm lucky to have such a generous husband, generous when it comes to money.

The green door opens on a cramped waiting room. Dim light, beige carpet, walls crowded with paintings of grassy fields. In the center of each field, a pair of lovers lies locked in a passionate embrace. The lovers' arms and legs are wreathed with snakes.

The receptionist comes out from behind her desk to greet us. "You must be Mr. and Mrs. Brower. Welcome to Zygote City."

"So this place is called Zygote City, too?" John says. I'd call his tone half-amused, half-suspicious, but I could be wrong. Who knows what goes on in that hole?

The receptionist smiles broadly. Her teeth are stained, crooked. "Officially, it's the Blankart Institute of Intersubjective Harmonics, but no one ever calls it that. We just say 'Zygote City,' and everyone knows exactly what we mean."

"It's funny," I say, "but you look just like someone we were talking to earlier this morning, at the hotel where we're staying."

She nods, her eyes flashing in the dim light. "Oh, yes, that was me. I enjoyed our conversation so much, I just had to race over here, across the golf course and through the woods, to chat a bit more before your treatment."

I stare at her, not knowing what to say. I try to picture someone running through those dense, gnarled woods. Boughs rake my face; roots curl around my feet. I shudder with imagined pain, imagined fear.

The receptionist laughs. "I'm just joking, of course. My sister works at the hotel. It must have been her you talked to."

"Oh," I say, chagrined. Why am I so gullible? I always want to give people the benefit of the doubt, even when what they're saying is absurd.

Maybe that's the root of the problem my husband and I have

come to solve. I'm eager to grasp onto whatever I'm given, desperate to believe anything, but John won't give me anything to grasp, anything to believe. I want to take him at face value, but he doesn't have a face, only a grass-covered mound, a hole, a spider.

John clears his throat. My buzzing thoughts scatter. "Does the doctor come out here, or do we go back there?" He points to the door behind the receptionist's desk.

"I'll just go see if the doctor is ready." She disappears through the door. I hope she wasn't offended by my awkward reaction to her joke. Embarrassment burns my cheeks. On the walls, the grassy fields swim in my vision.

John puts a hand on my shoulder. "Ready for the big event?" he says.

I take the hand, press it to my cheek. "Thank you for doing this with me."

"Of course. This is what I want, too, you know." Tenderness in his voice, or exasperation, or nothing at all, sheer neutral mask. *Spider, spider, spider…*

I squeeze my eyes shut, breathe deep. When I open my eyes, I see that the painted lovers' limbs are wreathed not in snakes but in chains, a network of entangling iron links. If the lovers' mouths were to part, I know a chain would stretch between them, binding their tongues.

Umbilical yoke, rooted in twin penetralia.

The door behind the desk swings open. A crooked smile in the dimness. "The doctor is ready for you."

"The treatment has two phases," says Dr. Blankart. "First, we'll have a little chat, all three of us together. Then, I'll meet with each of you alone." In the bright light of the conference room, his smile is almost blinding. "How does that sound?"

"Sounds great," John says. I squeeze his hand on the table. He doesn't respond.

"Wonderful." Dr. Blankart's smile glistens. He doesn't look anything like the night clerk from the hotel, his teeth's dazzling whiteness the only resemblance, but I can't shake the idea that the two men share a connection. *Mystic brethren of the shining teeth.*

"Excuse me, Doctor," I say, "but do you have a brother, by any chance?"

The smile darkens slightly. "I'm afraid my brother has passed on."

What a disaster. My thoughts howl and thrash. "Oh God, I'm so sorry, I didn't…"

Dr. Blankart raises a hand. "It's quite all right. A perfectly natural question."

My husband makes a noise I can't comprehend or name. A grunt? A stifled sigh? What is the vermin doing in there?

"Let's get started," says Dr. Blankart. "Do you have any children?"

"No," I say.

"How's your intimacy? Your sex life?"

"No complaints," John says. I nod.

"When you think of marriage, what's the first word that comes to mind?"

"Ring," John says.

"Chain," I say.

"And when you think of your spouse? Be honest."

"Nice," John says.

"Spider," I say.

I hear my husband shift in his chair beside me. I think he's turned to look at me, but I stare straight ahead into Dr. Blankart's smile.

"What's the second word that comes to mind when you think of your spouse?"

"Anxious," John says.

Vermin. "Twin," I say.

After a few more questions, Dr. Blankart rises from his chair. "Now for the second phase. Mr. Brower, please come with me. Mrs. Brower, wait here for one moment, and the receptionist will show you to the examination room."

John and the doctor leave together. I wonder what they'll talk about.

A painting hangs on the wall beside the door. I didn't notice it until I was alone in the room, but it's very beautiful, a night view of a city nestled in a wooded valley. Windows glitter warmly against the darkness; leaves ripple in the breeze like silk. The moon limns swirls of cloud above the valley, and as my eyes follow the swirls, I realize there are two cities in the painting, the city in the valley and a second city that comes into view only when the eye is elsewhere, a city wavering at the edge of vision. The first city's streets are empty, everyone tucked away indoors, but the second city is thronged with revelers, figures scurrying, dancing, writhing lasciviously. The revelers' bodies are wrapped in chains, wreaths of chains crown their heads, with chain-crammed mouths they call to their twins in the other city, calling through the curtains of the night, chanting, "Come out, come out, entwine with us…"

Someone knocks at the conference room door. Startled, I yelp, leap up, bang my knee on the edge of the table. The receptionist sticks her head around the door, smiles apologetically. "Sorry to startle you, Mrs. Brower. Whenever you're ready."

The lights in the examination room are turned very low. A speaker plays soothing ocean sounds. An overstuffed bean bag chair sits in a corner, and when I settle onto it, something crumples beneath me. Reaching under the seat of my pants, I retrieve a slim leaflet, perhaps left here to give me something to read while I wait for Dr. Blankart. What is he asking my husband about? What is John saying?

The cover of the leaflet shows a couple sitting together at a table. They gaze lovingly into each other's eyes, their hands clasped on the tabletop. Gaping holes in their chests expose knots of sturdy chains where feeble hearts once were. Above their heads float the words WELCOME TO THE BLANKART INSTITUTE OF INTERSUBJECTIVE HARMONICS. Someone has crossed out the institute's name and written, in a thin, spidery hand, ZYGOTE CITY.

I open the leaflet, squint to read its small print in the low light. *As the institute's Chief Harmonist, Dr. Buckley Blankart has carried forward his father's and grandfather's research into intersubjective harmonics (IH), defined by Dr. Blankart as "the application to human relationships of that science which my ancestor, the Rev. Ezekiel Blankart, christened general zygotics (GZ), that is, the study of universal bondage." Through the application of IH, Dr. Blankart entwines the chains that bind heart to heart, just as GZ's practitioners have bound city to hotel, hotel to institute, institute to city, city to brain, chains spreading through eternity, burrowing, penetrating…*

A hideous shriek interrupts my reading, so inhumanly awful it takes me a moment to recognize the voice. Pain prickles my bruised knee as I clamber up from the bean bag chair and rush out into the hallway. Another shriek, a heavy crash, and I'm running toward the noise, toward my husband, stumbling around corners in the labyrinth of the institute, and in my mind I see a grass-covered mound kicked open, a flailing vermin dragged out into the light.

A door slams. I turn a corner. Dr. Blankart is ahead of me, running down the hall with chains dangling from his hands, spilling from his pockets. He barrels shoulder-first into another door that bursts open to reveal the waiting room, its dimness bonfire-bright after the murk I've been sitting in. I race after him past the desk where the receptionist stands open-mouthed, crooked-toothed, across the beige carpet and through the green door, out into the clearing.

A dark bulk of tree-shadow lies on the grass. The sun is a red smear along the top of the woods, the moon high and pale among the lamp-poles. Wasn't it just morning? How long did I spend in that examination room, reading that leaflet?

Still running, I look past Dr. Blankart to see my husband loping toward the edge of the clearing. As John nears the curtain of trees, he glances back over his shoulder, and I glimpse the ragged hole Dr. Blankart made of his face. Chains twist around the bones the doctor laid bare, coil in emptied eye sockets, writhe between teeth. The grinding chains scream like a tortured animal as my husband plunges into the woods.

Dr. Blankart stops short, panting. He swivels his head left and right. As I sprint past him, he shrugs in resignation.

"I did my best!" he calls from behind me. "You can't say I didn't do my best!"

I run straight ahead, following John's howls into the clotted thickness beyond the clearing.

Slash of branches. Clutch of roots. I push through endless wreaths of dark drapery. From the corners of my eyes I see others keeping pace with me, limbs jangling as they whirl and caper. I run through the infinite night outside the world. Black leaves fill my mouth.

The moon hovers over the golf course, a pale moth above a green flame. The hotel is a dark slab against the stars. The chain protruding from my chest drags my faltering steps across the fairway, drags me toward the vermin I'm twinned to.

The black doors slide open. The glare of the night clerk's smile draws me into the blazing hole of Zygote City.

"Mrs. Brower," he says, "I'm so glad you've made it back safely."

As I near the desk, his teeth's pearly petals chatter. What I took for a smile is a rictus of radiant terror.

"I was terribly sorry to hear what happened to Mr. Brower," he says. "My brother called me from the institute in tears. He asked me to tell you again that he did his best."

I want to ask if he knows where my husband went, but I'm too exhausted to speak. I just look at his teeth.

Laughter fills the lobby, pealing across the faux-marble. I give the clerk a questioning look.

"The concierge is working late tonight," he says. "Her sister came by to keep her company. They love to joke, those two." I stare at him for a long moment. He clears his throat. "My brother told me that you did splendidly, by the way. Not everyone is receptive to the treatment, but for the open-minded, its benefits can be…"

I turn away. His voice is an insect's buzz, a murmur of blood in my ear. I stumble to the elevator.

The white-carpeted room is empty, freezing. When I switch off the air conditioner, its howl persists, shaking the arctic air. There are two air conditioners, I realize, one that can be switched off and one that can't.

From the window, I gaze across the golf course to the illuminated clearing, the squat, clustered buildings of Zygote City. Along the edge of the clearing, two gnat-like figures walk, scanning the woods. When the figures pass beneath the lamp-poles, I see the flash of tiny smiles.

I pull the curtain over the window. Standing in the howling cold, I stare at the print that hangs above the bed, the other print that hangs on the opposite wall. Have the pictures changed since this morning? No, the pictures are the same, but I see them more clearly now. They're not abstract swirls, wild and chaotic. They're painstakingly detailed depictions of two cities where two festivals are being celebrated. Both cities' streets overflow with wild revelry, dances and costumes and pageants and chains, each writhing, whirling celebrant in the city above the bed eternally bound to its partner in the city on the opposite wall, brother or sister, husband or wife. All things tangled and twinned in an ecstasy of everlasting gestation.

Where has my partner gone, my vermin twin, my darling spider?

He's gone to Zygote City.

When I step out of the elevator, the lobby still echoes with laughter. The front desk is empty; a sign propped on the white laminate says BACK IN 5 MINUTES, SORRY FOR THE WAIT. Across the faux-marble, the concierge and her sister the receptionist are whispering together. They cackle and guffaw, too caught up in hilarity to notice my approach.

"And then," the receptionist says, "the idiot got up and ran. He ran right into the woods, and… get this… she ran in after him!"

The sisters whoop and shriek. The concierge wipes tears of mirth from her eyes.

"Excuse me," I say.

When they recognize me, their stained, beautiful smiles turn to looks of chagrin, shame, horror. The receptionist begins to stammer an apology, but I raise my hand to silence her.

"I just have one question," I say. "Which way to Zygote City?"

They know exactly what I mean. The concierge points. "Out the door, to the road, turn that way."

It's a short walk from the hotel to the city—no walk at all, I suppose, since the hotel is in the city, used to be the old meeting-house, and the city is in the hotel, and the hotel and the city are in the institute, and everything is tangled up together in my brain's dark forest, yoked in a common bondage.

In any case, it's a short walk. Soon I'm wandering among weatherbeaten houses, wooden structures of another century. Firelight gleams in the windows; steeples rise from churches at crazy angles; awnings jut like jaws above silent storefronts. I wander the dusty streets, hunting for my partner, my twin.

Passing the mouth of an alley, I hear a clattering racket. I peer into the torchlight. A gaggle of men and boys, all ages from the cradle to the edge of the grave, are dancing and skipping around a pole, each bound to its shaft with a length of chain around his waist. They hoot and laugh and grin, their teeth flashing like lightning.

"You there!" the oldest of them shouts, beckoning me with a finger as knotted and veiny as an umbilical cord. "Come join the family reunion!"

I hurry away, still hunting. Behind me, the clang of metal blends with the scrape of boots as the dancers swarm from their alley to join the chase.

Outside a raucous tavern, a pride of ladies stands in a circle, drinking from jeweled glasses and swapping jokes. Their laughter makes a melodious counterpoint to the rattle of the chains wreathed in their hair, twined around their arms and across their bare shoulders. As I hurry past, they lift their glasses and smile, soft lips parting to show stained, crooked teeth.

Their beautiful smiles warm my heart, but I press on, still hunting. The jangling crowd of revelers swells behind me.

In a little park across from Rev. Ezekiel's meetinghouse, we find our quarry. The vermin sits perched atop a grass-covered mound, his eyes bright in the moon, blank as the moon. When he sees us approaching, his face takes on an expression of relief, or chagrin, or fatigue, or any of the thousand masks that flitter unbound in the spider-hole, the unchained and unrevealed spirit of my twin's secret heart.

Rushing forward, we flood the park, capering in circles around our cornered prey. "Come out, my little darling," I croon, and the throng takes up the chorus, chanting in time to our clamorous dance, "Come out! Come out!"

Sprawled on his mound, the vermin gazes dumbstruck, his mouth agape as he scans the spinning ranks. When I extend my hands toward him, beckoning him into the dance, he shrinks away. I tell myself I'm lucky to have such a sober, cautious husband, but I don't believe it. I lunge forward, grab his wrists, drag him toward me. I press my mouth to his. Throughout the city, the celebrants cheer.

Our kiss is long and deep, a sweet reunion after far, lonely wanderings. When our mouths part, I feel cold metal between my lips. The vermin's eyes shine with joyful tears as I grasp the umbilical chain that binds our tongues. Stepping backward, the revelers parting around me, I pull. My partner falls to his knees, his lips writhing lasciviously. I pull again. My twin moans in ecstasy.

A hand clasps my shoulder. Dr. Blankart is standing beside me, pride and wonder flashing in his smile. "Your technique is marvelous," he says. "We'll do great things together at the institute."

I'm sure he's right, but the institute can wait. For now, I have to finish my husband's treatment.

Gripping the chain, I pull with all my might. I pull until the grass-covered mound erupts, until the spider leaps shivering from its hole. I seize the unveiled truth in both hands, bring it to my mouth, and as my crooked, dazzling teeth sink into verminous flesh, the crowd's howl of triumph echoes through the city, the hotel, the institute, the brain, the universe, all the endless realms whirling in the festival bondage of Zygote City.

radiation exposure as emotional therapy

. . .

Casey Aimer

I'm flying under the aurora borealis
staring through frosted windshields
at green & purple radiation, soaking
their subtle energetic dance, wanting
these lights to randomly change me
through cell death & DNA damage.
Let them mutate my state of mind,
rediscover my creativity, like when I
was sixteen & every experience was
dramatically meaningful—I miss that
addictive pain of worlds-shattering
emotion. Overhead, ethereal paint
swatches jitter as ribbons in my eyes,
swirling as if reaching for me, touching
gently, transforming pain to inspiration.

That night I endure my first color dream.

how a satyr becomes real

. . .

Jennifer Jeanne McArdle

At the end of summer, satyrs must choose to become goat or man. Will you join the four-legged or two-legged herds after the end of the season? Soon the screaming cicadas will quiet, the iridescent butterflies, tall lilies, and fragrant wildflowers will disintegrate, the burning sunlight cool, and fervent nights will be frosty and still. Perhaps next summer the wine-god will call you again to stand tall, or harden your stomping feet, but there's no guarantee his whirlwind delirium will carry you up and transform you again.

In a moment of clarity, you realize the seriousness of your predicament: you do not want to be hominidae or bovidae. You want to split-hoof tip-toe that line forever, never stifling the notes of recklessness and freedom; domestication is not for you but is your fate should you not learn to help yourself. So, you pry yourself from the arms of a supple, languid wood nymph. You navigate the rocks near the caves by the sea, the waves crashing below you, making you stink of sea and matted fur, till you find the sphinx, who is woman and lion, eternally.

"You don't have to change. How can I be like you?"

The sphinx considers your query, if it's worth imparting wisdom or puzzles, if she hates that you want to be like her or loves your brazenness, if there are limits to her wisdom, and if she wants you to know her weaknesses. "Your magic is tied too closely to the summer, to one god whose mood is as temperamental as a dog day's storm, hardly sober, hardly reliable. Before his magic runs out, find a new patron, a new purpose."

You hear a low growl and realize the human-faced cat is hungry. She eyes your thick thighs, your broad chest; the chaos inside you fantasizes about the pain of being rent by ivory claws into red, wet confetti, of splashing in the stomach acid of an impressive legend, but no, you're different than your brothers and sisters still dancing in the fields. Something in you is clinging to the rocks, refusing to die.

She leaps at you, and you dodge. She's shocked you had the wherewithal, but also amused, and you use that pause to escape from the cave, climb up the stones, and reach the field. The sphinx has wings, you remember. She is not just two creatures put together, like you, but three, so you can't risk slowing down. You run, half-wishing you had four legs instead of two, you run half wishing you could hide in the human city and ask their wisest men for advice, but your heart denies easy solutions. Not a beggar man in the city or a kept goat, you know this, deep in your chest, it thunders through you, bulges your veins, bubbles your blood, rushing out of your lungs like a roar.

You cannot stop running through the fields, long grass collecting on your fur, scratching your naked skin, the pollen swirling around you, filling your sinuses, blurring your vision. You run through trees, hear the branches of the forest cackling, the magpies screaming insults, the juicy smells of ripe berries tempting you to stop and rest, but you keep running because these are all the things you need to leave behind if you're going to make yourself anew, if you're going to avoid shriveling up with them at the end of the season.

The air becomes colder and yet the sun still radiates pure summer light, the earth grows more barren, and the mountains loom before you, calling you to climb. These are the mountains where will is molded into something sharp and metal. You make your way up higher and higher as the vultures circle around you.

Above you is a goat unlike any you've ever seen before–he is not small and tamed. The wild mountain goat maneuvers through the rocks without struggle, and shakes a head decorated with long, twisted horns the length of half its muscular body. Your skin prickles from the chill, wants to be covered in the goat's long, dense fur.

You meet the wild billie on the plateau. He cocks his head to the side; a glorious shadow spreads out across the rock, stops at a hiss. A snake is coiled in the center of the plateau, muscles rippling, pattern scales twisting into nightmares of obscurity, screaming that you are not free or powerful, just a thing to be discarded. Has your god sent one of his creatures to punish you for escaping his cycles and games and drunken folly, dependency on fickle favor?

You hate this creature, how it mocks you with its whisper, the promise of a toxic, hallucinating death.

"You are nothing without my touch; without my madness. Your freedom is illusory."

For a moment, you nearly believe the serpent, but it was not the god who gave you the power to climb this mountain. The wind rushes at you, but your hair is growing thicker. Courageously, you leap at the serpent, pounding him with your fists, your hooves, your own horns, which have grown mighty. You pierce the monster through the neck, and it uncoils, goes limp. Foam fills your mouth, covers your face. The goat smiles, a face human and goat, eyes forward and sideways, predator and prey.

"You have become markhor goat, snake-killer, a free wild animal. A real legend, more solid than dreams," he tells you.

All year round, you will stay surviving in the mountains.

something so beautiful

. . .

J.D. Harlock

this light…
it's…beautiful.

still, I wonder
how somethin' so beautiful
can lay inside somethin'
as monstrous as
this machine

they say it's older
than us
they say it was built
by gods
maybe, it was built
when we were gods

when we commanded
the Earth,
and all that was in it,
the seas…risin' and fallin'
when we gave the word

I'm not sure
how you work it
or what it does
or why the folks waitin'
for us to fix it
want it so bad

but it ain't that hard to see

'cause it burns, like
a holy fire,
drawin' its power from
above, long after we couldn't
look to the heavens
no more

you know, I wonder
what's up there
I hear there's a light
that shines brighter
than anything
in our world

but I don't believe it.

sticking together

· · ·

Steven Mathes

True, we mistakenly assumed our noses had actually picked up some glue, probably from me being a slob with my retirement hobbies. Anyway, the spastic maneuvering, the awkward negotiations between two people wearing no clothing, the final acceptance of needing to pull apart, and the stinging wound of separation: it all resulted in a terrified giggle.

Our skinned noses did not bleed much.

During our morning walk, Virginia said little, and mostly stared at the icy path. I was no better. Images from last night's uneasy dreams still cluttered my thinking, not necessarily bad images, not necessarily good ones, but unsettling ones. I needed to process, not talk. Lingering flashes of conjoined bodies, of scalpels, of injury, of healing. My nose had already stopped itching, but not my mind. It felt like we were walking into the surreal. Actually, we were.

Someone fell down hard on a patch of ice ahead of us. This strange person had two faces. One does not see someone with that kind of disability, deformation, or whatever the correct term, at least one does not see them often, not in public. There were always reports, rumors that this old neighborhood harbored a fantastic history. Nobody mentioned conjoined twins, or people's noses fusing together.

But no matter, kindness required Virginia and me to do something more than ogle. We rushed over to help the fallen person. Or people.

"I dreamed this," I said.

"Please, Norman... Next time you dream, keep your nose to yourself," said Virginia.

She elbowed me, and leaned her head against me. She is better than I am at dealing with unusual people and events.

Anyway, we got to the fallen person (or persons), got them to their feet, and expressions on both of the fully-formed faces offered clear gratitude. An eyeball on the left face bugged because it was at the seam between them. They shared a single monobrow. The left face smiled faintly, while the right face frowned in solemn appreciation. The right face had to turn its eyes pretty hard to look at us, not having control of the shared head. I found myself trying not to look, but still trying to look them in the eye. Like trying to act natural, act correctly, when there was nothing natural, nothing correct.

Then it got solemn, maybe a little sketchy, to be honest about it. They, the two faces, reached up with one finger and touched the nose of Virginia, while a finger on the opposite hand touched mine. It gave me a shock, like brushing a live wire when changing a light switch, and the shock went right through my other hand, which was holding Virginia's. After, it left a slight sting that lingered, like there was some kind of life-force current that burned our nerves.

They spoke at last:

"Healed," said the left face.

"Mostly, anyway," said the right face.

"That's in thanks for your kindness," said the left face.

"Not that we needed it," said the right face.

"But beware of your dangerous power," said the left face. "No touching or you'll end up like us!"

The two-faced person hurried away giggling as if feeling naughty, and got into a nearby parked car, some sort of over-sized antique. Once safely inside those tinted windows, they could almost have passed for one normal person, although the thought of them driving raised questions.

"Norman, your nose," Virginia said.

"Don't tell me. Healed?"

"A little more than mostly. Don't tell me," said Virginia. "Just like mine?"

"Last night I dreamed of two people holding hands," I said. "Except it was just one hand connecting both of them."

"My whole night was weird," Virginia said. "But same as you. Stuff growing together was the theme. Plus blades and blood. Scary, but in a squirmy, funny way."

"Why did I think to marry someone who believes that squirmy is funny? Or at least that joking about something scary changes anything?"

"Everyone makes mistakes," said Virginia.

How do you define a stupid action, as opposed to an action that is inevitably human? Both Virginia and I trembled a little. Faced with all the evidence, both of us were stupid enough to instinctively reach out. Yes, we gave in to the urge to hold hands. The clasping of warm hands bare of our gloves soothed us. It comforted us, and neither of us thought much about anything except how much we needed each other. As if forty years together was not enough.

We covered the rest of our walk in the silence of denial. As we approached our little home with its dark windows, its ancient bones, I felt the truth of how accepted reality depends looking the other way. And maybe our noses were just fine to start with. Right?

"We'll never forget those two faces," Virginia said. "Don't fool yourself."

Conjoined twins often happened. That was a real thing. And

the nose incident could be explained. Yes, it would have been caused by glue. Obviously.

Except that the healing, not the unnatural being doing it, was the thing I could not forget. They (the perfect pronoun for someone with two faces?) gave off the impression of power like a stove gives off heat. What kind of being had Virginia and I met? Was this a single person with two faces? Or was it more properly two people with a single body? Did they share all or part of a brain? These felt like awkward questions to ask out loud, but they were honest questions that totally dodged the point. It was the sizzling power. That hit the point right on the nose, if you will forgive that accidental pun.

"The face on the left needed a shave. The one on the right wore a woman's makeup," said Virginia.

"The body that they both lived on? Or in?" I asked. "Was it female? Male?"

"I couldn't tell. Maybe they share the body equally. But maybe one of them dominates."

"You're saying they're a couple," I said. "Talk about having sex with yourself..."

"That's the silliest thing you've said today. And creepy. And politically incorrect."

At least she laughed when she said it. We had reached our walkway with its patches of black ice. I tried to let go of Virginia's hand so I could get my keys. At first I thought she was not letting go.

"Ow!" she said.

We held up our joined hands and pulled. Fused skin stretched between our palms, like smudges of taffy. This time I did not laugh, but that never stopped Virginia from joking.

"Into the glue again?" she said.

I could tell by her faltering voice that her humor was stretched. We braced against each other, and tugged. I slipped, and fell back on my ass while Virginia remained standing. But it was enough. At least we separated. This time my peeled skin really stung, and there were beads of blood oozing from the full raw expanse of my palm. Melting ice soaked into my pants, and my ass throbbed. My back spasmed.

I looked at Virginia in concern. Without thinking, she reached out to help me up, then snapped her injured hand back with that scared laugh. Her palm had beads of blood, too. I got up on my own. I admit that I was feeling sorry for myself.

We stood catching breath. I dangled the keys to the house, and otherwise talked sense to myself. Our palms were no worse than what you would get with a scraped knee. I told myself it was probably a known condition, something they had a pill or cream for. Some side-effect of being married too long. We would recover, even if we never met the person with two faces again. If we gave our imaginations a rest, the whole spooky condition might go away.

Believe me, I wished for no further encounters of that nature. I flexed my fingers, and everything worked. All we needed was a roll of paper towels and a drink.

One knows things are out of control when, while thinking the supposed worst, something even worse happens.

A child, a little girl, walked past our house, while an old truck came from the other direction. I swear, it looked like there was no driver, just a shadow. In a sickening example of bad luck, the child slipped and fell on the sidewalk, just as the truck skidded on the black ice. The truck swerved. The child tried to scramble out of the way. The truck spun, the back wheels jumped the curb, rolled over one of the child's legs, and she was pulled into the street with her leg tangled under the ratty, shadowy truck. I fell down again, trying to get there. Virginia fell over me. The car found purchase on some dry asphalt, and sped away. The driver, if there was one, apparently missed the memo about personal responsibility.

Virginia and I went through an elaborate, slippery process, almost as bad as when our noses were stuck, and we helped each other up, carefully. We did not stick. We went to the child. The child was of course screaming in pain and terror by the time we got there. Her knee was bent the opposite way any knee should bend, her pant leg torn open. Inside the tear her leg showed a substantial gash of torn flesh. Splinters of bone jutted out.

"Aw, crap," I said. "Aw..."

I felt like crying. Without thinking about germs, sanitary practices, or anything, I grasped the girl's bare leg above the knee. The need to stop her from bleeding got the best of me, or maybe it was just wanting to hold the poor child together. Virginia must have been thinking the same, because she grabbed the girl's bare leg near the top of her ankle. That same electric shock went through us, the one caused by the person with two faces.

Except the shock was way stronger. It felt like my hands were trying to grow into Virginia's through the little girl. I found I could not let go, even as the girl's leg got very warm.

There was nothing funny about it, but the little girl started to giggle. Virginia did not quite join in, but her eyes locked with mine in a vacant concentration so strong that I, at least, felt like I might faint. I also felt like I might throw up. It really did hurt.

The girl's bones snapped back into position with a noise loud enough to make me wince. Splinters swam into the gaps, and flesh closed together with a slurp. A faint musical hum came along with the crackle from the knitting flesh, or maybe the hum came from my spinning, sickened head. I knew of no drug that could make me feel this slipped out of joint, and I had tried some in my day.

Too soon for her, but not soon enough for my horror, the little girl was completely whole again. But at least it felt like the situation was stable, not getting worse, with no need to get better. The freaky buzz of further healing could not come if she needed no healing.

I was old enough to understand how strange stuff works. Anything improving always feels good while anything already improved (but not getting worse again) just feels normal. The memory of bad stuff fades. Gratitude fades. Or maybe it was the sick electricity. I knew the girl had forgotten the shattered leg, because she was a kid, and even her mind was cured.

I saw her boot in the middle of the street. I got it for her. I wished I could fix her torn pants. That would make me laugh because it would feel important when it was not.

"Oh, my pants," the little girl said. "I am so in trouble. My mother will never believe about that spooky truck. I am so in trouble."

"There's a lot of blood, too," Virginia said.

"How did that get there?" the girl said. "That's spooky. Like the truck had blood on it? How will I explain?"

She pulled on her boot, right onto the foot attached to her perfectly healed leg. She stood, flexed her boot, and tried a few careful steps on the ice, as if the boot were the only thing that needed testing, and not my sanity.

"Count those lucky stars, kid," Virginia said.

"I don't know what that means," the little girl said. "But thanks!"

Despite the ice, she ran back the way she had come, not even slipping much. The dark splotch from her bleeding reached right up to the seat of her pants. A kid. They rarely get hurt, but when they do, one just has to hope there are people to make it better. Her mother would freak, ask the girl what she got into. The girl would claim the truck wrecked her pants, pretend she just got dirty. Kids: how often do they say they sat in something disgusting, not human blood, just to stop the questions?

"Peace!" she called without looking back.

Forty years of marriage, and Virginia and I each knew the other's mind. It was not my place to make the unwelcome observation, to point out what kind of reality we had left forever. A new reality, superpowers being not necessarily bad, not good, just squirmy: the good and the bad were up to us, or at least we had the freedom of pretending so.

"What would you think, if your kid came home covered in blood?" Virginia said.

"Forget it," I said. "We have a good life. So does that girl."

We looked at each other for a long time.

"We both know it's some kind of magic," Virginia said. "We can't touch each other. That's already something out of a strange dream, and we can't pretend it went away. But that little girl might come back with her mother. We might run into that person, the two-faces person. Or someone."

"Surrounded by evidence," I agreed. "And responsibility. But magic? Forget it."

"I'm scared," she said. "So are you. But forgetting is for little girls. Superheroes have responsibility"

We helped each other as we went into our old New England colonial. Occasionally, we would touch skin-to-skin, but only for a second or two. Testing the limits. We tried kissing, just a peck, which was fine. Then we tried a longer smooch. Maybe a minute. It felt like we had been eating raw honey, the stickiness of our lips tasted sweet and the separation barely hurt. At least we proved we could touch for a moment, at least we could kiss a little, as long as we did not linger. More to the point, we had discovered healing people.

"I feel like a drug addict," I said.

"You mean that creepy feeling we had with the girl," Virginia said.

"I can't stand it, but it calls to me. I can't fight it."

"Did you notice your hand?"

I looked. The palm that had been torn by our separation looked perfect. Not only healed, not only free of blood spots, but younger. It was the hand of a younger man. I looked at my other hand, the one that did not carry that electricity. Still the hand of an old man. Virginia, too. Just partly younger. Her left eye had no wrinkles. Why was her right eye still old, and why did this remind me of someone having two faces in a single head, a head that people would pretend not to stare at? Would the youth in us spread? Too many questions. Both good and bad.

Not only did it feel addictive, it felt hilariously like the thing with money. More was better, but always dirty. And you had to get it without getting into trouble.

"I suggest we heal lots of people," said Virginia. "Fight creepy reality with creepy magic."

"Just sort of waltz into an emergency room?" I said. "Cure the masses?"

"Great idea. I'm sure that wouldn't attract any attention. Imagine if anyone found out what we can do. You want us locked up in a secret lab for study?"

"So what would you have us do?" I asked.

"Remember what I said to the girl?"

"No," I said.

"Count those lucky stars, kid."

"That's not exactly a strategy for life," I said.

"Those are words to live by, my darling. That's a strategy for living with power. The rest we make up as we go."

So now we count our lucky stars. So we make it up as we go. If one of us gets hurt jumping nursing home fences or bursting through hospital windows, the other has to brush the wound lightly, always stroking back and forth, never stopping in one place, like generating static electricity.

We absolutely refuse to sleep in separate beds, even though that speeds up the inevitable. We wait for the inevitable. Sure, there are mornings when we have to cut ourselves apart with a paring knife. We do it in the shower. Aside from the pain, the bleeding makes a mess.

sustain your afterlife by following rules that make no sense (but you have to follow them anyway)

. . .

Juleigh Howard-Hobson

There are no rules for dying, feel free to
die any way you can. The thing is, when
it comes down to the afterlife, *being* dead
does bring regulations into play. You
won't be able to cross water—even
floorboards painted haint blue will stop you, said

color being a representation
of the same stuff you can't cross. Damnation

sends you straight below, you won't get to hang
around, haunting people, revisiting
places you used to know, you'll bug out, gone
for good. Or, rather, not so good. The clang
of bell clappers will start inhibiting
your ability to still exist on

this plane, avoid them. Also avoid things
made from iron: nails, stakes, horseshoes, files, rings…

They'll punch right through the astral body you've

got and burn a hole in the middle of
you. Which has an effect on your after
life. Ghosts can fade, therefore it will behoove
you to understand: when push comes to shove
this is it. The last hurrah, top rafter,

end of the line for being a being—
unless you get to reincarnate, bring

yourself back around for another turn
of the wheel—but you'd've had to state that
before you died, so if you didn't, well,
too bad. It's this…or nothing. Once you learn
how things work, postmortem, you'll navigate
as smoothly as anyone. Facts propel

most regulations, protecting ghosts while
providing information that's vital

for most satisfactory other realm
inhabitations. The ways to float, ways
to pass through walls, ways to open cupboards
and spill the contents out. Death's a real scream
when you've mastered those. Some things you must stay
away from—selenite, cinqfoile, churchyards

(memorial parks, cemeteries and
 graveyards are doable). All hallowed land,

as a matter of fact, is a no go
zone for spectral persons. If you avoid
garlic, holy water, agates, bottles
(especially blue ones) hanging from low
branches of trees, silver (even alloyed),
mirrors, sage, willows, cats (they are hostile

to ghosts, they will hiss and arch up their backs
while swiping paws at you), salt (it's in snacks

as well as shakers), and people who sweep
new brooms while burning incense (tiresome
actions designed to drive ghosts out), you'll be
amazed at how freeing it is to keep
to all the rules and enjoy a welcome,
and most interesting unrest in peace.

it seeps in

. . .

Pamela Weis

Emily touched the window pane expecting her finger to become wet. But the condensation was outside or within the glass itself. It was wrong. They'd bought cheap windows. Or the installer had screwed up. With outside below freezing, that condensation should have turned to frost by now.

Inside the glass, then. Kept damp by the heat from the fireplace.

A rational explanation, but not a satisfying one.

Emily returned to her oversized leather chair, its worn arm rests familiar under her palms. The cat rubbed against her right ankle then reached up to claw the leather. Emily did not bother to stop her. The cat had long since claimed the chair as hers.

Theirs.

The cat's and Emily's.

She reached over to the side table and picked up her tumbler. Sweet bourbon swished in her mouth and cascaded down her throat, burning only a little. The really good stuff was in the liquor cabinet, saved for the next special occasion, which never seemed to come. She slid her chilly toes into her slippers and picked up her book. That condensation was going to drive her crazy. She'd talk to Jim about it the minute he returned from his work trip.

The cat, whose name was Stella, hopped onto Emily's lap and began to knead her thighs.

"Ow. Take it easy, girl." She pressed gently on Stella's back until her mottled calico body curled up. Emily's favorite way to spend an evening. A glass of bourbon, a good book, and Stella. All in front of the fire. Perfection, if it weren't for the damn condensation.

———

"I knew we should've had those windows checked before winter," she said. "Now we have to wait until it warms up again."

"Why? They can install windows in the winter."

Emily shook her head. "They'll make it worse."

Jim did not want to argue, not after being away all week. He laid the newspaper out on the coffee table and flipped to the crossword puzzle. End of the week, so this would be a tough one. But he preferred to do it alone. Especially when Emily was annoyed with him.

Emily watched Jim, waiting for him to call out a clue. Minutes passed. She'd make dinner instead.

"Burritos okay?"

"Hmm?" Jim looked up. "Oh, yeah, sounds good."

Emily did not want to cook dinner, but burritos were easy. She'd throw together a salad to make it healthier. Of course, the salads were never that healthy in the end. She couldn't resist croutons and a creamy dressing.

Stella stood by the sink and meowed.

"I guess it's your dinner time too. Okay girl, hang on."

———

It was the weekend. Jim and Emily stayed inside as snow piled up on their doorstep, blocking their way. They could have gone out the back door. They could have pushed hard to open the front and compress the snow. But they chose to remain inside where the fire roared and Stella curled up on the couch or on the carpet or on one of their laps and purred.

"That condensation is making its way inside," said Emily, touching the living room window again. Her test window. The furthest away from the fireplace. "I can write my name in it now. Look at this."

Jim was reading a book, his feet resting on the coffee table. He did not want to get up, but he groaned, put his stocking feet on the floor, and shuffled over to the window. "Let's see," he said, placing his right hand on his wife's right shoulder, standing behind her, so much closer than he'd been to her in days. She was warm. His hand was cold. But she placed her left hand across her chest, resting it on his.

"It's strange, isn't it?"

"I don't know, Em. It seems kind of normal to me. Doesn't this happen every year?"

"No, I would remember. This is new."

"Are you…" He did not want to argue. "Okay." He kissed her neck and went back to the couch. "We'll call someone to come and check it out."

"They won't be able to get out here for awhile. Not with this snow."

Emily went to the couch and snuggled up to Jim. He pulled her under his arm as if this were completely normal. As if they had not become estranged over the last several years. As if they had always been this affectionate with each other. Stella was pleased. She jumped up and snuggled down into the crevice between their thighs.

"Good girl," said Emily.

Later, when Stella hopped back onto the floor, Jim took

Emily's face in his hands and kissed her. A long sweet kiss like they hadn't done since first dating.

They went upstairs to their bedroom and made love for the first time in five years.

The snow did not let up. Three feet, according to the radio. That was more than either Emily or Jim ever remembered getting. And out where they were, on the prairie, it might have been more. Snow moved out there. Piled up, drifted, and only stopped when it hit something it couldn't push or smother, like their house. But they didn't seem to notice the snow. They spent so much time in bed, so much time wrapped around each other, their house could have blown away and they would have stayed in bed through it all, naked and oblivious. Stella curled up nearby, content with her humans creating so much heat.

The condensation began to seep in and drip from the window sill to the hardwood floor. The original floor in the old house. Now spoiled by a growing stain. In normal times, Emily would have noticed. Gotten a bucket, placed it beneath the window, used rags to sop up the water. But she and Jim were like a new couple who had just discovered sex and had no sense of time or responsibility. Stella had to pester them for food. Which, in turn, reminded them to eat. Thank goodness for cats.

"Is it getting hotter in here?" asked Emily on the second day, sweat pouring from her forehead.

"Only because you're here," said Jim, sweating even more, but unable to detach himself from his wife of so many years.

"I'm serious. I think it's too hot. We should open a window."

"No, don't do that. All that snow." Jim wiped his eyes and

threaded his fingers through Emily's hair. It was soaked. "Maybe I can braid your hair. Get it off your back."

Emily kissed his sweaty face. "Sure. That might help."

Jim straddled Emily's bare, damp back. He ran his fingers through her long dark hair and split it into three sections. He pulled the braid tight to hold as much hair as possible.

"I need something to tie it."

Emily reached for a small rubber band on the bedside table and handed it to him.

"Thanks. There. Better?"

"I suppose so. It was just nice having you do that. Felt good. Now come 'ere." She rolled over and pulled him down on top of her. Stella remained curled up in a corner of the bedroom, occasionally looking up to make sure her humans were still alive. Able to feed her when necessary.

Downstairs, the condensation continued to spread. It covered the interior walls of the living room and reached into the kitchen. Paint peeled. The hardwood floor warped. Mold began to develop underneath the area rug. When, at the end of the second day, Emily and Jim finally detached themselves from each other long enough to go downstairs and feed Stella, they did not notice.

Outside the snow remained; unmoved by the growing mess inside the house. The snow was just snow. There to be cold and keep the door closed.

During the night of the second day, Stella sat in the living room and watched the spread of the condensation. She batted at it as it crept under the area rug that covered the floor beneath the couch. She growled, hissed, but the condensation did not leave. It was not afraid of this little cat with a fierce attitude. Stella hopped up onto the couch and sat guard. The room was cold. The fire long gone.

Upstairs in their bedroom, Emily and Jim continued their love fest. They did not light a new fire. They did not notice the spread of the condensation. And they did not go to work. By the fourth day, their phones began to ring. Messages were left.

"Are you okay?"

"Do you think you'll make it in today? I know the snow is bad."

"Is your power out? Why haven't you called back?"

"Should I have someone come and check on you?"

"You need to call me back."

"You're fired."

These messages were for both Emily and Jim, though only Emily got fired.

But Emily did not know she'd been fired. And if she had known, she would not have cared. Sweat continued to pour down her body as she and Jim loved each other more intensely than they'd ever thought possible.

Stella popped her head in the bedroom every few hours to make sure her humans were alive. But by the sixth day, the stuffy bedroom had become unpleasant. Stella went down to the kitchen, hopped up on the counter, opened the cupboard, and pulled the bag of kibble down from the shelf. It landed with a *whoomp!* She tore with her claws and teeth until she ripped it open. Consistent, reliable food. For now, at least. Thirsty, Stella walked across the kitchen counter to the sink and hopped in. The constant drip from the faucet would have to do, as her water bowl had been dry for two days.

Upstairs in the pitch black bedroom, Emily sat up. "I don't feel right. Something is off."

"Are you sure? I feel okay." Jim was lying. He did not feel okay. He just wanted to slide against Emily's wet silky skin one more time.

"No, something's definitely wrong." She forced herself to crawl out of bed. When she tried to stand, her legs gave way and she toppled over onto the wet floor. "What?" The muscles in her legs felt like they hadn't been used in a year. The floor was completely damp with cool condensation. She wasn't sure what to be more alarmed by—her legs or the wetness.

"What's wrong?" said Jim, peeking over the edge of the bed.

"It's… I don't know." Downstairs Stella meowed at the sound of her humans moving around. "When's the last time we fed Stella?"

"I'm sure she's fine."

Emily crawled to the bathroom. Holding on to the doorknob, she pulled herself upright and touched her legs. So thin. Like all the fat had melted away. Light was not appealing in this moment, but she reached for the switch and turned it on anyway. She squinted at the mirror until her eyes adjusted.

Emily gasped. A gasp that grew into a cry followed by a slow, painful scream. "What is going on!" she wailed into the bathroom mirror. The person staring back at her was a stranger. A reflection of death. Emaciation. Decay. She looked like a bruised, melted candle. On the floor, the wetness touched her feet. It had followed her from the bedroom and now traveled up her toes, tracing the lines of her foot bones to her ankles. She sat on the toilet and watched the translucent condensation envelope her.

Jim stumbled out of bed and ran to the bathroom. "What's wrong? Are you okay?" It took so much energy to reach the door and get those words out that he slumped to the floor to catch his breath. Emily had locked the door. Jim's fingers felt the wetness on the wood floor beneath him. It crept up his weak, bruised, mushy thighs. Emily did not answer Jim's question and he did not have the energy to ask again.

Emily flushed the toilet and went to the bathtub. She turned on the water, poured in a cup of bath salts, and as soon as an inch of water had filled the tub, she crawled in. The part of her mind that was still rational and smart, knew this was a bad idea, but she wanted the bath so badly that she did it anyway.

"It'll be okay, Jim. It'll be okay."

Jim didn't respond, but she heard a faint snore coming from under the door.

The water was hot. Too hot, but she forced her body down and let the tub fill up around her. The condensation that had been covering her feet remained on her body like a thin film. Oil to the tub's water. It was not created from hydrogen and oxygen. It was something else. Something alien. She scrubbed her feet, arms, and legs but the condensation (or whatever it was) continued to creep up her body, moving even more quickly now that she was immersed in hot water. It crept up her neck, to her mouth, and down her throat. Emily gagged, afraid it would choke her, but like an amniotic sac, it only changed the way she breathed.

Her skin was slimy, even more so than before. And the coating of condensation prevented the water in the tub from penetrating her pores. Emily let the water drain. She slipped when trying to get out and hit her chin on the hard porcelain rim of the tub. She yelped. Outside the door, there was no reaction. Jim was completely out.

Emily was afraid to look in the mirror. Everything hurt. And now her chin was injured. But she gathered her courage and looked. Her bruised skin was more colorful than it had been only fifteen minutes before and the layer of condensation coating her body made her appear... fuzzy... out of focus. A red mark emerged under her chin where she hit herself. A pool of blood, kept inside the sac.

Emily opened the door and tripped over the sleeping Jim. It did not occur to her to rouse him. She pulled on a bathrobe and went downstairs. On the back of the couch, Stella sat guard. Her eyes were big and she reared up her back with a growl when she saw Emily. Emily, who no longer looked or smelled like herself.

"It's okay, girl, it's me." She stepped forward to pet Stella, but her legs gave way and she stumbled onto the hardwood floor. "Oh god!" Emily's left leg throbbed with pain. But having heard her voice, Stella seemed to understand that this was her human. She walked over and rubbed her face against Emily's back. "Good girl. Something is terribly wrong, Stella."

It was a struggle to get up, but she made it to her feet with the help of the old telephone table near the foot of the stairs. She walked to the kitchen and saw the massive bag of kibble open on the counter.

Emily sighed. "I guess I can't blame you."

Away from the bedroom, her mind began to clear, though her body was still completely enveloped. She went to the sink and washed her hands but the condensation would not budge. Brushes, scouring pads, nothing worked; only made her skin turn colors. A few tiny spots of red emerged on the backs of her hands, burst capillaries making their way through the epidermis, safely encased in the film covering her skin.

"Shit. What the fuck is this? Stella, I don't know what to do."

She looked around. Food did not sound appealing, though she knew she should eat. Stella sat on the counter near her bag of food and meowed. She ate a few pieces of kibble. Emily noticed that the part of Stella's face that had rubbed against her was damp now. She hoped whatever this was would not infect her cat too.

Infect. That's what it was. An infection. It had to be.

She walked to the refrigerator and finally noticed the squishing sounds on the floor under her bare feet. Water. No, not water. *My god, it's everywhere.* And gradually, Emily noticed… the walls, the windows, the cupboards… they were all coated with the condensation… the wetness… the infection. What was she supposed to call it? She touched the door of the refrigerator with her fingertip. It had no odor. No texture. No temperature. But it seemed to vibrate. Stella walked across the counter to stand near Emily, and meowed.

"I don't know, girl. Something strange. And I feel so… everything hurts. I'm weak. My body is falling apart."

Emily looked out the kitchen window. It was dusk. Just enough light to see that there was nothing but snow outside. The trees appeared shorter. Drifts came up to the windows. She wasn't going anywhere.

What was the date? She scrambled through her purse until she found her phone. Ten missed calls. Twenty text messages. The date was February 5th. The last time she'd looked at her phone it was still January.

Checking her voicemail was too overwhelming, but Emily flipped through the texts. Each touch of the phone made her fingertips ache, but she forced herself to do it. She backtracked to the earliest message. The screen of her phone became infected with the wetness from her body and after a few minutes of looking at panicked text messages from her mother, angry messages from her boss, and reminders from her pharmacy to pick up her meds, Emily's phone shorted out.

"Of course. Of course it fucking does that. Shit!" She threw the phone across the room where it landed in a damp puddle near the front door.

Stella bolted behind the couch and hissed.

"Sorry, girl."

Emily lay down on the couch and pulled a blanket over her legs. She felt cold down to her bones. The kind of cold that is impossible to get rid of. The kind of cold you feel when you are dying.

Stella hopped up on the blanket and snuggled in. The weight of the cat was somewhat painful, but also comforting. Emily fell asleep.

***

Jim woke up. His body was in even worse shape than Emily's and he had a craving. Not food exactly. Not sex either. He craved more closeness with his wife. A kind of closeness that was physically impossible. Or seemed like it should be, but he had an instinct that he could make it happen. To become one with her somehow. He knew this desire was irrational. Jim was a systems engineer. He was not one for fluffy emotional ideas of souls merging. He was systematic. Methodical. But the last few days had transformed him just as it had Emily. And to an even greater extent. He needed her.

Jim struggled down the stairs. He tried to speak, but his voice was hoarse and dry. Strange given the wetness on the outside of his body. "Em? Hon?" he finally managed in a raspy whisper.

At the foot of the stairs, he stepped onto the floor and walked, holding the wall for support, to the living room. There, on the couch, lay his Emily. Stella still curled up on her legs. He fought the urge to lay down on top of them both. To immerse himself in their scents and sensations. Instead, Jim sat on the floor next to the couch and gently nudged his wife. "Em? You awake?"

Stella stirred and let out a high pitched "mew," acknowledging Jim's presence and perhaps trying to tell him to shut the hell up, they're trying to sleep. Jim scratched Stella's head and went into the kitchen. Each footstep he took squished. Holding the wall for support, he made it there and opened the refrigerator. The inside was damp like everything else. He pulled out a jar of pickles and took a bite of one, but immediately spat it out onto the floor.

"Not right," he said, "just not right."

Jim was self-aware enough to know there was something very wrong, but did not seem to care about it as much as his wife. He followed his instincts and went back to the living room. Jim sat down on the edge of the couch where Emily slept. Stella hopped from the couch to the leather chair near the fireplace. She did not like getting her paws wet on this now completely soaked floor.

Emily stirred but did not wake. Jim leaned down and kissed

his wife on the cheek. Then, slowly, almost imperceptibly slowly, he crept up onto Emily so that he was lying directly on top of her, his belly touching her belly, his toes intertwining with her toes, his face nose to nose with her face. Emily did not wake. Her arms reached up and wrapped around Jim and pulled. Jim's body oozed down into Emily's like melting ice cream into sponge cake. She absorbed him. Brought him into her pores. Each cell, each strand of DNA, was taken in by Emily's body. Stella growled. She curled up into the furthest corner of the chair and tried to hide under the flap of the arm rest cover.

An hour passed. Then two. Then ten.

Stella leapt from one piece of furniture to another on her way to the kitchen, trying her best to avoid the wetness. She ate from the ripped bag of kibble on the kitchen counter and wondered if her remaining human would ever wake up.

A day went by.

Emily's body started to dry. As did the condensation on the floor and the walls and in the refrigerator. Everything began to dry. The snow outside melted and the pavement on the driveway cleared.

Emily woke feeling refreshed and new, as if she were emerging from a chrysalis, a long sleep during which everything inside of her changed and reorganized. She felt younger. When she stood up from the couch, strength shot up through her muscles—strength she hadn't felt in a decade.

Stella walked over and rubbed against Emily's leg. "What happened, girl?" She searched her memory for a record of the last several days but came up empty. "Where's Jim?"

Stella looked up at her and let out a short "mew."

The name "Jim" only vaguely had meaning to her. She knew he was her husband, but could not remember what he looked like, what he did for a living, or how they'd met. Rather she felt that he was an essence in her life. A kind of warmth with which she had been involved and was now a part of her. Like a cozy memory. After a few minutes of pondering Jim's existence, Emily let it go. She saw a pair of men's snow boots by the front door. They were dry now. Everything was dry.

"Let's get some breakfast," she said to Stella. The kibble bag was still on the counter. Stella was not an overeater. She'd only nibbled at it over the days since her humans had become engulfed in the strange wetness. She now stayed on the floor and waited patiently for Emily to scoop some into a bowl. Emily then folded the bag up, put a clip on the top, and placed it back in the cupboard.

"I wonder where these came from," she said, picking up a pair of reading glasses from the table. They sat next to a magazine about boating. Someone was interested in boating. It hadn't been her, not before, but now some part of her was intrigued. She put the glasses inside the pocket of her bathrobe and sat down at the table to read. In the background, Stella crunched her food. She was a good girl.

after now

. . .

Jordan Hirsch

He traces in the new mud, silky and anemic,
and the clay sticks to his finger. It hasn't rained here in years;
we've settled for building sandcastles until today.
Clouds came then burst, drenching us, briefly carving

gullies and trenches once the sand could hold no more water.
They didn't last long. Our ground is just sponge we set our
feet on.
What were these temporary micro-landmarks? Lakes? Puddles?
Streams?
We're too superstitious to name the beginning trickles of hope.

He digs out paths, bringing the soaked-in water closer to the
surface.
The curve of a cheek, the bow of two lips. Eyes wide, framed by
curling hair, all mud-brown.
She is breath-taking, etched features tattooed in the soil
that's threatened to forget her. He hasn't.

It's just one rain, but one rain can be a harbinger.

Hushed questions are all the same: if the planet's healing, can
we, too?
He wipes his muddy hands on his muddy pants–persistent
sun parting the clouds and steaming us back into our homes–

grabs a piece of stone and writes something
next to the portrait he's painted in canvas earth.
His words harden in the heat, moisture baking out of the clay,
more crucible than kiln, giving them permanence, at least until
they're trod underfoot.

"My love for you–it lasts."
And I wonder: who was she?

artifact

. . .

Laura J. Campbell

"You have quite the collection." Melody noted, as she surveyed Whitney's collection of carvings. They were all variants of the wild man image. Sasquatches, Yeti, furry men with club-like weapons, and other similar figures. She knew Whitney through a mutual friend who had been Whitney's roommate. She had been tasked with dropping off mail misdelivered to Whitney's old address.

"This is the OG wild man posse," Whitney grinned. "The wild man. An archetypal figure: the man who bows to no one. Only nature can break him."

Whitney picked up a moderately sized Bigfoot carving, fashioned after the images captured in the infamous Patterson video. "Believe it or not, I wrote a paper on the Wild Man archetype. It was published in one of those reputable journals that nobody reads."

"I make custom light fixtures as a hobby," Melody related, as she surveyed the carved beings. My chandeliers were featured in an equally esteemed and never read arts journal. Does Bigfoot scare you? He isn't real, you know."

"I beg to differ," Whitney replied. "About a decade ago I was out mountain biking with some friends, and I saw a Big Foot. I freaked out a little. Well, I freaked out a lot. I started doing the research on the geographic area, to see if there was anything out there."

"And?"

"A Sasquatch-like creature lives in the East Texas Piney Woods," Whitney reported. "A friend from the trip bought me the Big Foot statue as a joke. Now I collect the things myself. And, as you know, once you get an interest in something, the internet bombards you with ads for whatever that something is. Hence, I now own a platoon of these things. But I tend to stay away from the woods. I have no desire to see the real thing again."

"I grew up in the woods," Melody smiled. "There are weird noises and weird things out in the woods *all* the time. The secret is to not go out investigating them. You go on some backwoods biking adventure and see Bigfoot, that's on you. Still, I wouldn't want these statues in my house. They might attract the real thing."

"Images have power," Whitney replied. "Lots of little St. Francis statues in gardens. The image of peaceful nature. The opposite of the wild man, surviving the violence of nature."

"Are these statutes idols? Do they wield some sort of magic?" Melody asked, finding herself oddly fascinated by the statues, despite how grotesque some of them appeared.

"Most cultures embrace some concept of magic," Whitney replied. "Wizards, witches, shamans, and spells. Go into churches and temples–there are still sacred images around. Icons and statutes, some with purportedly miraculous powers. Socially acceptable magic."

"If there ever was any *true* magic on Earth, I doubt there's any left," Melody sighed. "We're all techno now."

"I have a theory that whatever magic survives on Earth is channeled through art. That art is our magic—it transforms dreams into actions. Movies, three-dimensional graphics, videos, games—these vehicles now perpetuate our myths and cast our spells. The ancient Greeks had their superheroes, we have ours. We still offer our tribute—our coin—to do them homage. Usually paid to the merchandising department."

"But they are just stories. They're not real."

"There are illusionists and there are magicians," Whitney replied. "Illusionists just appear to work magic, but others - artists, writers, musicians–inspire us to change. To think, to grow. To feel. To believe. To *act*. The modern shamans chanting their spells."

"Illusion entertains us, but magic changes us?" Melody summarized. "An interesting thought."

Melody entered her small studio space at the Silos at Sawyer Yards. The old rice silos and warehouse space had been transformed into sleek art studios.

She sat down to work on her latest chandelier. The occupation had started as a hobby to provide extra income; now the side gig was more profitable than the main gig.

She was making a purple chandelier for the entertainment room of a couple she had met at an alumni fundraiser a few months back. They had paid her up front, so she felt obliged to complete the piece expeditiously.

Melody worked all morning, fueled by uncooked toaster pastries and coffee. She stepped outside into the hallway to flex her back muscles and get her blood circulating after being hunched over her workstation for hours. She saw a discarded piece of wood in the hallway.

Hugh Sei, a sculptor who worked in wood a few studios away from her, had thrown out the wood. Melody went over and picked up the remnant, weighing it in her hands. The scrap suggested life, a soul whose song only she could hear.

She took it back to her studio; her instincts told her it was special in her hands.

A few days later, Melody was on the train going to work, sitting on a blue plastic seat. There was a young man sitting beside her. She had seen him several times before.

"I'm Melody," she said impulsively. It was very uncharacteristic for her to introduce herself to strangers. But he looked so frail, and his skin had an unhealthy pallor.

"I'm Lucas," he replied. "I've seen you on the train before."

"I don't like driving," she said.

"I don't like parking," he replied. "Well, more accurately, I don't like paying for parking. Med Center parking is crazy expensive. You think they'd give us sick folk a break. Like we don't have enough unexpected bills already. You work in Med Center?"

"I have a job at one of the museums. Do you work in Med Center?"

"No. I'm a patient, getting treatment for thyroid cancer." He pointed to a purple ribbon he wore. "I had trouble swallowing and thought it was no big deal. Now I'm undergoing radiation treatment."

"I'm sorry," she said, feeling oddly inadequate.

"Not your fault. You're an artist? You mentioned a job at the museum."

"More of a craftswoman," she said, almost as an apology. "I work in restoration and in my spare time I make custom chandeliers."

"My sister has a chandelier in her master bathroom. She's just a little dramatic. Chandeliers are a bygone decadence. They were meant to amplify fire, feeding off carefully positioned flames. The electric ones seem a little sterile to me."

"I like making the old-fashioned type better," Melody confessed. "But light is light."

"You practice making things that cut through the darkness. That has to be gratifying."

The train slowed, approaching Melody's stop.

"Best wishes for your chemo," she said, hoping that was an okay thing to say.

"Good luck with your chandeliers," he replied.

As she got off the train, Melody was gripped by the sudden urge to carve the piece of wood she had rescued. She could hardly contain herself during her work shift, the anticipation was so great.

Back at her studio, after work, she sat down and looked at the wood. And then she began to carve.

A masculine form began to emerge from the wood.

It took an hour or so of work, but she eventually recognized the carving's features.

She was carving Lucas, the young man from the train; but her carving depicted a healthier Lucas, with better body weight and a more robust physique. She worked all night, packets of instant coffee dissolved in hot water spurring her on.

Lucas was on the train again a few days later. Melody's face lit up when she saw him.

"I missed you," she smiled. "You were off for a few days."

"One or two," he acknowledged. "Scheduling snafus. Life's frustrations continue, even when you're dying."

"I made something for you," she said. "It isn't much, but I get these weird creative moments. My grandfather taught me to carve when I was little. I haven't done any carving since he died years ago. But apparently, it's like riding a bike; you don't forget how, once you know." She pulled out the sculpture and handed it to him.

Lucas took it in his hands as if it were made of solid gold. "It looks just like me," he said in amazement. "Well, it looks like I used to look—before I lost all the weight. I used to play lacrosse, and this is what I looked like then. Thank you. You have an amazing talent."

"You'll be back to health," Melody wished. "And back to playing fabulous lacrosse."

"Truth is, I played miserable lacrosse, even when I was healthy."

"Well, let's just focus on the healthy part, then."

Melody arrived at her studio after work.

"Hi," Hugh Sei greeted as she entered her workspace. He was the wood carver who had unknowingly donated the raw material for Lucas's statue.

"Hi," she replied.

"You're here later than usual," Hugh noted. "You need a ride home after you're done here tonight?"

"I can take the bus."

"This is a big city. You need to be careful. You weigh about ninety-eight pounds soaking wet. By the way, I was at Hugo's Cantina the other night and overheard Mark Ribatti bragging about you and some purple chandelier you were making for him and his husband."

"Come in and see," she said, ushering him into her studio. "It's nearly finished."

The chandelier had a purple glass core that sprouted six curved stems that each held six flame shaped light bulbs positioned on ornate glass platters. Jewel shaped droplets adorned the fixture, each capturing prisms of color.

"It's beautiful," he said. "It must be something, to create a functional piece of art. This piece has such a gorgeous old-fashioned vibe to it, yet it is so fresh and open. Like history without any tragedies."

"Thank you," Melody replied.

"I have a showing in a few months," Hugh said. "Maybe you

could work up a lighting piece on spec–we could have your light in the center of the room, and my carvings around it. I like the way your pieces capture and control light. You breathe life into things. It's a real talent."

"You flatter me."

"Enough you'll make a light for my show?"

"Yes," she replied. She paused, changing the subject. "Where do you get your raw supplies? The wood that you carve."

"A family-owned nursery and landscaping company in Seabrook," Hugh answered. "They have leftover pieces from various shipments of materials and conveyances of artifacts. One of their guys brings me a tub full of remnants and odd bits. I pay a bulk price. I sort them when I get them."

"That explains the variety," Melody noted.

"I'll put some coffee on in the breakroom," Hugh suggested. "Be back in a moment."

Melody looked outside his door. There was a smooth round log about sixteen inches long sitting dejectedly in the hallway outside of his studio space; it was marked '*basura*' so the janitorial staff would know that it was trash.

She knew it wasn't trash: she could make it something powerful.

She went and picked it up, taking it back to her studio. The wood was tough and dark.

She placed the log in a large drawer before joining Hugh for coffee.

Melody was on the train when Lucas got on at his station. He looked radiant as he sat next to her.

"You look happy," she noted.

"You're not going to believe this," he replied, "But my cancer is in remission. They're even suggesting that I may be cured."

"Cured?"

"Yes, ma'am," he answered. "I'm going in for more scans today, but everything looks good. Which means I must plan to live again. Things were so dire there for a moment that I made my own funeral arrangements. What hymns I wanted sung; I even chose a coffin. Very morbid. Now it looks like I have to worry about that thirteen-month apartment lease I signed and paying off my student loans."

"Thank God!" Melody said. "For the cure, not the student loans."

"I had some clients pick up a purple chandelier," she answered. She dug around her purse and pulled out a photograph of the completed work.

"It's beautiful," he told her. He unpinned the purple ribbon he wore and placed it in her hand. "Purple for purple. Consider the ribbon a down payment towards me buying one of your fancy lights. When I'm done paying off my loans."

"You're going to be so successful that I'm going to insist that you buy a chandelier for every room," she told him. "Including the bathroom."

"Deal," Lucas agreed.

As they approached her station, Melody found herself noticing that they were being watched by a young man with messy brown hair.

There was a newcomer in their midst.

Melody had a melancholy sense of optimism that she would not see Lucas many more times. He was getting better every day and once his follow-up visits were finished, he would no longer need to regularly ride the train.

Still, there was something comforting in knowing she had given him the statue. It was like she had given him a present for a new birthday.

The other young man, the one with the messy brown

hair, *was* on the train. He had a disturbing intensity about him; Melody could not look him in the eyes.

As she got to her stop, he watched her prepare to leave the train cab.

"Have a nice day," she mumbled out, feeling compelled to say something.

He did not reply. He just stared at her with his dark probing eyes.

She was oddly relieved to be on the platform. But his eyes never left her, until the train itself was out of range.

Even though the air was warm, Melody couldn't suppress the chill that went up her spine.

The next Saturday was a very rainy day. Lush thunderclouds congregated in the sky, dousing the city with frequent downpours to remind the good citizens of Houston that even though they had sent rockets into outer space, they were still at the mercy of the elements.

Melody sat in her studio, organizing her next paying project, a green-colored chandelier. Melody had designed a fixture to her client's liking. It was going to be made of spherical balls of inlaid stained green glass, suspended from a burnished copper central core.

She dimmed the lights and played some Schubert over her phone. As the lightning flashed across the sky, she started on the chandelier.

But by midday, she could no longer resist the temptation to work on the wood. She took the log into her hands and began to whittle into it, her eyes seeing exactly where she wanted to trim and mold.

It took hours, but she eventually saw a face staring out at her, the eyes hypnotic and penetrating.

The young man from the train, the one with the messy brown hair. The one who observed her with such disturbing intensity.

She put the wood down quickly and returned to making the chandelier.

Getting ready for work, Melody's mind was happy that she was nearly finished with the emerald-colored lighting fixture. Another piece had been commissioned, for a historic home, giving her another well-paying job.

Melody caught the train at her usual time and place.

The young man with the messy brown was already there, looking at her as she got on the train. She sat down, and tried to avoid eye contact.

He looked out of the window and smiled slyly, as if satisfied with some task.

She had the nervous feeling that his mission for the day had been to confirm which station she got on the train.

Melody's client had very exact specifications of the historical lighting fixture. The raw supplies to make the light, true to the materials that would have been available when the original chandelier was made, were on back-order.

With time to wait, Melody found herself picking up the unfinished carving. Perhaps if she saw more of the image evolve, her mind would be put at ease. She considered that she might be projecting her own apprehensions onto the young man; that hardly seemed fair.

She began to carve, the young man's upper body manifesting out of the wood: his carved image held a knife in his right hand. She put the wood down, troubled by what she saw.

Taking a coffee break. Hugh joined Melody in the communal kitchen.

"Why do you discard some of your wood?" Melody asked. "I see some decent pieces of lumber outside of your door. Maybe I'm a little cheap–I couldn't imagine discarding so much of my supplies." A copy of the invoice for the historically accurate materials for her next project had filled her with a certain amount of sticker-shock, even if she wasn't the one paying.

"Some remnants don't seem *right* to me," Hugh answered. "They seem to have too much energy. That may sound superstitious, but I'm afraid of bad juju, so I avoid certain pieces. No scientific or rational reason."

"I have a friend who could talk to you about vibes for hours," Melody said. "Bad vibes. Good vibes. Science. Magic hiding in art, as we become more scientific in our image making. He truly believes that some art is really magic."

"Maybe he has a point. Your work evokes science and art. You have a special gift for making the inanimate come alive. And the effect is entrancing. I could just stare into some of the chandeliers you've made for hours."

"They're lighting fixtures, not hallucinogens," she grinned.

As they talked, there was the sound of footsteps in the hallway. "Are you expecting someone?" Melody asked. "We're the only two here tonight, and no one ever visits me."

The footsteps were heavy and slow. They stopped outside Melody's studio space, as if searching for something.

"You wait here," Hugh said. "The door wasn't closing correctly earlier on. Some vagrants could have snuck in."

As Hugh entered the hall, there was the sound of footsteps retreating quickly, exiting the hall.

The door slammed shut behind as the intruder left.

Hugh reentered. "Whoever it was left the moment they heard me," he reported.

"Did you get a look at them?" Melody asked.

"It almost looked like a kid," Hugh said. "Some dude with

messy hair. He was just hovering outside your studio. I don't think he got in and took anything."

"Weird," Melody said, knowing who the intruder had been. *Why was he stalking her so diligently?*

"I'll make sure the building management fixes that door tomorrow," Hugh asserted. "The neighborhood is okay, but we can still get some shady types wandering around. Especially at night. And I'm giving you a ride home tonight. I insist."

Melody nodded, thinking about the young man with the messy hair. "Thanks," she replied. "I think I'll take you up on that offer tonight."

Melody was on the train. She was going straight home from work, not eager to be alone in her studio at night. Hugh had said he was taking the night off, and no one else was scheduled to be in.

The train doors opened and the young man with the messy hair entered and sat across from her.

"You're making another carving?" he asked spontaneously.

She felt her eyes betray her with affirmative acknowledgment. The carving of him has been hidden in a drawer; all he would have seen in her studio were chandeliers in various stages of completion.

"I like the one you did for cancer-boy," he said. There was darkness in his tone.

"He is cancer-free-man now," Melody corrected.

"I want to see mine."

She felt as if the floor had dropped out from beneath her. "I'm not finished with it," she told him. She felt compelled not to lie to him.

"That's okay. Just work hard on it," he commanded her. He looked at the map of stops posted above the doors. "McGowen is the next station," he said. "Your stop. I haven't figured out exactly where you live. Lots of lofts, condominiums, apartments, and a few old houses in Midtown."

She got off the train, feeling oddly violated. She stood on the platform, watching the train pull away. The young man with the messy hair stayed on the train, making sure she saw him. Implying with his gaze that he already knew which direction she turned to go home.

A bedraggled homeless man resting on a station bench looked at her. "How you are doing, girl?" he asked.

"I'm hanging in there," she replied.

As she walked away the homeless man asked her no more questions.

He sensed there was something stalking her that he wanted no part of.

Melody was putting her trash bag into the hall. She spied Hugh putting wood outside his door.

She approached. "Sometimes I think you throw out more wood than you carve."

"The batches are pretty big. So, not too much waste, really," Hugh chuckled.

"So, what it the rationale with throwing these out?" She spied a piece of wood in the pile, like the one she was carving, the image of the young man with the messy hair.

"This one," Hugh said, picking up that small log, "Is black-thorn—a wood associated with overcoming obstacles, but it also has long thorns that can cause nasty wounds. The Celts thought it was guarded by dark fairies. Think less Disney fairy, more Lovecraft fairy. There were a few pieces of it in the latest batch of wood I received. I've thrown them all out."

"It has bad vibes," she understood.

"Bad enough I don't want to mess with it."

She pointed to a piece of light-colored wood "That one has no vibes."

"If you say so. I can't read that piece. I don't mess with any piece I can't read. Even that stump of ash."

She picked it up. "Do you mind if I have it?" She gathered a few other pieces from the trash heap. The discarded fragments were her treasure.

"Once I put it outside my door as trash it isn't mine anymore," he replied. "Are you planning on using that piece of ash?"

"I have an idea for it," she replied. "Nothing malevolent, I promise."

"So, you're a good fairy, not a bad one?" Hugh asked.

"I'm not a fairy at all," Melody answered. "I have much more potential than that."

A few days later Melody was on the train.

The young man with the messy hair got on and sat next to her.

"You should be finished by now," he said. "You drink enough coffee to skip three nights worth of sleep and never notice it."

You have been watching me! Melody thought. She handed him a carving rendered from the ash, depicting him and his knife fighting off a bear.

He took it and rotated it in his hands. "Not what I expected," he said. "I was thinking of other uses for my knife. But holding this carving, those urges are suddenly gone. That isn't what I expected."

"Lucas wasn't expecting his depiction either," Melody reminded him. That much was true. She had heard that the best lies always contained elements of the truth. And she had now apparently cured both Lucas and the young man. She felt incredible: she felt proud.

"You know," the young man replied. "These things–these artifacts you carve–they reflect something inside you."

"I have a gift."

"Gifts are sometimes offerings," he suggested. "And some offerings are more fearsome than others. My thanks to you for this relic is a piece of advice: don't face your demons alone. You're not fighting them; you're negotiating with them. That is not a healthy option."

"I don't know what you mean."

"That statue you gave to the guy with the illness," he chuckled. "That reflected a malignancy deep within you. Something powerful and destructive is proliferating within you; but you still think you can defeat it all by yourself. This," he turned the statue in his hands, "Is this *you* fighting your nature? A beast metastasizing within your being? You wrestle with it. For now. But who do you want to win? The human being, or the magical creature you could become?"

"You're deluded," Melody announced. "You don't know anything about me."

"You practice a witchcraft you don't understand," he said, preparing to step off the train at the next stop. "But something in you yearns to wield that power. Not really for the good of others; you just like the taste of controlling other peoples' lives."

"Is this how you recoup your power? By suddenly seeming so philosophical?" *He was the beast*, she thought. *Now she had tamed him she was insulted that he thought he could lecture her.*

"The witch who controls the wood they would have burned her with has immense power," the young man nodded thoughtfully. "You need help. If this power of yours is only a delusion you have about some magical ability you think you possess, see a shrink. If you really are controlling others through your abilities, see a shrink *and* a spiritual advisor."

"I'm a good person."

"Everyone thinks they are a good person," the young man

stated. "Especially the evilest. Thinking they are the sole arbiter of good and right enables them to become what they become."

The doors of the train opened, and he stepped off.

Melody watched him as the train pulled away from the station, feeling an indignant wave of superiority well within her. How dare he suggest she was evil! She was not evil; she was *special*. How often humanity confused the two!

And Melody knew how to prove she used her abilities for the good of others.

Waiting back at her studio was a fresh lump of wood, ready for her knives to carve.

There were eight billion people on the Earth. All Melody needed to do was choose one to benefit from her exquisite gift.

nature's course

. . .

Colleen Anderson

Night's eye
a spider crawling slowly
webs spun, forever silvered
by the moon's cast, fishing
the light a sliver of memory drops
far into the spangled blanket
   plinking
     plopping
a hollowed sound, rolling soft
hallowed a wolf calls, alone
fuels thought—to run
heart drumming, spirit thrumming
loping beneath the lunar song
the obstacle, dark trees spear the sky
the finish line woven, threaded crystals
with spider's sorrow
as its web's beauty is broken
by the feral race of time

foundations

. . .

Camden Rose

Beth's house was falling apart. Every few years, she needed to replace the old wooden steps that descended into the waves during high tide or fix the cracks in the foundation. Small costs that allowed her to stay. As her life eroded around her, the water never left. The water was always there. The water always called.

No one loved her like the ocean did.

Which is why she'd chosen to stay when the contractor told her the foundation was rotting through. She had no money to fix it, but no heart to leave either. If she left, she would be leaving the one thing that she could always return to. And when he warned her of the hurricane, she couldn't find a way to explain why she couldn't make herself go.

A crash forced its way into her bedroom, pulling her with it. Beth fell through the window and into the waves. Pieces of her past bled through the water, cutting her. Old pictures of her and her husband. Part of her childhood bed. A hardcover book. She tried to grab something to hold onto, but nothing was stable enough.

Waves crashed around her, confusing up from down. She squeezed her eyes shut, hoping it would stop. It was all too fast.

Something sharp sliced her leg, her arm, her stomach. Blood mixed. Stung. She was afraid to open her eyes.

She thrashed. She kicked and screamed with an energy she didn't know she had, but all she could hear was the water infesting her. She tried to swim to where she thought the surface was. She wasn't ready to be claimed by the ocean. Not yet. Not like this. Not again. Back then, being taken by the water had been scary, but her mom had swum out and grabbed her just in time. Here, with no one to save her, it was terrifying.

Beth yelled, hoping someone might hear her. The water seeped down her throat instead. She started to choke.

She fought for breath, but pulled more water inside her lungs. Still, she couldn't stop her instincts. As she tried to find oxygen underwater, she only had one thought: *I'm not ready to go.*

The waves slowed. She must have made it just beyond the shore. Or she died. The water held her like a mother would hold her baby. Soft, caring, protective. Beth's heart thumped in her ears. She felt alive enough.

Something soft grazed her cheek and she instinctively opened her eyes to find it no longer hurt to see underwater. And she no longer struggled to breathe.

All the remnants of her life had drifted away. In front of her was a young girl, not over the age of seven, dressed in a swimsuit much like one Beth would have worn as a child. The girl smiled at her.

The child looked familiar, but Beth wasn't sure why. She smiled back. Maybe this was what heaven was like.

The child started to swim away, and without thinking, Beth followed. They swam to the surface.

The noise of the world appeared, with water lapping all around as they emerged. The moon shone down, more like a friend than a spotlight. Stars glistened above in a chorus of sparkles. As Beth trod water, she noticed that for the first time in the last seventy years, she didn't feel cold.

"Are you okay?" the child said.

Beth nodded. Surprisingly, she was okay. She felt herself for cuts, but instead of red lines all over her skin, she only noticed white scars that felt like they had been there for years. She couldn't remember where half of them came from.

The child smiled again. "Come on," she said and swam towards an island Beth had never noticed. Beth followed, able to keep up despite her age. She felt lighter. They waded onto the shore as the sun rose above them.

Before them were palm trees taller than Beth had ever seen. She felt a breeze coming from the North, and it carried a fresh airiness she had never experienced. Sand, black as the rotted wood under her house, stretched out on either side of her, but it didn't smell like it was dying. She breathed in the scent of salt and exhaled relief. No houses. No signs of human life anywhere. No one but her and the child.

Everything felt right. She felt more whole than she had her entire adult life.

"Am I dead?" she asked. The child shook her head.

"No, but not alive either. Somewhere… in between."

Beth started trying to find a response to that, but the girl giggled. It was full of happiness and innocence, something Beth had long left behind.

"Come on. I wanna show you something," the child said and grabbed her hand.

They headed off. Beth felt like she was in a bubble. She knew the black sand should burn her feet, but all she noticed was the grains tickling her toes. She knew the sun should beat down her neck, but instead she felt warm relief gleaming on her skin. She knew that practically she could never live in a place like this without access to amenities, especially at her age, but it felt right all the same. This new world beckoned to her with a hope she had forgotten.

The two of them walked for about an hour in silence, hand in hand, content to just be.

They found an exact replica of her house. It sat in the black sand as though it was meant to stay there, but it couldn't look more out of place. The two stories seemed extravagant now, among nothing but trees and sand. Beth noticed the first-story window had a scratch in the top left corner from where a neighborhood boy had thrown a rock when she was five. There were even stairs descending into the water, except these weren't dying like the ones back home. Not yet at least.

"Do you like it?" the girl asked.

Beth stared at her house. "What's your name?"

There was a pause. A hesitation as though the child was trying to remember herself. Beth found herself trying to remember something as well, but as soon as the thought started to form, the girl spoke.

"Anna," she said.

Beth smiled. She gave Anna a hug.

"Thank you, Anna. This is wonderful."

Anna hugged back. They went inside.

Everything was as Beth had left it, but different. She walked through the house, touching furniture that had no scratches. Dishes that had no chips. Doors that had no marks.

The house looked at least 70 years younger. Beth turned to ask Anna about the place, but the girl was already running upstairs laughing.

"I'll take the upstairs bedroom!" she giggled.

Beth smiled. She had lost that youthful excitement so long ago. It was nice to have it back.

She walked to the window, stared at the pulsing waves for a minute, tried to see if she could still feel the curious pull she had felt since she was a child. Nothing. She stared a moment longer, debating if she was happy or sad the water no longer wanted her, then decided she wasn't sure what she felt about anything anymore.

The days passed by as though everything was a dream. Beth and Anna spent the hours living in silence, not feeling pain or misery or anything in between. Beth couldn't remember the last time she had eaten, but she didn't feel the primal urge to have food either. Or water. Or anything she had needed before to live. All she had to do, in this magical place, was be. She didn't need to miss anyone or grieve her life anymore.

And that was enough until the voice in the back of her head started thinking something must be wrong if she was here, with Anna, like this. But it wasn't until they were on the back porch a week later that Beth finally dared to bring up the one thing she had been wondering.

She glanced out at the water. It had been calm every day they had been here. She was used to it surging at her presence, not piddling.

"Once, when I was younger, I went to the edge of the water and waded in," Beth started. "Then, I swam as far as I could."

Anna was quiet for a moment. Then she took Beth's hand. "You wanted to see what lay beyond the horizon," Anna said. Beth nodded.

They watched the waves together. Beth dug her heels into the wood. It was starting to rot again. Beth knew it was a sign. She wasn't meant to stay here forever. Neither was Anna. As much as they wanted to cling to life, it had already let go of them.

"My mom… she was yelling from the shore. I could see her screaming. I couldn't hear her above the waves, but I knew she was scared," Beth said.

"Some part of you died that day." Anna whispered.

"But, the rest of me always knew I would return when it was time." She looked at her younger self. "I think I always knew."

Beth had lost so much, but losing herself was the hardest of them all, even if she didn't know it at the time. Her near-death experience made her grow up. Made her forget what it was like to be a child.

Even so, she always felt drawn to the water, though it scared her. She never realized that call was from a past she had left behind, and the ocean was just a beacon to herself. The water was watching her, waiting for the day she left this world and went to the next.

"I'm sorry we couldn't stay forever," Anna said, staring at the darkened stairs.

"I'm sorry, too." Beth squeezed her hand. She felt whole again.

They looked out at the waves, the calm lapse of each one against the black shore.

"I think I'm ready now," Beth said.

"Me too," Anna responded. She smiled at Beth and Beth smiled back.

They started to descend the steps into the water, one at a time. The waves picked up, almost as if they were happy to welcome her home after so long. Beth wiped a salty tear from her cheek and continued to go further and further into the water. Anna dove under the waves with a grin and disappeared beneath the blue. Beth only paused for a moment before continuing forward.

With each step, the storm grew stronger, until Annabeth could feel nothing but its cool embrace, wrapping her body like a long-lost love. She opened her arms to its touch. She had never felt so whole, part of something so big. The water churned and she rested in its powerful waves.

No one loved her like the ocean did.

apocalypse house

. . .

Lauren Scharhag

"A riot of colors and religious iconography, this home was designed for apocalyptic times"
—Allison C. Meier, CNN Style

"And all should cry, Beware! Beware! His flashing eyes, his floating hair!"
—Samuel Taylor Coleridge, "Kubla Kahn"

i. mount erie

Even before he died, he was more legend than man, the dates of his life inconsistent across news outlets. When he was 12, his mother had a deathbed vision of his sacred destiny. Of course, she'd given him the name Isaiah, which was already a bit on the nose. Then he went and became a self-taught carpenter. Now, no one is campaigning for his sainthood, no reports of miracles performed, unless one considers art miraculous. He took odd jobs, restoring old buildings, a gig at Mt. Erie Baptist Church to hang sheetrock, where the Lord said unto him, *Make it oak*. So Isaiah got oak. As he measured and cut, he began to receive the symbols, reading God's cryptic communiques in shavings and wood grain, the symbols he believed contained a prophecy: the Rapture, the End of Days, the Fiery Falls. Prophets always have that air of mysticism. It doesn't matter how literally they take the Good Book's teachings. It doesn't matter that Isaiah was merely a parishioner, never a preacher. Such souls simply cannot operate within the bounds of the orthodoxy. God cannot possibly be orthodox. It can never be just words, it always has to be whirlwinds and burning bushes and other, even stranger manifestations. Like Amy Adams trying to communicate with aliens, prophets are God's linguists. (But you know what they say about translators and traitors.) The church job was only supposed to last three months but ended up taking three years, a holy trinity of annums. Photos of the artist reveal a tall, spare man, very upright, dressed in priestly back. He had hair and a beard worthy of a Golden Age Hollywood Biblical epic, bushy and wild as holy bramble. Give him a pair of sandals, a simla and a shepherd's crook, a stack of stone tablets, (though again, wood was his medium) and oh, Charlton Heston, eat your heart out. A prophet's brow, the sort of large, all-seeing eyes that you expect of both an artist and a recipient of divine emanations. The wrinkles and veins of his face seemed to flow outward from his eyes, like wings, like the tributaries of a river, his speech peppered with *Praise God* or *Praise the Lord* or *Hallelujah*, like punctuation. Instead of *full stop* he would say *praise God*. As in, *The Alpha and Omega – praise God, praise God. The flood is coming. It will transform into the lake of fire. Praise the Lord, praise the Lord, praise the Lord.* Like Tourette's, like a compulsion, he had to throw in words of praise every few syllables. The sanctuary was transformed, gleaming like burnished copper, like the feet of Christ. The stained wood panels interlock like universes, like heaven and earth, like human and divine. The cut patterns leapt from their backdrops and arranged themselves into new patterns in the prophet's brain. Smooth wooden walls like the insides of a ship, preparing for a lake of fire, a ship balanced on a river at the edge of the world. Isaiah had intended to return to Canada when he was done, but his mission took precedence. When the project was complete, Isaiah called it his Jubilee Year, time of forgiveness and redemption. To celebrate, he lit hundreds of candles (some say a thousand). God's signal fires.

ii. every prophet in his house

Isaiah's home was on Ontario Avenue, just blocks from the Niagara River, not four miles from the Falls. When he began crafting its adoration adornments, he started with a cross: 26 feet high, a 15-foot crossbeam bolted on. A true iconographer, Isaiah said it wasn't him, but God moving his hand. Instead of triptychs and marble and gold leaf, he went with humble house paint: crosses and diamonds, wheels within wheels (tipping his hat to his predecessors), five- and six- and eight-pointed stars, mandorlas like eyes, patterns within patterns, colors within colors. Living in God's shaken kleidoscope, in the belly of an alebrije, in a shining tabernacle. The number seven, three times. A petroglyph of Christ's body. A red rock encircled by green rocks to symbolize Goat Island, which splits the falls, and where, according to Isaiah, the sheep will be separated from the goats. Do you baa or do you maa? Over the falls there shimmers a perpetual rainbow, the ongoing promise of the Lord's covenant with Man. Some say the word "Niagara" means thundering waters. Isaiah says the roaring waters are the thundering voice of God. By 2012, it was mostly finished, so Isaiah turned his attention to touch-ups. All his wooden structures withstood the punishing northern winds just fine, but house paint is not so durable. So he busied himself painting and re-painting, especially the rocks, sometimes inscribing new patterns over the old.

Neighbors came, seeking guidance and the occasional loan. Niagara Falls isn't the tourism hotspot it used to be. Now it's like

so many other Rust Belt towns, whole blocks of derelict buildings, dead zones where we reap nothing but blight. Yet, it still
calls to artists. And when Isaiah made his house, tourists began
to visit again. Something about color and curiosities draws us in.
Something about the language of water, about life and baptisms
and the miracle of wine. Niagara Falls as the New Jerusalem.
Sinners rolling like barrels over the fiery falls. No matter your
purpose or beliefs, Isaiah's door was open. He dubbed it *The
Prophet Isaiah's Second Coming House*. He lived inside his art,
inside his icon, inside the hand of God itself. He was God's
hand. He passed away in the plague year. His neighbors
believed. Pilgrims continued to come. There is wisdom in water.
We are sentient bags of water. We ride a water-ringed stone
through space.

III. The Prophecy

Among Isaiah's bric-a-brac is a 300-pound boulder from Three
Sisters Island mounted to the front of his house, a microcosm of
our blue rock. Isaiah visited the island daily, certain that it was
the future site of the Rapture. His voice had flattened into an
American accent but still held a Caribbean lilt, …*God said in the
last days — hallelujah! — he will raise up the prophets — praise the
Lord! — and they will come from far countries*. Iroquois shamans
once made sacrifices on the island of food and gifts, and
communed with the great spirit He-No, the Mighty Thunderer,
who was said to dwell at the base of the falls. New Agers say if
you listen carefully, you can hear voices whispering at He-No's
cave. So was it the voice of God you were hearing, O prophet?
Or something else? Isaiah tells us that coming to the Lord's cross
is our final chance—we can choose salvation, or we can choose
to be lost. Floods and water will come, as in the days of Noah.
Only the water will turn to fire, undrinkable, unswimmable,
unquenchable. The end of the world was set for 2014. Ten years
later, we are still waiting. The prophet was always alone. No

wife, no children. But the prophet was never alone, praise God, praise God. He had his work. He passed through the gates, alone, hallelujah. Did you make way for us, Isaiah? Did you maa or did you baa? And was it a river of flame, a paradise, or something else that can't be articulated except through shape and color?

maximally extended

· · ·

Zachery Brasier

Nestled in the darkness of space, Traveler 3e9.425 watched as swirling disks of matter circled the absolute black of the Door's core. They watched remnants of solar systems—planets, moons, and asteroids stripped apart by tidal forces—trace terminal orbital paths in silence, glowing red, orange, and white in the Baseline (and Associated) spectrums.

Beams of energized particles cut glowing vectors through the maelstrom, shining out through interstellar space, starting a journey to the distant reaches of the universe. Energetic though they were, the beams were nothing compared to the tremendous forces Traveler 3e9.425 would experience as their vessel traversed through the layered corridors of the Door.

There was nothing to fear from those cosmic energies; it had been a long time since anybody had fretted about a ship being pulverized by radiative bursts. Even without a ship, floating pure in the vacuum of space, their body could survive most of what the universe could throw at it. The ship was really only there for locomotion and as a shield against the absolute upper end of energy. They thought back to those distant ancestors whose heritage they, and society in general, had long surpassed.

This would be terrifying to those ancient beings, the people inhabiting the distant medium-sized rock that the geneticists, ethnobotanists, and long-historians had pinpointed as the birthplace of the race.

Doors: corridors through spacetime. When a star of sufficiently heavy mass started cannibalizing itself on the Higher Metals, burning heavier and heavier combinations of subatomic particles, it could no longer maintain the outward pressure necessary to hold gravity in a stable equilibrium. A tipping point would be reached; matter would collapse on itself, transforming a luminous star into an object which bent the underlying fabric of the cosmos so profoundly that light, once fallen into its orbit, could not escape. But angular momentum from the original star was always conserved. As the Door formed, its internal structure bloomed into a series of nested regions, each with peculiar properties, each a separate room in a spacetime labyrinth.

Outside, the Door ravenously consumed the matter around it, feeding mass through its dark, externally featureless maw. The darkness hid the complexity inside, as well as the fact—if navigated correctly—there was another universe on the other side of the three-dimensional hole.

People had been traveling through Doors for as long as anybody could remember. Traveler 3e9.425 thought about the first person to discover these objects and put the math together. Wondering about that nameless, ancient being was a fun diversion, like speculating about when the first berry was plucked from a tree and eaten. Somebody had to be the first, concepts don't just emerge out of the ether, but it was a trip to imagine making that initial intellectual leap without knowing where it would lead.

Existential thoughts, they realized, were probably common

for people who traveled through Doors. The ships and bodies could certainly handle the trip; people had survived so much more in the long course of history. But behind that technological and cultural confidence was a slight twinge of panic. Nobody had come back through a Door. As far as anybody could tell, it was impossible. Once one made the terminal descent between the two outer layers there was no going back. For all their high-tech progress, light still won out in the end, keeping its velocity to itself: a ship would have to travel at a photon's speed to come back. This unidirectionality also meant that nobody had been able to verify the expected internal structure of a Door. That was still a mystery until they could see it for themselves.

On the other side there would be another universe: the same laws, nothing unexpected. So many people had traveled through this specific Door that there was certainly a civilization on the other side. Why wouldn't there be? Society had extended through the stars and established itself everywhere it had landed, an infinitely complicated self-similar fractal of modernity.

Paranoiacs had argued throughout the long course of history that this was all based on math and speculation: there was no way to know that anything existed on the other side, that the maps were right, that there wasn't a hidden quirk of reality, that the ships could even survive the trip.

It's all theoretical. *An unnecessary distinction.*

It's a one-way journey. *What isn't?*

The engines silently pushed the ship towards the Door. Few people understood how the interstellar engines worked; they certainly didn't. There was a time, so the long-historians said, when space travelers had to know everything about their vessels, had to be experts on all the myriad systems. It had also been a time when astronauts had used minerals held in a non-crystalline solid phase to see the wonders outside their ships. Shockingly primitive. But probably the best they could do.

Now as the incandescent patterns grew larger, the engines

had almost completed the first part of their job. In some layers of the Door, the eddies of gravity and time would carry the ship on a true path. In others, the engines would have to push themselves to the limit, fighting the nearly irresistible warpings of path and trajectory. Careful planning allowed ships to dive through the outer layer, into the interstitial region lying underneath, and then back out. For energy production. But once the Inner Layer was breached there were no mathematically valid paths to come back.

The outer layer grew wide ahead, disks of energized matter slipping below the vessel, battering the hull with radiation. Suddenly, a shell of energy coursed over the ship, bathing it in bright, monochromatic unworldly light, before receding towards a point directly aft. They were in the Door.

Angular momentum was the ruler here, preserved from the original star. Trapped photons, whipped into an ever-tightening spiral, streamed past the ship. They watched the light streak into a smeared starfield.

Below, a slightly elongated oval of radiation: the Inner Layer. The engines fired up, decreasing the apogee of their chaotic orbit. Surprisingly, they felt no fear when the engines nudged the ship towards the point of no return.

Another radiation bath—the Inner Layer breached. Spacetime coordinates tipped forward, transforming an inextricable path through space into one defined only by time. The sky had split into three layers: a disk of rainbow energy in the future, and one in the past. In between, a whole lot of nothing. Black vacuum in the Baseline spectrum. Of course, the region they were in was not any larger than the size of the Door as viewed from outside. But the trifurcated vista implied a deep eternity, endlessness in all directions.

Nothing to do now but wait. The massive collection of matter dictated the relationship between the past and future, forcing anything in this layer to proceed along one course through time. Not even the ultra-powerful interstellar engines could make a difference: they only changed directional trajectories.

While the causality rotation had not caused any noticeable sensation, as they waited they started to understand from a perceptual level what that strange theoretical language had implied. The disk in the future grew in size, but did not seem to get any closer. It simply morphed through an indeterminate period of time, gradually encompassing the whole forward visual hemisphere. The disk in the past slowly shrunk.

Viewing the sights, they felt fear, and reality briefly lurched. How long had they been here? They tried to interrogate their biological internal clock. Nothing. Simply an evolution of this alien sky. Well, they had wanted something new.

Climbing up the side of an imaginary globe, the swath of energy that composed the forward disk surrounded them; a Broadspectrum, three-hundred-and-sixty-degree shell of radiation. Then, it began receding into the past, opening another black region directly forward. In the future.

When the dark future had completely bifurcated the sky, the flow of time tipped back to its usual configuration. Flying forward meant forward in space once again.

And now there was something interesting to see: an incandescent Ring directly ahead, a thin torus glowing and filling space with titanic surges of radiation. They wondered how the heat would feel without the protection of the ship. They shuddered for just a moment at the thought. With causality back to normal the engines lit up again, and the weird timelessness of the last region gave way to something more expected: a vectored course through space.

Space, however, did not want them to approach the Ring. The fabric of reality had started to flow like water, pushing them away from glowing torus. The engines could handle it. Yet, the readings showed that the machines were totally redlined, pushed to their limit as they gradually approached the strange object ahead. They remained completely silent, and flew as smooth as if they were traversing a placid air current. Even without knowing how the engines worked, Traveler 3e9.425 could appreciate the engineering perfection they embodied.

They were also impressed by the sheer magnitude of the energies being thrown off by the Ring. Streams of time flowed around the ship, the causal relations now acting like objects, colliding into each other and disintegrating into energy blasts that rivaled the birth of the universe, visible when viewing all the frequencies at once. Even living in modern society, with all the wonders that were part of everyday life, this was completely outside of their experience. They watched in wonder as the dance of energy filled space, exploding across the dark sky in a surreal swirl of full-spectrum color. Dangerous, world-killing, star-collapsing color. Planetary life held nothing that could place the spectacle in context. As up-to-date as they were on trendy contemporary thought, it was impossible to conceptualize how a stream of time could act as an object; how it could collide, splinter, and vaporize.

The view was overwhelming when viewed in Totality. Back to Baseline.

Against a dark, starless background, the only visual cue that the ship was moving was the slow squashing of the Ring. They would have to come in close to the Ring near its equator, then skim over it at low altitude. Only some paths near the Ring led to the future and the next universe waiting there. The navigation computer was pre-programmed with a set of course corrections that would bring it near the toroid of energy at the right angle, swiftly firing the engines in lightning-fast bursts to traverse the absurdly-complicated, geodesically-determined orbital paths.

Once head on with the torus, the thick region of energy (uniformly bright, no clear differentiation on its surface) started to grow, signaling their approach. At the last moment, when it seemed they would crash into the glowing object, the ship pulled up, making hundreds of course corrections within a split second. They pulled into a poloidal course, tracing an arc in space, scraping over the top of the torus.

There was, naturally, no point of reference to track their movement over a uniform region of energy. Below and ahead, forming a curved limb, the universe simply glowed. Despite this they knew, at some deep, primally human level, that they were traveling at astronomical speeds. Embracing the moment, they howled with excitement. The view tilted up and back into straight black, speeding towards a disk faintly glowing in the sky.

Flipping the view aft, they could see the Ring disappearing behind them. Back to forward view, and there was a disk of stars directly ahead. It looked as if the whole night sky had been squeezed into a little circle.

Rapidly, this region approached and then in, a blink of the eye, burst into a normal celestial sphere, septillions of stars flecking the sky. A whole new universe.

They knew to look back. Behind them, one last disk had appeared against the firmament. It was indescribable beauty, infinite complexity; the whole history of their previous universe written in energy: the beginning to the end, splashed against a backdrop of stars, fading away.

As it vanished, the comms system lit up. A symphony of signals, isotropic sources of information. Lots of welcome notes. The ship's computer recognized every signal, and could read everything. Civilization once again, just like on the other side. Processing a fraction of the available data, they found a planet that looked interesting, having a large enough population to fit their tastes and dozens of explorable moons. A thought command to the ship, the stars tilted, and Traveler 3e9.425 flew on.

looking for death in northwest florida

. . .

Lauren Scharhag

Even I had never seen a corpse lying in the middle of the highway like that before, and I come from a zip code known as the Murder Factory. Florida traffic is its own malevolent force, like a tornado, born of colliding fronts: Jersey retirees and Ohio vacationers, Arizona spring breakers and Dakota snowbirds. I hadn't known that this is what I'd come to Florida to find. *Be still and know that I am God.* Death is the doorway to God. Sometimes, I think it really is that simple. A Jewish scholar told me once that the root for "be still" in Hebrew is actually "let go." I thought I did let go, of everything. I left it all behind and made the thousand-mile trek to get here.

When Death first appeared to me, he took the form of a snowy owl, white as the Florida sand. White as Epcot Center. White as the plastic shopping bags that snag on tree branches and strangle sea turtles, as the sheets covering traffic victims. Death said, *Build a scaffold. Make of yourself an offering to mosquitoes.* At dusk, I climb the lookout stations and wait for the six-pointed prick of their mouth needles. Despite all the rain, pine straw turns this whole place into a tinderbox. Off Santa Rosa Island, they're conducting munitions testing. Eighty thousand acres of pine in

237

Conecuh National Forest. Nothing prepares you for the scent of Christmas trees on tropical air, surrounded by grass so green it's almost neon. Just past the Alabama line, a floriculturist's harvest, acres of tiger lilies like a lake of fire. Death's brother lives here, too, the trickster god, Florida Man. Florida has the highest number of shark attacks in the country, and you will know this terrible twosome by their great white grins. Together, they take life and tell it slant, making everything as crooked as the peninsula on which we stand, which they are pulling, inch by inch, into the sea. Their supply of teeth is endless.

Next, Death sent me a bouquet of crows. He said, *Marinate yourself in key lime juice and lie down for the fire ants.* I spread my feathers over sandy loam, lie back, and wait for a sinkhole to swallow me, for a lightning strike to immolate me, for the graze of wild hog tusks, for the boa constrictor girdle. You'd think there wouldn't be a need for cryptids when there's already so much waiting to kill you, and yet, this place spawned Gatorman, Skunk Ape, the Sea Devil, the Wampus Cat. It's an urban legend that lovebugs were engineered in a laboratory at the University of Florida. Twice a year, they swarm and mate. Lovebug couples drift through the air, tail-to-tail. Copulation lasts two to three days; they live only two to seven. They join until the female is fertilized, at which point, she detaches, lays her eggs, and dies. Lovebugs have highly acidic body chemistry, and they are attracted to exhaust fumes. So, as the swarms die en masse, they stick to cars. If not removed quickly, their bodies will eat away at paint and chrome, leaving pits and etches, Death's Braille. Their black bodies clog radiator air passages, smear across windshield glass. More collisions. More ruined vehicles.

And gators—always gators. As with Florida Man, I am convinced there is a divine destructive force there, too. A chaos energy. Every morning, Florida seems to rise from its beds of white mist. Every day, rain. The sky split between sun and storm. A tug-of-war in heaven. These pale borders wide enough to slip through, into whatever world lies beyond the rift, beyond light and dark and hot and cold. This humidity is violence, is violence, is violence. When stalking avatars, you have to think like an avatar, but know this: you risk possession. When you catch them, they catch you right back.

Never had I seen so many Lamborghinis, so many Bentleys and Rolls-Royces. Never had I met so many wealthy European expats. Never had I seen so many shacks tucked away on dirt roads that don't appear on any GPS or map. So many people without transportation, walking along gravel shoulders with umbrellas to keep the sun off. On the Sound, the houseless fish from piers with cane poles. Someone tells me that human trafficking is a big problem in the hospitality industry, which explains why so many of the resort workers have Slavic accents and haunted eyes. They bring me key lime pie and sweet rum drinks garnished with orange slices. In the groves, I taste the bitterness of unripe citrus, all acid and pith. Razorbacks scream and rut in midnight forests. During cold snaps, invasive iguanas drop from tree limbs. Glass lizards shed their tails fleeing predators. There's an octopus marooned in a parking garage. Florida sand is so white because it is actually quartz crystals washed down out of the Appalachians. All of Florida is on eastern time, except the Panhandle, which is central. Hours disappear as you cross from one time zone to another. I don't know where they go. Somewhere, Death is waiting for Disney's frozen head to thaw.

My Midwestern instincts are useless in this land without storm cellars. I scratch at the earth and find only the ocean rushing up to greet me. Death's trail vanishes beneath pine pollen's sulfur-yellow drifts. Traffic is backed up on the I-4 where ghost hunters drive up and down, hoping to catch a glimpse or a snapshot of yellow fever apparitions who are said to be buried beneath the asphalt. Of orbs or phantom hitchhikers. Among the pirate parades and the perennial saw palmetto, among the pelicans and the red tide, the Spanish moss and the Pindo palms. Death's flag is a feather, an algae bloom, a drape of lichen, a fruit, a frond, a plastic sheet. I do DMT, the spirit molecule, trying to simulate the dying brain. All I see is a gate that is closed to me. Years ago, when we took my grandfather off life support, we all encouraged him to go with God, to *let go.* God is a vision of the dying. A spear in the side, your body filling up with toxins. When the Category 5 comes, we retreat inland, Ray Charles and Tom Petty on our playlist. At a Hattiesburg diner, Death and I meet up at last. He wears a yellow shirt, or it could just be dusted with pine pollen. I buy him breakfast. He puts hot sauce on his eggs and drinks his coffee black. A voice in my head says, *Let go. Let go. Let go.* This body is just another pit stop. Death says, *The road is all there is.*

baby brain

. . .

E.W.H. Thornton

CW: themes may be offensive to some readers

Jane nodded off while nursing for a handful of seconds and awoke to find that the baby had become permanently attached to her left breast.

Jane first thought it must be an error on her part but no, the more she investigated, the more certain she became that some sort of fleshen mass had permanently conjoined the baby's mouth and her nipple.

The situation unsettled Jane.

She called out to her husband. Guilt flowered inside Jane as she called out to him again with more volume since this was her husband's predetermined time to grab a few shreds of desperately needed sleep, but she knew he would understand. If anything since the baby's arrival they'd come to understand one another too much, the outer vistas of themselves shrinking until they shared the same singular, laser focus to the exclusion of all else.

Jane's husband entered the room, rubbing the spot above his forehead where a persistent headache he'd had since the baby came waxed and waned.

"Whallo?" he muttered, the words 'what' and 'hello' colliding in his mental fog.

"Sorry," Jane said.

"Is the baby all right?" he asked. Jane looked down at the baby and her left breast, and saw that the former appeared to be in no distress whatsoever.

"I think so."

"Are you all right?" She looked down at the point where the baby's mouth and her left nipple had merged.

"I don't know," she said, wondering how this might affect the upcoming Reveal Party.

***

Jane's husband went back to work because he had to.

Jane went to see the baby's pediatrician.

She entered the exam room to find a doctor a decade her junior seated before a computer and typing furiously.

"Come in," the doctor said without taking her eyes off the screen. "Sit down."

After a very long time the doctor stopped typing and looked at Jane with a start, apparently surprised she was still there.

"What seems to be the problem?" Jane revealed the baby and her left breast and explained her situation. The pediatrician looked confused. "So what's the problem?"

"The problem is that this shouldn't be happening," Jane said. The doctor frowned.

"The world as we know it is full of things that shouldn't be happening but are, not to mention things that should be happening but are not. What do you want me to do about it?" Jane struggled to respond. The doctor's gaze flicked back to the computer, a covetous expression on her youthful countenance.

"Please just help me," Jane implored. "This can't go on." The doctor sighed.

"Please get up on the exam table," Jane obliged. The doctor

produced a magnifying glass and examined the affected area. "Yep," she said. "That's a baby's mouth attached to a nipple, all right."

"How do you remove it?"

"Remove it? Forcefully? If you exercise a little patience it might naturally detach on its own after eighteen years or so."

"I can't wait that long."

"You know, it's easier to change your mind than your body. Consider: Females are the only creatures that are born with an empty room inside them that exists for the sole purpose of being inhabited by someone else. Consider—"

"Can you help me?" Jane cried out.

"What do you think I've been doing? Besides, I'm a pediatrician. Treating an adult woman like yourself would constitute malpractice on my part. Of course, if you went to a doctor for adults, treating the baby would constitute malpractice for them. Quite a bind you've fashioned for yourself." She sounded almost impressed.

Jane was forced to accept that the doctor was not going to help her. Her eyes flicked to the computer and she noticed her pediatrician had neglected to log out of her account. Jane decided she had to access it, though she would have to find some way to get rid of the doctor first.

"I have to fix this," Jane said. "I have to fix it now, before the Reveal Party. If this is still a problem by then it'll be bad for me— not just me, the baby, my husband, my co-workers, my friends, my family."

"Who's your husband?" The pediatrician asked, her interest piqued for what seemed like the first time. Jane told her. The doctor's face lit up.

"Wow, *he's* your husband?"

"You know him?"

"All doctors know about him! He's famous for being the stuntman who's survived the most injuries ever! Honestly it's incredible he was able to impregnate you given the damage his genitals have endured over the years." Jane was confused. She'd never noticed her stuntman husband being afflicted with such catastrophic injuries. She wondered if they were thinking of the same person, then had an idea.

"You know, he came with me." She told the baby's pediatrician. "He's filming in the Whole Foods across the street. If you —" There was no need for Jane to elaborate on her lie, the doctor was gone, her chair overturned on the sterile floor, the door to the exam room hanging open where the doctor had burst through it.

Jane sat down before the computer.

She wanted to look at her own medical records so she could search for any possible hint of a prior malady that might explain what was happening to her, but she also wanted to access the records of other patients to see if this had happened to anyone else, and what they'd done about it.

Jane couldn't find her own records and she was on the verge of giving up when she happened to find a case thirty five years ago that bore a strong resemblance to her own. She'd just managed to photograph the computer screen displaying the basic information when the pediatrician returned.

"Wow," the doctor said wonderingly. "I'm still starstruck. I had no idea they were filming the next Whole Foods movie just across the street, I can't wait to see it. I know everyone is tired of the Grocery Cinematic Universe these days, but I think *Whole Foods 4: Hummus With A Vengeance* is going to take things in a fresh, gritty direction. It was great meeting your husband. They didn't allow pictures, but he did give me an autograph.'The pediatrician held up a piece of paper with her husband's name written on it. "Can you tell it's written in blood? It started out red but it looks kind of brown now."

"What should I do about this?" Jane gestured at her chest and the baby. "The problem isn't even just that the baby is constantly suckling, it's only my left breast, so the right one isn't getting drained, it's so full it hurts."

Her pediatrician's smile imploded. She sighed wearily while walking over to a nearby cabinet. She opened it and, after a great deal of fishing around, withdrew a plastic contraption the size of a soda bottle.

"Here." She tossed it to Jane.

"Go milk yourself."

Jane returned home to find that her husband's skin was coming loose, detaching from his muscles as it grew increasingly pliable and gelatinous in a process that spread from the top of his head to the soles of his feet.

"What happened?" she asked, keeping her tone neutral as she struggled to hide her revulsion.

"I don't know," Jane's husband replied. "My headache's gone, that's a relief." He gently poked his skull. "It's softer than ever, but at least it doesn't hurt anymore."

Jane's husband continued his work as a stuntman in a limited capacity, only appearing as flammable clothing or parachutes or any other fabric routinely subject to danger.

Her husband's new state created new difficulties. Not only did everyday chores he'd once readily performed become prolonged, exhausting ordeals, but the worst part by far was the lose skin's effect on his face, the way it obscured his eyes and mouth to render his expressions virtually unreadable.

Jane showed her husband the picture she'd taken at her pediatrician's office depicting the basic medical records of the only other woman who'd had her condition, and asked him to try to find her. Jane's husband obliged and spent much of his free time online, scouring social media accounts and online support groups and mommybloggers of all stripes. Despite his efforts he found no trace of her, ending each day with nothing to show for his work except hands that looked like waffles due to the keyboard's imprint on his loose skin.

He experienced much more success with maintaining Jane's presence on the various social media platforms she was too exhausted to maintain. Once in a while she would review his work and be both amazed and mildly disturbed by how well he imitated her, liking the things she liked and disliking the things she disliked and commenting how she would comment and RSVPing for the Reveal Party just as she would have, despite her growing reservations. He also performed the unglamorous grunt work of blocking the endless legions of dummy accounts bombarding Jane with vapid targeted content: quotes set against stock landscape backgrounds and said things like "Pregnancy is a sickness heavy with future possibilities. —Friedrich Wilhelm Nietzsche." Other phrases had no attribution, sentences like "We float in a sea of others' pain," and "People often keep secrets of which secrecy knows nothing," and "Do we love the people in our family or do we just know them too well to bring ourselves to fully hate them?" and "The greatest tragedies are personal and silent" appearing out of thin air and landing without purpose.

The baby couldn't cry on its own since its mouth was permanently occupied, so instead it channeled its outbursts through Jane, who would correspondingly scream for extended periods of time.

A few days after her husband's condition revealed itself, Jane woke in the middle of the night to find that a portion of her husband's loose flesh was penetrating her body, that it had narrowed into a thousand filaments so fine she hadn't felt them burrowing into her skin.

Jane released an eruption of screams that were for once hers and hers alone. She cried out for her husband to wake up, and while she couldn't see his eyes open, his muttered "whallo" was cut off by his own revolted outburst as he saw what his body was doing.

"What's happening?!" he cried. Jane had no answer beyond her panicked outbursts. The baby was awake now and its screams were intermingling with her own to the point where she could barely breathe. "Grab onto something!" Jane's husband scrambled out of their bedroom as quickly as his sagging flesh would permit, stumbling and groping his way through their living room and kitchen.

It was only when he'd reached the opposite end of their shared domicile that he finally reached the end of his skin's tether and could begin pulling with enough force to uproot it.

Jane had been fortunate enough to wake up before the tendrils could burrow deeply into her, though that was no consolation in the moment. While her husband's skin had been extremely careful to inflict no pain during its invasion, it felt no similar compunction as it was forcibly removed. Each tendril resisted its extraction, writhing and scraping as it flailed for purchase inside her, and Jane was forced to endure what felt like ages of itching and burning until the entire system was finally extracted to become a twitching heap on the floor.

Jane could only watch as it writhed and shivered in a way that looked more liquid than solid, boiling with the synchronized chaos of swarming ants.

The mass withdrew, sliding out the bedroom door as her husband reeled it in, pulling hand over hand to gather it up as he worked his way back toward Jane. She was going to tell him to stay away but it seemed he had already reached the same conclusion, and he hovered just outside the bedroom doorway.

They both waited to speak to one another until the baby, and therefore Jane, was done screaming.

They waited a long time.

Jane's husband moved out.

———

Jane went back to work because she had to.

Her coworkers welcomed her return with open arms, each one repeating the phrase they had been taught during mandatory sensitivity training.

Jane returned to her desk and saw that a picture of her sonogram remained on her cubicle wall in the exact spot where she'd pinned it up what felt like a lifetime ago. She remembered showing the image to her coworkers half a year ago, a shape of hazy meaning she was for some reason obliged to share with all and sundry. They dubbed it adorable, but it did not feel adorable; the thing taking up space inside her felt heavy and ungainly and occasionally invasive, like an invited guest who had overstayed their welcome, oblivious to their host's growing discomfort.

Jane went to the lactation room three or four times a day, a converted broom closet whose single window had been covered with aluminum foil and duct tape to ensure privacy. Images related to nursing covered the walls, medical diagrams of mammary glands, multiple frescoes depicting great moments in the history of lactation that ranged from Romulus and Remus suckling at the teats of a she-wolf to the actress Heather Graham breast feeding in the two thousand nine film *The Hangover* directed by Todd Philips and starring Bradley Cooper and Zach Galifianakis in twin breakout roles.

She spent much of the time at her desk scouring the internet for any trace of the woman who'd had the same condition as her thirty five years ago. She found nothing and tended to circle back to her own social media accounts for the tiny dopamine hit she'd come to depend on, but despite her husband's best efforts they were still clogged with useless maxims inflicted by a seemingly endless torrent of dummy accounts, things like "People, like windows and dams, are most notable when they break," and "Faith emerges at the point where hope becomes intolerable."

The way the mysterious patient had utterly erased herself seemed so impossible in the age of internet ubiquity it made Jane wonder if the patient had somehow managed to utterly detach from reality, something Jane wished she had thought of herself. She was fantasizing about just how wonderful residing in an impenetrable shell of anonymity would be when one of Jane's coworkers told her the boss wanted to see her in his office. Her general exhaustion conspired to keep the world at a distance, and it was some time after she took a seat across from her boss that she realized she was being fired.

"Whallo?" she muttered, clawing her way back to full conscious awareness.

"I said we're giving you leave, Jane."

"Unpaid?"

"Is there any other kind?"

"When can I come back?"

"That's not up to me."

"Who is it up to?"

"I don't know, you'd have to ask them. I am proud to bestow this beautiful parting gift." Jane's boss placed a cardboard box atop his desk with the reverential air of a father giving away his daughter at her wedding. "The finest cardboard money can buy, guaranteed to hold objects like nobody's business." Jane's boss sensually stroked the box, which responded with an affirmative shiver. "Naturally, security will be escorting you out of the building. Don't worry, it's just standard procedure." Jane's boss nodded to a space behind her. Jane turned and saw a security guard looming over her, a human paunch cocooned in black kevlar. "Now, to ensure a safe transition, we are going to have to taze you in advance. Don't worry, it's just standard procedure, purely a precautionary measure, routine."

As the security guard withdrew the taser gun from his belt Jane seized the box and held it up as a shield. Her boss exclaimed "Look out, it's made of one hundred percent recycled materials!" but it was too late. The steel barbs shot out to become lodged in the box and commenced channeling their powerful electric current. The box screamed in pain and Jane threw it in the security guard's direction. The box opened its mouth to expose rows of fangs that clamped down on the security guard's left forearm. He screamed and commenced flailing in a futile effort to dislodge his gnashing aggressor. Jane's boss leapt up and attempted to pull the box off the security guard before he became hurt enough to qualify for paid medical leave, and Jane fled.

She clasped the baby tightly to her breast as she ran for what felt like the first time in years, fleeing not just her attackers but her own troubled mind, struggling not to think of the effect losing her job would have on the upcoming Reveal Party as she snatched the sonogram picture off the wall of her cubicle and escaped the building with it.

Jane fell asleep for a few seconds while milking herself and awoke to find that the breast pump had become permanently attached to her right breast just as the baby had become permanently attached to her left breast, an intimate union of flesh and plastic that made it difficult to tell where Jane ended and the appliance began.

She fainted, lingered in unconsciousness for an indeterminate period of time, and awoke to find that the breast pump and the baby had merged with one another.

Jane reflexively called out her husband's name before remembering he'd been forced to remove himself from her life, managing only a meager "Whallo," before lapsing into silence.

She informed her husband of the situation over the phone, and he offered his sympathies. She looked at her social media and saw another dummy account had posted 'Do we die or finally escape ourselves?' and 'History is poor decisions romanticized.'

The new biomechanical organism continued to grow. Jane wondered how long this could go on, how long she could stand it, where her limit was; what would happen when she finally exceeded it.

Jane awoke in the middle of the night from unfathomable dreams and found that her husband was in bed with her. A large mass of gelatinous flesh linked him to her chest, and through the midnight gloom she could see that the biomechanical entity was no longer attached to her but drifting toward the greater mass of her husband's globular body via a crude conveyor belt fashioned from his mutable flesh.

"Whallo you doing?" she mumbled.

"Jane, I can take it away," her husband said in a voice dripping with sympathy and loose flesh. "I can be like a seahorse, I can bear it myself, you don't have to carry it alone!"

Jane reached out, clawed her way through the loose skin and wrapped her fingers around what was, at her best guess, her husband's throat.

"Give it back now."

"Jane—" He choked through his constricted windpipe. "Think— About it— Everything— You've been through—" Jane squeezed harder until speech was no longer an option.

"Give it back right now, or I swear to god, I will kill you."

The flow of his skin reversed itself. Jane let go as the biomechanical organism was reattached to her chest and the majority of her husband withdrew to the opposite side of the bedroom.

"I'm sorry," he croaked.

Jane examined the entity on her chest, confirming that everything had been returned to its appointed place. She considered demanding that her husband surrender his key to their home but realized there was no point, there would always be some tiny aperture he could ooze through to get back in her life. If only she knew how the woman who'd survived the same ailment thirty five years ago had managed to endure it, the violations and infiltrations and-

Jane's eyes went wide.

"I know how you can make it up to me," she said. "I have an idea."

***

Jane assumed the best posture she'd exhibited in weeks, raising the biomechanical entity attached to her chest up to her laptop's camera for inspection.

"Wow." Her distant physician marveled. "That's fucked up." Jane angled the screen back a few degrees, tilting the camera further upward to make sure her pediatrician couldn't see her husband ooze into the computer.

Once data was on a computer it was never really gone. The complete medical file of the mystery woman who'd had her condition thirty five years ago had to be on a server somewhere. Jane just had to keep the doctor connected and talking long enough for her husband to find the data and send it back to her.

"Have you ever seen anything like this before?" Jane asked.

"No, but given the vastness of the universe, it's safe to assume I haven't seen most things."

"Whallo's going to happen to me?"

"Are you familiar with what happens when a butterfly comes out of its cocoon?"

"Yes..."

"It'll be like that, except the cocoon will be, you know, you."

"Are you serious?"

"Often. Not always."

"What can I do?"

"Given the constraints you're currently operating under, not much."

"Isn't there some way to mitigate the damage? Giving birth to this thing could kill me."

"The same was true of the infant you birthed. It didn't bother you last time."

"The last time was different."

"How?"

"It was natural."

"You're right. Giving birth is a completely natural process." Jane's doctor cupped her chin thoughtfully. "Indeed, most abominable things are."

"You have to help me. There must be something you can do."

"That all depends on you. What do you want, Jane?"

Jane was suddenly baffled. She couldn't remember the last time someone had asked her that. It was as if she'd somehow lost her capacity to want things for herself, that it had become a vestigial part of her that had naturally fallen away, her desires shed and abandoned like flakes of dead skin.

Jane hesitated too long and could tell the doctor's attention was beginning to wander. Aware she could terminate the call at any time, Jane blurted out the first thing that entered her head.

"I want you!" Jane's doctor gave her a dubious look, but at least she had her full attention. "I want you to be an integral part of me and my husband's life. We can do a ménage à trois, proto-second wave feminism thing like the trio that created Wonder Woman. You know, one full time breadwinner, one full time caretaker, and someone who splits time between the two roles. It won't be perfect, but what relationship is in this workaday world?"

"You want me to help raise…" Jane's doctor directed a pointed finger at the biomechanical entity embedded in her chest, "that?"

"You'll love it. Parenthood is a wondrous adventure. Also my husband could use his connections as a stuntman to get you a role as a background actor in *Piggly Wiggly 3: Cornstarch of Madness*."

"I'll have to think about it." The doctor moved to end the call.

"One time offer!" Jane cried out. "This is a very in-demand

position. We have hundreds of other qualified applicants vying for the role. I need a hard 'yes' or 'no' right now."

Jane's doctor pursed her lips. Her eyes fixed on Jane as if she was noticing her patient for the first time.

"It seems like…" The doctor's eyes flicked to the biomechanical entity. "A struggle."

"Yes." Jane nodded emphatically. "But a glorious struggle. Arguably the greatest struggle, perhaps only comparable to serving in a war. As the saying goes: 'The only way to have it all is by giving a significant portion of it away.'"

"Wow. Profound. Did you think of that yourself?" Jane shook her head.

"No, some dummy account spammed my social media with it, but the point still stands." The doctor's expression grew distant, then snapped into fixed resolve.

"All right!" she declared, slapping her thigh for emphasis. "By god, I'll do it! And that background actor role is a sure thing, right?"

"Absolutely!" Jane affirmed.

"Great! Say, now that our relationship has entered this profound new phase, I have some information that might help. It seems another woman had a problem similar to yours thirty five years ago; do you want me to send you her personal information?"

"Uh, yeah," Jane stammered, "If it's not a problem."

"No problem at all." Jane's doctor struck exactly two computer keys. "There you go. By the way, would you come and pick up your husband? He seeped out of my computer and has been puddled in the corner for a while. I think he accidentally made contact with a video game while he was in the internet, he keeps muttering things like 'learn the meta' and 'play your class' and 'fucking kill yourself', it's a little distracting." Jane stared at the full medical records of the woman who'd had her condition thirty five years ago, mouth agape. "So Jane, now that we-" Jane slammed the laptop shut as a chill resonated through her body, a shock so nerve-wracking even the biomechanical entity shuddered, eliciting a foreboding creak from the semitransparent chitinous material encasing it.

A dazed Jane checked the time. It seemed like she had just enough spare hours between now and the Reveal Party to do what she had to.

Jane put a shirt on, steeled herself, and went off to see the woman who'd had her condition thirty five years ago.

—Hi, Mom.

—They control the weather with lasers from space. The solar panels, they're huge, the size of aircraft carriers, you think all that power is just for sending radio signals?

—It's nice to see you too.

—They're using the lasers to change the weather to trick people, to deceive them into thinking global warming is real.

—Mom, I have to ask you about something important.

—They want to trick people into thinking the world is over-populated, to trick them into not having children.

—And by 'people' you mean 'white people', and by 'they' you mean 'Jews'.

—There's new evidence.

—That's not why I'm here, Mom.

—Tell me your e-mail address.

—I'm not going to do that.

—Why not?

—Because you'll send me ten links a day, all of them… I'm not going to argue with you about this, that's not why I'm here, I need your help with something that's real, that matters.

—Do you think deceiving the whole world doesn't matter?

—Look

—Because it does.

—LOOK! LOOK AT IT! LOOK AT WHAT HAPPENED TO ME!

—Oh. That. I guess congratulations are in order.

—Is that really all you can say?

—Please cover yourself.

—The same thing happened to you.

—I suppose it did.

—I was the one. I did to you what it's doing to me now. The same thing.

—Yes.

—How do I not remember?

—We all forget the vast majority of the... unhelpful things we did as children. If we remembered every instance of our early youth when we were selfish or cruel, we'd go mad with guilt.

—This is the stuff I needed you to tell me! But no, you refuse to speak to me about anything other than insane conspiracy bullshit.

— I tried to tell you.

—No you didn't.

—I did. Who do you think has been creating all those dummy accounts to post on your social media? I conveyed what I could. It's not my fault you broke off all avenues of communication.

—No, it is completely your fault, Mom. I didn't want to cut you out of my life. It's one of the hardest things I've ever had to do.

—There's a cabal of satanist pedophile elites.

—But you gave me no choice.

—It doesn't matter who's in power, they all serve the same master.

—I want to love you.

—They abduct children from all over the world.

—But you make it impossible.

—They drain their blood to make a serum that keeps them from aging.

—Literally impossible.

—They replace the children with holograms. The parents never know.

—You care more about that shit than you do about me. You should've told me it was like this.

—What could I have said that would have changed anything? 'Hey, you shit yourself and your hair falls out, have fun.' What are you going to tell *that* when it grows up? How can you possibly say it in a way that doesn't hurt?

—How did you manage to free yourself?

—Who says I did?

—But you survived.

—That's debatable. The act of parenting teaches you things about yourself you would rather never know.

—So you hide it. Let it fester.

—They encourage sexual depravity in schools, they want to trick children into thinking it's normal.

—There are a million real bad things in the world you could actually help with. You could have helped me, but no, it's not important enough, it's not saving the world, it's not making you a cosmic messiah.

—Have you ever actually been to Australia? Have you seen it with your own eyes?

—You don't know how much seeing you like this hurts. It feels like I'm talking to the person who murdered the real mother I loved. Who loved me.

—You can see Chicago from the other side of Lake Michigan. No curvature there.

—Well, this has been enlightening, but there's somewhere I have to be.

—Fine. Walk away.

—I'm going to the Reveal Party.

—The Reveal Party? You're actually going?

—Yes.

—They'll eat you alive.

—Yes. I'm counting on it.

the reveal party

Anna Silverburgh greeted Jane with a firm hug.

"Jane, so glad you could make it, you look wonderful!"

"Thank you Anna. You look positively breathtaking," Jane said, hoping to make up with hyperbole what her voice lacked in enthusiasm.

"You're just in time, we're about to start."

All the parents had pooled their money to rent out one of the mid-sized ballrooms at a Best Western Hotel. The space was almost completely full, and Jane was forced to run a gauntlet of social niceties as she worked her way toward the stage erected at the center of the ballroom.

Half of Laurie Tate's face had been annexed by something that resembled an oversized Venus flytrap made of skin, the two flaps sealed by a membrane of scar tissue. Its stiff, intertwined cilia teeth protruded a foot or so into the air where they quivered like antennae in concert with the motion of Laurie Tate remaining eye.

"Great to see you."

"You too."

Jamelia Wittles, who'd birthed twins, had two large red teratomas emerging from the back of her legs. Both lumpen masses of bulging tissue were dotted with teeth and bone and tufts of hair, while their tiny slit mouths moaned in protest with each step she took.

"It's a pleasure to see you."

"The pleasure's all mine."

Jim Thurgood was difficult to recognize since the vast majority of his body was covered in drooping semitransparent cysts where shapes of vague life drifted through what appeared to be a mix of blood and Pedialyte.

"Hey, what's up?"

"You know, the usual."

The room fell silent as Anna Silverburgh mounted the high circular stage at the center of the ballroom. She plucked the microphone from its stand and addressed the parents through a bulletproof smile.

"Hello everyone, and welcome!"

Polite applause.

"Let the Reveal Party commence!" Anna Silverburgh beckoned offstage. Laurie Tate accepted the microphone and replaced her atop the stage.

Laurie Tate raised the microphone to the remaining half of her mouth not annexed by the fleshy Venus flytrap and spoke the words.

"Everyone before me has done it incorrectly. I have learned from their mistakes, and I will do it correctly." She returned the microphone to its stand and began.

The long, stiff tendrils emerging from the Venus flytrap curled back upon themselves in a motion like burning paper, then burrowed one by one into the span of scar tissue dividing the two lobes. They tensed, straining with all possible effort. For a long time nothing happened, then the length of flesh gave way all at once, tearing apart with a sound like broken bone punching through flesh.

A clear gelatinous substance spilled out along with a small figure consisting of something that looked like Spanish moss made of brain matter.

Polite applause.

Laurie Tate bent down, picked it up, and cradled it in her arms as she left the stage.

Jamelia Wittles took her place and said the words.

"Everyone before me has done it incorrectly. I have learned from their mistakes, and I will do it correctly."

She held her legs together and the twin teratomas began to merge. Neither of them had enough teeth or hair to form anything resembling a face on their own, and the same was true after they joined with one another, their crude effort at bringing the necessary facial features into being resulting in failure as only the vaguest hints of what might be a nose emerged while the eyes and mouth were barely implied by thin slits filled with teeth or hair.

The thing that wasn't a face peeled itself off Jamelia Wittles, sloughing away to land on the stage with a wet plop where it commenced flailing like an insect stuck on its back. Jamelia Wittles bent down and picked it up, no mean feat considering what her legs had been through.

Polite applause.

Jamelia Wittles was helped off the stage by Jim Thurgood, who took her place.

Jane worked her way toward the edge of the stage, knowing she was next as Jim Thurgood took hold of the microphone and said the words.

"Everyone before me has done it incorrectly. I have learned from their mistakes, and—"

The fluid filled cysts covering his body all burst at once, spraying pungent, yellowish red liquid across the stage and onto the nearest parents who lifted the plastic sheets they'd brought in anticipation of being in the splash zone. Jim Thurgood collapsed while a hundred thin slivers of pale meat flopped.

Polite applause.

Jim Thurgood crawled around the stage, gathering up what offspring he could. He stepped down, muttering "Good luck" to Jane as he staggered away.

Jane removed her shirt, climbed atop the stage, and held the microphone to her mouth.

"Ev—" Jane coughed. She could feel the biomechanical entity's eagerness, its profound desire to be born. It was ready, but was she? She was on the verge of fleeing when she saw a familiar face in the crowd, then another, then another.

They were all here. The doctor, her husband, her mother, her coworkers and boss and the security guard who'd tried to taze her and the box that was still chewing on his arm—They were all here! All of them smiling and making encouraging gestures, radiating solidarity!

Jane realized there was no such thing as 'ready'. There was only blind hope, leaps of faith, trailblazing into the great unknown, and it was sometimes difficult, but without it life wouldn't exist, not really, not in any way that mattered.

Jane raised the microphone to her lips.

"I promise I will try my best."

She braced herself, took a deep breath, and began to push.

Jane was ripped in two.

Her body split apart vertically, a divide that went from the crown of her head down to her groin, separating the halves of herself.

A Perfect Golden Being emerged, tall and fit and radiant and beautiful, absent blemish of any kind.

The crowd erupted into rapturous applause, cheering so hard the ballroom seemed to shake.

Jane's two parts looked at one another from where they'd fallen.

The Perfect Golden Being opened its Perfect Golden Mouth and began to scream.

Before long, everyone joined in.

***

Communion.

rolling over indecision

. . .

Brian U. Garrison

Icosahedron is as fair as fair can be
when tempting fate among twenty options.

Dodecahedron is presumably also random
if you've narrowed your options to twelve.

Decahedron can decide among ten options,
unbiased, but since when is any waypoint
so clearly delineated?

Octahedron may prove handy
if you're needing to decide
which arm to chop off the giant squid
first, but you're probably safest
to sever them all as soon as possible.

Cube is what many people are familiar with
for random numbers, but life is no game,
and the rolls stopped feeling random years ago.

Tetrahedron flips everything down to four.

Coin, or a similar thin cylinder,
can give you yes or no.

But everything comes down
to one thing. Are you alive?
Yes!

pilgrim in the ruins

. . .

Mike Adamson

Once these halls thronged with joyous life, but now they are home to the crow and the field mouse, and to the climbing ivy whose frayed emerald tendrils outline arch, buttress and column. The golden leaves of autumn are swept by the wind's broom in cloisters where once song and chant made the living stone hum.

So hard it is to come back, a lone figure in hooded robe, who walks where the dreams of yesterday are the desolation of today. How did we come to this? All was vibrant in the belief of life everlasting, of spirit indomitable, yet now the wind taunts my memories as it plays a demon's fife through crumbling towers.

It was not war, nor pestilence, neither plague nor famine, but the ultimate weakness of the animistic human spark. For we placed ourselves above the world and fancied humanity some intermediary between the mortal and the divine, closer the other than the one; but this was fallacy, and presumption to sit down with the gods when we are of Earth born; and imagine proximity to heaven excused every excess. Nature shall have the last laugh, and to see the swallows' nests high on walls of once-polished marble reminds me of this. Where roofs are fallen in and the rain makes a ruin of chambers once inviolate, and where the dust of the years stirs only to the prints of big cats and their prey, these are mute testimony to the fall of all our high towers.

But the sun shines. Long rays of light through arched cloisters and surviving high windows write a beauty upon floors and make magic of dust motes in the air, and the hurrying squirrel in the downswing of the year is the ever-diligent messenger of next season's life. The green that forces through the flagstones seeks its own destiny, and in this there is music, the harmonies underpinning all. Where the wind-blown soil gathers, the seed drifts in and the forest, one sapling at a time, strides into the worlds men make.

Why did I come back? Are the years not sufficient, the depredations of time not acute enough, to make clear the message all civilization is cyclical and, no matter our best intentions, from dust we came and to dust we shall return? I look across the valleys and rivers from the high promenades, and feel the world thrum to its own rhythm, a high, clear note purer than bells and beyond human imitation. That was our error, perhaps—to believe the inventions of our clever hands superior to the ordered universe which gave rise to us.

Maybe it is just that simple. In the living world is our blueprint; in a harmony of its forces, our kingdom. As the wind blows, as the rain erodes, as the Earth moves, as fire burns, let the interplay of these poles be the furies that drive all within the physical plane, while the infinite layers of the universe recede like stairs to the unreachable stars, ours to climb one gleaming step at a time.

I breathe the sweet air of the hills, rich with the tang of humus and life now, as I walk the ancient halls, and with quickening step I find a strange beauty, a simple joy that brings laughter to lip. Yes! I came back for a reason, not to grieve for what was but to see all that remains, the glittering potential that awakens in a single idea. Without ever knowing from whence proceed the powers, I gesture and the dirt and leaves are swept aside before me, a path of pure white stone opens to my tread, and the ivy recoils from the walls. I ascend the stair to the Chapel of Heaven's Light, the tall tower of soaring windows surrounding the Font of all Wisdom, a simple spring that played in this place of meditation. A tired hand strokes the dry stone and the filth of years is swept away, and water gushes forth once more.

Let it be! May the purity of intent overcome, and play the fabric of reality as the fine instrument it is—powerful as the storm, delicate as a moonbeam. Nothing is impossible, nor was it ever—only beyond the grasp of the blind.

In the airy tower, sunlight shafting all around me through the stoutly-glassed portals, I give voice to an ancient chant whose reverberations fill this place, and in their overlapping medley of waves I bathe in spectral energy. I barely feel my feet leave the floor as I ascend between the soaring windows to hang gracefully in defiance of all earthly bonds and revel in the balance of each force with its neighbor. Through closed eyelids I see them come, first the birds, crows and swallows, then sparrows, even a hawk. They flutter into the corridor and line the edges of the fountain below me; and are joined by the mice and voles, mink and squirrel, and I know should I send my thoughts forth on the simple breath of the mind, others will follow. Deer and wolf, wildcat and bear.

Perhaps humans will come too. Perhaps some will remember all that went before, and want something new and better, and word will pass from mouth to mouth, that one who knows floats serenely in the sunrays. And they will come, just perhaps, to listen to the whispers of the pilgrim who teaches in the ruins.

hopscotch

. . .

Amy Grech

Sitting cross-legged on the stone wall near the playground at recess, I watched the other girls playing hopscotch. Today, I would join them. I stood, pulled my socks up, and approached tentatively. "Can I play, too?"

The girls started at me for a minute then they huddled like football players. I couldn't tell what they were saying, but I was sure they were talking about me. I waited eagerly for their decision. Just when I started to walk away, Judy rushed over. "Follow me," she beckoned, smiling.

I stared, astounded...

We played jump rope; Judy watched me adjust the tempo, so we could jump at the same time.

A group of girls gathered to watch—the dynamic-jump-roping-duo—strut our stuff. I adjusted the rope and started to jump, swinging it in wide arcs. Judy joined me when I nodded. When we were synchronized, we said a song that went like this:

> Fudge, fudge
> Call the judge.

> Mamma had a newborn baby.
> Wrap it up in tissue paper,
> Send it up the elevator.
> First floor, stop!

The girls gasped when they saw the dynamic-jump-roping-duo's feet hit the asphalt at the same time.

> Second floor,
> Turn around.

Thunderous applause erupted on the playground as we turned in opposite directions without tripping.

> Third floor,
> Touch the ground.

The others cheered when we touched the asphalt without losing the rope...

"I thought you wanted to play with us, Hope." Bewildered, Judy stared and waved her hand in front of my glassy, hazel eyes.

"Huh?" I blinked and found myself back on the playground without a rope.

"I do, Judy!" I winked.

"Okay, follow me."

She led me over to the rest of the girls standing by the hopscotch board.

"Can I join you?" I asked timidly.

"Do you know how?" one of them asked.

"No, no one ever showed me." I started to cry.

Judy patted my shoulder. "It's okay, Hope. Let me teach you."

I dried warm tears from my face with the backs of my hands.

The other girls looked on as she taught me. She grabbed a pebble and handed it to me. I took it and waited anxiously for her instructions.

"Toss it on one of the squares."

I threw the pebble; it landed on the square with a **3** in the middle.

"What should I do now?" I bit my lip.

"Hop on one foot 'til you get to the one your pebble landed on, pick it up, and hop off the way you came." Judy winked.

I was afraid I would fall when I tried to hop onto the third square and retrieve my pebble. The others started at me with impatient eyes; reluctantly, I started my maiden journey onto the playground's highwire.

I hopped onto the first square with the grace of a dancer, but I soon became clumsy when I saw the other girls watching my every move. I started to lose my balance when I hopped from the first to the second; I fell trying to hop to the third, like a highwire walker who has just realized how far away she is from the ground's safety.

The others laughed. Judy didn't, but she didn't run over to see if I was okay either; she just stood there listening to her friends' laughter. I saw her grinning

I lay sprawled out on the hopscotch board for a long time, feeling humiliated; I wanted to cry, but I didn't want the others to know they hurt me.

I started at the light blue sky and watched clouds shaped like balloons, cats and people go by. *Those aren't clouds, they're real people!* The others crowded me, blocking my view of the peaceful sky; now I started at their angry faces.

"Get off *our* hopscotch board," they demanded, circling me like vicious sharks.

I rose slowly, shoulders drawn up and my head lowered, to sit on *my* wall...

Judy and I played jump rope again; the applause never ended.

a river, a tree

. . .

Deborah L. Davitt

If you could look inside of her,
you would see
all the arteries and veins reaching for one another
like the branches and roots of some great tree
somehow commingling,
brushing shyly through the capillaries,
while the venules and arterioles keep their distance,
splitting out from their sources like rivers;

each vessel, each *vas*, bounded by a triple layer
of elasticized flesh, the *tunica intima, media, adventia*:
the intimate clothing of each knotted cord
through which our lives flow—

if you could see inside her,
with her life so delicately arrayed
like a tree
    a river
        a net:

how could you not perceive the whole of her

(the magic, the miracle)
without wonder—
how could you not weep
to see the vessels
broken
      shattered
           emptied?

never already always

. . .

Jennifer Hudak

Akma swims in eternal darkness, watching over seeds in the nursery. The seeds and Akma are both darkness. The darkness is both an absence and a presence. The seeds will never burst. They have already burst. They have always been bursting. There is nothing but the seeds, and the nursery, and Akma.

Akma has a vague awareness of kin, but not as something separate from herself. In the eternal darkness, there is no distinction between any of them, just as there is no distinction between her and the nursery, or between the nursery and the seeds. Akma knows her kin the way she knows her own consciousness. Together, they are a whole. They are always. They are complete and unchanging.

And yet in the eternal darkness of the nursery, the seeds flicker. It is a paradox. In order to flicker, the seeds must be dark, and then not dark. Which means there must be a series of moments, connected by a *then*. When the seeds flicker, they create tiny bursts of now, of past and future. A suggestion of space, immense and endless.

Akma knows she mustn't follow the seeds. She has always

known. She has never not known. To follow the seeds would mean chaos, and danger. It would mean the end of the nursery.

But the nursery has no end. Neither does it have a beginning. It is a paradox.

The flickering of the seeds offers a clarification of the darkness. An organization into self and other. Already Akma has a sense of herself as separate: from her kin, and from the nursery. Separate from the seeds, and from the command not to follow them. If there is a command, then Akma is the one being commanded.

Akma is a *one*; she is distinct from another. She is an individual. A *presence*.

The darkness, too, is a presence. It, too, is distinct. She feels it around her in every direction; she feels direction itself. She understands that she might swim first one way, and then another. She might swim in a circle that forever retreads her previous path, or she might point herself in a particular direction and swim and swim until she reaches a place she has never reached before.

Wherever she swims, the darkness is eternal. It does not change. But even so, Akma knows that she has.

She has *changed*.

Akma knows she musn't follow the seeds, but the fact that she can feel her own weight, can feel waves of light and sound, means that it is already too late. It means that there is such as thing as *late*, and such a thing as *already*. The flickering seeds have made of Akma a being that exists not only some*where* but some*when*.

Somewhere: *here*, in the nursery, with her kin, who manifest not only as thoughts but as massive, ethereal shapes looming in the darkness, bodies pressing all around, above and below and alongside. Akma, too, exists as a body, distinct from both seed and kin.

Somewhen: *now*, in this moment. Swimming through a darkness that laps her fins as she passes, that eddies in her wake. She circles round the seeds in her care. She sees them flicker and flare, and knows that they must burst—not now, not in this moment, but in one of the moments yet to come.

One of the seeds in Akma's care flickers brighter than the others. It has become as distinct from the other seeds as Akma has from the rest of her kin. It trembles and quakes, nearly overcome by the light inside it. For the first time (there is a *first*, there is a *time*) Akma swells with possibility. With *potential*.

When the seed bursts, Akma follows.

Together, they explode in all directions, becoming vast. Akma is no longer a body in a place. She is all bodies, in all places. She is atoms colliding and bonding; she is a black hole swallowing itself. She is every star and all the planets that circle them, and she is the space in between. She expands and expands; even if she swims in one direction only, she will never reach the end of herself.

Akma tries to remember the nursery. She tries to remember her kin. She tries to remember the other seeds, and wonders what they will do without her to care for them. But the nursery is in the before. There is no before. Since the seed exploded, there is only after. It is a paradox. Akma has become a new kind of darkness, one that sparkles with the flickering of millions of seeds.

She has become a beginning. She will become an end. In some faraway future, so distant it may as well be never, Akma will have grown so vast that all her stars will cool. All her lights will blink out, one by one, and her seeds will wither to particles that drift apart forever. She will become eternal darkness once again.

But Akma is still between beginning and end, between past and future. No matter how far she swims, she cannot touch either. There is only now. There will only be now. There has always only been *now*.

In this space, a planet begins to distinguish itself from its kin. It flickers and flares. It trembles and quakes. It is not a seed. It will not burst. But it will not stay the same, either. It will become something new, over and over again. Akma watches it, and waits.

forest hills

. . .

Stewart C Baker

They rise all along the coast, these hills, coated in firs and elms and vast branching oaks, their contours impossible to trace, their slopes impossible to survey. In the beach cities, people avoid them, speak quietly of the way they seem to be more distant than they should on foggy days and how their curls of fallen greenery sometimes spell out words from half-forgotten love songs. That the hills hold the spirits of those unready to pass from this world or unwilling.

You were always drawn to them, these hills, even before you met Marc. Certainly since he left you, his fingers cold and stiff and unable to grasp a single winter rose.

In your younger, freer days, you loved their distant solitude. You would wander through the breeze-flung mist for hours, seeing no sign of anyone save markings, chipped and crude, which made memories of birches, forget-me-nots of pines.

The fear the hills inspired appealed to you; ignoring it made you part of a beautiful world that others were too meek to access, too modern to deserve. You used to drive as far as the roads would take you and hike until your legs went weak, then sit and watch the green rolling dampness of the meadows dip and wave as wisps of fine grey cloud blew over. It changed you.

It defined you. The sound of the sea would follow you after-wards for weeks, smashing itself against a shore somewhere far out of sight.

Then you met Marc.

You lost interest in your visits to the hills—at least, you told yourself you had. You told yourself it was Marc you'd been looking for, out there away from everyone. That the connection with a numinous something you'd felt had just been the longing of a lonely mind.

You never told Marc about your hikes, about that quality in the air that made it seem as though unheard voices had just died away, how sometimes you would feel eyes looking out from just inside a cave you'd already explored and found empty. You never told him how at least a dozen times you'd been absolutely certain there was someone there behind you, how you'd felt the barest hint of a hand on your shoulder, a breath on your ear, before turning to find yourself alone except for trees and trees and trees.

All those long, lonely years together with Marc, you felt sure you must be happy. You would wake in the night with his arm around you and tell yourself that this was what you wanted—what you needed. That the tightness in your chest was a frag-ment of dream that would burn away like fog in the afternoon sun. You closed your eyes and pictured birds above the ocean until sleep let you back in.

Then the cancer happened. The cancer Marc would never believe you were the cause of, no matter how many times you told him. The guilt you felt every time he lost another pound from chemo, his life shedding from his body along with his hair and his pride and his hope. That hospital antiseptic smell on everything. After the funeral, you were so drained you just felt relieved it was over.

And now at last you find yourself back in the hills, alone again and older. More alone, you think, if such a thing is possi-ble. You walk for days at a time, trying to find a patch of forest where the lodgepole pines are arranged just so, where the eyes you swear are watching have the weight and warmth of Marc's.

After a year of this, you give up. You take one last trip to the hills and just walk, not looking, not feeling, not caring, until you're exhausted. You stop before a heart-carved birch too young to have earned it; you sit at its trunk and pull its whip-like branches around you and listen to the waves roll over each other somewhere far below.

You sit and you wait and you listen, long after the night fog sticks your shirt to your body with damp. You sit and you tell yourself that maybe now you will feel that old, familiar sense of connection. Maybe now. Maybe now.

It's only when the sun pierces through your sleep-crusted eyelids that you finally let yourself admit that Marc is gone, that he always would have been anyway. That there was never anything you could have done about it.

The fog is breaking up in the heat and sunlight, and away to the south you can just make out the edges of a city. You stand and stretch and walk toward the sound of the ocean, the sound of a child's laughter. It's just like the old days, and yet it's as far from them as possible.

Now, when you walk down from those hills, nothing comes with you. No waves, no fog, no raucous gull's cry. Nothing can follow you, because all of it is there before you. Perhaps it always was.

interstellar catalog: fog

. . .

Shana Ross

On this world there is a near constant mist; you must learn to navigate clouded terrain. On foot or flying the uncertainty of wisps and fuzzy sightlines. No one minds the damp, you get used to it. On this world they love their sweaters.   Sighs are softer.   Even strangers clasp your hands, often and earnest,   in case you need them on the way. In case you are needed.   Yet still it is dangerous to fly blind.

On this world, early on, they decided it would be worse to learn where things ought to be. To navigate with expectations instead of treading carefully, feeling your way, every time. Certainty is for the foolish and selfish. For the inevitable crash. They built their cities on wheels.   They relocate everything constantly — the buildings, the sidewalks, the gaps.   Even the rich man's castle will not stay put from generation to generation,   or, for that matter, three weeks from now.   And on the days where the fog lifts, the whole world goes to high places — a rooftop, a mountain, the narrow bridge out of the valley where all the people live — everyone is curious to see what home really looks like,   knowing that too is already changing.

not for human consumption

. . .

Stuart Docherty

After your funeral, the glitter, stretching down to the river by the train station and up to freeway in the north, rustled into town. The exact time is unimportant, save to say that it occurred around midnight or one am, while most people were asleep. Initially, I had planned for the build-up to be slow, to release more and more across successive nights. But, as with most things done in the heat of strong emotion, I found myself spurring on the distributors with greater and greater aplomb. As a consequence, in certain parts of the city, the glitter became so heavily accumulated that it started to build up and spill over into balconies and onto rooftops, blocking whole streets and doorways. But further afield, this flutter took place slowly, the small mounds of plastic accumulating as gentle as autumn leaves, filling the streets and alleys, sprinkling the rooftops and sidewalks, and the train tracks and carparks. That was how it began.

After that first release, I had one special moment of quiet with the glitter. Just the city, the glitter and I. Though, I kept my distance. Afraid, perhaps, or just simply uncertain, though I enjoyed the small sounds it made as it was moved by the wind. Then, buoyed by some courage, I walked among it. When it was clumped together or seen from afar, it took on that metallic, grey-black sheen that refused to stay still or be identified by one singular name. But when I moved closer, the individual pieces became clearer, became distinct—sitting there in all the expected and varied colours: the blues, greens, yellows, and reds. It was just like your hair, the way it would change with the light and surprise me with its newness, even if I'd seen it thousands of times before.

In those first few days, it was difficult to ascertain a precise public reaction. There were many competing voices and lots of clamour. But it is important to note that the glitter was never arranged in a way to cause harm or disagreement, though this inevitably occurred with the changes of the wind. I was unable to control its accumulation in the narrow side streets or in doorways. Indeed, many of those disgruntled voices were the type to sweep the streets outside their house routinely, the type with clean-cut lawns and hedgerows. You remember Mr and Mrs Appleby, across the street? That first morning, I watched her watch him shake it from the oak in front of their house, grumbling while he did it.

Yet I observed many who embraced the glitter. At its apogee, children tunnelled into mounds of it, disappearing from sight before emerging from the peak, scattering small particles of it far and wide. It stuck to their cheeks and in their hair as they screamed and hollered. Down by the river, where we used to walk together, couples, hand in hand, strolled through it, kicking up piles and laughing and chasing each other. Now and then, I found messages, small piles of glitter piled up to form words and phrases: "Janey loves Tom," "S.O.S.," or a simple heart.

But not everyone took part in the glitter. Many were timid, even hostile to it. It is difficult to say if this was caused by fear or annoyance, for the origins of the glitter were never revealed—of that I was adamant. It is easy to judge those hostile to the glitter, for many of us abhor change and mystery, and if the glitter created an atmosphere of anything at all, it was of mystery and change. These people, I expect, had suffered in their own right and couldn't bear to face it in the world. People want to be moved, not pushed.

And, over time, the glitter moved in ways unexpected. It built up in some areas and scattered in others. A change that most of the population simply accepted, adjusted for and moved on. It wasn't a quick change, but to call it lackadaisical is antithetical; it moved as it liked.

Commentators have suggested, entirely after the fact, that its movements should be judged and studied with various techniques, if ever an event just like it is to repeat. One such commentator suggested that the limits of its spread were important. Another, that the topography was crucial and that, by analysing aerial photographs from the time, we could find the locus, the heart of it. But the results of these inquisitions have never been revealed and, as time has gone on, interest has faded.

After a few weeks, the spread reduced and the distributors had stopped resupplying. In due course, the public interest in the glitter faded, too. I, of course, knew why, for it was my pen that signed the cancellation notice.

Towards the end, I started helping with the clean-up; many were sweeping the streets, gathering up all of it to be hauled away by the city government. But I kept mine and stored it in boxes. As always, joy becomes embarrassment, becomes shame. Those same boxes take up more than half of the attic now, alongside the rest of your things. I haven't opened one in years but, now and then, reach into my pocket for a pencil or a handkerchief and there it is; stuck to the tips of my fingers, the metallic, plastic sheen of glitter.

departure

. . .

Lorraine Schein

When we became silver, we left behind you who were flesh, those remaining bound to the Earth-settled worlds.

Shorn of skin, our organs had floated past us: lungs, hearts, brains unspooling, red and yellow bodily liquids streaming into the void, frozen into contorted icicles floating in space.

Manta-ray winged, we soared on the currents of space-time, dove through the black hole slit pupil of the Cat's Eye Galaxy.

The gaseous plasma simulating dopamine and oxytocin filled us with radiant emotions, thrilling us as we roamed through the vacuum, then vibrate in joy as we sailed, gliding along the neon pulsar winds flung from the shock waves of dying stars.

When we became gold, we radiated the brighter light of the first stars, when time moved faster. Now we could communicate instantaneously in luminous psi quanta.

Merging together, we orgasmed in endless pulse upon pulse, the universe throbbing with us as we raced towards its unknowable end.

the disappearance of 'ways of being'

. . .

Cullen Wade

Nobody knows precisely when *Ways of Being* went missing. It burst into national news in the third week of January three years ago, but I learned of it a week prior, when I got a call from a journalist asking if I had a copy. I didn't. I'm not in the habit of watching movies I worked on. "But it shouldn't be hard to track down," I told the writer.

"You wouldn't think so," she replied, "but nobody seems to be able to find it."

Ways of Being was hardly the most noteworthy picture I'd worked on. Though it had been seen by millions, it was neither beloved enough to be a classic nor niche enough to be a cult item. It lived in that bland middle ground where self-appointed cinephiles would exalt it just for being overlooked, and when people asked me about my career I would remember it about half the time.

The first public mention of the film's disappearance seems to be a Bluesky post by someone named India Slawson from January 8th: "why isn't 'ways of being' on any streaming or vod service? I didn't think it was THAT obscure." A self-reply followed an hour or so later: "ok nobody seems to be selling a copy either. please tell me I didnt make this movie up."

General recognition of the film's absence from the world got off to a slow start. For all anyone knew, it was a mundane matter, a 50-year-old movie that fell through the cracks. But India Slawson had not been mistaken. The film had disappeared from every streaming service's library. Rips had vanished from file hosting sites. Torrents were empty. Physical copy owners went to their shelves to find discs that refused to play, tapes that showed only snow, and obliterated box art. A few weeks later, someone went digging in the studio vault but no negative, interpositive, or exhibition print could be located. Clips and trailers had evaporated. Nobody could even find the script. The movie seemed surgically excised from reality.

No one denied *Ways of Being* had existed. This was not mass hallucination; everyone agreed, even the fringiest conspiracists, that the film was real. It had an IMDb page. References and writeups remained in all the expected books and websites, both contemporary and archival, but the associated promo stills were blacked out, like redacted bits of someone's FOIA-ed FBI file. Youtube reviews and video essays still mentioned the movie, but if they cut to a clip you'd see nothing but glitch mosaic, hear nothing but a voidsome whoosh.

People wanted to know if other films, or books or albums, had suffered the same fate. Hobbyists nervously checked their collections and worked through Letterboxd lists, making sure everything was still there. As far as anybody could tell, only *Ways of Being* was missing. But it was immaculately missing.

The journalists left me alone at first. When the news blew up, they wanted to talk to the actors, a few of whom were still alive. Queries only came my way when they couldn't get ahold of (or got turned down by) Simon or Kate. But somebody soon worked out that no crew member above me in the credits was still living.

This presumably made me important, since the film itself, and not just its disappearance, was starting to captivate the public. All this in spite of my reputation as an awful interview. I always gave the same answers: no, I do not have any standout memories of working on the film; I vaguely remember the director being an okay boss; no, I do not have a theory as to how or why it vanished. I did think it was interesting, I said, that nobody knows for sure how long it had been gone. We as a public seemingly woke up one day, decided that of all movies, we wanted *this* movie, and couldn't find it.

That last bit was the quote they used in the parade of thinkpieces—or rather, the parade of variations on the same thinkpiece:

"Like an average Joe whose eulogy is full of superlatives he never earned when alive; like an estranged lover we can't stop thinking about; like a bulldozed childhood home we dream of returning to, *Ways of Being* has been granted an indelible glamor by virtue of its inaccessibility. It isn't quite that we don't know what we have until it's gone—the fact of its being gone allows us to invent what we had."

They all said crap like that. To the commentators, whether *Ways of Being* was a good film had become immaterial. The public, though, seemed certain. TikTok was full of tearful paeans to how moving, fearless, and ahead of its time the film had been. #JusticeForWOB was huge, though nobody could ever figure out quite what justice meant in this context.

In early March, someone cleaning out their phone storage came upon a forgotten video, taken five years prior, of a dog and a cat snuggling atop a laundry pile. Somebody in the next room was watching *Ways of Being* on TV, and the clip gave us about four muffled seconds of the film's audio. The video had north of 400 million views when it, along with all the reuploads and copies on local, offline and cloud storage platforms, disappeared 21 hours later.

Hearing a snippet of the movie seemed to validate the

fandom's faith in it as a lost masterpiece, but the clip's swift and comprehensive deletion suggested some agency at work, keeping the film from being seen. The sole intelligible line, "You'll want to watch your back in there"—spoken by an actress who had been dead for thirty years—became a rallying cry for the #JusticeForWOB movement, like a desperate message from the film to its devotees, urging them to be wary of whoever or whatever was trying to erase it.

Not long after the "Watch Your Back" clip, a group of enthusiasts from the *Ways of Being* subreddit crowdsourced a screenplay reconstruction. Leveraging the memory fragments of a few dozen fans, they managed to knock together a reasonably faithful facsimile. With an all-volunteer cast and crew, they mounted a microbudget remake. Everybody was on edge thinking the script would get erased, or the locations would catch fire or the memory cards would melt, but none of that happened. All was done in as much secrecy as the ragtag team could manage. For the most part, they succeeded in keeping the project out of the public eye. The completed film was shown at invitation-only screenings, and a limited number of analog copies were given out along with an injunction against ever uploading the film to the internet. Everyone involved bought life insurance policies. There was talk of a curse that had killed off most of the original cast and crew. Never mind that the film was 50 years old, and plenty of us were still alive besides. A growing group viewed my mortality as a piece to some puzzle. Although I am nearing 80 and still smoke when the mood strikes me, when I die they will inevitably cite the curse.

Rather than try to pick apart the legal complexities of owning intellectual property that did not currently exist, the studio quietly bought the rewritten screenplay and greenlit their own professional remake. I got the call on a Monday from an associate producer whose parents might not have been born when we made *Ways of Being* the first time. Simon, the original star, had been hired to direct. He was an experienced director, having made several pornos in the late '70s under a pseudonym, but they were doing their best to keep that part hushed. They offered me the DP job. When I protested that I didn't know a thing about lenses, the kid assured me it didn't matter, they would probably shoot digital and make it look like 35mm. I still thought I was unqualified.

"Charles," he said, "can I call you Charles? You're a very important person to this project. You're the first above-the-line crew member who's still available." I knew by "available" he meant "alive."

"I know," I said. "I get emails from the weirdos. I had to change my number."

"When you start doing press for this project," he said, presupposing my acceptance, "I hope you won't call the audience weirdos."

"You're asking me to do a job I know nothing about. I was a set dresser. And I haven't worked on a film in a decade and a half."

After more one-sided negotiation, we settled on the job of production designer. More responsibility—and money—than I wanted or deserved, but at least in the neighborhood of my skill set. We would shoot in Vancouver, where the original was made, and I had two weeks to report to the hotel they'd booked for me. The only research I could do was watching the fan film, so I asked the AP if he could get me a copy.

"I'll send it by courier. But you should know that as far as this production is concerned, that video does not exist."

Sitting down to watch the remake was like meeting the daughter of someone I went to summer camp with. Echoes of a brief, intense, mostly forgotten relationship in the basic features of the person in front of you. I did not remember *Ways of Being* being this ponderous. It wasn't the actors—the pro-am performers were quite good—but every line and setpiece was imbued with canned portent, self-conscious about being a Momentous Work. The "watch your back" line was practically given with a wink to the camera. Where able, they'd returned to the original filming sites, but bland location lighting clashed with the elevated shooting style. I had to remind myself to pay more attention to the mise-en-scéne. When you seek out your old friend's daughter hoping to jog your memory of them, only to find her a wholly different person, you don't tend to notice how she accessorizes.

As I watched the actors shoulder their way through this dingy rendition, I wondered if we would be making a '70s period piece. The fan film was contemporary out of necessity, but I had a feeling my producers would want to recreate *Ways of Being* as closely as possible, despite it being a spiritual betrayal. We weren't making a period piece the first time, why should we make one now?

Around the midpoint, something happened that is difficult to explain. It was during the scene where Simon goes to Kate's house to ask her for the key. The air around me thinned, as if I'd been lifted to a new abrupt elevation, trespassed into uncertain territory where earth laws held less sway. The actor playing Kate, or rather the actor playing the character portrayed by Kate, stood before a window covered by floor-length drapes. The drapes were wrong. They were a dusky cornflower when they should have been the color of midday sky. Somehow the icepick wrongness of that small detail rocketed me into a memory of those drapes, of their softness when handed to me, of hanging them under hot lights. Of being young and making art. Then the actor playing Kate playing a young woman in trouble moved her hand without looking, clutched an anemic cornflower curtain, pulled it open a few inches, and the too-real skyline of 21st-century Vancouver punched through the window with a lens flare announcing its intrusion. And just like that, I was crying.

———

Simon was no help. Every producer I approached told me to try someone else. Certain I was being given the runaround, I figured Simon might be able to swing some more weight, but he was there for the paycheck and uninterested in litigating what he considered minutiae. The digital matte work would likely be outsourced to somebody in Eastern Europe during post. "I'm the production designer and I don't even get to meet my whole art department?" I asked. I was told I could probably Zoom with them.

Apparently the commitment to getting everyone back from the old film did not extend deeper into the art department than me. The internet listed no specific credit for a scenic artist on *Ways of Being*, but there was one for "painter": someone named Ellen Shaw, for whom there were no other credits, no photo, and no information. I sifted through decades for any recall of this person, but I hadn't been lying to the reporters—there was nothing memorable about the making of that film. The only clear memory, swept out of some corner of my brain by that cold unaccountable gust, was of those quilty sky-colored drapes.

Kate was easier to talk to than Simon. She'd been retired longer than any of us, and was brought onto the remake in a ceremonial producer role. She didn't remember Ellen Shaw either. "Why are you so interested in the scene painter?" she asked me.

I tried to explain, but it felt like describing a dream. Ellen Shaw's sky was an artifact, I said, a relic of a human hand, buried in glacial ice but with veins still primed and tender. If our aim was to drag this movie out of whatever sinkhole it fell into, Ellen Shaw deserved the chance to redraw her heavens. Sometimes to know how something should be done, you have to see it done poorly, and the fan film's sky was dishrag condescension, the color of the drapes was wrong—

Kate stopped me. "Wait, are you actually complaining about the curtains' shade of blue? Literal blue curtains?"

"What do you mean?"

She chuckled. "It's something the kids say, when you make too much of something. You're seeing meanings that aren't there —the color signals grief and longing, that kind of thing. 'Sometimes,' they tell you, 'the curtains are just fucking blue.'"

Rumors of the remake had leaked. I started getting calls from the weirdos again, but suddenly the weirdos didn't seem so weird. One introduced herself as Esa, no last name, and though she couldn't have been long out of her teens, her *Ways of Being* knowledge was uncanny. We were barely past pleasantries when she started listing my own filmography and other tidbits about the cast and crew like rattling off her multiplication tables. I felt my resolve not to engage with these people crumbling in the face of her earnestness, and before I could stop it, I heard myself say, "What do you know about Ellen Shaw?"

I read her pause as surprise, not with the question itself, but that I'd asked one at all. "Well, it's obviously a pseudonym."

"Obviously?"

"A shoutout to Peter Ellenshaw, or maybe his son Harrison, or maybe both. Famous matte painters. Pretty much the whole fandom agrees it's an Alan Smithee situation."

"What makes you all so sure?"

"You worked in a lot of art departments back then. How many women do you remember?"

I didn't have to answer out loud.

"Scenic artists are notoriously hard to track down because they often went uncredited," Esa continued. "But I happen to know the exact number of female matte painters working on all the English-language film productions in the 1970s. Wanna guess? One. Her name was Jena Holman. This Ellen Shaw person is presented as an unlikely gender, with no other credits, no guild memberships, no bio, and the name is a cheeky reference to a legend in the field. It's bogus."

"If I'm understanding you," I said, "none of you... enthusiasts has ever tried to track down this person because you don't think they exist?"

"I mean, those backdrops didn't paint themselves. The only person who might know for sure who did them is, well, you. But to my knowledge, nobody has seriously considered that it was a woman named Ellen Shaw."

"Would you be willing to seriously consider it? I'll make you a deal. Proceed on the assumption that Ellen Shaw is a real person and see what you can learn about her. In exchange, I'll tell you everything you want to know about this project I'm working on."

As I suspected, we were setting it in the '70s, and I found myself taking an active role in the set decoration. I was hoping if I spent more time with my hands in the soundstage, I might meet another wash of sensory memory. The studio where we'd shot the old interiors had long ago yielded to a mini-mall which later became a hotel and now housed mixed-use lofts with a vape shop at street level, so we were working in a new facility elsewhere in town, whose bright green cyclorama screamed mockery whenever I looked at it. I focused on details as much as I could. Like trying to find those drapes.

Four weeks into pre-production, Esa called me back. "Ellen Argiano, of Whitefish Montana," she said without preamble. "Maiden name Ellen Shaw."

"Who is she?"

"Housewife, and amateur landscape painter with ambitions. But you're probably better off asking who *was* she. Her husband reported her missing on March 1st, 1977. The same week you wrapped shooting on *Ways of Being*."

"Montana?" I scratched my stubble. "That's a stretch."

"She's the only painter named Ellen Shaw I could find in the whole northwest. And the date of her disappearance could be a coincidence, but…"

"Do you have a photo?"

"Check your email."

In my inbox was a scan of the article where Esa had gotten most of her information: a local artist profile from a 1972 edition of *The Whitefish Pilot*. According to the author, the 44-year-old Ellen Argiano had a vibrant personality, seemed to sit still with difficulty, and leapt between topics in conversation. She talked about her urban upbringing, her preference for low horizons, her approach to color, and her love of the movies. "People seem to respond to my paintings as if they were friends," she said. The journalist called her "a small-town artist with big-city drive," and asked if she planned to go pro. "I've been lucky enough to sell some pictures," she said, "and it's the best feeling in the world. But, well, there's so much to do at home, my husband travels for work, the children—I dcn't know where I'd find the time. One day, when the stars are right."

Three photographs accompanied the profile. One was a staged shot of Ellen at her easel. Hippie hair, a turtleneck, quick hands, concentrated joy. To my disappointment, her face did not ring any bells.

Something about the second photograph made my skin cold. It was taken in the family living room—where the interview was conducted, according to the article. Ellen on the edge of an easy chair with four children gathered, straining a smile that anyone could tell was fake. In the corner of the room, what could only be her husband, in a dark coat, eyes casting tempests at the camera, hands at his sides in what, notwithstanding the smudge of stipples and half-century-old ink, were almost certainly fists.

On the facing page was the third photo: a closeup of one of Ellen's landscapes. She had not been lying about the low horizon. The Whitefish Range's grandeur was a mere suggestion, a bit of marginalia underlying the real attraction: burnished firmament that seemed cannon-shot rather than lain upon the canvas, a heaven blanket woven from clean winds of home. A piece of me, not the piece that was looking at a laptop on a hotel bed, wheeled and spun into the painting, leaning back and tearing aloft where despite that crumbling newspaper's yellowy grayscale, my marrow knew the sky's uppermost reaches, between the riots of cloud, was the exact blue of my long-lost drapes.

<hr>

One of Ellen Shaw Argiano's four children was dead, and two others turned up no accessible contact information. The fourth, her oldest daughter, was named Italia and lived in Wenatchee, Washington, where her father had moved them shortly after Ellen went missing. On the phone she sounded tired, and reluctant to speak. In fairness, my vague story about having worked with her mother back in the '70s probably did not inspire much trust. I got to the point: "Do you have any of your mother's paintings? Or do you know who might?"

A voice of sand. "I don't want to talk about those paintings, sir. If that's all you called for, I'll be saying good night."

Against my better judgment, I plowed ahead. "If you don't mind me asking why?"

A long pause, then an exhale. "Those paintings destroyed my parents. Please don't contact me again."

Having told Esa I was certain we had the right person, I was anxious for more information on the next phone call, and she came through. Ellen's husband, Derrick Argiano, was a train engineer on the Empire Builder's Whitefish to Wenatchee leg. Five years after Ellen vanished, the moment she was legally dead, Derrick remarried.

"But are you ready for the firecracker?" Esa asked me. "Derrick died at the beginning of last year. January 3rd. Five days before India Slawson's first *Ways of Being* post."

A universe of noises in the phone static as we both went silent. Neither of us knowing what to make of it, both too nervous to speculate out loud. Finally I managed a mild, "Anything else?"

"There were some issues of *The Whitefish Pilot* missing from the online archive, so I called their local library. They didn't have the papers, but they did have something else. One of Ellen's canvases."

I traveled down to Seattle and booked a ticket on the Empire Builder. There was snow on the riverbank as the train passed into Wenatchee, and the tracks followed the water for a long, long time, over a bridge and under a highway, at a speed that made the shallow wash stand still. As the train waited at Wenatchee Station, I thought about Italia Argiano.

Like everything else in Whitefish, the public library looked like a ski lodge. I entered the dim vestibule, and before I could get my bearings, it hit me. There, right there, between a bulletin board advertising kids' storytime and a rack of local interest pamphlets, with yellow dust upon its frame, hung an Ellen Shaw landscape.

It wasn't the one I'd seen in the newspaper, but clearly its cousin, and I'd had no idea it would be so big. Up close, textures of cloud and windswept tree were photorealistic, but the color was fantasy-body extravagant. I was right about the blue. It seemed to put out both light and heat. Standing in its vastness, I knew the landscape had no earthly business as the product of a weekend dabbler. Ellen Shaw had missed her calling as a scenic artist, a movie magic sorceress. Or maybe she hadn't. Maybe it was denied her.

The manager, a man no older than I imagined Esa to be, asked distressingly few questions about why I was interested in the painting or its maker. He didn't even haggle. I asked him if he was sure he wouldn't get in trouble for selling it to me, and he rubbed his eyelids.

"We walk by that thing every day," he said. "I think we all kinda forgot it was there."

Back in Vancouver, I hung the painting in the middle of Kate's apartment set, making it the unavoidable centerpiece of the scene. It didn't make sense in a humble working-class apartment, but nobody seemed to care. It looked stunning between the windows, hung with the curtains I'd finally found in the perfect shade of sky.

We'd wrapped principal shooting by the time I got the last email from Esa. Attached was another smudged scan, a police report. A Jane Doe had been pulled from the Wenatchee River, just north of town. Caucasian, aged 30 to 50 years, but otherwise so mangled as to prevent identification. No signs of sexual violence. The document was dated March 6th, 1977.

The body of Esa's email was brief, and in all lowercase. "cold case. best of luck with the film." It was the last I heard from her.

When I met virtually with the digital matte team in Serbia, I sent them detailed shots of Ellen Shaw's skies with instructions to do them justice. The jolly group of they/thems and bearded bros greeted me warmly, thrilled to be working with "a legend." They did a beautiful job. The film opened in 3,000 theaters, and I did not read a single review. I did not look at box office numbers. I deposited the checks. *Ways of Being*, the new one, was a thing that now existed. And so far, it hasn't disappeared.

Ellen got a credit for the painting, amid the rest of the art department, but that didn't feel like enough. I made a single request during post-production, a request I fought for and proudly managed to ram through. The very last image anyone would see in the resurrected *Ways of Being*, for as long as it lasted. A solo title card at the end of the closing credits:

In Memory, Finally, of E.S.A.

two gardens

. . .

Jason P. Burnham

Dear Alonzo,

Please, do not throw this letter away. Not without reading it, at least. I hope you will stick with me until the bitter end, even through the parts that sound, to put it mildly, improbable. I think it will be as much worth your time to read as it was worth mine to write.

Now, where to begin? What better place than the beginning?

I remember standing in front of the beings of the Multi-Universal Mind like it was yesterday. (This is all true, I swear it. Please, *please* stay with me.) The meeting chamber was a cavernous, echoing space, lodged precisely, strategically, painstakingly in the Lagrange point analogue of the multiverse's space-time-plane continuum. The rows of creatures seated menacingly above me are shrouded in the darkness of my memory. The Multi-Universal Mind, or the MUM, do not permit you to remember fine details of their appearances so as to maintain the mystery of their identities, their origins. But I remember the feelings, the words, the ultimatum.

The ultimatum was this: I could stay in my timeline, my version of the universe, dying of amyotrophic lateral sclerosis or

I could move to a new timeline, a different iteration of the multiverse. Seems like an easy choice, right?

Wrong. There's always a catch.

Let me explain. Amyotrophic lateral sclerosis is a progressive and ultimately fatal degeneration of the body's motor neurons. You might be more familiar with it if I tell you that Lou Gehrig and Stephen Hawking both died from it. Both of those people existed, and were also famous, in your timeline, so even if their names are not ringing a bell, I know you'll be able to look them up. Anyway, the disease destroys the nerves that control voluntary movements. How does that kill you? At first, it doesn't. You might have trouble moving an arm. Or a leg. Or you might have a little trouble swallowing, a catch in your throat. You would probably brush it off (like I did) and think it would go away. Maybe you were just too tired (read: me), stressed from working too many hours.

But the muscle weakness progresses to the point that you can no longer swallow, that you can no longer breathe without the assistance of a mechanical ventilator. Eventually you are a heap of skin and bones kept alive by machines. Did I mention your brain keeps working normally while your muscles fail you, fiber by fiber?

Did I mention that I got diagnosed with this at age thirty-three? And that my son was only three years old at the time? And that my life expectancy was down to just three years by the time I finally got diagnosed?

You are probably saying to yourself, "Take the other timeline! The one where the ALS goes away! Duh! How is this even a question?"

Like I said, there was a catch.

One of my greatest fears was that my son would not remember me. What is your first memory? Mine is from when I was about four years old, and my mom put my sister on the hood of the car while she was still in her car seat, and the car seat slid off the hood and onto the hot summer asphalt. Don't worry, my sister was fine; she has a doctorate of philosophy in theoretical biostatistics. After that, I remember someone in kindergarten peeing in their little blue plastic chair and later that year, I recall losing a reading contest to a girl with black hair and bangs named Stephanie from the class across the hall. But that is the sum total of my memories before the age of six. So what did that mean for my son? He *might* have one fleeting memory of me? Maybe he could remember the color of my hair? Or that one time I yelled at him? Memory is so random, and we can't choose what stays with us. What if all he got was something terrible? And worse, what if it was good?

So yes, I wanted to go to an ALS-free timeline. But that is not what the MUM offered me. What I got instead was this: stay and die of ALS, not knowing what will happen to my son and wife when I'm gone *OR* go to a new, ALS-free timeline where I have no spouse and no children.

What? (Stick with me here, *I know.*)

I had to decide—the MUM is busy and important and even if there is a chance they exist outside of time, you do not get forever to make up *your* mind.

The guilt of leaving him was crushing. Yes, I know he had my wife, his mom. Don't get me wrong, my wife was *supremely* capable. She is the reason he was such a great kid. But we all loved each other very much, and I knew that she too would be wrecked by my premature death.

It was a one-way ticket, the MUM said.

Staying meant slow deterioration, a body atrophying into dust while the mind raced on. A heavy dust, a burden to those sweeping, trying to keep the wind from blowing it away. Just one more week. Just until the end of kindergarten. Just until the end of summer. We can shape it into a semblance of him until… until…

Leaving meant rebirth, virility, vigor—no wasting away. But no children, no life partner. It was selfish, I told myself, selfish to stay. I would be doing it for me. To watch what I could watch until I could watch no more. Better to leave and not be their life-long void. Better not to impose my progressive corporeal burden upon my wife and son.

I could not cross back over into my old timeline, my old universe, the MUM said. Once I chose, I could not change my mind.

So I decided to take myself out of the equation. But when I arrived in my new timeline, I thought, "What do the MUM know?" They are only an unknowable, all-powerful conglomerate of space-time-plane affecting mystery-beings, after all. Their memory alteration techniques worked against them. Or against me, I am not sure which.

I knew as soon as I left that I had made a mistake.

I worked. Math classes nobody understood the names of. Theoretical physics that only a few people on Earth could fathom. No family to hold me back, even though all I wanted was for them to be with me, to hold me back. Science was all I had, and it was so supremely lonely. But I kept on because I told myself that if I could just get past that one irreconcilable mathematical fallacy, then maybe, *just maybe* I could cross over and tell them I had made a mistake.

After I reconciled one mathematical inconsistency, there was another. And another after that. Each time that it seemed I was on the precipice of solving the crossover problem, the only thing that succeeded in making it across the threshold was another piece of my sanity.

So naïve. Why would the MUM have lied? Why would they have told me I could not cross over if I truly could not? What could they possibly stand to gain?

These thoughts have haunted me for forty years. Their persistence, the inability to shut out their cacophony is what drove my research productivity. The less time I gave myself to think those thoughts, the more I could hold it together.

But a dried husk is no match for a flame, the consuming conflagration of absence. All the years in dark, dusty libraries, laboratories with toxic chemicals. My blood type is rare and the shape of my thorax unfavorable. Nobody on the planet can donate their lungs to me. The pulmonary fibrosis caused by a lifetime of exposures has eroded away my alveoli, leaving me with anatomical cavities mirroring the holes in my soul left by my family's imprints. The physical and the metaphysical conspire to accelerate my demise.

My oxygen exchange capacity is critical. If I take off this mask even for a minute, it takes me an hour to recover. Writing this letter is slow, laborious, but it will have all been worth it if you make it through to the end. With breathing and writing each individually so taxing, a change in humidity could be what kills me.

In our pulmonary fibrosis support group, I remember when Kathy's husband Tom came to our therapy session without Kathy for the first, and only, time. She had been in the hospital for weeks, slowly suffocating. Much like me, her anatomy was unfavorable for lung transplantation. She got a little worse every day, sitting around, waiting, hoping a small pair of lungs would come through the door in a cooler. But the cooler never came.

One night, after a particularly strenuous fit of coughing, Tom told us Kathy motioned for a pen and paper (not unlike these upon which I write I imagine). By that point, she had to wear an oxygen mask and oxygen nasal prongs just to maintain her breathing. The prolonged coughing session was so tiresome she couldn't speak. When Tom handed her the paper, she wrote simply, "Done." He knew immediately, Tom told us through tears. Kathy nodded when the nurse asked if she was certain she wanted the morphine drip. Tom held her hand until she died, a mere sixty seconds after stopping the oxygen. She had enough morphine in her to prevent air hunger and Tom said it was the most comfortable he had seen her in a year.

That's what I can expect. And soon, too. Perhaps that's why I'm out here in the garden, writing this letter to you; I wanted to have a chance to write something more than "Done" to the ones I love.

Maybe a letter can cross over. I'm not sure who the courier would be. With forty years of strict devotion to the mathematics of multiverse travel to the detriment of functional human relationships, I'm not sure there's anyone left that doesn't revile me that could possibly deliver the message. And in order to do it, they'll still have to solve that last irreconcilable problem…

I've always liked it here in the garden. It reminds me of the park where we used to play. The one by the house. The one where a butterfly landed on my shoe. You always brought it up, months, maybe even a year after it happened. I remember being surprised you had formed memories that far back, to a time before you could even *say* butterfly.

There are lots of butterflies in the garden today, bud. You would love it.

The MUM let me keep my memories of the time we had together, though I'm not sure why. Those precious scraps of happiness are what kept me going, kept me pushing the envelope, making that next breakthrough. People say I'll be famous for generations.

But I don't *care*. If I could take it all back, I would have stayed. Every last drop of optimism I have, I am wringing from this sack of emaciated bones and distilling into this letter. Maybe it will reach you. I can only hope.

I love you more than any words I can write. More than any words that have ever been written or could ever be written. I don't know what is more selfish, coming here, or telling you now that I regret it. If I had understood then that my old timeline would still happen without me, I never would have left. I would have enjoyed those last three or four years, even if it meant I had to do it from a hospital bed, immobile and mute.

I should have stayed, buddy. I should have stayed. I don't know if you remember me. You were so little when I left. But if the memories aren't there, know that for a blink in cosmic time, someone loved you more than anything in this entire multiverse. And that's coming from someone who's been in two different versions of it.

I hope you made it with me all the way to the end of the letter and that you thought it was worth it.

With all the love in my heart,
Your Dad

In a shadowed, cavernous chamber at the equilibrium point of the space-time-plane continuum, a voice spoke in a language that could be understood no matter the origin of the audience. "We believe conveyance of this letter invalidates our non-interference mandate," said The Primär, their tone dark as the shrouded countenance from which it reverberated.

"We cannot show them the way," agreed another voice.

"We are not showing them, merely providing lighting for the path," said the Defender from their chamber alcove. The Defender was the most experienced member of the MUM—it allowed perspectives not otherwise available to the rest. The Defender's alcove was enclosed, as usual, to permit uniform diffusion of the chemicals required for clarity of interpretation.

"Explain," said The Primär. They were the overseer of the proceedings and though the MUM decided by cohesion voting, what The Primär and Defender said often held weight in the minds of the others.

"The progenitor was allowed passage to drive discovery. His grief, his sorrow were his companions, but also contributed to his premature expiration. Had he persisted, he would have made the final connection, allowing humanity to finally join the Multi-Universal Mind," said the Defender, the synthetic gases floating around them in the alcove.

"How does transmission of this letter to the progeny further humanity's development?" asked The Primär.

The Defender was prepared and did not hesitate in their response. "The lineage persister will be motivated to join another timeline where the precursor has not perished, but has also had to leave his family behind. The lifetime of the precursor's absence will be strong enough to drive reconnection."

"This was your plan all along."

"Humanity is the last without representation here. *We* are incomplete without *them*. To achieve balance for all, they must join us," finished the Defender, hoping their experiences would sway the MUM.

"I'm not sure they're ready," rumbled The Primär. "We disagree in principle with allowance of these actions, but conclude that technically it violates no directives."

"Then the letter shall be channeled?"

"Perhaps against our better judgment, we will let the cohesion vote proceed."

Had anyone watched the Defender through the chamber's fading penumbra, they might have seen a look peaceful, but triumphant.

Under a cerulean sky flitted black stripes on orange. A monarch descended on a warm breeze, alighting finally on a flower nestled comfortably in a verdant garden. On a nearly identical planet, in a garden very like this one, a letter had been written as a last act of love, of apology, from father to son.

"Why are you crying, Daddy?" asked a young boy.

"Check out the butterfly, bud. Isn't it beautiful?" asked the father.

"Yeah!" The boy paused, recalling a story he had heard. "Did a butterfly land on Grandpa's shoe a long time ago and you saw it?"

"It sure did, bud. It sure did," said Alonzo.

the girl who swallowed
a star

. . .

Erwin Arroyo Pérez

At first, the star was small—
      a sugar pearl,
      a bright bead on her tongue.

She swallowed it whole—
      it did not burn.

Then, her ribs
      unfolded like solar panels.

Her spine
      stretched into a bridge of light.

The sky
      bent toward her like a magnet.

She breathed,
      and helium threaded her lungs—
      golden, thin, weightless.

She heard
>the geometry of sound—
>laughter spiraling in endless spirals.

She stepped,
>and the ground reconfigured.

She walked,
>and continents redrafted themselves.

Then came the astronomers,
>palms blistering with clocks,
>mouths spilling numbers,
>coordinates, equations.
>'Come back,' they said.
>'Come back
>down.'

She laughed,
>and her ribs unraveled into auroras.

She wept,
>and her tears fractured into moons.
>She exhaled,
>and gravity forgot itself.

The sky
>was no longer above her;
>it was her.

And so,
>with one last shuddering breath,
>she stepped forward—
>not up, not down,

but into

     the spaces   between—
     where no maps could follow.

a mathematician's guide to being normal

. . .

Sam E. Sutin

Class doesn't even start for another ten minutes, yet you're already the sweatiest you've ever been in your life.

It's the first day of high school—you barely slept last night, you don't know anybody, and if you don't fit in immediately you think you might die. Or throw up. Probably both, and possibly in that order.

Being **normal** has never been more important.

You're navigating to first period when a girl trips in front of you, her untied laces snagging beneath the soles of her sneakers. You watch her arms flail like windmills as she falls, the *snap* of her glasses against the floor spreading goosebumps across your skin. Pencils spill across the linoleum like spilled intestines. Someone nearby is laughing—several someones, judging by the echoing chorus rising around you. It's your worst nightmare brought to life, and your first reaction is a shameful wave of relief that it isn't happening to you, followed quickly by sheer empathetic terror for the poor girl who's just become the laughingstock of the entire hallway.

The question is: do you help her?

Sure, it would be the *kind* thing to do, but at what cost? This girl is already damaged goods, and initial impressions are *every-thing* in high school. Is this *really* the first person you want to be associated with?

God, you're already overthinking things. With effort, you unclench your jaw and try to cram some rationality between the lobes of your brain.

What would a *normal* person do?

<u>Definition</u>: *In linear algebra, a matrix is normal if it commutes with its conjugate transpose. These are the "well behaved" matrices—the ones that don't twist or distort vectors too much as they interact with them.*

Sometimes, you think to yourself, being normal means not being a dick.

You square your shoulders, take a deep breath, and gather a few rogue pencils rolling surreptitiously for the stairs. Shoelaces is back on her feet, and you can see she's doing everything she can to hold back tears. You offer her the pencils, giving her a sheepish smile you hope comes across as an 'it happens' sort of expression.

Her name is Elaine, and in two days she will already be the best friend you've ever had.

It's the second week of classes, and by some miracle you're still alive. A wooden prop sword/makeshift bathroom pass swings heroically at your side as you enter the restroom. There are two girls huddled excitedly around the trashcan. They know you're a freshman—can smell it on you like bad perfume. Between bursts of hysterical giggling and intermittent puffs on a shared vape pen they show you the YouTube video they've found on how to light a fire in a school trashcan without getting caught. They ask if you'd like to join them, or if you'd rather be prissy about it instead.

You regret leaning the sword against the opposite wall; you should've known the castle would have dragons.

> _Definition:_ In differential geometry, a vector bundle is normal if it encodes the ways in which one can move from a point on a submanifold to the ambient manifold without staying within the submanifold itself. In other words, normal bundles tell you how much wiggle room you have when inhabiting a larger space.

You leave the girls to their petty arson and return to class, sheathing the bathroom pass until destiny calls upon you once more. Ten minutes later, you follow your class outside in single file, fire alarms shrieking above your head. When Elaine runs up to tell you two sophomores have been suspended for setting a trashcan on fire, you pretend to be as shocked as she is.

Sometimes, being normal means understanding what you can and can't get away with.

Somehow, it's already October, and you can't believe you actually have *friends*. You taught Elaine how to tie her shoes without making fun of her, and in return she's bullied all her middle school friends into being nice to you. You've fooled them all into thinking you're vaguely interesting, and to be honest you're not really sure how you pulled it off, considering how cool they all are. Théa is the only person you've met in real life who's seen *Revolutionary Girl Utena*, and Penelope makes you laugh so hard you start oinking like a pig. Blake is quite possibly the most beautiful person you've ever seen, but she's usually hanging out with the junior boy who asked her out on the third day of school. He's nice enough, but it's never as much fun when he's around.

You were just starting to believe that being normal wasn't as hard as you thought, and then you found out Théa had cancer.

You didn't know girls your age could even get ovarian cancer. The doctors caught it early enough to be confident in a full recovery, but that hasn't stopped you from screaming into your tear-soaked pillow until your vocal chords sizzled like a stovetop. You've never felt so helpless, and you have no idea what to do.

Definition: In complex analysis, a family of functions is normal if it can be written as a pre-compact subset of the space of continuous functions. Put simply, functions in a normal family cluster together, rather than spreading out widely.

On Halloween, you, Penelope, Elaine, and Blake show up to school in matching Pitbull costumes. It takes Théa until third period to realize the shaved heads are real. If anyone thinks five copies of Mr. Worldwide sobbing uncontrollably in the hallway is strange, they keep it to themselves.

Sometimes, being normal means sticking with your friends when things get rough.

It's your first high school party, and it is everything you hoped it would be and also a complete disaster. You got to watch two drunk seniors make out on one of the couches, but you didn't have a chance to drink anything yourself because the alcohol ran out in the first thirty minutes.

Blake is sick and Théa is spending the night at the hospital, so it's just you, El, and Pen huddling against a back wall, nervously rubbing your buzzcuts in what has quickly become a synchronized nervous tick. You're surprised when Blake's boyfriend makes an appearance, but not half so much as when he tries to kiss you in line for the bathroom.

The next day he texts you saying he was drunk and begs you not to say anything to Blake since he really *really* likes her, and besides if you tell her he'll say that you tried to kiss *him* first and then she'll never speak to you again. You don't *think* Blake would believe him, but even the thought of her mad at you sends butterflies spinning around your stomach. Is it worth the risk? What if she *does* blame you and then all the others side with her and start ignoring you? You've only just gotten friends and if you lose them now everything will fall apart and you'll get super depressed and it'll be like 9/11 all over again, and you can't even tell your parents because if your dad knew he'd kill you or the boyfriend or possibly both and either way you need him to stay out of jail until he's paid for college.

Your heart is pounding against your ribs like rain on a tin roof. You need to chill out, think rationally. You need to be *normal* about this.

> Definition: In algebraic geometry, a scheme is normal when each of its local rings are integrally closed domains. When you look at normal schemes up close, there isn't anything important hidden outside the structure.

Sometimes, being normal means not keeping secrets from your friends, even when it hurts.

You make a new group-chat with everyone but Blake, stoically explain the situation, and *then* freak out and have a meltdown over FaceTime. Like an adult.

You go to Blake as a team, and then you all egg her (ex)boyfriend's house. Théa even tags along, but she has to wait by the car. Because of the cancer. Blake is actively sobbing as eggs catapult from her hands, mascara smearing across her cheeks and unrelenting fury burning in her eyes.

It's all very poetic until Elaine tells her she looks like an emo Mr. Clean. Then an egg takes Elaine full in the face, yellow viscera exploding across the tiny bristles of her hair. Elaine shrieks, returning fire. Suddenly eggs are flying in all directions, arcing through the night like yolky grenades. You take several unprovoked hits, and also a few that were probably justified. As the dust settles Théa calls you all idiots, then screams as one last egg smashes against her temple. Blake throws back her head and howls in triumph, eggy tears still staining her cheeks.

You've always been a little intimidated by Blake – by her charm and her beauty and the way the world seems to bend around her, projecting her image larger than life. Now, as she stands cackling before you in the moonlight like some demented raccoon, you'd be lying if you said she didn't look a little insane.

You're pretty sure you'd die for her.

That night, the five of you pass out in a tumble of towels, tissues, and empty pints of ice cream. Somewhere in the early hours of the morning you find Blake's hand in yours. It takes you another two hours to fall back asleep.

***

Elaine and Penelope have a crush on the same boy, though 'obsession' might be a better word for it. You don't really know what all the fuss is about, but his hotness seems to be common knowledge to most of the school. His name is Declan, and he's on the swim team, so he's got, like, abs and stuff. Blake is on the swim team, too. You can smell the chlorine on her skin when you sit together in the hallway before class. El and Pen keep trying to get her to set them up with Declan, and she likes to complain to you and Théa about how annoying they're being. (You suspect Théa secretly thinks Declan's hot too, but you don't say anything.) Ever since her breakup, Blake's sworn off men, and you've joined her in solidarity. Talking about how gross boys are with Blake has quickly become one of your favorite hobbies.

As the weeks go by El and Pen start acting really nasty to each other. Yesterday Elaine called Penelope a bitch and then Penelope tied Elaine's shoelaces together, which was a low blow, given her history. So now they're not speaking. Blake can't stand either of them at the moment, and you feel like you've been strapped to one of those medieval torture devices that pulls you in seven different directions at once.

How did normal people deal with infighting like this?

Definition: In group theory, a subgroup is normal if it is invariant under conjugation. In normal subgroups, the elements of the subgroup remain constant regardless of what is happening outside in the larger group.

You go to Théa, and the two of you hatch a plan that, looking back, was definitely super unethical. On Friday you called Elaine, Penelope, and Blake separately, wailing about some sort of complication with Théa – that she was in critical condition at the hospital and that they all needed to come spend the night in the ER as soon as ASAP as possible.

One by one they burst into Théa's room, only to be brought up short by the large banner hanging above her bed with the word 'Mantervention' written across it in pink and purple crayon. Elaine and Penelope are irate (which, like, _fair_), and Blake gives you a pouty face that features prominently in several of your dreams over the next few weeks. Nevertheless, your first ever Mantervention (and yes, there _will_ be more) is ultimately a smashing success. Elaine and Penelope both agree to both stop trying to date Declan, and you're shocked at how quickly things return to, well, normal.

Sometimes, being normal means putting the hoes before the bros.

(Still, two years later when you walk in on Théa and Declan making out in an empty classroom, you can't resist giving her an awkward fist bump before shutting the door again. You respect the art of the long play.)

For Christmas your mother buys you a scale for your bathroom, which will soon go down in history as the single worst gift you've ever received.

You start weighing yourself every morning before school and observe, to your horror, that the number keeps creeping higher and higher. None of your clothes seem to fit right anymore, and when you wear a belt, you can feel your belly bulging over its constricting embrace. You know gaining weight is something that happens in high school, that what you are experiencing is most likely ~puberty~, but that doesn't change the fact that every time you look at your thighs, they seem a little rounder.

Definition: A real number is considered normal if each digit in its infinite decimal expansion has the same natural density. If you were to look at a normal number in its decimal form, each of the digits 0-9 would appear approximately 10% of the time.

You decide to keep track of the calories you eat each day. They're just numbers, after all, and you love numbers. Numbers can't be bad for you. You also start watching weight-loss YouTube videos and follow several Instagram accounts that show you how to make yourself look skinnier in pictures. You develop a habit of staring at yourself in the mirror and hating what you see.

Sometimes, you decide, being normal means having the right proportions.

Your biology teacher hands you the exam you took last week. You got a 68%. Shame bubbles up like boiling water, and you cram the test into your backpack and pray that no one saw the sickly red condemnation scrawled across its surface. At lunch, everyone is going around comparing their grades, talking about which questions they missed and how many points they think they'll be able to get back. You mumble something about math homework and scurry away before they remember you're three weeks ahead. Why can't everything be as easy as math?

<u>Definition:</u> *In set theory, a function is normal if it is continuous and strictly increasing. To picture a normal function, imagine climbing an infinitely tall staircase where each step is never shorter than the one that came before.*

After politely reminding you that if you carry on like this you'll never amount to anything in life, your parents sign you up for tutoring after school. You're too embarrassed to tell your friends, which means you don't have a good excuse for missing Elaine's Quiz Bowl competition the following week. She's definitely a little upset with you, but it's what you deserve for not studying hard enough. You'll do better next time.

Sometimes, being normal means avoiding mistakes at all costs.

It's Valentine's Day, and all anyone can talk about is *boys*.

Neil Buchanan has been wriggling his eyelashes at Elaine all morning, and to your horror she's been wiggling hers back.

Even worse, Penelope is practically drooling over a senior on the wrestling team and keeps literally swooning whenever he walks by.

Even *worse*, Blake gets no less than *six* roses from secret admirers, which has your stomach in a trefoil for no good reason. Sure, one of them had been from you, but you'd bought roses for all your friends, because that's what girls do for each other.

You are pretty sure that's what girls do for each other.

And then *you* get a rose from the boy who sits behind you in English. You're pretty sure his name is Terry, and you're quite positive you haven't exchanged so much as a 'hello' with him all year.

Oh, god.

Oh, *god*.

It's not that you're *not* interested in boys, that would be crazy. You can appreciate the curve of a bicep or the ridge of a jawline as well as anyone, but to you it's always felt more like admiring a well-crafted piece of art than some primal, carnal desire. Boys didn't make you *feel* anything—make you laugh or cry or swell with pride the way you do with Elaine and Penelope and Théa. The way you felt around...

Definition: You can normalize a vector by dividing each of its components by its length, converting it into a unit vector, which has a magnitude of one.

Maybe you're just being picky. Everyone knows dating is the most important part of high school, and nobody ever said being normal would come naturally. It was something you *did*, not something you *were*.

Sometimes, being normal means cutting away the pieces of you that didn't seem to fit.

After class, you corner Terry by the stairs and ask him through gritted teeth if he'd like to watch a movie with you on

Friday. He looks like a petrified piece of wood but is able to jerk his head up and down, which you suppose is probably a yes. El and Pen practically tackle you to the floor when you tell them. Blake sighs dramatically and says it looks like the ban on boys is finally over. For some reason, this makes you feel like your soul is dribbling out of your nostrils.

You've started skipping breakfast in the mornings. If you're going to have a boyfriend, you can't have him dump you in a month because you've gotten fat. You get a little lightheaded during precalculus sometimes, but you've never needed to pay attention in there anyway.

Dating is exhausting. You don't know how Elaine does it. Despite the perpetual avalanche of homework and the Quiz Bowl team advancing to nationals she still manages to suck face with Neil Buchanan at least six times per day. They're always laughing when you see them together.

You wish Terry made you laugh like that.

It's not that he isn't funny, he just isn't funny to *you*. On St. Patrick's Day he tried to pinch your butt for not wearing green and you shoved him into a locker so hard he got a bloody nose. You felt bad enough to let him kiss you on the lips before World Geography, telling yourself it was the dried blood that almost made you gag.

Every day you feel forced to choose between your boyfriend and your friends, and if you choose what you *actually* want everyone looks at you like you just kicked a puppy.

What do you mean *you left Terry on read Friday night to go watch anime with Théa?*

What kind of girlfriend would want *to go to prom with her friends and not her boyfriend???*

Sometimes it feels like high school is one giant river, and while everyone else is rafting down the rapids you've been caught in one of those little whirlpools that form on the edges, turning endlessly in circles as life washes past you round the bend.

Worse yet, something weird is happening with Blake. It's like someone's stuck magnets behind your eyes, because whenever she's around, you just can't stop *looking at her*. You've always liked hanging out with her—who wouldn't?—but now there's a physical sensation in your chest, an irresistible itching that turns every minute you aren't with her into a moment wasted.

You don't think she's noticed—*pray* she hasn't. It's weird, and you know it. Obsessing over your friends isn't normal behavior—it's clingy and possessive and gross, but try as you might it *just keeps happening*.

You can feel yourself slipping. Your grades are getting worse and despite only eating celery for lunch you've gained *another* 4.3 pounds in the last month. You've been trying so hard to be normal, pushing yourself so damn hard, but it feels like all you've done is spin yourself around the whirlpool that much faster.

Definition: In ring theory, a ring is normal if every localization at a prime ideal yields an integrally closed domain. Similar to normal schemes, one way to think of a normal ring is to visualize it as a self-contained universe—if something 'should' belong, it already does.

Sometimes, being normal means having everything you need without having to try. Sometimes, being normal is just something you're born with.

You failed another biology test, and now your parents have grounded you for screaming at them while they were busy screaming at you. You're locked away in your tower when Blake sets a school record in the 200-meter freestyle, and now you understand what it felt like when Mr. Giles got crushed to death in *The Crucible*. (It doesn't help that the words "More Weight" now come to mind every time you step on the scale).

Blake says she understands when you try and explain why you couldn't make it, but you can tell she's disappointed. Her hair has already grown back down to her ears, and the chlorine has turned it softer than you thought possible, like silk between your fingers. You could run your hands through it for hours, drinking in the scent of her...

Then Terry crams his sweaty, hairy body between the two of you, and Blake says she has to study for a quiz she missed before scooping up her bag and vanishing around a corner. But you know she took that quiz already because she said so last week and you remember everything she's ever said to you, committing each tidbit to memory like one of your Spanish vocab flashcards.

No one seems to have time for you anymore. Elaine keeps saying she's super busy, but she always seems to have time for Neil. You swear she's got him on a leash like a dog; whenever you text her about hanging out you can practically hear his tongue lolling in the background.

Penelope isn't any better. After months of basically stalking that senior boy he finally developed enough of a brain to notice, and now they're practically conjoined at the hips, if not the lips.

Even Théa seems too busy to work you into her schedule. Her hair was straight when she started chemo, but it's grown back curly, and the TikTok she made about it went super viral. Hank Green even stitched it; she's like a local celebrity. You're pretty sure the fame has changed her. God, you can't believe you're feeling jealous of a *cancer survivor*. What kind of person does that?

Definition: A topological space is normal if, given two

disjoint closed sets, there exist neighborhoods surrounding each that are also disjoint. Normal spaces are the topologies in which you can "push apart" any two closed sets by using open ones.

Maybe having friends was a mistake. It felt good at first, but now all they seem to do is bring you misery. It was stupid to let yourself care about them so much when they obviously didn't feel the same about you.

Sometimes, being normal means not letting anyone get too close.

It's 1am when Blake calls you in tears saying she's outside.

Bringing her up to your room would be too risky (you're pretty sure your dad was lying when he told your mom he'd sold the shotgun), so you climb out your window and half-scramble-half-slide down the gutter drain like a pudgy fireman with Velcro for fingers. You pray it doesn't make you look too much like an idiot, but then Blake is crying into your shoulder, and nothing exists but the feather-soft kiss of her hair on your skin.

She was at a party (one you didn't even know about, much less get invited to) and her sleazy ex kept trying to get her alone to 'apologize' for being a shitbag, and after an hour she tried to leave but he stopped her and asked her to prom in front of *everyone* and when she said no he called her a bitch and then she slapped him and someone caught it on camera and now the whole school is going to think she's psycho and if her parents see she was out partying she'll be in such deep shit and you're the only person she could go to and—

And it turns out you aren't the only one feeling neglected by El and Pen. They're always locked away with their boys, Blake says, and Théa is shit at texting. (You're actually pretty bad at it yourself, but seeing as how you always respond to Blake's texts within about five seconds it's understandable she wouldn't know this.)

You know Blake is going through a lot right now, and you feel a little guilty about how good it feels for her to come to you in a time of crisis. You definitely *don't* kind of secretly wish she had crises more often, because that would be a super fucked up thing to think.

You're so caught up in feeling guilty about feeling good that you almost miss it when she *apologizes to you* for being weird earlier that week. It wasn't about the swim meet at all—she gets that parents can be crazy. It's just—and *please* promise not to hate her for saying this—it's just she really, *really* doesn't like your boyfriend. It's crazy, she knows, but she can tell he doesn't make you happy and that you deserve better and that even though it sounds obsessive she just *can't stop* thinking about you and him and how gross it makes her feel inside.

You are suddenly acutely aware of each individual follicle of her skin that is touching yours, your senses coming alive as her words wash over you.

Through some combination of the revelation, sleep deprivation, and, let's be honest, mild starvation, you feel the last of your walls melting away like candle wax. Tears flood your eyes, and before you can stop yourself you're whisper-wailing about how your entire life is falling apart around you, about how all you want is just to be *normal* and how being *normal* means having a *boyfriend* and getting good *grades* and *starving yourself* and how you've been alone for so, *so* long and now you're ruining the one good chance you have to be happy.

It's Blake's turn to hold you as the sobs wrack your body, the movement of her fingers across your back sending tingles down your spine as she tells you everything is going to be all right. If it had come from anyone else you wouldn't have believed it, but as Blake's hands cup your cheeks and her tears mingle with yours you wonder if anything might be possible.

<u>Definition:</u> *In multivariable calculus, a vector is normal if it is perpendicular to some object or structure. Normal vectors help you define directions on a surface or curve at a given point. Specifically, they are essential in determining one's orientation.*

You break up with Terry over text, which is kind of shitty but also you don't care. The girls come over with face masks and half a handle of vodka Penelope stole from a homeless guy who'd tried to pee on her one time. You pretend to be really distraught but to be honest you haven't felt this good in weeks.

Sometimes, being normal means going your own way.

It feels like the five of you haven't been together in years. Decades, even. You give Théa some tips for styling curly hair and Penelope shows everyone a demo of her boyfriend's mixtape. (*He said I could show it to anyone I wanted—he's, like, super talented and confident about this stuff*). Elaine says she wished Neil was creative like that, and Blake pretends to choke to death on your bed. Her dead body gives you a wink that comes close to putting you in the grave alongside her, which honestly wouldn't be the worst thing.

There's a warm fuzziness that hangs over the room like a blanket, and as your cuddle puddle slowly sinks into sleep Blake makes a point of pulling you up close to her, one arm draped lazily around your shoulders. You can feel the smooth skin of her leg pressed against yours, the gentle heat of her breath on your neck like a summer breeze.

It's going to be a very, very long night.

You feel healthier than you have in a long time, which you grudgingly admit is probably because you're eating again. You'd been hiding out during lunch so no one would see you dumping your sack lunch in the trash, but recently Blake has been conspicuously dedicated to tracking you down. Every day she sits quietly as you force yourself through the food in front of you, unable to look her in the eye. It's agonizing and humiliating and exhausting and quite possibly the kindest thing anyone has ever done for you. Sometimes you cry from sheer frustration, and she holds your hand and runs her fingers through your hair, which is causing some very confusing things to become connected in your brain.

Classes are also more manageable now that you're not too dizzy to pay attention. It also helps that Penelope has been studying with you a lot more since she dumped her boyfriend. (*I can't believe he was sending those songs to so many other girls!*)

You get a B- on your next biology test. It feels really fucking good.

Definition: In Galois theory, an extension of fields is normal if every irreducible polynomial that has at a root in the extension splits into linear factors. Thus, if a polynomial has one root in a normal extension, then all of its roots must be there as well.

Sometimes, being normal means having a little bit of help be all you need to get back on your feet.

There's a music festival this weekend, and not only are your parents letting you go but Blake asked if she could come by early to do your makeup. You've cleaned your room at least eleven times, and it doesn't occur to you that this might be suspicious until you hear her feet on the stairs.

You sit very, very still on your bed, trying not to stare too openly as Blake adds glitter around the rhinestones already dotting your face. You're acutely aware of how close the two of you are sitting. Of how red her lower lip is getting as she chews it absently, the way she always does when she's concentrating.

Blake leans in a little closer to adjust a loose rhinestone, her thumb brushing against your cheek as if wiping away a tear.

Your eyes meet.

You've never been big on eye contact, always shied away from the intensity of staring at someone—*into* someone, and knowing they were staring back. But, for the first time in what feels like months, you don't look away. There are gentle flecks of grey hidden amongst the hazel of her eyes, flickering and kaleidoscoping hypnotically the longer you look. You feel yourself pouring into her, your soul bared, every inch of you on display. Tension crackles between you, electric. You can practically feel the potential energy dancing across your skin. She gives you a shy little grin, the freckles on her nose crinkling in tandem with the corners of her eyes. Your stomach drops away as the world disappears beneath your feet, plummeting downward as your heart casts you out into open air.

The words slip out before you can reel them in, cascading past your lips in a whirlwind of reckless need:

Conjecture: I don't think I've ever wanted anything more than how badly I want to kiss you right now.

The words hang in the air between you, frozen. You've forgotten how to breathe, every cell in your body ablaze in heartrending anticipation.

Definition: In abstract rewriting systems, a normal form refers to an object that cannot be rewritten any *further using the rules of the system. It is a completed jigsaw with no more pieces to add. It is a dish cooked to perfection.*

326

"Oh, thank fuck," whispers Blake. And then her mouth is on yours, lightning forks across every inch of your skin, and the scent of chlorine surrounds you as the world dissolves into the smell of her hair and the taste of her lips.

Sometimes, being normal means accepting exactly who you are.

for pico-8: a fantasy consolation

. . .

Esteban Gaspar Silva

t=0
--patterns persist in temporal memory--
function _draw()cls()
-- [[to create and to clear]]--
--perpetually--

-- each orbit traced in simple mathematics--
--cosine waves pulse through finite space--
for i = 0,99
-- ninety-nine loops --
-- dancing --
-- spectral --

--functions of protocol--
do circfill(64+cos(t/99+i/32)
*40,64+sin(t/50+i/32)
*40,1,8+i%8)
--one hundred circles rejoice in pixel paradigms--
--each a new metaphor--

t+=.0093

-- time increments as movement and as divination--
--[[forever]]--

end

end

mirrorcat

. . .

Robert Dawson

The floor-length mirror showed two cats, sprawled on the carpet a meter apart. One of them was my Dextro; the other had the same black front paw, but on the left side. It would have been a cute kitty picture for my Facebook page—if only there had been any cats at all on the carpet by my feet.

Was this one of those video shows featuring elaborate practical jokes? Had somebody snuck in and replaced my mirror with a one-way mirror into the next apartment? I scrutinized the mirror for the foggy image of half-silvered glass, but my wrinkles and crow's feet were as sharp as ever.

Dex had found a second way to get into trouble with mirrors.

"MRAAWWWRR!"

My skin had tingled with shock, and I had looked around the living room of my apartment for the source. My hindbrain said "sabre-toothed tiger," but the only feline around was Dex; and he never snarled like that.

"MRRRAAAAWWWWRRRR!" Dex stood on his hind legs at

the balcony door, tail as thick as the brushes the technicians use to scrub the big flasks in the lab, swiping at the glass as if he wanted to tear his way through it into the night. "MRAAAAWWWWRR!" The window clattered under the fury of his claws.

I put down the tablet with this month's *Organic Chemistry Review*. What could be out there? A raccoon? But the outer walls of my apartment block were five sheer stories of concrete and glass. Maybe a bird? I walked over and checked the shadows on the balcony carefully, then inched the door open, jamming my leg in the gap in case Dex decided to carry the war to the enemy. When the crack was wide enough, I stuck my head out. The balcony was empty: not so much as a pigeon perched on the railing.

"See, Dex? Nothing! Nothing at all, you silly kitty!" I pulled the door fully open. Dexter fell silent. He stepped to the sill, stuck his nose out cautiously, then went out onto the balcony to make absolutely sure. I let him look around in puzzlement, then picked him up, put him back in the living room, and closed the door. There was silence, then a hiss like gas escaping from a pressure valve. A moment later he was rampant again, snarling and spitting, eyes blazing fury at his own reflection.

Well, if that was the only problem… I got an old tea towel and some masking tape and covered over the bottom of the pane. Dex sat and watched me silently, wondering wide-eyed at the strange things that humans did. When I had smoothed the last strip of tape into place, he made no attempt to dislodge the cloth, but stood up and walked silently away. Nothing to see here, folks. I reheated my tea, picked up my tablet and started to read.

I'd been having my own problems with mirror images, at work. I was trying to synthesize a drug that might cure a common form of breast cancer, the same one that had killed Mom twelve years ago. (It might have got me too, but at Mom's insistence, I got genetic testing. That led to a preventative bilateral mastectomy at forty. The cytology report said I'd been just in time. They offered me reconstructive surgery, but I decided not to bother. A lab coat isn't very flattering anyhow.)

Theory said that if we could synthesize the right-handed isomer of a certain chemical—we called it *d*-sigma-disjunctase for short, its systematic name takes three lines to write out—we could use it to shoot tiny doses of cyanide into tumor cells and kill them dead, without hurting the patient. That was what the oncologists on the team said, and it looked good on paper. My job was to figure out the synthesis. The left-handed version's cheap and plentiful, a few hundred dollars a kilogram: you can find stuff more expensive than that at Bulk Barn if you look hard. The trouble was, *l*-sigma-disjunctase isn't synthesized one step at a time, benzene ring by hydroxyl group: if it had been, we could just have repeated the synthesis starting with mirror-image molecules. But the molecule's complicated, and nobody's ever assembled it by hand. It gets peed out in a vat by genetically modified yeast cells, and you can't just tell a yeast cell "no, other way round!" And so I was reading every paper on unusual synthesis techniques I could find, looking for tricks I could borrow to assemble that elusive molecule that would have saved Mom.

A few minutes later I was interrupted by another unearthly yowl. Dex had found his reflection in the darkened television screen.

By the end of the evening I had masked, with cloth or brown wrapping paper, the bottom parts of three windows, the shiny black front of the dishwasher, the oven window, the bathroom mirror and the full-length mirror in the hall. The television screen and my computer monitor had shawls draped over them. As I got into bed, I wondered whether Dex would find his reflection in his water bowl, and what would happen when he tried to attack that. I smiled at that thought and went to sleep.

The next day, after my lecture, I phoned the vet from my

office. "Hi Paul! It's Sandie Pfeiffer here, Dextro's mom. You'd never believe what he did last night."

"Go on."

I started to tell him about the war against the Mirror Cats.

Part way through he laughed. "That's a thing, Sandie. Cats don't have an abstract enough sense of self to realize that the cat in the mirror is *them*, and sometimes this happens. You did the right thing covering the shiny surfaces up."

"I can't leave my windows covered forever."

"Wait a few weeks. Then uncover them one at a time. Do the windows during the day, so the return of the reflection isn't sudden. If that doesn't work we can try him on a tranquilizer, but I hate to do that if we don't need to."

"Me too." In my fourth year of university, the year Mom got her first cancer diagnosis, I'd had a bad experience with some pills that a friend had said would help me study for my finals. Once I realized there was a problem, it had taken me three months of therapy and self-hypnosis to get out of their grip. Maybe I was being overcautious: but I vowed to myself that medicating Dex would be the last resort.

He snickered. "Oh, and do you know what the psychiatric term for the fear of mirrors is?"

"Go on."

"*Cat*-optrophobia."

I groaned. "Paul, that was *awful*. But thanks for the advice. I'll let you know how it goes."

For a few weeks the apartment looked as if it was prepped for painting. Ralph, the building superintendent, joked about vampires not being able to see their reflections. Dex paced the rooms, looking curiously at the cloth and paper where there had been shiny surfaces, but made no attempt to claw it down. Finally,

I felt I could wait no longer, and when Dex wasn't around I peeled the kraft paper off the dishwasher, then rattled kibble into his bowl. He appeared as if out of nowhere in the kitchen door, walked past the shiny black surface to his bowl and began eating.

By the next evening there had been no attack on the dishwasher, so I uncovered the bathroom mirror. The masking tape had already dried on a little bit. I poked at it with a fingernail. It seemed like a nonpolar-solvent sort of gunk. In the lab I'd have tried hexane, but I fetched WD-40 and a plastic scouring pad and scrubbed away. This was longer than I'd spent in front of the mirror in a while: I kept my eyes on the glass, ignoring the gray hair half a meter beyond. Slowly the adhesive dissolved into a fragrant white goop; I used a few drops of shampoo to emulsify it and wash it away, then Windex to get off the last traces. Primitive, but safe without a fume hood. Dex was sitting on a chair, watching me. I considered putting him up on the counter to see his reaction but decided against it. *Don't make a big thing of it,* Paul had said. *Just let him forget it.*

Over the next week I took down the remaining covers, one at a time. Sometimes Dex would come up to a newly-revealed surface and look at his reflection curiously, with maybe a quiet growl—but he never reverted to the shrieking hellcat of that first night. For some reason his digestion seemed a little sensitive— every few days I had to clean used kibble off the floor. Paul checked him over, said it was probably just delayed stress, sold me a bag of special cat food—and that was that.

Until, two evenings later, Dex didn't turn up for his dinner. I went off to find him, but even in a small apartment a cat can find a lot of places to hide, so I wasn't too worried. I'd just about given up looking when I looked in the bedroom mirror and saw two cats, Dex and another one whose black forepaw was on the left. *How had that other cat got in here?* Could it have slipped in yesterday with Ralph when he came to change the stove element? Could a cat get from one balcony to the other? No, those balconies were at least five meters apart. I looked directly at the floor.

There were no cats there. Not even one.

I looked in the mirror again. Two cats.

"What the hell?" I said, more loudly than I'd intended. Either there was something wrong with my mirror—or there was something wrong with me.

One cat yawned and stretched; the other stayed put. How could a mirror do that? Maybe vampires didn't have reflections, like Ralph said. But even if vampires were for real, Dex and—Levo?—were on the wrong side of the glass. They *only* had reflections. Did that make *me* the vampire?

Okay. Deep breaths and take an inventory. Was I asleep? They say you can't read in a dream. Something to do with brain anatomy. I walked into the living room, picked up my tablet, and glanced at the article I'd been reading. It was written in the usual stuffy third-person style, but once you scraped away the fluff it made sense. I carried the tablet over to the mirror and took a photo, choosing the angle carefully.

The photograph showed two cats in the mirror, none in my apartment. Could this be an optical illusion, like when magicians use mirrors to hide an assistant on stage? I waved to myself with my left hand, stuck out my tongue. Mirror-Me reacted as you'd expect. The mirror seemed to work just fine—except for cats.

Was I going crazy? Should I call Ralph? Maybe 911? Or 119? I got myself a glass of water, sat down at the kitchen table, and thought about the situation, while my heart slowed to normal. If this was a hallucination, this was the time to get to the hospital: right now, while I still knew it wasn't real.

But I wasn't suicidal, depressed, or panicky. I felt perfectly normal, except that I'd imagined a couple cats in a mirror. I didn't see any reason to involve a psychiatrist in that, and I didn't want to be locked up and medicated. Sure, I could have used a few months' leave, but not in a hospital; and not at the cost of rumors at work that Professor Pfeiffer was losing her marbles. I could imagine the gossip around the department: *living by herself, no company but a cat, and you know they had to relieve her from lab work last year? A nervous breakdown, somebody in HR told me. Maybe she could share a lab with the grad students, just so somebody's there to keep an eye on her. For her own safety, of course.*

No thanks! This one I was going to handle by myself—if I could only understand what was going on. I forced myself back to the hall, and paused just short of the corner. Could I face this? I stepped forward: no cats. I gave my mirror-self a shaky thumbs-up: the mirror was working normally again. Time to go and reheat that stew for my supper. No work this evening, I promised myself, and I'd try to get a good night's sleep. I turned, walked toward the kitchen, and nearly tripped over them. Two white cats, each with one black forepaw.

This couldn't be an optical illusion. There wasn't a mirror in sight. Either I'd been working *way* too hard, or Dex had brought Levo home for a playdate.

I felt a little dizzy, and got down on my knees. I scratched both sets of ears, and checked the cats out carefully. Identical sizes and markings. Both neutered toms. Brothers? But the man who'd sold Dex to me had said all the other kittens in the litter were other colors. I wished now that, even though he was an indoor cat, I'd had Dex chipped. It wouldn't help this crazy situation, of course, but I'd have given a lot to see Paul's face when both cats showed the same RFID number.

If they did, of course.

Should I put out a second bowl of kibble? No, Mirror-Me was surely feeding Levo too, even though I couldn't see her doing it. But just to be safe I added another half-scoop. I put my stew in the microwave and poured a small glass of red wine. The cats ate politely, taking turns at the little china bowl. I took my dinner out of the microwave and ate it. Just as I finished, one of the cats —Levo—retched loudly and threw up.

I got a paper towel and cleaned the floor, then scratched his head to show there were no hard feelings. "Poor little guy..." Paul had looked Dex over and said there was nothing wrong—but that was just Dex. Should I take Levo in for a separate check-up?

I couldn't do that. Not while there was even a tiny chance that I might walk into the clinic with an empty cat carrier, explaining to a mystified receptionist that the little guy wasn't feeling well. That way lay the locked ward. Levo purred and rubbed his head comfortingly against my hand. The two cats seemed to be in about the same physical shape—maybe both a bit thin. That new food was meant to be easy to digest. Was Mirror-Me feeding them the same brand? Or at least the mirror image of it.

Mirror image! No wonder the kitties had been sick. Dex's food might be vet-supplied and organically sourced, but it still had hundreds of chemicals in... and most of those molecules were asymmetric. Dex's kibble wouldn't be good for Levo, and anything Dex ate in the apartment beyond the mirror would upset his tummy too. What had Alice said to her cat at the beginning of the book? "Perhaps Looking-glass milk isn't good to drink."

Smart girl, Alice.

But apparently Looking-glass kibble didn't taste bad enough to deter a hungry kitty. I picked up the almost-empty bowl and put it on top of the fridge. Dex would have to eat only when I was around to stop Levo from trying to share. And Mirror-Me would have to do the same.

Would she know that? Of course she would—she was me, after all. A professional chemist. Fifty-three years old. Living alone—I'd definitely have noticed if she'd been in the habit of bringing guys—or gals—home with her! She went to bed when I did, even shared my understated taste in clothes. But did her thoughts match mine *exactly?* For Dex and Levo's sake, I decided that I'd better make sure. I took a sheet of paper and wrote in scrawly mirror writing:

CAT FOOD HAS ASYMMETRIC MOLECULES!
YOU FEED YOUR CAT, I'LL FEED MINE.
LOVE,
ME

I picked up the sheet and the bag of cat food and carried them into my bedroom.

I needn't have worried. Mirror-Me appeared at the same moment, bearing identical items. I gave her a grin and (as mirror-images do) she did the same. And that was the end of the cat puke on the floor.

I'm embarrassed to say that it took me almost a week to figure out the next step: I guess I still had the whole affair compartmentalized under "pet care" and "mental health." But one day the penny dropped: I came home from the lab that night with a sealed factory-fresh jar of l-sigma-disjunctase, and Mirror-Me and I put our jars on the floor in front of the mirror. And then we put the lights out and went to bed, because that's what you do when you're waiting for Santa Claus.

Next morning the jars were just where we'd left them. The Fisher Scientific label on mine was still as legible as ever. I picked it up, waved it at Mirror-Me, and the gullible gal waved her jar back at me with the same sheepish smile. *Well, it was worth a try, wasn't it?* I pushed my jar into the mirror: it stopped a couple millimeters away from hers with a *clunk*. Like jars do when you bang them into mirrors.

What should I do? Rub the powder into the mirror? Put a collar on Dex and tape an envelope of l-sigma-disjunctase to it? That might work, but like many apartment cats he didn't have a collar, and I didn't want to take the time to run out and buy one. Dex rubbed against my shin. "How do you do it, little guy?" I asked him. "How do you get over there?"

I thought about it. This had all started when Dex had failed to recognize that cat in the mirror as himself. Cats are conscious (oh, yes, Herr Doktor Professor Schrödinger, they are.) So, if consciousness is a quantum thing, like Penrose thought, maybe Dex and Levo managed to break some sort of quantum entanglement, so that they could act separately. Dex had thought Levo was a different cat: could I do that too? Could Mirror-Me? I had once been pretty good at self-hypnosis, and I could manage lucid dreaming. Could we put ourselves into whatever special state of mind the cats had been in?

I drew the bedroom curtains, lit a candle, and stared into the flame. It had been thirty years since my therapy, but my mind had not forgotten the way to that place. Fifteen minutes of relaxation and yoga breathing got me there; then, careful not to break the spell, I visualized my mirror image. *She is not me. She is another, an other. A stranger, an intruder…* No, not that. It wouldn't do to arrive in Looking-Glass-Land looking for a fight. *She is a colleague. She does her work, I do mine. We respect each other. We support each other.* I repeated the words to myself like a mantra. I visualized Mirror-Me standing motionless as I walked toward her, and a shiver of primitive fear ran down my back. If this worked, I'd have a doppelgänger. Or become one.

I'd have to risk it. This could save thousands of lives, could have saved Mom's life if somebody had done it in time. Victory was close, so close, just the other side of the mirror—all I needed to do was to take that last step and seize the prize.

I picked up the jar, turned it so the label could be seen from in front, and walked toward the mirror. (This was crazy.) I'd seen the two cats side by side. (But I'd never actually seen one do this.) The worst thing that could happen was bumping into the mirror. (The cats could do this.) Mirror-Me was walking towards me, matching my steps. (Well, cats could lick their butts, too. I wasn't a cat.) I took a slow breath, trying to make myself believe. *You are not me, I am not you.* We were only a few feet apart; I shut my eyes and deked to the right, not slowing, trying not to think of my nose crunching into the mirror.

It was if I was walking into a vertical sheet of ice-cold water. Or maybe boiling-hot; my nerves registered not heat, not cold, just a thin bright pain. I kept my eyelids squeezed tight. What if I got stuck forever, halfway through the mirror? I bent my knees, put the jar gently on the carpet, and backed away, feeling the burning razor-edged boundary recede again. When I opened my eyes, I was looking at myself. I reached slowly out and touched the hard sane glass. Mirror-Me, pale but triumphant, touched the same spot in perfect synchrony.

By our feet were small brown jars. I picked mine up and *yes!* The label was in mirror-writing! I and I grinned in triumph.

"Right, sis!" we said. "Let's take this stuff in to the lab and try it in vitro. And if it works, next week we'll swap some sour-dough starter!"

Yeasts aren't picky eaters like cats. They can digest both glucose and its mirror image. Throw in a few simple nutrients and trace elements, and they multiply like mad, and turn out whatever else their genes tell them to. If I gave Mirror-Me a vial of the yeast that they use to make *l*-sigma-disjunctase (we had a culture at work that we used for experiments), she'd be able to take proper care of it. And when she gave me one from her lab in return, I'd do the same.

***

The Nobel Prize Banquet is held in a grand indoor courtyard at Stockholm City Hall, called the Blue Hall even though it's made of bare red brick. In just a few minutes I was going to be escorted into that banquet by a handsome Swedish prince. I turned to the ornate gilt-framed mirror in the ladies' cloakroom for one more look at my dress, fancy enough to make up for all the high school and university proms that I'd found excuses to stay home from. I grinned to Mirror-Me; we took a deep breath and unentangled ourselves. It had got easier over the years, though we still couldn't stay independent for nearly as long as the cats could.

"Now *this* is worth getting dressed up for, Alter-Ego."

"You bet, Shadow. Hey, they did say we could bring a guest. Want to come to the party on my side? Imagine their faces!"

"No way. They say the food's going to be incredible. I don't want to miss it. Enjoy!"

"You too!"

I blew a kiss, she waved. Then we let ourselves entangle into a pair of mirror images again, turned, and strutted toward the reception hall. When we got back to our hotel rooms, we'd have quite a story to tell the cats.

five rivers you must lay your eyes upon: a travel guide by gervaise the grizzled

. . .

Gabrielle Bleu

Hark, readers! The Peregrinating Peryton brings to you a new guide for your wanderings. Whether you read our fine publication digitally, in paper broadside, or via your crystal nexus, we are pleased to bring you another sight-seeing guide by the famed Gervaise the Grizzled. In her many years of life, undeath, and life again she has tracked down top destinations all across the lands of Angvaux, the seas beyond, and the caves beneath.

We were lucky enough to catch her upon her return from the realms of the Count of a Thousand Caverns, where she engaged in perilous games of chance and skill with the Count and his denizens (reportedly among them the Dogtooth Dauphine and her Stalagmiteal Squire). Fresh from winning the most high-stakes game of boules likely ever played, Gervaise was kind enough to offer her recommendations for "Five Rivers You <u>Must</u> Lay Your Eyes Upon."

"This is not a suggestion but a directive," she told our editor.

Read on for Gervaise the Grizzled's five riparian recommendations. Beware angry perytons, and good health in your travels! May your peregrinations be enlivened by the rushing of water.

Few can say they have traveled as far or as frequently as I, Gervaise the Grand, Gervaise the Geographic, Gervaise the Grizzled! While much of my knowledge will follow me for a second time to the grave, kept secret and safe behind spell-runed silver teeth, I nevertheless have deigned to share the secrets of five of the loveliest waterways. The editor, thrice-cursed dog-tongued being that they are, has suggested that appending my riverain secrets to the chittering of bats would not be in keeping with what the readers of the Peregrinating Peryton have come to expect from the publication. I have instead supplied a numerical list, even as the very nature of rivers defies enumeration.

5. I recommend the river of Ateio to all my friends. To my enemies as well. Friend and enemy alike cannot fail to find the heron that never ages, wading in the clear waters of the Ateio. Whatever our relationship status, our association will not shield you from the gaze of the bird. Look into its eyes and feel yourself aging; know your own approaching end. Know too, that the heron knows no end. It has always been in this river, water up to its knobbed knees, and it always will be. Mammoths walked along the riverbank, and the heron watched them. Trilobites darted between its legs, and now their riverbed-bound bones press hard into the underside of its feet. You passed along the bank at my suggestion, and the riverbird saw you too. Someday, the moon will erode into nothingness, and the heron will still wade in the waters of the Ateio, its gaze unperturbed, withstanding the siege of age.

In my youth, (now far, far gone) I found the heron and its keen eyes a good reminder of the transience of all things. Returning to the Ateio and its singular heron, now that I am Grizzled, is like returning to gaze at an old friend.

4. A unique trait of the river Gollur is the stones beneath the waters. If you reach beneath the current and pluck up a stone, it transmutes upon breaking the surface into whatever sort of

stone the grasper desires. The lovely agates of the Gollur riverbed, grey and orange and yellow, do not frequently remain agates once removed–more frequently they become emeralds, silver nuggets, sapphires within the traveler's hand (though this traveler has oft remarked that children pull forth agates that remain agates, just as content with the stone's original form as the river is).

Gervaise the Grizzled, myself, that is, came away from the last visit with a delicious piece of rock candy, to sate her plummeting blood sugar.

I must warn your readers that there is a strict limit of one rock per person per visit to Gollur–and visits are limited to once per person every sixteen years. The sole exception being should one of those years coincide with an albino bull being stuck by a falling star in a meteoric event, in which case that year counts for double. The keepers of the river do not want tourists carrying away their whole riverbed in one go, of course, and historically have struggled with the erosion caused by overzealous visitors. Policy unlikely to change until the next significant glaciation event replenishes the river with newly plucked rocks.

3. This river has no name. You must find it, beyond the plains of Lunarmar, trickling down from the highest peaks of the mountains of Allcyro. The water is frigid, coming from the lonely polar peaks, high above even the tepid warmth of moonbeams.

I warn you again, the water is freezing.

Nevertheless, I urge you to visit, and dunk your head beneath the water. Your childhood best friend will be waiting there, grinning up at you from the riverbed, caught in the idle of a game the two of you once played. They wave, but do not invite you down, for they are waiting for the you from years ago to reappear. For as long as you can hold your breath, watch and wait for a youthful version of yourself to appear and resume the game. Should you have a high enough lung capacity, you can watch the game. If you must withdraw your head for a breath, the forgotten rules of the game will rush back to your mind; the sound of the laughter shared with your best friend; the secrets passed between the two of you **(see editor's note 1).**

2. Lo'on is a hydrographical wonder. Or perhaps a meteorological wonder. The specifics are a point of contention in the neighboring village Tempsheim, which I would highly recommend visiting for its quaint roof tiling and unique buttressing **(see editor's note 2).**

But the main attraction is the river Lo'on. The water of the Lo'on moves in such a sluggish and solid manner that you can walk across it. With nothing more than a brisk pace, you can cross from one bank to another in a straight line. Of course, if you are in the mind for a more leisurely stroll, you will merely end up a short distance downriver, carried only slightly southward by the slow-moving stream.

The downside of this scenic river vista is that while the river moves along at a speed that makes the pace of snails look like hawks, actual hawks are made to look slow by the wind that blows across the Lo'on. Scarves and dangling jewelry are not recommended on this visit, lest the rapid winds whip them away from the unwary tourist.

The locals of Tempsheim have been embroiled in a hotly contested debate for decades on whether the high-speed winds merely give the river the illusion of running slowly, or if the slow-moving river has given the otherwise unremarkable wind speeds a much more rapid feel.

A good walking tour of the river Lo'on is sure to put you in either a ponderous mood, or in energetic spirits, whichever side of the debate you chose to uphold. Either way, you will come away feeling just a bit out-of-sync with the speed of the world you return to, beyond the river's touch. Be sure to bring galoshes with water-tight soles, and a sturdy windbreaker, if not also a shielding incantation to ward against bad weather while traveling the Lo'on.

1. The river Ramloc is a must-see location for the more

gastronomically inclined. Stand on the shores with your gaze upriver and wait, as the water winds by. Eventually, a gentle whistling will meet your ears, and then a boat will meet your eyes.

The flat-bottomed boat that traverses Ramloc's waters carries a mountain of fruit. The boatrunner's bounty glitters in the sunlight, a dazzling array of delicate pinks, vibrant greens, and joyful yellows no matter the season. Whistle the tune along with the boatman and he will poll towards you, to give you a gift from his cargo in thanks for the shared music. Their hat will hide most of their face, keeping them in cool shade as they work. You will still be able to notice their gentle smile as they hold out a fruit to you over the narrow divide of water between their boat and the riverbank. You will not be able to remember any other details from her face afterwards. Take whatever she offers you. Take a bite.

It will be like nothing you have ever tasted. It will taste like a singular moment long passed. Green apples like the dock I fished from in my youth, long toppled into the lake. Quetsches like afternoons spent watching the migratory flights of now-extinct birds. Mirabelles like the face of a grandmother that I must have once had. Surely even Gervaise had this, once.

I do not know what the fruit will taste like to you.

Let the juice pool in your mouth as you chat with the ferry-woman. Savor it. Even as the years progress before you and the memories the fruit brings dancing to mind fade, you will never forget the taste of the fruit itself.

I have been many times to the river Ramloc to speak a while with the ferryman. I have had a different fruit each time, never willing to re-try the original proffered gift, the memories and taste of which I now carry behind my tongue, behind my rune-safe silver teeth. It is many memories to carry, especially for one as Grizzled as I.

My knowledge of rivers spent, I return now to my domicile to sleep, and perhaps even to rove the singular river that can only be found in dreams. Alas, I have failed to enumerate this final waterway for your readers, a secret sixth river, a gift in my parting.

Should the reader visit my most beloved quinate of rivers, and find them lacking, I would suggest they pass from waking to dreaming, and attempt to meet me at the shores of the Slumbering River. Should they succeed, we must stay awhile, and we must gaze upon the river together. So rare is it to come upon a fellow traveler in dreaming, that it is an imperative we share the fleeting moment at the riverside. We will discuss the rivers of our youth, and the bridges we find ourselves always drawn to return to. We will gossip on the fickle turning of waters and of memories. We will have a grand time on the shores of the Slumbering River. And perhaps, on waking, you will even remember it.

Editor's note 1: This peregrinator would advise against trips to this nameless river with the same childhood best friend who you hope to see a child version of on the riverbed. Nothing ruins a girls-weekend trip more than learning that while you saw a childhood version of Hildeth Cooper beneath the waters, it was not a child version of you that she saw on the bed of that nameless waterway.

Editor's note 2: Join us in the next issue of the Peregrinating Peryton for Olivine Briarblight's tour of "Top Six Architectural Astonishments of Angvaux That You May Look Upon if You So Desire" for a description of the shapes the tiles make when the roofs of Tempsheim think you are not looking.

contributors notes

Mike Adamson holds a Doctoral degree from Flinders University of South Australia. After early aspirations in art and writing, Mike secured qualifications in both marine biology and archaeology. Mike was a university educator from 2006 to 2018, has worked in the replication of convincing ancient fossils, is a passionate photographer, master-level hobbyist, and journalist for international magazines. Short fiction sales include to *Metastellar, Strand Magazine, Little Blue Marble, Abyss and Apex, Daily Science Fiction, Compelling Science Fiction* and *Nature Futures.* Mike has placed stories on over 270 occasions to date, totaling over 1.4 million words.

Casey Aimer is a cyberpunk poet and editor who holds master's degrees in both poetry and publishing. He works for a non-profit publishing science research articles and is founder of *Radon Journal,* an anarchist science fiction publisher. His poetry has been featured in *Strange Horizons, Worlds of IF, Apparition Lit, Star*Line,* and many more. An SFWA and SFPA member, his work has been a Rhysling Award finalist and *Soft Star Magazine* contest winner. He can be found on Bluesky and Casey-Aimer.com

Colleen Anderson is a multiple-nominated and award-winning author with published works in seven countries. Her writing has appeared in *Weird Tales, Cemetery Dance,* and *Fantasy Magazine.* Among her achievements, Rhysling Award-winning poem

"Machine (r)Evolution" can be found in Tenebrous Press's *Brave New Weird*. Colleen's literary talents have twice won her the SFPA's Dwarf Poetry Contest. Her poetry collections—*The Lore of Inscrutable Dreams, I Dreamed a World*, and *Weird Worlds*—are available online, as well as, her fiction collections, *A Body of Work* and *Embers Amongst the Fallen*. *Vellum Leaves and Lettered Skins* will be published in 2025 by Raw Dog Screaming.

Robert Bagnall was born in Bedford, England, in 1970, and stood for parliament for the Green Party in 2024. He has written for the BBC, national newspapers, and government ministers. Five of his stories have been selected for the annual 'Best of British Science Fiction' anthologies. He is the author of sci-fi thriller '2084 - The Meschera Bandwidth' and two anthologies, each of which collects 24 of his ninety-odd published stories. He can be contacted via his blog at meschera.blogspot.com.

Stewart C Baker is an academic librarian and author of speculative fiction, poetry, and games. He is the author of *The Butterfly Disjunct: And Other Stories* (Interstellar Flight Press) and co-wrote the Nebula-nominated *The Bread Must Rise* and Nebula-award-winning *A Death in Hyperspace*; his shorter works have appeared in *Asimov's, Fantasy, Flash Fiction Online, Lightspeed, Nature* and other places. Born in England, Stewart has lived in South Carolina, Japan, and Los Angeles, and now lives within the traditional homelands of the Luckiamute Band of Kalapuya in Oregon—although if anyone asks, he'll usually say he's from the Internet.

Devan Barlow is the author of the *Curses & Curtains* series of fairy tales-meet-musicals fantasy novels, and the collection *Foolish Hopes and Spilled Entrails: Retellings*. Find her short fiction and poetry in various anthologies and magazines. She reads voraciously, and is usually hanging out with her dog. devanbarlow.com, Bluesky @devanbarlow.bsky.social.

Madeline Barnicle received a PhD in mathematical logic from UCLA, and now lives in Maryland. You can find more of her writing at madeline-barnicle.neocities.org.

Gabrielle Bleu writes luminous science fiction and fantasy. When not writing, she watches birds, admires lichens, and plays the accordion. Bleu's work tends to explore the boundaries of time, monsters and myth, the reach and limits of language and memory, and the concept of cats. Their work has appeared in *Archive of the Odd*, *Hexagon*, the Gargantua anthology by Air and Nothingness Press, and in *Astral*, *Alien Fiction*, among others. Find more of Bleu's work at gabriellebleu.com.

A queer, disabled Latina originally from South Texas, **Lisa M. Bradley** now lives in Iowa, the traditional homeland of the Iowa, Ponca, and Winnebago tribes and the Meskwaki Nation, among others. Her poetry has appeared in *F&SF*, *Small Wonders*, *Nightmare Magazine*, *Fantasy*, and many other venues. Her first collection is *The Haunted Girl* (Aqueduct Press). Her debut novel is *Exile* (Rosarium Publishing). She also co-edited, with R.B. Lemberg, the Ursula Le Guin tribute poetry anthology, *Climbing Lightly Through Forests*.

Learn more at www.lisambradley.com or on Bluesky, @cafenowhere.bsky.social.

Zachery Brasier is a science fiction writer and visual artist residing in Salem, MA. His stories have been published in *Apocalypse Confidential*, *Corner Bar Magazine*, *The Pink Hydra*, and more. Find him as Element115Art on most platforms.

Pixie Bruner (HWA/SFPA) is a writer, editor, and cancer survivor. She lives in Atlanta, GA, with her doppelgänger and their deranged cats. Editor of *Memento Mori Ink Magazine*'s "Morsus Vitae", her Elgin-nominated book *The Body As Haunted* was published in 2024. (Authortunities Press). Her words are in/forthcoming from *Space & Time Magazine, Hotel Macabre Vol. 1* (Crystal Lake Publishing), *Amazing Stories, Star*Line, Weird Fiction Quarterly, Abyss & Apex, Penumbric,* Angry Gable Press, and many more. She wrote for White Wolf Gaming Studio. Werespiders ruining LARPs are her fault. 2024 SFPA Pushcart Prize nominee/2025 Rhysling Award Chair.

Jason P. Burnham loves to spend time with his wife and children. He dearly misses his dog. A butterfly once landed on his shoe. He is writing a cosmic horror bureaucracy game for Choice of Games.

Laura J. Campbell Over eighty of Laura Campbell's short stories have appeared in *Chilling Crime Stories, Road Kill: Texas Horror by Texas Writers Vol. 6, Reader Beware: A Fear Street Appreciation Anthology,* and other publications. Most of Laura's recent works are available on Amazon. Laura's short stories "From the Garden" and "416175" can be heard on Spotify's 'Scare You to Sleep' podcast. When she is not writing, Laura can be found running alongside Houston's bayous or attending live music performances. She is encouraged in her writing by her children, Alexander and Samantha.

Charles Chin (he/him) was born in Oak Ridge, Tennessee. Raised by scientist parents to be a scientist himself, he needed a creative outlet to offset the rigid worldview of doctoral degrees and data science. He still writes about science, but on his own terms. Should you come across Charles in the wild, know that he prefers rum over whiskey.

Emmie Christie's work includes practical subjects, like feminism and mental health, and speculative subjects, like unicorns and affordable healthcare. She has been published in *Factor Four Magazine, Small Wonders,* and *Flash Fiction Online,* among others.

Her fantasy romance novel, *A Caged and Restless Magic* debuted Feb 2024. She also narrates for *Strange Horizons*. Find her at www.emmiechristie.com, her monthly newsletter, or BlueSky.

Rodrigo Culagovski is a Chilean architect, designer, and web developer. He has published in *Flash Fiction Online*, *Nature*, *Levar Burton Reads*, *Future Science Fiction Digest*, *khōréō* among others. He misses his Commodore 64. Pronouns he/him/él. SFWA | Codex | ALCiFF On Bluesky as @culagovski.net

R.A. Daunton is an award-winning screenwriter, author and musician from Edinburgh, Scotland. Some of his previously published works include "Man/Maid" for *Black Sheep Magazine*, "From the Hollows" for *Event* and *PULP*, "The Forty Winks of the Narcoleper" for *Winter Splinter*, and "Edin" and "Padlocks" for an upcoming anthology by Hex Arcana Publishing. His short films, "A Whole Host" and "Wooden Masks" are currently doing the rounds on the festival circuit and can be viewed at various festivals around the world and online. You can find him at www.radaunton.com and on Instagram at @radaunton.

Deborah L. Davitt was raised in Nevada, but currently lives in Houston, Texas with her husband and son. She's worked as a technical writer on contracts involving nuclear submarines, NASA, and computer manufacturing. Her prize-winning poetry has received Rhysling, Elgin, Dwarf Star, and Pushcart nominations and has appeared in over seventy journals, including *F&SF* and *Asimov's*. Her award-winning short fiction has appeared in *Analog* and *Lightspeed*. She's published six novels and a TTRPG. For more about her work, including her Elgin-nominated poetry collections, *The Gates of Never*, *Bounded by Eternity*, and *From Voyages Unreturning*, see www.deborahldavitt.com.

Robert Dawson teaches mathematics at a Nova Scotian university. His stories have appeared in *Nature Futures*, *Year's Best Military and Adventure SF*, *Tesseracts*, and numerous other periodicals and anthologies. He believes the world needs more bicycles.

Stuart Docherty is a British writer and poet based in Tokyo, where he writes, eats too much, and pretends to speak Japanese. You can find his work at ergot.press, *Maudlin House*, and Black Hare Press.

Mark Fiddes lives and writes in the Middle East. His third collection *Other Saints Are Available* (Live Canon) followed *The Chelsea Flower Show Massacre* and *The Rainbow Factory* (Templar Poetry). He is this year's winner of the Ledbury International Poetry Prize, having also won the Ruskin Prize and the Oxford Brookes University Prize among many others. Recent work has appeared in *London Magazine*, *The Irish Times*, *Southword*, *Shearsman Magazine* and *The Madrid Review*. He regularly appears at events such as Versopolis and the Emirates Literary Festival.

Adele Gardner (they/them, https://gardnercastle.com/) has a poetry collection, *Halloween Hearts*, released by Jackanapes Press (https://www.jackanapespress.com/product/halloween-hearts) and over 500 stories, poems, art, and articles in *Analog, Clarkesworld, Strange Horizons, PodCastle*, and forthcoming in *Asimov's*. A graduate of Old Dominion University (MA, English literature), Florida State University (MLIS), and the Clarion West Writers Workshop, this genderfluid, bi night owl coedited SFPA's *Dwarf Stars 2022* (https://sfpoetry.com/ds/22dwarfstars.html) and guest-edited the Arthuriana issue of SFPA's *Eye to the Telescope* (Issue 27, January 2018, https://eyetothetelescope.com/intros/027intro.html). Fifteen poems won or placed in SFPA's Rhysling Award, the annual PSV Contest, and the Balticon Poetry Contest.

Brian U. Garrison is President of the Science Fiction and Fantasy Poetry Association (SFPA). His poetry has waited at a bus stop in Montpelier, Vermont; popped out of a vending machine in Boston, Massachusetts; traveled to Tuscaloosa, Alabama (among other cities) aboard Asimov's Science Fiction; and flown to Mars aboard NASA's MAVEN mission. His chapbooks include *Micropoetry for Microplanets* (Space Cowboy Books) and *New Yesterdays New Tomorrows* (self-published). He lives under a tall, leafy tree in Portland, Oregon. Find him online at bugthewriter.com.

Born in Ukraine and currently residing in California, **Elana Gomel** is an academic, an award-winning writer, and a professional nomad. She is well-known in the academy for her work on speculative fiction and narrative theory, including books such as *Science Fiction, Alien Encounters, and the Ethics of Posthumanism* and *The Palgrave Handbook of Global Fantasy*. A member of Horror Writers of America (HWA), she is the author of many short stories, two collections, several novellas, and eight novels of dark fantasy and science fiction. Her stories appeared in *Best Horror of the Year*, *The Dark* magazine, *Apex*, and many anthologies. Her latest novels are *Nightwood*, a fairy tale about exile, marriage, and monsters (Silver Award in the Bookfest 2023 contest) and *Nine Levels*, a mythological fantasy.

Amy Grech has sold over 100 stories to various anthologies and magazines including: *10 by 10 Flash Fiction Stories*, *Apex Magazine*, *Even in the Grave*, *Gamut Magazine*, *Microverses*, *Punk Noir Magazine*. *Roi Fainéant Press*, *Tales from the Canyons of the Damned*, *Yellow Mama*, and many others. Alien Buddha Press published her poetry chapbook, *A Shadow of Your Former Self*. She is an Active Member of the Horror Writers Association and the International Thriller Writers who lives in Forest Hills, Queens.

You can connect with her on
Bluesky: @amygrech.bsky.social,

Medium: https://medium.com/@crimsonscreams,
X: https://x.com/amy_grech, or
visit her website: https://www.crimsonscreams.com.

J.D. Harlock is an Eisner-nominated American writer, research, editor, and academic pursuing a doctoral degree at the University of St. Andrews, whose writing has been featured in *Business Insider, Newsweek, The Cincinnati Review, Strange Horizons, Nightmare Magazine, The Griffith Review, Queen's Quarterly*, and *New York University's Library of Arabic Literature*. You can find him on LinkedIn, Twitter, Threads, & Instagram.

Jordan Hirsch writes speculative fiction and poetry in Saint Paul, MN, USA. Her debut chapbook *Both Worlds* is out with Bottlecap Press, and her work has appeared in *Strange Horizons, Apex Magazine*, and other venues.

Find more at jordanrhirsch.wordpress.com.

Liam Hogan is an award-winning speculative short story writer, with stories in Best of British Science Fiction and in Best of British Fantasy (NewCon Press). He volunteers at the creative writing charities Ministry of Stories, and Spark Young Writers. Sci-Fi collection: *A Short History of the Future* (Northodox Press). Fantasy: *Happy Ending Not Guaranteed* (Arachne Press).

More at http://happyendingnotguaranteed.blogspot.co.uk.

Juleigh Howard-Hobson's poetry has appeared in *Amazing Stories, The Dead Lands, Midnight Echo, The Audient Void, Dreams and Nightmares, Under Her Skin* (Black Spot) *Vastarien: Women's Horror* (Grimscribe), and many other places. Nominations include the Pushcart, Elgin, Best of the Net and Rhysling. Her latest book is *Curses, Black Spells and Hexes* (Alien Buddha). An active member of both the SFPA and the HWA, she lives in a suitably haunted house on the edge of the known world. Bluesky: @juleigh.bsky.social X: @poetforest

Jennifer Hudak is a Nebula-nominated speculative fiction writer whose work can be found in venues such as *The Magazine of Fantasy & Science Fiction*, *Lady Churchill's Rosebud Wristlet*, *The Sunday Morning Transport*, and *Strange Horizons*. She is a 2018 graduate of the Viable Paradise workshop and a member of the Codex Writers' Group. Originally from Boston, she now lives with her family in Upstate New York where she teaches yoga, knits pocket-sized animals, and misses the ocean.

Find out more about her at JenniferHudakWrites.com.

Geoffrey A. Landis is a poet and writer by night, and a NASA scientist by day. His writing has appeared in over twenty languages, and his poetry published in magazines and anthologies from *The Magazine of Fantasy and Science Fiction* to *The Journal of Humanistic Mathematics*. He knows more about mathematics than the average human (a Ph.D. in physics will do that), but if you have serious questions about topology, better ask Greg Egan. He's the author of two poetry collections, the novel *Mars Crossing*, and the story collection *Impact Parameter (& Other Quantum Realities)*. He's won Hugo and Nebula awards for SF, and most recently won the 2024 Rhysling award for best short poem for "What No One Now Remembers."

Akis Linardos is a writer of bizarre things, a biomedical AI scientist, and maybe human. He's also a Greek that lived across the globe and eventually plans to return to his cave in Crete, to write what words of beauty he can until the self-destructing empires of the world implode. Find his words at *Apex*, *Strange Horizons*, *Uncharted*, *Heartlines Spec.* and visit his lair for more: https://linktr.ee/akislinardos.

M. Lopes da Silva (he/they) is a bisexual and non-binary trans masc author and artist from Los Angeles. He writes pulp and poetry, and lectures about the political power of desire. Weird-punk Books just released his fiction collection *Infinity Mathing at the Shore and Other Disruptions*, in March of 2024.

Native New Yorker and award-winner, **LindaAnn LoSchiavo** is a member of British Fantasy Society, HWA, SFPA, and The Dramatists Guild. Titles published in 2024: "Always Haunted: Hallowe'en Poems" [Wild Ink], "Apprenticed to the Night" [UniVerse Press], and "Felones de Se: Poems about Suicide" [Ukiyoto]. Forthcoming: "Cancer Courts My Mother" [Prolific Pulse Press, 2025] and "Vampire Verses" [Twisted Dreams Press, 2025]. Book Accolades earned: Elgin Award for "A Route Obscure and Lonely" and the Chrysalis BREW Project's Award for Excellence & Readers' Choice Award for "Always Haunted: Hallowe'en Poems" and the Spotlyts Story Award from Spotlyts Magazine for "Apprenticed to the Night."

Blue Sky: @ghostlyverse.bsky.social

Steven Mathes lives miles from the nearest pavement with a spouse and a dog. When he isn't writing, he tends a garden. He gardens because he likes to cook. He cooks because he is passionate about eating. For tonight's supper, he plans to toss cauliflower with a generous amount of good olive oil, then (because he has run out of unicorn dandruff) sprinkle it with ground sumac. He will roast it in a convection oven at 350 for around 45 minutes. He is a full member of SFWA.

Jennifer Jeanne McArdle lives in New York and works in animal conservation. A list of her previous publications can be found here: https://jenniferjeannemcardle.blogspot.com/.

Cliff McNish's middle-grade fantasy novel *The Doomspell* is translated into 26 languages, and his ghost novel *Breathe* was voted by The Schools Network of British Librarians as one of the top adult and children's novels of all time. Amongst other places, his adult stories and poetry have appeared in Nightjar Press, *Stand*, *Confingo*, *Ink Sweat & Tears*, *The Literary Hatchet* and *The Interpreter's House*. Facebook: cliff mcnish; Instagram: @cliffmcnish

Saundra Mitchell (she/they) has been a phone psychic, a car salesperson, a denture-deliverer and a layout waxer. She's dodged trains, endured basic training, and hitchhiked from Montana to California. Her short fiction has appeared in periodicals including *FORESHADOW*, *Vestal Review*, *SmokeLong Quarterly* and more; it has also appeared in anthologies including *A TYRANNY OF PETTICOATS*, *FORETOLD*, *GRIM*, *TRUTH & DARE*. She is an Indiana Author Award winner, an Edgar finalist, as well as a Lambda and Pushcart nominee. She is the author of nineteen books, and resides in Maryland with her wife, daughter and two terrible, wonderful cats.

Kurt Newton's poetry has appeared in *Extrasensory Overload*, *Katabatic Circus*, *Space & Time*, *Eye to the Telescope*, *Sublimation*, *Apocalypse Confidential*, and *HWA Poetry Showcase XI*. His recent collections include, *Songs of the Underland*, *A Troubled Sleep*, *The Ever-Evolving Alphabet*, and *The Body Snatchers*. A new collection, *Moonlight Apocrypha*, is forthcoming from Island of Wak-Wak.

Erwin Arroyo Pérez is the founder and Editor-in-Chief at *The Poetry Lighthouse*. He also teaches English literature and works as a translator. He holds a Master's degree in English Literature and Linguistics from Université Paris Nanterre and King's College London, specialising in Victorian literature and poetry. He has studied under poet Sarah Howe and novelist Benjamin Wood, shaping his approach to creative writing. Erwin's poetry has been published in *Ink Sweat & Tears*, *Wildscape*, *The Nature of Our Times*, *The Winged Moon*, *ResPublica Politics*, *The Jewel City Review*, Nanterre University Press, and other American and British literary magazines and anthologies.

Marisca Pichette is a queer author based in Massachusetts, on Pocumtuck and Abenaki land. Her work has appeared in *Strange Horizons*, *Clarkesworld*, *Vastarien*, *The Magazine of Fantasy & Science Fiction*, *Fantasy Magazine*, *Asimov's*, *Nightmare Magazine*, and others. Her poetry collection, *Rivers in Your Skin, Sirens in Your Hair*, was a finalist for the Bram Stoker and Elgin Awards. Her cli-fi novella, *Every Dark Cloud,* is out now from Ghost Orchid Press.

Camden Rose is a queer author who loves seeking out magic beneath the everyday world. Her works have appeared with *Inner Worlds* and *Heartlines Spec*. She lives in the Pacific Northwest with her spouse, black cats, and collection of books and board games.

You can find her online at www.camdenscorner.com.

Shana Ross is a newcomer to Edmonton, Alberta and Treaty 6 Territory. Qui transtulit sustinet. A Rhysling nominated author, her work has recently appeared in *Augur, Radon Journal, Paranoid Tree, The Deadlands* and more. She is two years into a campaign of befriending the local magpies. Just in case.

A. M. Sahu writes whimsical, heart-first fiction about curious people, unexpected adventures, and the magic tucked inside everyday moments. Being an engineer with a head full of stories, she delights in blending reality with just a hint of mischief. When she's not writing, she's sipping chai, day-dreaming or sharing musings on her Substack. She's working on a full length novel and can be found on social media — @amsahubooks

Lynne Sargent is a queer writer, aerialist, and holds a Ph.D in Applied Philosophy. They are the poetry editor at *Utopia Science Fiction magazine*. Their work has been nominated for Rhysling, Elgin, and Aurora Awards, and has appeared in venues such as *Augur Magazine, Strange Horizons*, and *Analog*. Their work has also been supported through the Ontario Arts Council.

To find out more visit them at scribbledshadows.wordpress.com.

Lauren Scharhag (she/her) is an award-winning author of fiction and poetry, and a senior editor at *Gleam*. Recent honors include first place in the 2024 Rhysling Awards (long form category), and the 2024 Roadmap Short Story Competition Top 50. Her latest releases include *Screaming Intensifies* (Whiskey City Press), the *In the King's Power* series (self-published), and *Ain't These Sorrows Sweet* (Roadside Press). She lives in Kansas City, MO.

https://linktr.ee/laurenscharhag

Lorraine Schein is a New York writer and poet. Her work has appeared in VICE *Terraform, Strange Horizons, Scientific American*, and *Michigan Quarterly*, and in the anthologies *Wild Women* and *Tragedy Queens: Stories Inspired by Lana del Rey & Sylvia Plath. The Futurist's Mistress*, her poetry book, is available from Mayapple Press. Her book, *The Lady Anarchist Cafe*, is out now from Autonomedia.

https://autonomedia.org/product/the-lady-anarchist-cafe/

Esteban Gaspar Silva is a Mexican immigrant educator, storyteller, and community organizer based in Brooklyn, NY. Through his work as a high school teacher, he explores the intersection of cultural identity and narrative, developing innovative curriculum that connects literary genres like Magical Realism,

Afro-futurism, and Cyberpunk with social justice. His creative practice spans multiple mediums, including music, poetry, and short fiction, examining themes of queerness, immigration, and economic liberation. He also releases abrasive rap music under the name Curanderx://

Unbeknownst to **Robert E. Stahl**, his body is an empty shell telepathically controlled by a brain in a jar which was buried long ago under the floorboard of his home in Dallas, Texas. Consequently, his days are filled with the urge to write: stories, letters, articles, whatever. At night he listens to music, and when he finally drifts off to sleep, the brain laughs, a humorless, pitiful sound as it jiggles alone in the dusty darkness.

When **Sam E. Sutin** is not writing fiction he is Sam Macdonald, a graduate student pursuing his Ph.D. in mathematics in Lincoln, Nebraska. He has publications in both speculative fiction magazines and mathematics journals, and enjoys rock climbing, strategic hammock placement, and the Axiom of Choice.

Laura Theis writes in her second language. Her work appears in *Poetry, Oxford Poetry, Magma, Rattle, Berlin Lit,* etc. Accolades include the Alpine Fellowship Writing Prize, Oxford Brookes Poetry Prize, AM Heath Prize, Mogford Prize, Studio Faire Fellowship and a Forward Prize nomination. Her debut *how to extricate yourself,* an Oxford Poetry Library Book-of-the-Month, was nominated for the Elgin Award and won the Brian Dempsey Memorial Prize. *A Spotter's Guide To Invisible Things* received the Live Canon Collection Prize, and the Arthur Welton Award from the Society of Authors. Her latest publications are *Introduction To Cloud Care* (Broken Sleep Books) and her forthcoming children's debut *Poems From A Witch's Pocket* (Emma Press).

E.W.H. Thornton work has appeared on *The NoSleep Podcast,* in the *BlazeVOX Journal, Unorthodox Fiction, After The Storm Maga-*

zine, and the *meat4meat* anthology. They maintain a blog presenting magazine content from pre, mid, and post World War Two era America, with a focus on the golden age of pulp fiction. It can be found at https://thegilcedcentury.tumblr.com. They also occasionally write about the more bizarre, lurid, and tragic aspects of video game history at

https://www.giantbomb.com/profile/lostsol/blog/.

D. Matthew Urban hails from Texas and lives in Queens, NY, where he reads weird books, watches weird movies, and writes weird fiction. A collection of his stories, *Shaky Pictures of Vanished Faces*, was published in 2025 by Cursed Morsels Press, and his work has appeared in such venues as *Cosmic Horror Monthly*, *Tales from Between*, and *Fraidy Cat Quarterly*.

Find him on Twitter and Bluesky @breathinghead or on the web at https://dmatthewurban.com.

Veda Villiers (she/her), 23, is passionate about speculative fiction and poetry that probes the complexities of the human experience. Her works have appeared and are forthcoming in *Gamut*, *Radon Journal*, *Heartlines*, *Trollbreath*, and *Star*Line*. Though her day job keeps her busy, you can find her at @Veda-Villiers on X (formerly known as Twitter).

Cullen Wade (he/him) is a writer, horror critic, and high school teacher. He is the author of *S(p)lasher Flicks: The Swimming Pool in Horror Cinema*, out in 2025 from McFarland Books. His work has appeared in *Paste Magazine*, *Night Tide Magazine*, Spindle House Press, *Horror Homeroom*, *HorrorGeekLife*, and *Deaf Sparrow*. He lives in Charlottesville, VA, USA, with his wife Emma, cat Bishop, and rescue pit bulls Hazel and Libby. Follow him on Bluesky @cullenwade.bsky.social.

Pamela Weis writes fiction during those few moments of clarity between her day job as a web developer and the rest of her life. This is challenging. But it keeps her sane. She has a background in Anthropology and Theater and a mountain of debt to prove it. She plans to write weird little (and big) stories until her fingers are too arthritic to type. She lives in Northern Indiana with her husband and their two black kitties, Nyxie and Shuri.

Anne Wilkins is a sleep-deprived New Zealand teacher who writes in her spare time. Her short fiction has appeared or is forthcoming in *Apex Magazine, Cosmic Horror Monthly, The Dark, Small Wonders, Elegant Literature,* and more. She has won the June 2024 *Elegant Literature Prize,* the 2023 *Autumn Writers Battle,* and the 2023 *Cambridge Autumn Festival Short Story Competition,* among others. Her love of writing is fuelled by copious amounts of coffee, reading and hope. Anne is supported in her writing journey by her ever-patient husband, two wonderful daughters, and two feline writing assistants.

Learn more at www.annewilkinsauthor.com.

Joe Wood is a novice speculative fiction writer. Having graduated from Canisius College with a BS in Psychology and a BA in Creative Writing, he now studies School Psychology at SUNY Oswego. His work has appeared in the *Eunoia Review, 365 Tomorrows,* and *Sci-Fi Shorts.* During his free time, Joe enjoys going on hikes with his wife Lauren (who is considerably faster).